One for the Gods

Also available from Alyson
by the same author

THE LORD WON'T MIND
FORTH INTO LIGHT

One for the Gods

A NOVEL BY

Gordon Merrick

THE SEQUEL TO THE NATIONAL BEST-SELLER *THE LORD WON'T MIND*

alyson
books
LOS ANGELES • NEW YORK

Manufactured in the United States of America.
Printed on acid-free paper.

This trade paperback is published by Alyson Publications Inc.,
P.O. Box 4371, Los Angeles, California 90078-4371.
Distributed in the United Kingdom by Turnaround Publisher Services Ltd.,
Unit 3 Olympia Trading Estate, Coburg Road, Wood Green,
London N22 6TZ, England.

First published in 1971 by Bernard Geis Associates
First Alyson edition: May 1996

10 9 8 7 6 5 4 3 2

ISBN 1-55583-291-1

For Jeannie Sakol

One for the Gods

A ship's whistle hooted in the night. The blond American closed his book and sat in the soft light of a kerosene lamp and tried not to hope.

After a moment of total immobility, he sprang up and crossed the bare whitewashed room and went out onto the terrace that hung over the port. Lights bobbed on the water below. Launches were running between the quai and a steamship lying at the entrance to the harbor. People bustling about their little business. Coming from Athens? Going to Athens? As if it made any difference.

The terrace was too high for the American to distinguish individuals as they clambered ashore in the dark so he made no effort to concentrate on the arrivals, although there was one head he felt sure he would recognize even at this distance if it should appear. He stood with godlike detachment, watching the human ants scurrying about beneath him. The sound of excited voices drifted up to him.

Was the beloved voice among them? Even at this distance, he felt sure that his ear would catch its unique note. It was an absurdity to hope to hear it, since not a soul in the world knew that he was here on this small Greek island. He had only himself to blame if nobody attempted to rescue him from the shipwreck of his life. An apt metaphor, very nearly the formulation of fact.

He turned his back on the picturesque scene below and retraced his steps, skirting the area of the terrace that looked as if it were about to cave in. He seated himself once more in the rickety straight-backed chair at the unpainted wooden table and pulled the kerosene lamp toward him. He looked at his book but didn't reopen it. He wondered how long it would be before the unreasonable hope died. And was it really hope? He would never know unless it were fulfilled. Otherwise, what? Would he stay on in this crumbling ruin of a house, slowly dying with it into time? Why not? He had made the acquaintance of death—whether voluntary or involuntary didn't seem important—a new acquaintance but not an unwelcome one. There was much to be said for being dead. The hazards of rescue were perhaps more to be feared than the oblivion he had found here.

He thought of the day of the trip from St. Tropez to Porquerolles, the day he had first known, no matter how much he had tried to close his mind to it, that the years of unbroken tranquility were ending. He felt as if an eternity of torment separated him from that day, but it had been only the time it took to sail from France to Greece, the time it took to test and reshape everything he had thought himself to be.

He felt already, after barely a week here, that he was taking on a new, dim identity. Kyrios Carlos, as some of the shopkeepers had begun to call him, since apparently "Charles" was a sound the Greeks couldn't pronounce, and "Mills" became something he might eat three times a day. Kyrios Carlos, the silent foreigner who had unprecedentedly bought a house. Give him twenty years or so and he could turn into the island's colorful old eccentric. By then, his unborn child would be fully grown and a total stranger to him. His child? Of course. There was little room for doubt, no justification for the disclaimer of a question mark.

He wished he could decide whom he was punishing. Himself? The others? If he could find the answer to that question, he would be able to glimpse the shape of the future. He knew that he deserved punishment, but he was far from sure that he was qualified to administer it. Was his being here an evasion of it or a submission to it? As he was discovering about most questions in life, there was no clear-cut answer. Therein lay hope's resilience.

His mind was timing imaginary movements on the port. So many minutes to collect oneself at the point of debarkation and get into the center of the built-up area of the port where there were lighted shops and cafés. So many minutes being passed from hand to hand until the old man who spoke English was found.

So many more minutes for the ritual interrogation, with perhaps some ouzo or retsina thrown in. A little more time for a guide to be produced, and the final eight minutes or so to get up to the house. It could happen. If anybody really wanted to find him, it would be possible. Nobody could just disappear off the face of the earth.

He opened his book. As he did so, his straining ears picked up a sound. He sat without moving as the sound grew nearer. He leaped to his feet and stood motionless, as a thrill, like light fingers running over him, crawled up the skin of his back. The unmistakable footsteps were mounting the last rise to the house. For an instant, his ears lost the sound, or perhaps his mind distrusted the boon of what he so longed to hear. He caught another sound. Voices? His mind clouded in protest: he couldn't face both of them. The sound of hurrying feet again, just outside now. His heart stopped at the knock on the door.

o   o   o

We must take a step back in time and break in on a private conversation.

"Is it true you two go in for fidelity and all that?"

"I don't know about 'all that' but fidelity, yes. Does that sound terribly quaint?"

The two young men were strolling past the bare central square of Porquerolles, elegant in the French way without containing any single elegant element, in the wake and out of earshot of a small band of holiday friends. Ahead of them was a stand of wind-twisted pines beyond which could be glimpsed a curve of white sand and the intense blue of the Mediterranean. The sun was hot and harsh, soaking up color, so that the gaily dressed party looked somehow ghostly against the black pines. Only the blue of the sea survived.

"I find it not only unlikely but damned inconvenient for me," the dark young Frenchman persisted. His name was Guy de Sainval and he was very rich. "I think you and I could have something very exciting together."

"The thought has crossed my mind," Charlie Mills, the blond American, lied. He lied not because Guy was rich and, having

5

bought two of his paintings, was something of a patron, but because he had had this conversation with so many others that he had developed a set of stock replies in order to get it over with as quickly as possible. Life with Peter had made him resent people making passes at him, especially men; the implied assumption that he could be had was an affront.

"You see?" Guy flashed him a suggestive smile. He had a face that interested without attracting Charlie, a witty, intelligent face, fine-boned, like an aristocratic bird. "Fidelity is altogether too limiting. Especially for an artist. Even normally married couples don't attempt it."

"But that's just it. We're not a normally married couple so we've made up our own rules. It's really no great hardship. We like it that way. What about you and Harry?"

"That gangster? If you'll forgive my speaking so of a compatriot of yours. All my friends warned me against him. They were right. I'd get rid of him in an instant for someone like you."

"Just so that we could be unfaithful to each other?"

"Yes. Absurd, isn't it? But one must have someone to be unfaithful to." They both laughed, although Charlie's laughter was not wholly spontaneous. Something was wrong. He didn't like to joke about something so deeply ingrained in his life and precious to him, but it wasn't that. Was it too soon to be in Europe for pleasure? The war had been over for five years but evidence of its agony was still vivid and pervasive. Was that why he had felt a shadow over the day, the drive from St. Tropez in expensive cars, the voyage out to the island on the regular tourist boat, which, for this run—though some magic of Guy's—had been entirely reserved for them, all in order to taste what Guy described as the only perfect *bouillabaisse* in the world? Frivolity in a vacuum? Graveyard gaiety?

Recently, in the brief panic stirred up by the outbreak of war in Korea, they had almost abandoned their holiday. Charlie was beginning to wish they had. He hadn't wanted to come on this excursion; it was going to use up a whole working day. He had allotted a daily hour-and-a-half for the beach but at whatever time was convenient to him, and alone with Peter, so his concentration wasn't broken. This was an exception, a triumph of Guy's insistence over Charlie's will.

He was finding it difficult to adjust to this unfamiliar life of

6

social promiscuity and luxurious idleness. He and Peter had chosen a life that seemed, by contrast, austere.

Their converted farmhouse in Connecticut was comfortable but small. Their cars were serviceable. Charlie was deeply absorbed in his painting and spent his days at it. Peter was fascinated by the hobby that had become his career, dealing in art, but found time to cook for them and run the house.

Together, they had never frequented a homosexual world. They had found their friends among their neighbors, professional people, married couples with children, and among the rich, whom Peter cultivated as clients. Charlie's earnings were irregular and often meager but there had never been any question between them of keeping separate financial accounts. Peter paid, and was quite able to, but he had to keep considerable sums of cash available for his business affairs, and they had never been given to extravagance.

This lavish, lax, azure coast was basically alien to them, but there was more to it than that. Something was wrong; Charlie knew what it was, but he wasn't yet ready to put a name to it.

"This is a beautiful place," he said, as the immaculate curve of beach, the clean blue depths of the sea became more clearly visible through the trees.

"Ah, but wait till you taste the *bouillabaisse*. It's rare that one can introduce somebody to perfection. If I can't seduce you, perhaps the *bouillabaisse* will."

"It sounds messy." Charlie laughed his enforced holiday laughter.

"Of course, you two are the sensations of the season. You're both so wildly attractive and so alike in many ways. Nobody believes for an instant in this fidelity. Everybody's trying to decide which of you they'd prefer to have. For me, there's no question. Peter is utterly charming but it's all open and obvious. You have a mystery. It's very intriguing."

"That's me, all right. 'The Mystery Man'." Charlie's eyes traveled over the small group ahead of them, squinting against the sun. It had further subdivided itself. The Courtin girl was flanked by Peter and her brother Jean-Claude. It figured. The two other women walked hand in hand. Harry skulked around the edges, kicking up dust with heavy feet. To Charlie, the center of any group was always Peter, and he was definitely so now. His golden head was almost white under the sun. He somehow moved with quick jaunty grace even though he was walking slowly. He was gesturing with his hands, obviously casting his spell over his companions. Of them all, he was the one who seemed wholly alive, lifting them all on the surge of his light-hearted vitality. Charlie's eyes lingered briefly, irresistibly, on his bottom.

"You've been together—how long did somebody tell me?—ten years?" Guy was continuing. "You must have been infants. Do you really expect me to believe that neither of you has strayed in all that time?"

"That's about the way it's been," Charlie said, achieving an approximation of the truth. The year they had been separated by the war didn't count. He knew as surely as anything could be known that Peter had never been unfaithful to him.

"Your past must be absolutely strewn with broken hearts. Look at the Courtins. Both Anne and Jean-Claude are madly in love with your friend. And here am I, glued to your side, eager to fill any idle hour."

"It's a great comfort, I assure you," Charlie said with a laugh, lightly touching the other's shoulder.

"Peter went to Paris last week, didn't he?" Guy asked, abruptly dropping his bantering tone.

"Yes. He's working on a deal."

"I know about it. He's trying to get some things from the de Belleville collection. It will be a triumph if he succeeds. They've never parted with so much as a spoon, though God knows they need the money."

"I hope he manages it. It's for a very important client."

"Oh, he'll doubtless charm them out of everything they possess. He came back Thursday, didn't he?"

"Did he? Yes, of course. He took the Wednesday night train back."

"Do you think it at all curious that Jean-Claude was away on Wednesday night? He and Anne were to have dinner with us, but he dropped out at the last minute. He said he had to see some friends in Cannes."

Charlie's heart felt suddenly strained and heavy. The muscles of his face were stiff, but he managed a smile. "You *are* a trouble-maker, aren't you? I really don't see how Peter on a train has

8

any connection with Jean-Claude in Cannes."

"You're sure he was on the train?"

"Of course. He called me from Paris on Wednesday and was back Thursday morning." He was getting angry now, angry with Guy for such outright bitchery, for forcing into the open the agonizing thoughts he had been trying to suppress, angry with himself for permitting suspicions that left all his nerves feeling raw and exposed.

"I'm no doubt imagining things," Guy said. "I shouldn't have said anything but all is permitted in love and war, n'est-ce pas?"

"Of course," Charlie said cuttingly. "It's a familiar story. Some people can't stand seeing two people living happily together. This whole conversation bores me."

They were saved further acrimony by a pause ahead; the others had reached the shade of the trees and stood waiting to regroup.

"We remind me of some idyllic Renoir," Madeleine de Montrécy exclaimed in her chuckling fruity voice as Charlie and Guy approached. "Look at us. I think we're too lovely for words."

"None of us is nearly round enough," Peter objected. They all laughed as they set off once more on a path through the scattered trees. Peter detached himself from the Courtins and fell into step beside Charlie. As he did so, they looked deep into each other's eyes and told each other, invisibly to anybody else, how pleased they were to be together. Charlie put his hand on Peter's neck and gave it a squeeze. As he dropped his hand, he allowed it to brush against Peter's bottom in a discreet caress, reaffirming his possession of his body. The look and the physical contact assured him that his suspicions were absurd. He and Peter existed only for each other.

After a few moments they emerged from the woods onto the broad curve of sand. They straggled across it, blinded, to the water's edge. The sea was held by two rocky promontories in a still, blue cove, hissing faintly as it rippled up over the gently shelving shore. There was nobody else in sight. In a moment, they had taken possession of their chosen area. Towels were flung out, shirts and shorts were dropped, they all milled about together, nearly naked, copper-brown from the sun, exchanging and applying lotions and oils, settling themselves in. Madeleine had been right; they made a lovely ensemble, with the exception of

9

Harry, who was hairily bullish with a sullen, sensual face, and Madeleine herself, who, being fortyish, required courage to display herself with the others but carried it off with an air. She was the only one who had passed beyond that magical time between the early twenties and the early thirties when age can mercifully be forgotten. Anne Courtin had a sweet, immobile child's face with staring devouring eyes and a grown child's body with adorable breasts softly nestling within the meager confines of her bikini top. Jean-Claude Courtin offered a startling contrast to his sister. The tallest of the group, his dark brows swooped dramatically, his eyes were soft and liquid, his mouth ripe. His long-limbed body was sleek and smoothly fleshed with little muscular definition, rich and voluptuous. Geneviève, Madeleine's friend, had a trim, elegant boy's body, as did Guy. Charlie and Peter, the two "blond gods" as they had sometimes, embarrassingly, been called, were physically very nearly twins, yet Charlie gave an impression of athletic masculinity that in Peter was somehow converted into delicacy and gentle harmony.

They were all wearing the minimal garment that the French call straightforwardly a *cache-sexe,* a sex-hider. It performed its function with reasonable discretion except in the case of Charlie, whose prodigious parts seemed to strain at the scrap of cloth at his loins, emphasized and magnified by it. Eyes roved, were held, dutifully dropped, returned to it. They all reacted in their various ways. Madeleine, after a long and detailed scrutiny, decided that it was vulgar and typically American; the Americans were always guilty of excess. Guy lusted to see it in action. Anne, knowing her brother's tastes, wondered how he could have chosen Peter. Harry angrily envied it; with a thing like that he wouldn't have to go on hanging around Guy. He could have the whole world. Peter felt his usual twinge of proud jealousy at its exposure, Geneviève stared with fascinated horror, seeing in it all that she loathed and feared in men. Jean-Claude had earlier abandoned any hope of possessing it and resented it now for its hold over Peter.

Charlie was so accustomed to the attention he was attracting that he was scarcely aware of it and in due course stretched out on his stomach on a towel. Others dropped into supine positions. Madeleine finished unfolding an object she had been carrying, which turned out to be a backrest with a small parasol attached. Jean-Claude and Anne stood in front of each other, painstakingly applying oil to every available inch of themselves. Peter picked up a shell lying at his feet and studied it for a moment before dropping it in front of Charlie.

"Pretty," he said. He wandered off, studying the sand. He was an inveterate beachcomber.

Madeleine engaged Charlie in conversation about painting. Names rolled off her lips with impressive familiarity; she knew everybody who had ever made a mark in the Paris art world. She implied that she was prepared to take Charlie under her wing. He didn't bother to point out that Peter was a highly qualified dealer, which she knew, and had always handled the business side of his work. He didn't believe in blurring the line between work and social contact. Just because they had been properly introduced, how did Madeleine know he was worth being taken under her wing? She had probably seen the two things Peter had allowed him to sell to Guy, but they were little more than quick working studies. He sensed here among the people he had met a self-satisfied cliquishness he didn't like; if one knew the right people, one would be launched. He took pride in his independent solitary struggle; he had found in it a solid core of self-respect. As he chatted, his eyes roamed, watching the others.

Harry had plunged into the sea. Peter was halfway down to the western promontory, moving slowly, crouching frequently and digging about in the sand. Jean-Claude and Anne were nearby, still oiling each other. He heard them murmuring together and then they set off, arms draped around each other, in Peter's direction. He felt the clogging around his heart again and his muscles tensed. Should he follow? Jesus. Didn't Peter have the right to stroll on the beach without being spied on? Anyway, Anne was there. He breathed deeply and slowly relaxed, but he remained watchful as he responded politely to Madeleine. He saw the brother and sister slowly overtake Peter, who gave no sign that he was aware of their approach. When they joined him, Peter suspended his search long enough to show them something he had found; they stood close together as they passed it around among themselves. The grouping dissolved and the Courtins moved on ahead, pausing frequently and turning back as Peter crouched over another find. They were nearing the end of the promontory. Before they reached it, Peter stopped and straightened and stood alone for a moment before making a running dive into the sea. Jean-Claude and Anne turned back and waved, but continued on their way. Charlie's eye was caught by a rock formation behind them and for some minutes he forgot his surveillance as he explored its forms and colors, making compositions in his mind. When he returned with a mental jolt to the world around him, he immediately scanned the empty sea. Out there where the beach ended and the shore became a tumble of rocks, Peter's bobbing head would blend into the landscape. Anne was clearly visible perched out on the very end of the promontory. Jean-Claude wasn't with her. In one swift movement, Charlie was on his feet, brushing sand off his arms. Guy was immediately at his side.

"*C'est magnifique*," he said, his eyes fixed on Charlie's crotch. "*Mes hommages*. Why don't we all take everything off? We can be naked here. I don't believe in exercising my imagination needlessly."

Something seemed to explode in Charlie's mind. Revulsion shook him. All these people were vile. He wanted to find Peter and take him away from here. He wasn't worried about Jean-Claude. Peter would be no more interested in his advances than Charlie was in Guy's, but the atmosphere made him feel dirty, dirty for Peter as well as for himself. It seethed with sex; these people had nothing else to think about. He was tempted to tear off his trunks in an act of provocation and defiance. His hand went to the fastening as he looked at Guy with a dangerous smile. The thought of Peter restrained him; Peter would hate for him to expose himself, even without any sexual connotation.

"I think I'm in favor of the imagination," he said.

Guy laughed. "You lead me on. Very well. I'm very clever and very persistent. It will make the summer exciting."

Will it now? Charlie thought. He should have made more of the opportunity to get away when it presented itself a week or two ago, but he hadn't known how to without hurting Peter's feelings. The summer had been Peter's idea. When they had come to Europe before, it had been on Peter's business and they hadn't had time to really absorb it. It had been Peter's idea to give Charlie a chance to work in new surroundings, in a new light, surrounded by new forms. He had found the house and made all the arrangements. It would have been unkind to suggest so soon that it wasn't working out. Still, he could invite the Kingsleys for dinner and encourage them to talk to Peter about Greece. It might work.

As Peter rounded the promontory and headed into the next bay, he caught a glimpse out of the corner of his eye of Jean-Claude climbing along the rocks after him. His heart accelerated so that it became difficult to swim. He let his legs drop and eased over onto his back and floated, waiting for the excitement to subside. He could still turn around and go back to the others. There was no point in a brief encounter with Jean-Claude out here; it would only add to the weight of guilt and frustration that had been accumulating in him for the last few days.

Frustration, really, more than guilt, frustration at being able to have only brief secret moments with Jean-Claude. He supposed he ought to feel more guilty but he knew he wasn't really doing anything bad to Charlie, given the circumstances. He could even imagine making a case for himself in the inconceivable event that he had the opportunity to do so. It had nothing to do with their life together. He was as much in love with Charlie as ever. He hadn't asked to be struck by a sudden uncontrollable infatuation with Jean-Claude. It had happened, and surely it was better to do something about it and get over it than to let it eat away at everything that was most precious to them both. It had been getting so that he couldn't make love successfully with Charlie without thinking of Jean-Claude. If that trick had failed—it was too appalling to think about.

Of course, he couldn't hope for Charlie to accept any of this, any more than he would, if the situation were reversed. If he caught Charlie doing what he'd been doing, he would kill him, or kill himself, or both probably. Then why was he doing it?

In the past, when he had been violently attracted to someone, the normal complications of life had always given him time to reason himself out of it. Meeting places had to be arranged. Stories had to be invented. By the time you did all that, you realized it wasn't worth it. Here, living as they did, practically naked all day long, a look was almost as complete a commitment as an embrace, and the final step was such a small one that it seemed idiotic not to take it, like a swimmer up to his waist in water making a big fuss about getting wet all over. He had as good as been to bed with Jean-Claude before they had even touched each other. That was the only thing that had made it possible to take the vast and almost unimaginable step of being unfaithful after all these years. He had fought it and resisted it and had been terrified by what he had sensed it was doing to him. Life without loving Charlie was a contradiction in terms.

Life *was* Charlie and always had been since he had first set eyes on him, not even knowing that passion between two men was possible. Even after Charlie had banished him from his life and got married, even when he was more or less doing the streets of New York, changing bedmates every night and sometimes a couple of times during the day, too, it had never changed, even though he had longed and prayed for it to. Charlie had only to say the word to get him back. Always Charlie, so that he had been quite unprepared to cope with the predicament of Jean-Claude.

He had been tempted to extricate himself by advocating the Kingsleys' Greek project, but he was afraid Charlie would suspect something after all the trouble he had taken to arrange the St. Tropez summer. Besides, he had looked into Jean-Claude's eyes once too often; the commitment had been made.

The alternative had been his desperate plot to spend what he truly hoped and believed would be a therapeutic night with the boy. Do it and get it out of your system. If it hadn't worked out like that, it was because Jeannot had revealed to him a side of himself he hadn't known existed, a dominating male side with a lust for possession, rather than being possessed. Totally uncharacteristic. A sexual aberration. Thinking of that night and of the few hurried, anxious occasions since, he felt a turbulence all through him—heart, loins, a tingling even in his hands and legs—so that he had trouble keeping himself afloat. He knew the boy was near, probably watching him from the shore, hesitating to make a move for fear of contravening some intention of Peter's. Peter had that sort of power over him. He wondered if he dared risk taking him up under the trees. If he did, he must make very sure that it was for no more than ten minutes, absolute maximum.

He heard the thrashing of water and his heart surged up suffocatingly. He let his body straighten into the buoyant sea and turned and saw Jeannot churning toward him. His eyes swept the shore. Anne was the only person in sight, alone at the end of the promontory. Jeannot flailed the sea with his arms in a final stroke and came gliding up to him. His brows arched up thrillingly into his temples. His dark eyes were soft with desire. Peter longed for the moment that was bound to come—tomorrow? the next day?—when he could look at him with indifference. He knew that if he could spend a whole uninhibited day with him, it would be over. The boy would bore him into his senses.

"Hello, child," he said into Jeannot's eyes. Mesmerized, he allowed him to slide up against him and their mouths met above the water in a salty kiss. Peter's sex stiffened and he gave his trunks a tug to allow it to ride up against his belly. He kicked the sea to back away. "That's enough of that. People can see us."

"Only Anne. My lover, I've wanted you so. I couldn't stay away any longer. Didn't you know I was waiting for you on the beach?"

"I knew. I was about to come in."

"We have a chance to be together. Why do you waste it?"

"It's not safe. I'm not safe around you."

"You talk as if you are not your own master. You're too young to be tied down. I want you. Why don't you take me?"

"Listen, child, I'm almost thirty-one. That's a hell of a lot older than you are. You'll find out things. I'm not my own master because I don't want to be. My life's the way I want it. No matter how much I want you, there are more important things. I've told you. You said you understood."

"I do understand, or did. But things change all the time. I'm more in love with you than I've been with anybody in my life. It's more every day."

Their arms and legs waved slowly to keep them afloat, touching constantly, sliding across each other caressingly. Only the necessity to keep moving restrained Peter from taking the boy in his arms. "Just remember, *I* haven't said anything about love. I might've said almost anything else but not that. I'm nuts about you, but that's sex, child. Don't get it confused."

"All right, but for sex we must be together. When can that be?"

"Whenever I can manage it, like yesterday. Maybe tomorrow.

15

Shopping's a good excuse. We've got to be damn careful."

"I don't know how long I can be careful with you." He took a deep breath and sank beneath the sea. Peter felt his hands on him, lifting his sex out of his trunks so that it rose fully into erection, stroking it, peeling the trunks down over his feet. He didn't resist, though his eyes kept watch on the shore; it felt glorious to be all naked in the sea. It was amazing what a difference the little scrap of cloth made. Jean-Claude surfaced with a great blowing of water and tossed his thick, dark hair back from his eyes. He laughed as he held up two pairs of trunks. "We are all ready for each other now. Underwater, you're a beauty—do you say that? You're so beautiful. It's unbelievable."

"If you lose those, we'll have to stay out here all day. Come on. We better go in."

They struck out for shore, not very purposefully, letting their bodies glide against each other. Jean-Claude dived and rolled under him like a porpoise, his hands and legs and chest constantly brushing Peter's sex, keeping it erect. When they reached shallow water, Jeannot took him in his arms and pulled him down and they sank together, briefly locked in a submarine embrace. All of Peter's body was suddenly sensitized and electrified by a gathering orgasm.

He struggled to the surface, gasping and shaking off water. "Hey, wait. Jesus. Let's sit here and cool off. We've got to get our trunks on."

Jeannot made another lunge at him and lifted him and grappled him toward shore. Peter laughed and struggled, slipping about in his arms, half-in and half-out of the water. Jean-Claude beached him with his legs still submerged and slid down over him and took his sex in his mouth. Peter's body gave a great leap and he fell back under the sun, his eyes closed, and lifted his hips in surrender to Jeannot's worship. In an instant, he remembered where he was, remembered Anne, remembered that the whole world could see them. He struggled up with a little cry and snatched his trunks where Jeannot had dropped them and plunged back into the water. His knees almost buckled as the orgasm threatened to overwhelm him, but the sea calmed him and the crisis receded. His heart was racing with panic.

Advancing into the sea, he forced himself to glance over his shoulder and survey the beach, prepared to see the whole party

16

lined up as witnesses. Anne was still there, but there was nobody else. When he was in up to his waist he stood and waited for the tumult in him to subside completely. Maybe this would be a lesson to him. Maybe now he could free himself from this ridiculous infatuation. He was trembling with the frustration of the interrupted climax.

He heard splashing behind him and his trembling increased as Jean-Claude moved in beside him. His sex lifted achingly; it felt as if it would remain erect forever.

"Why didn't you let me finish?" Jeannot reproached him.

"Are you out of your mind? Anne could see us."

"She's watched me before. She would have warned us if anybody was coming."

"Jesus. I don't go in for public performances." It was unbearable to feel Jeannot so close and not be able to do anything about it. He was seething with thwarted desire. He was almost sorry he hadn't let him go ahead since, as it turned out, nobody would have seen. Except Anne. He must be losing his mind if he was willing to let the girl watch. "Don't you understand?" he burst out. "Anybody could turn up any minute. I told you we have to be careful."

Jean-Claude sank down until the water was up to his chin and moved around in front of him. From the shore, they would look innocent enough, but the proximity of Jeannot's mouth to his straining sex made his heart begin to pound again. He wished it was possible to do it underwater.

"Now you're angry," Jeannot said contritely. "Let me just look at you. I've never had a chance to really look at you." His hand drifted toward Peter's sex.

"Don't touch me," Peter warned him hastily. "I'm almost coming."

Jeannot brightened. "Yes? Me too. I think I could come just looking at you. Are all Americans big there?"

"Lots of them are bigger." Peter stood with his feet apart in the shifting sand, his hips thrust forward so that his sex rose tautly before him, magnified by the water, long and straight, an arrow of flesh.

"Amazing," Jeannot murmured.

"I shouldn't think you've had many complaints, as far as that's concerned."

17

Jeannot smiled. "No. We're a good match. A good pair. Is that right? But that's what's so amazing. I'm much bigger than you everywhere else."

Peter felt once more the preliminaries of orgasm in the tingling of his loins. Could they make a dash for the trees and find some satisfaction there? No. He obviously couldn't trust himself to observe any reasonable precautions. He swung his hips forward so that the head of his sex surfaced. "Up periscope. Damn the torpedoes." He burst into laughter and felt his tension pass. He doubled over with laughter. This was more like it. He would laugh himself back to sanity. He laughed still more when he caught a glimpse of Jeannot's puzzled, tentative smile. "Have you really let Anne watch?" he asked when the laughter had subsided.

"Of course, if she happened to be there. She's in love with me. We've always known everything about each other."

"Knowing and seeing are two different matters," Peter said. His mind skirted a memory he still couldn't face without a shrinking of the spirit, a sense of impoverishment and lasting humiliation. He hurried on, "Just don't try any tricks like that again. I don't see how I can face her."

"But that's of a foolishness. She's in love with you, too. She wants us to be happy. It will make her happy to see us together. She would love to see you now. I would love to show her my beautiful lover. I've told her about what you've taught me."

Distaste and an unfamiliar excitement mingled with his hunger for the boy. It would take very little to make him despise him. Already, he felt safer, already the urgency of his desire had eased. He felt that the moment was near when he could look at him and feel nothing. With an effort of will, of which he would have been incapable only five minutes ago, he turned from him and dropped down into the water and pulled on his trunks so that his erection was trapped once more against his belly. "Put your pants on," he called over his shoulder as he sprang forward onto the water with a splash and swam vigorously away, waiting for the exertion to reduce his sex to normal.

When he turned back, Jean-Claude was standing on the beach, properly covered, waiting for him. He splashed out of the water to him, alert to his own responses, hoping that the last few minutes had speeded up the process of alienation. Jeannot stood with

18

a hestitant smile on his ripe lips, his eyes guileless and welcoming. He didn't speak but put his arm around Peter's shoulders and hugged him awkwardly, boyishly. It was such a simple expression of need that Peter was immediately disarmed; he would have to get through another day of torment.

They walked the fifty-odd yards back to the promontory where Anne had been sitting all along. Peter braced himself to speak to her naturally, to act as if nothing unusual had happened. Her staring eyes were on him when they joined her.

"You're so lovely," she said without stirring, staring up at him from the rock on which she was perched. "You two looked absolutely divine all naked together. It must be heaven to make love with you. Jeannot's very lucky."

Her open acceptance of their physical intimacy struck a quick, responsive chord in him; he did get weary of playing straight for all their straight friends. Charlie had always taken more naturally to the deviousness behind which he insisted they hide their life together. As if they were fooling anybody. "I'm not sure how lucky either of us is," he said. It was the first opportunity he had had to speak openly to her. "Jeannot knows I tried not to let this happen."

"Would your friend be very angry if he knew?"

"Yes, very. Worse than that. I don't expect Jeannot to have any secrets from you, but you mustn't let anybody else know."

"Yes, of course. But you must be more careful, too. I've told Jeannot. If he loves you, he must put your feelings before his own and be grateful that he has had you even for a night."

Peter looked down into the odd child's face. His eyes wavered to the breasts nestled in the bikini top and then met her extraordinary gaze. A little spasm of tenderness for her passed through him. "You're a funny one," he said with a smile.

"No. I know about love and its pain. I told Jeannot to leave you to your friend but then he told me you wanted him, too. I was glad you could arrange it last week."

He looked at Jeannot and met dark eyes full of longing. Anne was fanning the flame; the fire was not yet out. The inexplicable passion that had driven him from their first meeting came pounding up in him. His scanty trunks became a painful confinement. The presence of a witness was oddly liberating, giving a stamp of public recognition to their liaison, which in a more rational mood he would have preferred to avoid but which now added a unique thrill to the moment. On an uncontrollable impulse, he reached out and took Jeannot's hand. The contact was like a blow, almost making him lose his balance. His chest heaved and his rigid sex slid up at an angle along the top of his trunks. "I want him, all right," he said. "He knows that."

Anne laughed softly. "It is quite obvious that you both want each other, but we should go back. Kiss as lovers should and then we must go."

He looked into Jeannot's mesmerizing eyes and felt a compulsion to do as Anne suggested. He knew that if they kissed, they wouldn't stop there. Anne's presence was no restraint. On the contrary, she was a spur. He must be getting depraved in his old age. His sex almost burst from its confinement at the thought of her watching him take her brother. He shook his head slowly.

"No," he muttered to himself. He turned abruptly and stepped out onto a rock hanging over the sea. "You two go on," he said. "I'm—"

He commanded his muscles to function and dove in. The shock of cold water immediately steadied him. He wasn't very pleased with himself. What was this exhibitionistic bit? Letting Anne watch. Getting a hard-on in front of her. If he wanted to make a public spectacle of himself, why not do it with Charlie? That was who he belonged to, always had and always would; he would love to have it publicly recognized as a marriage, which was what it was.

He had figured out that he had been separated from Charlie, in the sense that he had thought they would never be together again, for exactly 146 days of his active sexual life—the duration of Charlie's marriage to a girl (he didn't count his year in the Army, during which he had been completely neuter, regardless of the way it had ended)—and in that time he had been had by about 200 guys. If he had had any great urge to experiment, he would have done so then. What was he trying to prove? That he could have somebody the way Charlie had him? Great. That was firmly established now, at the risk of destroying his whole life. He had to pull himself together. He would probably go to Jeannot tomorrow morning because he had more or less promised and, besides, there had to be a last time after today, but that would have to be it. So long as he was sure that his obsession with Jeannot no longer threatened his love for Charlie, he wanted that to be it.

He swam hard, determined to get back to the party before Jeannot and Anne.

❄   ❄   ❄

Charlie immediately spotted the Courtins coming back along the promontory. They had probably been together all the time, Jean-Claude just out of sight on the other side of the rocky point. There was still no sign of Peter. He was doubtless off somewhere exploring on his own, the way he liked to do. Charlie took a long breath of relief. He had been a damn fool to be so upset by Guy's silly, malicious remark. He would have been an even bigger fool to go rampaging after them, as he had been tempted to do. The fact that Jean-Claude was so obviously swooning over him wasn't Peter's fault; people were always falling in love with him. Who could blame them? He turned back to the group with a private smile on his lips and encountered Harry's eyes. Harry responded as if the smile were intended for him; Charlie saw the truculence in his face lift slightly.

"You liking it here OK?" Harry asked, the attempt at cordiality coming out guarded and surly.

"Yes, sure. It's wonderful," Charlie said coolly. He never pretended to like people when he didn't. Life was full enough of pretenses just winning some measure of acceptance.

"Course, you're not here for long. Couple of months?" Harry launched into a snarling attack on living conditions in France, the strikes, the shortages, the vicious shopkeepers. "One thing," he concluded, "you don't have trouble here with staff. Not like at home."

Charlie contained his mirth. Staff, yet. He wouldn't have been surprised to learn that Harry's parents were servants. "Servants aren't really one of my big problems," he commented politely.

"Guy lets them walk all over him, but I don't go for that. I expect service and no crap."

"Well, naturally," Charlie agreed, with a tremor of spent laughter in his voice. He looked back down the beach and saw Jean-Claude and Anne still ambling along toward them. He felt a slight stirring of anxiety for Peter. His gaze shifted and then he saw him, the golden head moving along the water at an angle that would bring him to shore ahead of the Courtins. He was swimming flat-out, making speed. Charlie kept his eyes on him, the sight of him more than usually welcome because of the moment of anxiety he had felt for him. He watched as he ran up out of the sea, the beautiful symmetry of his body glistening in the sun. He stopped and called something back to the brother and sister and then turned and came jogging down the beach, all swift and lithe and bursting with youth. A great wave of love rose in Charlie as he watched his approach.

Peter circled around the others and dropped to his knees beside him. Charlie looked up over the swell of the crotch to the lightly heaving, flatly muscled abdomen, lingered over the broad full definition of the chest muscles, completely hairless, before he met the smiling blue of his eyes. Peter's regard was eager and devoted; it touched Charlie with special poignancy because of having doubted him.

"I've been swimming and swimming," Peter said. "It's gorgeous."

"You're pretty gorgeous yourself." He maintained his social guard, making it something he could have said to any of them, but he exerted a slight pressure with his arm against Peter's.

A small frown creased Peter's brow. After what he had been through, he would have liked Charlie to tumble him over, hold him in his arms, kiss him on the mouth. He giggled as he imagined this unlikely occurrence and put his hand on Charlie's shoulder as he lowered his head to his ear. "You're beautiful. Has anybody said anything about lunch? I'm starving."

"I think it's in the offing. I could use a drink."

"So could I. Let's try to get them moving soon."

Peter chuckled. "You have only to say the word to Guy."

Charlie sensed a keyed-up excitement in him. The exhilaration of a morning of physical activity? Sexy. He felt the same way himself. Perhaps there would be time before lunch to do something about it. He studied Peter's hand where it rested on his thigh, long-fingered, big-knuckled, powerful. He inhaled the clean salty tang of his skin, underlaid by the faint musky animal smell that had always intoxicated him. He wished they were alone. It required a real effort of control not to touch him, caress him, lay his hands all over him. He looked at his large smooth nipples and smiled to himself, knowing what he could do to Peter when he touched them. His eyes lifted and swam into the extraordinary sweetness of his face, alive, responsive, incapable of any meanness. It was absurd for him to go on looking so like the boy of under twenty whom Charlie had seduced and whose first lover he had been. Charlie had only himself to blame that he hadn't been his only lover. People generally took Charlie, quite accurately, for only a year or two older than Peter, so he supposed he was holding up pretty well, too.

They were leaning against each other, heads close, murmuring together when Jean-Claude and Anne rejoined the party. Jean-Claude stopped and brooded down at them; neither looked up. Anne took his arm and led him over to Guy and Madeleine.

Slowly, the party started to reorganize itself. They had their final plunges and gathered up their things and straggled back through the trees to the inn, a band of immaculate gypsies. Guy had taken all of the half-dozen rooms at the establishment for the day and they all went up to shower and change.

As soon as they were alone in the room where they had left a little traveling bag earlier, Charlie peeled off his damp trunks. Peter was immediately self-conscious and uneasily postponed stripping as if the morning had left some telltale mark on his body. His response to Jean-Claude was so intense and immediate. He hated it to be any less with Charlie, as it had been recently. He bustled about, keeping clear of Charlie, avoiding looking at him. He picked up the trunks Charlie had left on the floor and spread them out on the windowsill. He opened the bag he had packed for them.

"God, I'm thirsty," Charlie said behind him.

"Yeah, me too. Let's just wash the salt off and go find the bar." Once it was established that they weren't going to linger in the room, Peter was able to relax. He pulled off his trunks and placed them beside Charlie's. He tossed fresh shirts and shorts out onto the bed. "Which do you want?" he asked. They wore each other's clothes, or rather owned a joint wardrobe.

"I don't care. I'll take that blue shirt if you don't want it. How goes the flirtation with Jean-Claude?"

Peter's ears were instantly alert for undertones in the question but found none. It was light and playful. He laughed, "How goes yours with Guy?"

"I really had to lay into him this morning. He tried to make some insinuation about your trip to Paris last week."

Peter's heart skipped a beat. "How do you mean?"

"Oh, something about Jean-Claude having gone somewhere Wednesday night and whether you were really on the train. I don't know what it was all about."

Blood rushed to Peter's cheeks. His hands trembled as he leaned over the bag pretending to look for something in it. "Silly fucker," he said, hoping that his voice would work. "How did he think I got back?"

"I don't know. I suppose you could've taken a plane to Nice. It sounds complicated even for an experienced old roué like you. Getting from Nice to St. Raphael to pick up the car. What if I'd come to meet the train? I almost did, as a matter of fact. Let alone the danger of running into somebody we know."

Peter's scalp crawled as he was presented with the risks he had run. He continued to rummage in the bag, but Charlie's accurate account of his movements on Wednesday afternoon and Thursday morning had given him time to compose himself. He felt sure that his blush wouldn't show through his tan. "Guy must be getting desperate for you," he said dismissively. "Where's the damn—? Oh, here it is." He pulled out the comb he had been clutching all along and threw down the bag and turned as Charlie laughed.

"Oh, he's mad for me. I got a gilt-edged proposition. I'm supposed to take Harry's place." Charlie was standing idly at the foot of the other bed, naked, a hip thrust out rather in the attitude of Michaelangelo's David, his cloudy purple eyes smiling at Peter. His regard deepened as Peter's met his. "I guess we're irresistible," he said. "You certainly are."

Peter felt a twinge of apprehensive withdrawal. He picked up a shirt to cover himself. "I just happen to be in love with you, in case that comes as a surprise to you. How about that drink?" Even as he parried Charlie's look, he felt everything happening the way he wanted it to. There was a welcome stirring in his loins. Had Charlie's coming so near the truth frightened him into his senses at last? He looked at Charlie's superbly tanned body, so like it had been almost eleven years ago except for a little more hair on the chest, still his first and only love. His sex jutted forward and nudged the shirt. There was nothing equivocal

24

about that. His eyes dropped to Charlie's imposing sex, extended, as he knew it so well, in prelude to erection, curving out slightly toward one thigh, heavy with promise and power. He threw his head back and laughed with the sheer joy of knowing that everything was working right and tossed the shirt from him.

Charlie looked at him approvingly. "That's my baby. I'd recognize him anywhere. Are you planning to get a drink like that?"

"Drink?" Peter asked through laughter. "I just happen to've brought the stuff. The eternal optimist." He snatched a tube from the bag and advanced to Charlie. As he did so, he watched the massive sex swing out straight from his thighs, lengthen thrillingly, swell, lift its darkly shining head.

"You mean, the drink is going to have to wait?" Charlie's brows rose devilishly, his smile was assured and possessive. He put a hand on the back of Peter's neck and held it tight.

"It sure is." Peter reached out and took Charlie's sex in his hand. It sprang up under his touch. "Oh, oh, oh," he murmured. "I don't think I'll ever really believe it. I saw them all eyeing it this morning. If they could see it now, they'd faint dead away."

Charlie laughed. "I don't remember you ever fainting."

"I might some day. I think it's growing." He squeezed the tube into the palm of his hand and began to apply lubricant. "It's so hot and hard and enormous."

Charlie laughed again and put out a hand for some of the lubricant and ran it between Peter's buttocks. His other hand stroked Peter's sex.

Peter growled deep in his throat and swayed against him and rested his forehead against the side of his head. "What are you going to do to me, mister?" he whispered. It was a private joke and laughter shook their bodies, exciting them further as they stood close against each other. Peter wanted Charlie's hands on him, he wanted to feel the weight of his body bearing down on him, he wanted the great column of flesh inside him, raging through him, exploding into him. He wanted to be taken, used, totally possessed, as only Charlie could ever possess him. His legs began to tremble as Charlie's hands teased him toward orgasm.

"I think I'm going to come in about three seconds," he said with a little giggle. "Take as long as you can, darling. Make me come twice. That'll be heaven."

Not long afterward, the other members of the party heard groans of pleasure and muffled laughter issuing from behind the thin partitions of the Americans' room. This was followed some time later by a succession of hoarse, triumphant cries.

Guy looked across his room at Harry with a wry smile. "Really. After ten years. They must have been telling the truth. Lucky Peter. I'd say he's getting quite spectacularly fucked. A pity you're not so well equipped. There might be some excuse for you."

When the sounds began, Jean-Claude stamped around the room, flinging clothes about. As they continued, he sank onto the edge of the bed all huddled up in himself. Anne hummed a little tune in an attempt to cover what was taking place on the other side of the partition. At the cries, Jean-Claude tore his hands through his hair and burst into tears. He had recognized Peter's voice. Anne went to him and stood over him and stroked his head soothingly.

"He has told you how it must be," she said.

Madeleine and Geneviève were stretched out on their beds getting a moment's rest. Geneviève sprang up angrily.

"I must say—" she exclaimed. "I find it too disgusting. They might wait until they're in their own bed."

"They're Americans, dear." Madeleine chuckled fruitily. "They lack our weary sensibilities. Did you look at Charles this morning? What can you expect, with such an instrument? There will always be somebody to play it."

The party reassembled under a grape arbor in the kitchen courtyard and drank pastis while Guy conferred intently with the untidy little cook-proprietor. Charlie and Peter were the center of all eyes, either envious or jealous or disapproving. The blond gods glowed with well-being. They all noticed Peter's tendency to hug Charlie's side. Guy soon cut between them and led Charlie into the midst of what was beginning to look like a witches' orgy. A wood fire was blazing in an open stone hearth and a great iron cauldron was set on a grate over it. A good many assistants were milling about, presumably the proprietor's family judging from their age span, tending the fire, carrying pots back and forth, chopping tomatoes and onions.

"You see, it's very important that it should be done very quickly just before we eat it," Guy explained. He indicated a table where a quantity of gleaming headless fish were heaped up in several piles. "Some places, they cook the fish with their heads on. They are necessary for the flavor, but not pretty to see. Darius cooks them separately and adds the bouillon. A detail, but important."

Charlie's eyes were held by patterns and forms. He turned instinctively to point something out to Peter, but Peter wasn't there. It really was a bore being with others all the time. He politely gave his attention to Guy, who identified the great variety of sea creatures by their French names, the obscenely scarlet *rascasse*, the creamy-gray *loup de mer*, the *congre*, as well as *langouste* and spidery crabs and an odd little shellfish Charlie had never seen before.

"We are eight," Guy went on, totally absorbed in the operation. "There is no point in doing it for fewer. Otherwise, I'd have asked just you, With Peter, of course. At least a dozen varieties of fish are essential for it to be right."

The activity seemed to accelerate around them. Children were chopping herbs and smashing garlic in a mortar. Darius advanced on the fish with a long, murderous knife that looked homemade and deftly chopped the bigger ones into thick slices. The cauldron began to bubble fatly, making a thick plopping sound. A woman added wood to the fire. The bubbling grew more rapid, the cauldron began to sing. The kitchen brigade rushed at it, bearing pots and copper cans and flung their contents into it. Darius scuttled after them, adding a platterful of *langouste* and crab and slabs of fish.

"There," Guy said with a sigh of released tension. "It's most important that all the fish not go in at once. Otherwise, half of them are overcooked. In exactly fifteen minutes we will eat." He turned to Darius who was swabbing his brow with a great white rag. "*La rouille est déjà préparée?*"

"*Mais bien sûr, monsieur le comte. Tout est pret.*"

"*Bien.*" He turned back superbly to Charlie, a medieval prince regulating his household. "Now you will see. I've arranged all this just for you. After what I've just heard, I'm beginning to face the fact that I'm wasting my time, but no matter."

"What you've just heard?"

"My dear!" Guy smiled a thin aristocratic smile. "Upstairs. Such an orgiastic hue and cry. Such groans of ecstasy."

Charlie blushed. "Oh, dear. You could hear us?"

"Of course, but don't look like that. It was a joy—vicarious certainly, but the imagination ran rampant. You and Peter don't sometimes go in for group activities? Gang-bangs, I think you call them. I might be satisfied just to see you at play."

Charlie thought of his year alone in New York while Peter was in the Army and blushed again. "No. I'm afraid not."

"No? Ah, well, patience. I wish I could say that's the motto of the Sainvals. Actually, it's 'The Devil Take the Hindmost.' A rough translation. I don't suppose you could be the devil?"

Charlie laughed. "Are you the hindmost?"

"Gladly," Guy said with a suggestive smile.

They mingled with the others as a last pastis was poured. Madeleine had taken charge of Peter. Charlie heard her rich voice pouring over him. "—at the party tonight, I must speak to Clo-Clo about you. But how absurb of me. I'm so stupid. I keep forgetting that you're *the* Peter Martin. You look so sublimely young. How is one to believe that you're also a very shrewd businessman?"

Charlie avoided Anne and Jean-Claude and exchanged pleasantries with the rather discontented-looking young woman called Geneviève, about whom he knew nothing except that she seemed somehow attached to Madeleine. He felt her snub him, which intrigued him until he thought of what Guy had just told him. His jaw set with anger. Was she cutting him because he was a queer? What in hell did she think her host was? All his protective aggressiveness was aroused. Granted, he and Peter should have thought of the possibility of being heard. They wouldn't have abandoned themselves quite so completely if it weren't for this awful enveloping atmosphere of sex. They weren't queers like these others. They were two people who were in love with each other and had made a decent life for themselves. Just watch it, lady, he thought belligerently, prepared to attack if she made the slightest ambiguous or derogatory remark.

In a few moments, Guy was herding them all in to lunch. "Àllons, mes enfants. A table. Nous sommes servis." They filed into a dark, cool dining room, all blackened wood and copper, and gathered around the only table that had been set. Guy took Charlie's arm and insisted he take the place of honor at his right. He let the others fend for themselves. Charlie saw Jean-Claude crowding close to Peter, but just as they sat, Anne cut in between them. Trying to save her brother from making a fool of himself?

Taking over Peter for herself? No matter. He had no further worries on that score.

A steaming tureen was borne in and ladled out, inspiring sighs and groans as the soup's aromas were released. It was followed by platters of fish, which they spooned into the rich bouillon, which was in turn topped by thick, toasted slices of French loaf smothered in "rust," the fiery rust-colored, garlic-laden *rouille*. There was a suspenseful pause as they all gazed at their brimming bowls and then Guy gestured to Charlie to begin as he took the first spoonful. They all followed suit, and there was a chorus of appreciative cries and greedy moans as the full impact of the superb mess struck them. They fell to in earnest and the only sound was the clunk of spoons against pottery and the smacking of lips. Anne broke the silence with sudden laughter and they all burst out laughing with her.

"*Quels cochons que nous sommes*," Guy announced delightedly.

"It's fantastic," Charlie gasped as he came up for air. They began to chatter happily. They ate, and ate some more, washing it all down with beakers of a chilled rosé of Provence. As he reached his capacity, Charlie felt himself drifting into a contented, stupified lethargy. He glowed with the sun, and the memory of Peter's body in his arms, and with whatever was taking place in his overfed stomach. The contented, inordinately healthy-looking group had finally achieved a sort of wholesome harmony. He smiled at Guy with an approximation of genuine affection.

"You were right. It *was* perfect. You're a prince among men."

"Aha! You see? I warned you. You will be seduced by the *bouillabaisse*."

When the dishes were removed and were replaced by a huge bowl of grapes and figs and peaches, he became vaguely aware that the harmony was dissolving. A preoccupied look had settled over Guy. The others shifted about restlessly and snatched at the fruit without eating it. As Charlie struggled back to a state nearer to consciousness, he remembered other meals with Guy and realized immediately what was up, although he was surprised that it was on the program here. He took a bunch of grapes and began to pop them lazily into his mouth. He saw Guy signal to Harry and then rise.

"Well go prepare," he announced. He looked down at Charlie.

"You're coming?"

"I don't know if I can move."

"We'll be waiting."

Geneviève was already on her feet. Madeline followed more slowly until only Charlie and Peter and the Courtins were left at table. Charlie looked across at Peter. "Do you want to?" he asked.

Peter shook his head.

"But you must," Jean-Claude broke in. "It will be bliss after the meal."

"Charlie doesn't want to," Peter pointed out. "I don't either, particularly. It doesn't do anything for us."

Peter glanced at Jeannot and saw the hurt disappointment in his eyes and was not immune to it. He felt much surer of himself since the glorious interlude with Charlie before lunch. He could afford to let the boy down gently without fear of repercussions with Charlie. He was working his way through this odd, unwanted episode without damage on any side. "Oh, well, what the hell," he said, looking at Charlie, "I suppose we have our duty as guests. This is a big deal for Guy. I guess we'd better join the party."

They all rose, Charlie bringing up the rear. He was aware that Peter had allowed Jean-Claude to settle the question, but he knew how tiresome it could become to keep on running all the time when you were being pursued. A harmless sop.

He trailed the others up the stairs and followed them into the room Guy was occupying. The lacquered box containing the pipes was already open on a table, the spirit lamp lighted and Harry was heating and shaping the glob of opium with miniature instruments. The others were stretched out on the beds. Guy beckoned to Charlie and took his hand and pulled him down beside him. He complied with Guy's wishes in the same spirit he supposed Peter had given into to Jean-Claude. What harm could it do? "You should loosen your shorts," Guy directed.

"They're loose enough," Charlie propped himself against a pillow, only half-reclining, with one foot on the floor. Peter settled on the other bed and Jeannot immediately stretched out beside him. Anne took a place by Geneviève, who was watching Harry's preparations with intent hungry eyes. The opium sizzled over

30

the fire, and Harry dropped it into the little bowl of the long straight pipe and turned and offered it to the assembly. Guy waved a languid hand at Geneviève, who reached for it greedily and pulled on it with blind concentration. Harry returned to his flame. Charlie looked at Peter and their eyes met. They lifted their eyebrows slightly in an expression of the deep solidarity between them that set them apart from everybody else, complete in each other, indestructibly and happily alien. Charlie's eyelids dropped contentedly; this could go on for some time, only two pipes for eight people and some of them used to four or five pipes at a sitting. When the next one was ready, Guy lifted his hand and touched his shoulder. From the way he moved, Charlie realized that Guy had already had his first.

"For you," he said dreamily. "It's very fine. The best I've had for some time."

Charlie puffed dutifully, pulling the smoke deep into his lungs, wishing for something miraculous to happen. So far, nothing had. At least now he could go to sleep. He waited for the pipes to go the rounds, just barely awake, hoping that he looked as if he were in some sort of mystical trance. When the pipe came back to him, he waved it away. "No, I'm fine." He pulled himself to his feet. "I've got to have a nap," he said to no one in particular. He passed behind Peter and lightly touched the back of his head. As he did so, he saw that he had Jean-Claude's hand clasped in his, hidden down between their thighs. His jaw dropped with a gasp and his heart leaped up painfully. His eyes shot to Peter's crotch to see if there were any telltale signs of excitement there, but he saw nothing.

"I'll be right along," Peter said.

Charlie forced himself on out of the room. As soon as he closed the door, he wanted to go back and pull Peter to his feet and drag him away. Of course, holding hands didn't mean anything in this set. They were all constantly pawing each other. He couldn't expect Peter to make a scene about it in front of everybody. He had himself permitted Guy small physical intimacies simply because it would have seemed prudish to object. He still didn't like it. He didn't like any of it. He felt revulsion stirring in him again. They didn't belong here. They didn't belong anywhere. Nobody understood anything about decency and loyalty and devotion. He wished they could lock themselves up some-

31

where away from the world. He stumbled into their room and threw himself on a bed and was asleep.

When he woke up, his eyes immediately sought Peter. The bed beside him was empty. He was on his feet in one bound. He stood looking around him, bewildered. He had no idea what time it was. He ran his fingers through his hair and arranged himself in his shorts as his erection subsided, and hurried across to Guy's room. He knocked on the door. When there was no answer, he opened it and looked in. It was empty. He remembered seeing Anne and Jean-Claude going into the room next to theirs. Where else? He crossed back and knocked again. Silence. He opened the door. Nobody. His heart was racing as he flung himself down the stairs. He careened into their midst; they were all sitting out in front of the inn under an awning, their things gathered around them, ready to go. He came to an abrupt halt, gazing at them with confusion. Peter laughed.

"Guess who's been asleep. I was just coming up to wake you."

He saw that Peter was in the same clothes he had worn for lunch. He looked fresh and glowing. "Didn't you have a nap?"

"I was so full after that lunch I had to go have another swim."

Charlie nodded. As he did so, his eyes were caught by wet swimming things hanging over the edge of Anne's basket, hers and Jean-Claude's. They made an interesting composition. "Have you all been swimming?" he asked.

"Just these three children of the deep," Guy said waspishly. "The rest of us followed your sensible example. Can you imagine what a plunge into cold water would do to your digestive system after such a meal? If their bathing costumes weren't wet, I wouldn't believe it possible."

The innuendo was overtly malicious. Charlie looked at Peter and caught a gleam of anger in his eye. An expression of solidarity was called for. "Peter has a stomach of iron," he said and was warmed by the look of gratitude Peter shot him.

The party they were all going to that night was being given by the Graumonts, out near the end of the peninsula beyond St. Tropez. Peter and Charlie had barely got back to their rented villa from the elaborate lunch excursion before it was time to dress for the evening. The Graumonts were representative, not of the increasingly popular St. Tropez of the gossip column, but of a small, almost invisible stratum of the immensely rich who had acquired their great vacation estates in the twenties or earlier. The Mills-Martins, as Charlie and Peter jokingly referred to themselves, had been given entrée to this exclusive world by clients of Peter's, who were constantly outdoing each other to win his favor; it depended on his good will whether a prized piece would find its way into the collection of one or the other of them. The Mills-Martins had been armed with introductions. Charlie, as a little-known American painter, would have been obliged to expend some effort to make his presence known; Peter was courted. Since they had both been brought up with all the advantages, as the saying goes, they weren't surprised to find themselves consorting with an elite. The only surprise, particularly to Charlie, was in being accepted everywhere 'as a couple. Their subterfuges were brushed aside with invitations to "you and your handsome friend," or "both of you, of course—I'm sure neither of you lets the other out of his sight." The Mills-Martins had become a social reality. Peter, laughing delightedly, had threatened to begin introducing them accordingly.

They dressed for the party in pale slacks, bright scarves and picturesque adaptations of fishermen's shirts, which was accepted formal evening wear in this corner of the coast. They set out in the convertible they had bought and planned to take back to the States, Charlie at the wheel.

"Listen, baby," Charlie said when they were on their way, "I hope you don't go on letting Jean-Claude monopolize you this evening. I don't like its getting to the point where Guy feels free to make cracks."

"I know. You're right. I do find him sort of appealing. He's such a baby for such a big boy."

"Babies can be damn nuisances sometimes."

"You're right. I've already told him not to carry on so in public."

"You mean it's all right in private?"

Peter laughed to cover his slip. "You know what I mean. I don't know whether you noticed, but he was determined to hold hands when we were doing the dope-fiend bit this afternoon. I'd have looked silly if I'd made a fuss in front of the others, but I told him afterward that I didn't like it."

Charlie had wondered if he would mention it, and his doing so confirmed his trust. Still, he felt he had a right to reaffirm

33

what Peter already knew, that he didn't like that sort of sloppy, promiscuous physical contact, not primarily out of jealousy or perhaps not out of jealousy at all, but because it didn't measure up to the standard of conduct they had set for themselves.

"He was mooning at *me* when we first met. You notice that didn't last very long."

"Yes, well, you can be pretty forbidding. I don't seem to have the knack."

"Maybe it's because you don't want to."

"Maybe, in a way. I told you, I think he's sort of sweet. I'm not as tough with people as you are. Still, I don't notice everybody running around making passes at me."

"Doesn't holding hands count as a pass?"

"Not really, here. You know that. Look at Guy. He isn't exactly standoffish with you."

"Guy is a tough, grown-up man. He knows he hasn't a chance in hell of getting anywhere with me."

"OK. OK. You're perfectly right. The next time he even looks at me, I'll knock him flat."

"I'm not joking, you know."

"I know you're not, Champ." He leaned over close to Charlie and put his hand on his knee. "Don't worry. I've made it perfectly clear you're the only person who means anything to me. I won't let him forget it."

"Fine. That's all I'm talking about."

Peter drew a little inner sigh of relief. He had never lied to Charlie. Long ago, he had sworn to himself that he never would but he had never before allowed himself to be pushed so close to betraying his resolve. He didn't know what he would do if he ever got really cornered, except tell the truth and take the consequences. Which made it all the more imperative to get himself disentangled as fast as possible. Jeannot had frightened him this afternoon. He had been withdrawn and moody, and when Peter had warned him not to count on the morning meeting, he had given him a look that hinted at layers of instability that Peter hadn't suspected in him. He had looked as if he might be capable of anything. Peter was going to have to handle him very carefully so that he wouldn't be provoked into making a scene that might involve Charlie and give the whole wretched game away. Peter felt a touch of panic; it had been so thrillingly perfect with Charlie at noon, convincing him that he had averted a serious crisis between them. He couldn't let anything go wrong now. He was going to have to keep very cool for the next day or two. It was already a strain to have to choose words that told the truth and yet covered his enormous lie.

They were driving through vineyards and olive groves in the gathering dusk, catching glimpses of the sea when the road rose. As they progressed, the road grew narrower and rougher.

"Do you know where we're going?" Peter asked.

"I think so. Guy gave me pretty careful directions. There should be a turn to the left soon. They apparently own that whole hillside. The house is on the other side, the Porquerolles side."

They reached the turnoff and began to climb through a forest of cork trees. Charlie switched on the headlights. It was almost dark. He could see lights moving on the road ahead of him. The road wound upward in a succession of tight turns. Charlie handled them with finesse, enjoying his skill. When they reached the crest of the hill, a vast panorama of sea was spread out before them. Distant lights indicated where they had been for lunch. They began the descent and after a few more turns they saw below them, on a high cliff jutting into the sea, a great expanse of roof surrounded by lights.

"I guess that's it," Peter said. "It's big enough."

"The rich are so damned rich here. All the houses are fabulous. Did you ever read that Veblen book? Conspicuous consumption must've been invented here."

"Home is going to seem awfully dinky after all this grandeur."

"I'll take home any day."

"Me too." Peter put his hand on Charlie's knee again and gave it a squeeze.

After a good many more twists and turns, they came to a stop in a wide graveled area in front of a huge, bare, floodlit Italianate facade, unadorned except for a columned doorway. There were some twenty-odd gleaming cars parked haphazardly in front of it. When they entered, they encountered a uniformed manservant, who said, *"Bonsoir, messieurs,"* with a bow and an arm extended in the direction they were to take. They passed through handsomely furnished reception rooms and came out onto a sweep of terrace above landscaped gardens and a swimming pool suspended over the sea. They were greeted by their hostess, who owned theaters and who detached herself from a group near the door. "There you are. I'm so glad you could come. The two most attractive young men on the coast." She offered them a limp hand, palm down, to be kissed. Neither of them had acquired this practice. "My husband is somewhere about. He'll be so pleased to see you. I hope you'll find everything you want. Ah, René. These are two very special American friends." She pronounced their names as they were confronted with the familiar face of a politician who had been Prime Minister recently for a few weeks. After a further brief exchange they moved out into the party.

People wandered about the terrace and down in the garden around the swimming pool. Music was playing somewhere. There were a great many extraordinarily decorative women and sleek, immaculately groomed men. A manservant presented them with a tray of drinks from which Peter selected champagne, Charlie whisky. They spotted Guy and drifted over to him. He was with a celebrated playwright and academician with a startling aureole of white hair who quickly fell into absorbed conversation with Peter. Guy put his hand on Charlie's arm. "Come. I must introduce you. Everybody is dying to meet you. Ah, there's Edwige." He led him over to meet a handsome woman, who was, he explained, a distinguished actress. Charlie had almost been an actor and loved the theater and theater people. He found the woman dazzling even though he was unfamiliar with the French theater and her name meant nothing to him. He did a double-take when he caught sight of Marlene Dietrich in the center of a nearby group. He turned instinctively to point her out to Peter, but Peter was nowhere in sight.

Drinks were passed continually, as were mounds of gray caviar. People gathered into groups, drifted apart, formed new alliances. Everybody had a great deal to say, most of it bright and witty. They switched easily into English when it became apparent that Charlie's French was limited. He had a long, illuminating conversation with a very famous painter. He caught glimpses of Peter from time to time, once with Marlene Dietrich. Trust Peter. In due course, the guests' attention was called to an enormous buffet, at the end of the terrace, spread with lobsters and truffled *foie gras*, hams, smoked salmon, elaborate salads. He was pleased to encounter Jack and Martha Kingsley beside it.

36

"Another stowaway," Jack Kingsley exclaimed. "I thought we were the only lowly Americans who'd been allowed in."

"You let one in and before you know it they've taken over," Charlie said. They had known each other casually in New York and therefore had all fallen on each other like old friends when they had met by chance at the port. Jack had been the victim of some Madison Avenue debacle that had left him with a good deal of money and no job. Instead of fighting back, he had bought a boat and sailed away. The boat was in the harbor after an Atlantic crossing.

"Where's Peter?" Martha asked. She was a pretty, relaxed blonde who looked a good deal younger than her husband. He had a weathered look appropriate to the master of a sailing yacht and close-cropped hair becomingly gray at the temples.

"He's somewhere around. With Marlene Dietrich, I think."

"Cradle-snatching now, is she? There're a couple of babies a-round I wouldn't mind seeing in the movies. Martha won't let me out of her sight."

"Now that Charlie's here. I don't need you any more. Run a-long and play."

"When you put it like that, I wonder if I'd better. Never get married, Charlie boy."

"I've already made my mistake," Charlie said with a laugh. They were the sort he was used to associating with, treating him and Peter as if they were simply good friends, with never a sexual allusion or a hint at their true relationship.

"You two guys haven't reconsidered our proposition?" Jack inquired.

"I've been thinking about it, Jack. In fact it's been on my mind all day. The thing is, I'm really sort of Peter's guest here. He's paid three months for the house. You can't blame him for not wanting to just throw it away."

"He shouldn't think of it like that. He'd make it up by being on board with us. You can't spend money at sea. And just think of it. Sailing around the Greek islands. A real experience you'd never forget. It's great fun here, but hell, we've all had it in a dozen other places."

"Well, you know *I'd* love it. I've always wanted to go to Greece. And sailing—well, it would be fabulous. But aside from everything else, I'm not sure Peter can. He's got a deal cooking that he's got to keep an eye on."

"Well, we certainly want both of you. We have to be four to handle the boat or it would be an awful sweat. Hell, we've got dozens of people begging us to take them, but we think the four of us would really hit it off. We don't want another couple. One girl is enough."

"It's just possible that they're not as mad about us as we are about them," Martha suggested amiably.

Charlie smiled at her. "You should see me in the morning. Anyway, I've got work to do, too. That was the point of taking the house instead of traveling. I've got a show coming up next winter."

"Think about it some more," Jack urged. "We're going to hang around here for another week or two. We'd really like you guys with us."

"Look, why don't you talk to Peter? I was going to suggest it. I don't want him to get the idea that I don't like it here but if you talk him into it, I'd go like a shot. The hell with work. I'd make up the time somehow."

They left the table with laden plates. Charlie saw the Courtins and smiled and nodded to them. Peter wasn't with them. He followed the Kingsleys to one of the numerous tables scattered about the terrace and grounds and ate with them while Jack continued to extoll the wonders of the proposed cruise. Charlie grew increasingly enthusiastic. He had handled small boats all his life and loved sailing. Greece was a remote and cherished dream; it had never occurred to him that he might actually see it someday. To have it offered to him under such ideal conditions was irresistible. He felt completely at ease with the Kingsleys. Jack's man-to-man manner made him feel manly. Martha somehow spared him the dilemma that women generally posed; if you responded to them naturally, they began to get ideas and you had to beat a hasty retreat; if you were cool to them, they went around telling everybody you were a pansy. With Martha, simple friendship seemed possible. He supposed the Kingsleys were that rarity, a happy couple, like the Mills-Martins. If they knew about him and Peter, as they certainly must, they apparently didn't care. They would be easy people to spend a month or two with. It wouldn't be the perfection of being alone with Peter, but it promised a clean, hardy antidote to the decadence he felt here. He didn't know what Peter thought of the idea;

they never seemed to have a chance these days to discuss any-thing seriously. They had let the Kingsleys' invitation slide as not fitting in with their established plans.

"You've got to come to dinner with us," he said. "I'll check with Peter and fix a date for the next day or two. You can talk to him. Unless it interferes with his business, I'm all for it."

Peter had garnered other invitations in the course of the evening—a dinner at Cannes, an offer of an introduction to Pi-casso, who was somewhere around Antibes, some special gala night in Monte Carlo. He had dutifully avoided Jeannot so that when, some time after food had been disposed of, he appeared beside him, Peter was unprepared to be plunged once more into his private conflict.

"Come. I must speak to you," Jeannot said abruptly. His eyes looked as if they weren't quite focusing and his hair was in slight disarray on his forehead. He looked as if he had had a lot to drink. Stirred-up and dangerous, aroused from his usual placi-dity, his attraction was electrifying. Peter set himself to resist it.

"We can't talk privately. Not here. Don't be silly," he said in quiet admonition. They were standing on the fringes of a group that had gathered at one end of the pool discussing the possibility of a swim.

"I tell you, I must talk with you. I can't stand it any longer."

Peter looked quickly around him. Charlie was nowhere to be seen. Better to get him away before he said something that would attract everybody's attention. Again, he felt that the boy might be capable of anything. He looked at him and nodded. "All right," he said.

Jeannot turned and disappeared quickly around the back of the dressing pavillion. After another quick glance around him, Peter followed. Jeannot was waiting for him and put his arm around his shoulder and led him to a path under the trees.

After a moment, they came out into a small clearing at the head of steps leading down to the sea. Light from the party filtered through to it. Jeannot stopped and pulled Peter to him and kissed him avidly.

Peter drew back with a little laugh. "Take it easy, I'm only going to stay a minute."

"I'm not surprised. All evening, you flirt with everybody, but you can't even look at me."

"Don't be an ass. Being polite to people at a party isn't flirting. And it's none of your business anyway. We're not setting up housekeeping, so don't start getting ideas."

"You're mine." He ran a hand down to Peter's crotch and found his sex and gripped it. Peter resolutely pulled the hand away before he could be further aroused. Jeannot burst out, "Why do you do that? You want me, but you always pretend you don't. It's been like that all day."

"All day? What about this morning? I almost let you make me come in front of Anne. What's pretending about that? Come on. Tell me what you want to say."

"Everything. Why can't we go somewhere now? I can't wait until tomorrow."

"You're really nuts. You know that's impossible. Charlie's beginning to get ideas. I'm still not even sure about tomorrow."

Jeannot seized his arms and shook him. "What do you mean? You've promised. You say shopping is always a good excuse."

Peter's first impulse was to pull himself free and hit Jeannot if he made any more trouble, but he knew it was safer to humor him. He didn't want complications that might keep him here more than a minute or two. "I just said I wasn't sure," he said placatingly. "You never know when something might turn up. I'll probably make it, but we both know this can't lead anywhere. You mustn't take it so seriously."

"I must take it seriously. I'm in love with you. I want you to be in love with me and then we'll be together always."

The grip on Peter's arms was tightening. Jeannot was stronger than he realized. "You can't turn love on and off when you want to. You know that," Peter said as if he were addressing a child. "I've told you I'd have to break it off if Charlie gets the least bit suspicious. You're not helping any."

"If you try to break it off, I'll tell Charlie everything. I warn you."

"Now, Jeannot, don't say things like that. You're not a shit. You're a sweet guy and I've loved what we've had together. Let's keep it that way."

"You speak as if it were over." The tensions within him were visibly surfacing. The instability Peter had become aware of earlier was manifesting itself in the wild, jerky rhythms of his speech. "I know what it is. You're not happy with the way we make love. I know now. You want me to fuck you. Charlie fucks you. He fucked you before lunch. How do you think that made me feel, with everybody listening? I heard you. I'll fuck you. I'll make you shout like that for me."

Peter's longing to strike out at him was nearly irresistible but he warned himself that he might only make matters worse. "For God's sake," he said roughly. "You know perfectly well we both want it the other way around. But what the hell—if you want to experiment—well, we'll see. That's enough of this now. Leave it for tomorrow. I've got to go back to the party."

With a quick movement, Jeannot seized Peter's shirt at the collar and yanked. Buttons flew and the shirt ripped down the middle. "There. Go on back to the party now," he shouted.

Peter stepped back and his fist lifted. In the split-second it took him to direct the blow, he envisioned the consequences. He didn't think Jeannot would put up much of a fight, but he couldn't be sure. If they really slugged it out, neither of them would be able to put in an appearance. He needed time to figure out how to get out of this predicament. He had to make Jeannot go back so that at least Charlie would know they weren't together. His hand dropped to his side, but his fists remained clenched. "You really are a shit," he said out of the depths of his anger.

"I don't care," Jeannot cried wildly. "It is better for you to hate me than to go on like this." He grabbed the top of Peter's trousers with both hands and yanked again. More buttons popped and there was another sound of tearing fabric. The brief silken thing, even flimsier than his swimming trunks, that he wore as underpants was gone with one quick painful rip. The trousers fell down around his ankles. He was trembling with rage, but all he could think of was to make Jeannot go back to the party. The forbidden memory nudged his brain, less memory after the years of scrupulous obliteration than a series of reflexes triggered by involuntary physical exposure, all commanding violence. He almost wished for somebody to find them like this: it would free him to attack. His fists ached with longing to smash into flesh. This was part of the memory, too, along with the enforced shaming frustration of his impulse to fight back.

Jeannot's voice sounded appeased when he spoke again.

"There. Now you are naked the way I want you," he said softly. "I've never seen you naked before without your being hard. You're so beautiful."

"I doubt if you'll ever see me hard again." Peter was surprised he could speak through his choking rage. "Please, Jeannot. There's nothing more you can do here. Please go back to the others."

"No." He fumbled with the ruined shirt and got it off and threw it on the ground. His hands were everywhere, touching all the places he had discovered where Peter was sensitive. Peter's body felt dead except for the blazing anger that shook it from head to foot. Jean unfastened his own trousers and released his sex and pressed it against Peter. "Now. We are together. Now you will get hard."

"Please, Jeannot. We've been here too long already." His voice broke with desperation. "I'm begging you. Go back. Let everybody see you."

Jean-Claude's hands continued to roam over him and hold him as he moved around behind him. He slid his hands down to his thighs and pulled him in tight against him. Peter felt the hard, naked flesh pressed up flat between his buttocks. Christ. Did the disgusting shit think he could compete with Charlie? "You see?" Jean murmured. "I will fuck you. You will be happy."

"All right. Tomorrow. I'll let you do anything you like tomorrow. Just go now."

"No. I want to make you hard."

"Then we'll be here all night. Do you think I'm enjoying this? I've never been so angry in my life. If you ever want me to speak to you again, go, for Christ's sake."

"You mustn't be angry. Everything I do is because I love you. I'll suck your cock. You like that."

"What'll it take to convince you that I can't do anything now? The only reason you're still alive is because I want you to go back."

"I want to see you hard with me."

"Oh, Jesus. Forget about that. I'm too angry now. Listen. Maybe we don't have to wait till tomorrow. I'll try to come tonight."

"Yes. Tonight. Now." He turned Peter in his arms and took his mouth in his. His tongue probed deep. Peter suddenly felt it as a violation of some sacred, private area of himself. His hands grew insistent again. Peter waited long enough not to appear too obviously repelled and then drew his head away.

"All right. Now go."

"You promise you will come tonight?"

"I'll come if it's humanly possible. I'll have to wait for Charlie to go to sleep. Otherwise, I swear I'll be there in the morning."

"No. Tonight. Promise."

"All right. I promise." The appalling possibility that Jeannot might come to the rented villa crossed his mind but he had to deal with the immediate peril. "It may be very late. Just wait for me."

"Yes, I will wait. Anne says I must think of you first."

"Button yourself up," Peter ordered brusquely. "Now listen. Go right back there. Make sure Charlie sees you. Find him and ask him if he's seen me. Make it clear that you've been looking for me. You understand?"

Jean tucked himself in and fastened his trousers. His hair was no more disordered than it had been before. "Of course, my lover. What will you do?"

"That's my problem. Just get going."

"I can count on you?"

"Yes, definitely," he said to speed Jean on his way. He would go as soon as possible to prove to him that nothing he could do would ever stir his body again. That should settle it once and for all.

Jeannot hesitated and then gave his sex a final caress and turned and went back up the path. Peter pulled up his trousers and retrieved the tattered shirt and put it on as best as he could. He had to hold everything closed. The little undergarment was beyond salvaging. He left it where it lay. He continued to be shaken by waves of anger, but he hadn't time to give in to them now. He would settle with Jean-Claude tomorrow.

Although it had seemed an endless nightmare while it was going on, he realized that the incident hadn't taken much more than five minutes. Something to the good. He would have to try to get away from here without anybody seeing him, rush home to change and get back as fast as he could. The drive would give him time to make up a story for Charlie. He didn't know what he would say if anybody saw him now. A fall? Not very convincing. With his fly ripped open and his shirt in rags, he looked quite simply as if he'd been raped.

Clutching his clothes together, he started off cautiously after Jean-Claude. When he saw the dressing pavillion looming up in front of him, he turned off the path away from the pool. It was rough going. The ground sloped away and rose again. There was a good deal of undergrowth to slow him. Every root that tripped him, every spikey branch that tore at his trousers added to the anger that burned in him. When he thought of Jean-Claude, unscathed, enjoying himself at the party, while he stumbled around in the dark with his clothes torn off, he wanted to shout with frustrated rage. At least he should have found Charlie by now. Seeing Jean-Claude should keep him from imagining things for a while. If he could make it home and back in under an hour, if Jean-Claude did as he was told without wasting any time, Charlie might not even notice that he was gone. He *would* notice that he'd changed his clothes. How in the world was he going to explain that? Even as he tried to fabricate some plausible tale, he knew he was going to have to tell the truth, the truth arranged slightly, perhaps, but still the truth. He was going to have to admit going off into the dark with Jean-Claude. If he could think of some mitigating excuse for doing that, he could pose as an innocent victim. Which was what he had been, goddamn it. Charlie would be furious with Jean-Claude. There was the danger of confrontations, of angry words, of the whole truth coming out. Could he invent some other culprit, an unknown stranger, and keep Jean-Claude out of it? No, not with Charlie. He stumbled over a rock and swore violently.

He had reached the last rise leading up to the great house. He broke out of the trees and stood watchfully for a few seconds on the edge of a large clearing. Through lighted windows ahead, he could see people working in the kitchen. He was safe from guests here. He ran up the last steep ground and made a dash around the side of the house and across the parking area to the car. It occurred to him with a lurch of his heart that Charlie might have taken the keys, although he usually didn't when they were together so the car would be available to both of them. His breath caught as he pulled open the door. The keys were dangling from the dashboard. He leaped in and was away.

The road was mercifully free of traffic. As far as he remembered, there was no risk of taking a wrong turning. He drove as fast as he dared. He hadn't really noticed how long the trip had taken earlier. He calculated that he'd been driving about twenty minutes when he turned into the drive through the vineyard in which the rented villa was set. He raced upstairs and let the clothes fall off him and left them on the floor. He was washed and dressed again in minutes and back in the car. At this rate, he wouldn't be gone much more than three-quarters of an hour. He was panicky all the way back as he encountered turnings and forks in the road he hadn't remembered. He had the feeling that the return trip was taking much longer. He came at last to the left turn he knew now and triumphantly gunned the car up the hill through the cork trees.

When he was once more under the bright lights of the terrace, he felt as if he'd been gone for days. As he stepped out, he wondered whether he should blend into a group and let Charlie find him as if nothing had happened or go to him directly. He was spared the choice. Charlie had obviously been watching for him and was immediately standing in front of him.

"Well. You decided to come back." His voice was ominously calm and his face set and his eyes steely as he surveyed the fresh costume. "You've changed your clothes? What's the story?"

"I had to go home. It's all right. I'll tell you all about it later."

"I think we'd better go now."

"I've just got back. Isn't it too early?"

"Some people have left already. We won't be the first. I know you weren't with Jean-Claude. He's been here. Who did you go off with?"

"Don't be ridiculous. Nobody. I just had to go home to change."

"Just like that. I'd like to know what's going on."

"Shall we say good night to Madame Graumont?"

"You couldn't have let me know what you were up to, could you? It didn't occur to you that I might have been worried."

"I'm sorry, Champ. There was nothing I could do about it. You'll understand when I tell you."

"All right. Let's go."

The atmosphere was tense between them as they left their hostess and went out to the car. Peter couldn't think how to begin without immediately adding substance to Charlie's displeasure.

"You're not going to like this," he said when Charlie had the car in motion. "I don't either, as far as that goes. I beg of you not to make more of it than it's worth."

"You really have me guessing. You go home in the middle of a party to put on a new outfit. Go ahead and tell me about it."

"I want to. It all has to do with Jean-Claude, of course."

"I see." Charlie felt as if he had been hit in the stomach but he didn't show it. "Then I think you'd better be very careful to tell me the truth. I'll find out if you're lying."

"You don't have to use that tone, but never mind. After what you'd said, I decided just to ignore him this evening. He cornered me eventually and said he wanted to talk to me. I refused but he began insisting, and I decided it was as good a time as any to tell him to lay off, to stop running after me. Besides, he was drunk and sort of wild and I was afraid of what he might say in front of others. We were beside the pool so I went with him a little beyond it where there're trees and a sort of clearing and steps going down to the sea. That's were it happened."

Charlie's grip tightened on the wheel as Peter went on. He was intent on every word, weighing it, subjecting it to lightning scrutiny for hidden implications, waiting to pounce on a discrepancy. His chest and stomach were aching with the conflict of doubt and outrage, trust and despair. The thought of anybody handling Peter, above all of harming him, aroused in him a passion of protest. If Peter were telling it as it really happened, he would gladly kill Jean-Claude. Could he believe it? Was it really convincing?

"All I could think of was to go on reasoning with him so he would leave me." Peter quickly concluded his account, suggesting that Jean-Claude had only looked at him rather than touched him after ripping his clothes. "I had to get away and change. There was no way of letting you know."

"And you expect me to believe that he did this without your having encouraged him in any way?"

"How could I encourage anybody to do a thing like that?"

"I don't mean tonight. I mean the last few weeks. You've let him hold hands with you. What else have you let him do? Have you let him kiss you, for instance?"

Peter's instinct for truth made him hesitate for a fatal instant.

46

Would it be so bad to admit to a kiss? "You know I don't go around letting people kiss me," he protested a beat too late.

"Is that supposed to be a straight answer? I think all the rest of it might be a bit more believable if you'd said yes."

"I agree it's unbelievable. I was stunned. Wait till you see my clothes."

"Clothes are apt to look a bit the worse for wear if you've been out fucking under the trees. Why did he look so tidy? Had he taken his clothes off, perhaps?"

"He was ripping and tearing at me, I tell you. I didn't touch him."

"That's odd, too. If anybody tried to rip open my fly, I'd really bash him. Unless I wanted him to, of course." His breath caught in something like a sob as he said it. He was turning the knife in his own wound. He couldn't believe the worst, but he had caught Peter's hesitation and he was sure now that he had led Jean-Claude on in some way. If Peter were really lying, he would have made up a better story, but he was surely editing the facts in some way. That such a thing could have happened, even seeing Peter's part in it in its most innocent light, made him sick.

"I wanted to hit him, God knows," Peter asserted with persuasive passion. "I was afraid once might not be enough. He's stronger than you'd expect. If it had turned into a free-for-all, I was afraid everybody would find out. You'd have hated that as much as I would."

"Yes. Well, let's restudy the whole scene. For the sake of argument, let's say that Guy asks me to leave a party and go for a little stroll with him. I know perfectly well what he has in mind, so I say no. We'll have to assume that I temporarily lose my mind and agree." That he was actually having this conversation with Peter was inconceivable, but he went on implacably. "So there we are in the dark and if I let him move in close enough to tear off my shirt, I must know the moment is coming. He makes a grab and I'm ready to move fast. If I don't want to hit him for some reason, I run and there I am back at the party, a little out of breath but intact."

"It's not going to help for you to make some sort of lousy joke of it."

"Oh, no. That wasn't a joke. It was a perfectly reasonable reconstruction of a perfectly familiar situation."

"All right. That's the way it would be with you and Guy. But can't you understand how I was thinking? You'd just spoken to me about Jean-Claude. If I got in some sort of a mess with him, it would've seemed as if I hadn't paid any attention to you. I just wanted to keep it quiet and get it over with as quickly as possible until I could speak to you."

"I still have the feeling that you're leaving something out," Charlie said coldly.

"What? I've told you I found him sort of appealing. I admit I've known he thinks he's in love with me. I guess I was touched by it. I wanted to help him get over it. Maybe I shouldn't have. But I swear to God I never dreamed he'd be capable of anything like tonight."

"Well, that sounds a bit more honest. Maybe you're ready to admit to a few more things." He didn't want to hear any more. He wanted to stop the car and jump out and run, run anywhere to get away from this. But he knew how to exploit Peter's basic honesty and he was blindly determined to get the truth. He felt as if their whole future depended on it. He took an iron grip on himself and said quite lightly, "You might as well admit you've let him kiss you."

"Well, yes. I—"

"I don't think I want to make a catalogue of all the things you might have done. He's had a good look at your cock. I can't imagine his bothering to pull your pants off without playing with it a bit. Are you sure he didn't show you his?"

"All right, if you want all the sordid details. Yes, he opened his pants. He had a hard-on. I didn't. That's the difference."

"Really lovely. I suppose you know I'm going to beat the shit out of him myself tomorrow. Tell me this. Under different circumstances, can you imagine going to bed with him?"

"Not after—" He checked himself. The question had been phrased so that it was easy to evade but he realized that an attempt at honesty in answering it might achieve more understanding between them. Charlie's unyielding manner was making him begin to pray for understanding. He began again, "Oh, Christ, how do you expect me to answer that? You know you're the only person I've ever cared about. But—hell, things happen sometimes. Damn rarely. Practically never, really. Two or three times in ten years. It's just a kind of chemical reaction. It doesn't

48

mean anything, but it's hard to control when it's going on. I admit I got pretty worked up about him for a little while, but it's all over. I don't mean just because of tonight. What happened before lunch today—that was real. You know that. That's all I want, you, you doing the things we do together."

Charlie's jaws were clamped shut. He felt as if he could break the wheel in his hands. This wasn't going to end here. "Well, I suppose I ought to thank you for telling the truth," he said evenly, "but I can't pretend I like it. I feel as if I don't even know you. Things happen! Is that your way of saying you've been to bed with two or three other guys?"

"Good God, no. I'm just talking about being attracted sometimes."

"Well, things like that don't happen to me. I don't let them. That's the way it's always been. That's what I've always believed in. If I found out you'd been sleeping around, it would be all over."

"You know I feel the same way." Peter's heart pounded up with alarm. Charlie spoke with such cold finality. He had to enter a plea for forgiveness in case this thing went any further. He added hesitantly, "Still, if something did happen with you and somebody else, I suppose I'd have to accept it somehow. I can't imagine life without you."

"I can't imagine life without you so long as you're the person I've always thought you were. If things changed, the hell with it. I need you. *You*. Not somebody who gets into nasty little messes with hysterical kids. Just don't forget it."

Peter could think of nothing to say. Although he was badly frightened, his mind was rapidly sorting out Charlie's words, assessing the situation. The main thing was that Charlie still thought he hadn't been to bed with Jean-Claude. How was he going to silence the boy? Charlie's threat to beat him wasn't idle talk; it was just the sort of thing he would do, rushing off to defend their honor. He felt the danger in Jean-Claude like a timebomb ticking away toward the blasting of their lives. He would certainly have to go to him in the morning. He knew he could demonstrate that he was of no use sexually to him any more. Would that be enough? If not, he would have to plead with Anne to intervene. She had some control over her brother.

They completed what remained of the drive in silence. As soon as they reached the house, all lighted up as Peter had left it, Charlie got out of the car without a word and went straight in and mixed himself a drink in the living room, where bottles and ice had been left out by the cook-maid who was included in the rental. He was still seething. His hand shook as he lifted the glass to his lips. He took it out to the terrace and sat in a canvas chair. He was aware of Peter trailing along behind him. He approached and put his hand on the back of Charlie's neck and stroked it.

"I'm sorry. It was awful but we can forget it now. I suppose I could say it's taught me a lesson, but this sort of thing happens so rarely that I don't really need any lessons. Beautiful darling. It's all right now, isn't it? Please don't make anything more of it."

"I don't know. Maybe in the morning you can make it sound as if you were telling all of it. I don't want to go over it all again now."

"Would you like me to stay and have a drink with you?"

"Not particularly."

Peter lingered miserably. It was so awful. He was beginning to feel deeply ashamed, but he couldn't see how any of it, except for tonight, could have been different. Last week, Jean-Claude really had represented a threat to everything he felt for Charlie. This morning before lunch had been proof that he had met the danger and overcome it. He couldn't allow anything to go wrong now. Perhaps by morning Charlie would have worked it out in his mind and they would be secure and together again; he was completely shut off from him now. Peter touched the back of his head again, longingly. "Well then, I'll go on up. Come up soon."

When he was gone, Charlie finished his drink in several long swallows and got up to get another. He went back to the terrace and sat, his throbbing head resting in one hand. Forget it, he counseled himself as the second drink began to calm him. If Peter had been lying, it could only be because he and Jean-Claude had been having an affair. This quite simply wasn't possible. Oh, possible. Everything was possible if you set your mind to it. There had been Guy's innuendoes about the trip back from Paris. Peter was out and about for hours during the day while he was at work. He and Jean-Claude had disappeared long enough this morning for anything to happen, which was one more reason why it was impossible. If anything were going on, Peter would take great care not to give him any grounds for suspicion. Still, he was going to make sure. He had no intention of living with doubt. He sprang up, tempted to go back to the party and confront Jean-Claude. And make another faggotty little scene? He went in and replenished his drink and returned to the terrace and sat. He would find out in the morning and if, as he was almost sure, Peter had been more or less telling the truth, he would give Jean-Claude a beating he wouldn't forget. Christ, faggots. How he hated them.

In the past, in periods when things weren't going well between them and life had sometimes seemed unbrearable, he had spent hours picking meticulously over the past, assembling a case history, trying to understand why his life had taken this course. He had seized on every small milestone, arranged them in chronological order, learned the sequence by heart. Somewhere as it unfolded in his mind should lie the answer to why all his life was bound up with, all of himself was dependent on, another man, yet he had never found it.

It had all started at school, of course. From the age of sixteen, his sex had begun to attract attention. For a long time, he didn't know whether he was supposed to be proud or ashamed of it. It was simply commented on as one of the school's phenomena. One year's jokes and hints and glances became the next year's acts. Somehow—it had had something to do with a boy who wanted to measure him—he was introduced to a secret circle that engaged in mutual masturbation. After the measuring boy, he was approached by another, who muttered something about "doing it" and led him down into the basement to a dusky, dusty room where athletic equipment was stored. There, they unfastened each other's flies, liberated their by-now erect sexes and rapidly stroked each other to orgasm. That was all there was to it. Thereafter he was approached regularly and repeated the routine with a number of others. It was a day school in the suburbs of Philadelphia and the encounters always took place somewhere on the school grounds, never at home. It was a practice he associated with school and although it was secretive, he couldn't think it was bad because all the others were doing it, all the ones he cared about, the athletes, the leaders, the good-looking boys.

"You ought to do it with McClelland," one of his regular partners said one day when they were buttoning their flies. "He's almost as big as you are."

He had never paid much attention to anybody's size except his own; he supposed he wasn't really interested, but he was pleased to learn that Eddy McClelland was a member of the circle. He was captain of the football team, a school hero, not a particular friend, but one whose looks and style he admired. He dressed beautifully. He looked forward to Eddy's approaching him, since that was the way it had always happened and it wouldn't have occurred to him to make the first move. A large part of their last school year had passed when, at last, as they were leaving the locker room together, Eddy brushed a hand against his and led him across the grounds to the driveway where they parked their cars. Eddy went to his.

"Get in," he ordered. They drove a few blocks and parked on a residential street and there, seated side-by-side, they went through the familiar ritual. Charlie usually didn't look while it was going on, but now he stole a glance at what he held in his hand. It staggered him, and the realization that he was bigger made him feel almost deformed.

After that, he avoided doing it with any of the others. The first indication of a tendency to find a male mate? He didn't know if Eddy felt the same way, but they constantly found occasions to be alone, sometimes several times a day, in daring and original places, out on the grounds hidden by shrubbery, in a deserted classroom, so he assumed that something special had been established between them. He didn't know then that they had taken so long to get together because Eddy had never before made the advances.

On their graduation night, after he had disentangled himself from his family, he hung about at Eddy's side and Eddy seemed to expect him to be there. When the crowd had begun to disperse, Eddy nudged his hand in the way he had and they made their way quickly out of the gym, where the ceremonies had taken place. Outside, he directed their steps across the dark grounds toward the squash courts. There, to Charlie's surprise, Eddy opened a door, which he seemed to know would be unlocked, and they entered. They were in some area behind the courts. Faint light entered from somewhere, but it was quite dark.

"Take your clothes off," Eddy murmured. "There's a bench here to put them on." His hand was on his arm to guide him, and then Charlie could feel him undressing at his side. Charlie did the same. When he had stripped, he could feel Eddy's naked body moving in close to him, handling him, guiding him until somehow he was on his back on some sort of hard mat and Eddy was on top of him, naked in his arms. This bore no relationship to the simple ritual they had performed before.This was his whole body writhing against another in an act of intense intimacy and union. It was so unexpected and momentous that it passed in a daze. Afterward, he remembered his lips shaping a kiss against Eddy's cheek in the convulsions of orgasm. He hoped Eddy hadn't noticed it.

Another milestone? Would none of the others with whom he had "done it" have dreamed of exchanging a kiss? Was he already responding to these childish games with some fixed, warped element in him that the others didn't share? He had genuinely thought of the "games" as part of schoolboy life and had expected them to end with college. The last thing that would have entered his head was to seek an occasion for their continuation. In the first few weeks at Princeton, however, he had become increasingly aware of a youth he encountered regularly in the communal washrooms of the dormitory where he lived. He knew he was a class ahead of him and therefore didn't speak, but he admired his aloof, sensual, aristocratic face and his fine, sleek body, which looked as if it had been formed by aristocratic exercise—riding, squash, swimming—well-muscled but unadapted to hard labor. He was sorry that the rigid social isolation of the freshmen made it impossible for him to know him, but he didn't let himself think anything more than that.

One morning, Charlie was in the shower and the young man, whose name he learned later was Hal, was standing only a dozen feet away drying himself. Charlie, as usual, was admiring the lovely flow of the lines of his body as he moved. He turned suddenly and their eyes met. Charlie started to glance away, but the intensity of the regard held him. The look traveled down through his body and hit his groin. Things began to happen that he had to conceal by turning his back, but not before he had seen Hal's gaze drop to the troubled area, not before he had caught a glimpse, as the other lowered his towel, of what was obviously, boldly, in such a public place, the beginning of an

53

erection. Charlie turned on a blast of cold water to calm himself and quickly finished his shower. When he turned back, Hal was gone. Obviously it hadn't meant what he had thought it meant. After a moment's disappointment, he decided that it was just as well. He had known that that sort of thing wouldn't go on here. It was a thing of the past. It would be ridiculous, now that they were all grown men. He went back up to his two rooms, which, thanks to his family, he didn't have to share with a room-mate, thinking as he climbed to the top of the building that if this were prep school, he could have hoped for the young man to intercept him somewhere along the way. Why even think about it? He flung off his bathrobe in his bedroom and realized that he was still tingling with the shock of the look that had been exchanged. His sex stirred and he stroked it and felt it stiffen under his hand. He wondered if he should do himself to get it out of his system. There was a knock on the door. He snatched up a towel and crossed his study to answer it, knowing who it would be before he opened it. Hal stepped in without a word and threw off his robe and they were in each other's arms, Hal's mouth on his, his tongue running along his closed lips. It took him a second to realize what was expected of him and then he opened his mouth and they welcomed each other with their tongues. The slight roughness of their freshly shaved skin seemed a bit odd to Charlie but he forgot it in the unfamiliar thrill of kissing. His visitor backed him to the sofa and they fell onto it, grappling with each other, their legs thrashing, finding their satisfaction in the pressures of their bodies and in their eager, exploring hands.

"Jesus," Hal muttered when it was over. He sprang up and wiped himself with Charlie's towel, his back slightly turned. "Are you going to be home this evening?"

"Yes. Sure."

"Shall I come up about ten-thirty?"

"Yeah, that'd be great."

He pulled on his robe and departed as silently as he had come, leaving Charlie in a trance of happiness. So it wasn't all over. On the contrary, there were sophistications to be learned here; kissing added a whole new dimension of delight. That night, with the light on, frankly and abandonedly in bed for the first time, Hal introduced him to oral play. It had never occurred to him

54

that anybody would want to take his sex in his mouth, but Hal did, and the sensation was electrifying. When it came his turn to reciprocate he did so without enthusiasm, dreading the ejaculation. What would it taste like? Since Hal had swallowed his, he supposed he would have to do the same. When the moment came, he managed it, but it gave him no pleasure.

If he had any lingering doubts about whether to regard his prodigious sex as an asset, they were dispelled now. Hal came every night to worship it. He wanted it everywhere, in his mouth, against his cheeks, in his armpits, lying along his chest and nipples, between his thighs. He led Charlie through an elaborate ballet of shifting positions as he massaged his whole body with it. Charlie found it flattering and exciting, but embarrassing too, since he felt no similar obsessive passion for Hal's, though it was very handsome in its way. Looking back, he found it amazing that he had been indifferent to so many things that later had given him such joy and ecstasy. Had he forced his body to find pleasure where it didn't naturally exist for him? If he had refrained in time, would his sexual urges have been redirected? He and Hal had been meeting nightly for a week or more when he arrived carrying a tube of something. Once in bed, he reached for it and began to apply an oily substance to Charlie's sex. Charlie assumed that this was an elaboration of his phallic worship; he wanted to see it glistening and have it move more voluptuously over his body.

"I've taken care of myself," Hal murmured inexplicably. They rarely spoke when they were in bed and never referred to their love-making before or after it. In a moment, he moved around and by the position he assumed and by his urgently guiding hands, he indicated that he wanted Charlie to enter him. Everything in Charlie recoiled from the act. He knew vaguely that it was possible (Something about Oscar Wilde? Words looked up in the dictionary?), but just the thought of soiling himself was almost enough to make him physically incapable of performing it. Hal's desire communicated itself so strongly that he was almost forced to comply.

As Charlie felt himself entering, a strange new sensation seized him. He slid deeper into him and he was gripped by a lust for possession. This beautiful body was his. Everything that Hal was, was his. He lunged into him and Hal cried out. His sex seemed to swell gigantically as it took possession. Hal's acceptance of it, his hips lifting and working to have more, was a total submission to him. He drove into him and his penetration became huge and complete. He took him fiercely and Hal surrendered himself to him with cries of rapture. His orgasm was an immense planting of himself in the other. He shouted as he felt himself pounding into him, flooding him with himself. He collapsed onto him, spent and triumphant, having tasted finally the full joy of his sexuality. He had often wondered whether everything would have been different if, at that time, a girl had offered herself to him as totally and rapturously as Hal.

The experience left him with a craving for more. He wanted to possess the whole world. Everybody he met became a potential bedmate, but he quickly began to discriminate as he never had at school, until Eddy McClelland, studying the texture of skin and hair, the shape of a hand, the curve of a mouth, the look of eyes and, of course, the drape of trousers at the crotch and what it seemed to offer. He never made a move to take what he wanted but somehow, perhaps because there was a circle here too into which Hal had dropped his name, his conquests multiplied. When he became active in the undergraduate theater, the field widened, and his aspect of life became more overt. There were those who hinted at it quite openly. He received his first declaration of love, which stunned him and which he rejected as silly and exaggerated, but it unexpectedly set him to thinking about Eddy. The thoughts led to an exchange of letters between Princeton and New Haven and a meeting for a night in New York. The prospect was more exciting to him than he had had any reason to anticipate. He wondered if Eddy had been learning things, too. The thought of kissing him made him tremble inside.

But Eddy didn't kiss him so he didn't attempt to kiss Eddy, and it quickly became apparent that they both had the same idea in mind. Because it was Eddy, he lay on his stomach and went through the motions, all muscles tensed, of trying to satisfy him but he had no intention of letting him succeed. The idea appalled and terrified him. (He had even got over that, although it hadn't happened to him often: once with Peter and a few times when Tony introduced him to multiple coupling during Peter's

56

Army service.) The night with Eddy hadn't been a success, but all through it words of love had hovered on his lips. It was inconceivable that he would say them unless Eddy spoke first, and they died forever when Eddy said as they were parting, "If we don't look out, we'll end up falling in love with each other." He had laughed and Charlie had forced himself to join in.

If he had had the courage to speak out, would the hopelessness of it have awakened him to the danger he was courting? Would it have made him realize that as long as the world forbade love between two men, the only chance of happiness lay in conforming? He had returned to college with a tormenting yearning and an even greater contempt for endearments so that he never went to bed a second time with those who used them, but he did learn to talk and laugh and joke while making love, which he found made it a much more rewarding experience. His silent coupling with Hal began to seem as incomplete as his abortive play with Eddy, although he continued to receive him regularly at night all through his freshman year.

By the time he finished college, he was an experienced and, for those who wanted him in the way he preferred, a quite breathtaking lover of men. Because it had all taken place within the framework of normal school life, he had no feeling of having committed himself to a future of vice or perversion. He wasn't a pansy or a fairy or a queer; he knew some of those and they disgusted him. When he met Peter as a house guest of his grandmother's during the summer after his graduation, he had had no sense of corrupting an innocent when he introduced him to pleasures that, nearing twenty, Peter could have been expected to have discovered for himself by then. It had been just harmless fun, except the boy had succeeded in finally overthrowing all his guards. Peter had fallen so openly and articulately and passionately in love with him that it was impossible for him not to declare his own passion. He had fought it, even to the point of going through with his disastrous marriage, but only very briefly had there been any doubt in his mind that he had to be with Peter. The words once said couldn't be withdrawn. They had held him for eleven years. It couldn't change. Peter wouldn't let it change.

He eased back in his chair and looked up at the star-filled sky. He thought of sailing under them to Greece. The nasty little incident this evening had distracted them from things that really mattered. He would settle with Jean-Claude in the morning and then go by the Kingsleys' boat and make a definite date for dinner. And if it turned out that there was more to the story than Peter was admitting? Disagreeable things still happened inside him when he thought of it—the churning stomach, the accelerating heart. He needed another drink. He pulled himself up and went in to find the bottle. Remember, he warned himself as he poured a generous refresher. His own fidelity hadn't always been as perfect as he liked to pretend. But Peter had been away, he thought defensively. He had been going out of his mind with longing for him and loneliness. True, but if his living with a man was such a fluke, as he also liked to pretend, if he found it so hard to understand how Peter could be attracted to a pretty boy, why hadn't he found a girl to keep himself company? Peter would have found that much easier to accept if he had ever discovered anything and, having been married, Charlie no longer found girls so inaccessible as he had when he was growing up. No, it had to be boys. He thought of his chance meeting in a bar with Hal when Peter had been gone only a few months and he had still been resolutely celibate. The bar had been a discreetly semiqueer one in the East Fifties and he had not gone there on the make but simply to try to get through another hour without Peter. Hal had been the first person he had seen when he entered, very glamorous in a superbly tailored captain's uniform. They hadn't met for nearly five years. They fell into each other's arms. Their greeting was more intimate than it could have been elsewhere; they held hands for a moment.

"I never expected to find you in a place like this," Hal said. "I thought you were married."

Charlie had forgotten how beautiful his voice was, probably because he had never said much. Otherwise, this was the same young man he had so supremely possessed; the look of the green eyes still gave him the shock he had felt that morning in the shower, the aloof smile, the refined sensuality of the mouth summoned him to reestablish his mastery over them. "I *was* married," he said. "For about four months. What about you?"

"You of all people shouldn't have to ask that. You're still a civilian?"

"I had a slight case of polio as a kid. It seems that one leg is an eighth of an inch shorter than the other. Nobody will take me. It's driving me nuts."

They talked about their lives since graduation. Charlie explained that he had quit his job in a publishing house and was devoting himself to painting. Peter was introduced into the conversation, since this had been Peter's idea and Peter was keeping him. They laughed about a Princeton man being a kept boy. Peter was stationed in California. So was Hal. They commented on the coincidence. Suddenly Hal stared.

"Good God. You couldn't be talking about Peter Martin by any chance, could you?"

"Of course," Charlie said proudly.

"Good God Almighty. That divine creature. If anybody could make me forget you, he could. He's in my outfit. Of course. I understand now. He looks like you. I knew something was bothering me but I couldn't place it. All that golden hair. You lucky devil."

Charlie laughed softly. "I think so."

Hal wanted to know all about him. Why wasn't he an officer? Charlie explained that he didn't want to be, that his father was a general and Peter was very antimilitary. Why hadn't he gone to college?

"He was about to go to West Point when we met. He'd missed a couple of years of school. We decided to stay together and he resigned his appointment. He's taken a lot of courses at Columbia."

"That's the kind of story I like to hear. You don't hear many like it. You're going to live happily ever after? Vows of fidelity and all the rest of it? Needless to say, I haven't found anybody else like you, so I'm still playing the field. Maybe some day." He paused and the green eyes gave Charlie another jolt. "I suppose you know what I've been thinking."

"I've been thinking the same thing."

"Is there any chance of doing more than thinking about it?" Charlie reluctantly shook his head, but Hal went on, "It wouldn't really be infidelity. I found you first."

Charlie had already thought of that. It made a difference, but not enough. What if Peter picked up with one of his old lovers? No, he couldn't let himself do it. "Christ, Hal. Don't tempt me. Now that we've been around a bit, we'd be fantastic together. I know that."

"Don't you have any patriotism? What about the morale of the services and all that? I could lick the Germans singlehanded if I had another day or two with you. You're attempting the impossible, old love. It's easier for Peter because he doesn't have much opportunity to play around. But you. If you don't break down with me, you're bound to with somebody else sooner or later. I've always adored you. I wish you'd let it be me."

"I hope you're not right. If I can say no to you, I should think I could say no to anybody." (Famous last words. He had met Tony only about a month later.)

"Thanks for putting it like that. Well, knowing Peter, I can see your point. I'd gladly turn in my captain's bars if I though I had a chance with him."

"You don't."

"You're that sure of him?"

"Surer than I am of myself, unfortunately."

"Lucky lads. Both of you."

The bastard, Charlie thought as he wandered restlessly around the moon-washed terrace nursing his drink. Hal was another one he would gladly tear to pieces if he could get his hands on him. Peter seemed to have a knack for letting people get him into trouble through no fault of his own. At least that was always his version of it. Unfair, he reprimanded himself. The trouble with Hal had almost broken him. Charlie had never doubted his story. Besides, they had been separated. Almost anything could have been forgiven. Jean-Claude was different. Right here under his nose. Even if Peter had led him on a bit, it was unpardonable for Jean-Claude to think that Peter's friend would sit by while he took over, attacking Peter, trying to have him in front of practically the entire party. No matter what had brought it on, he would be sorry for that.

Charlie's glass was almost empty. He considered refilling it but decided against it. He wanted to be up early and out before Peter was awake. He took a final swallow and went into the living room and snapped off lights and stretched out fully dressed on the sofa. He wasn't going up to Peter. He couldn't go near Peter as long as a doubt remained.

He slept fitfully, waking with a start to reach for Peter, sinking back into sleep with foreboding clutching at his heart. The sun hadn't been up long when he abandoned further attempts at sleep and tiptoed upstairs. He took his time to prepare himself for the day. Peter ususally slept till eight-thirty or nine. He couldn't pay his morning call any earlier than that. He had plenty of time, too much time.

Their clothes were spread about in closets and bureaus in various rooms and he was able to find shorts and T-shirt and sandals without going into the bedroom where Peter was sleeping. He mustn't wake Peter. He mustn't see Peter. Peter might undermine all his resolve. When he had had a light breakfast, it was still too early to go, so he spent some restless time pacing about the downstairs room he had set up as a studio. Partly finished canvases were propped up against the walls, on chairs and, the one he had started day before yesterday, on an easel. He couldn't look at them. They all looked wrong. His heart was beating erratically and there were odd constrictions in his chest and stomach. The woman who worked for them arrived at eight, and he could wait no longer. He left word for Peter that he had gone to town to get a color he needed and left.

He drove around the back of the town and took the bayside road until he reached the turn that climbed to Gassin. At the first rise, he saw the house and driveway. It had been pointed out to him several times; he had never been there. He came to a stop near a long converted farmhouse under a great cork oak and got out. The stillness peculiar to houses where people are sleeping enveloped him. He moved lightly along a gravel path, wondering if he dared break the stillness by knocking or calling out. A neat old woman emerged from a door and greeted him. "Ah, bonjour, monsieur," she said, with a smile, in a muted voice. "Monsieur Jeannot left word that you should go right up. He's waiting for you."

Charlie stared at her without seeing her. A great, cold emptiness opened up in his stomach. His mind seemed incapable of thought, but the awful knowledge was lodged in it. The old woman had taken him for Peter.

So it was all over. All the years of devotion and contentment smashed. He thought he would thank the old woman and go, but she was looking at him questioningly. He had to be absolutely sure. He collected himself and managed to smile with stiff lips. "Let's see. Waiting—where—" he said. That was all right. Peter had been here, but he couldn't have come so often that they had established a routine.

"Right up to the right," the woman said, indicating the door through which Charlie saw a staircase. "Where I showed you the other morning. The door at the end of the corridor."

"Oh, yes. Thank you." He forced himself to move. His mind began to function more normally. It was over, but he would bring the whole structure of their lives crashing down in his own way, on his own terms. He would make Peter wish they had never met. He reached the foot of the stairs. He needed a moment to make sure he was completely in control of himself. He was frightened of what might happen when he saw Jean-Claude. He forced himself to start up the stairs. When he reached the top, he was shaken by a gust of rage. Peter had been here; he had hurried down this hall eager and lusting. Rage drove and freed him. He went quickly to the door and tried it gently. It opened before him. He stepped silently inside. Jean-Claude was lying on a big bed with his back turned, a sheet pulled up over his hips. Charlie's eye was held by a tube of lubricant on the bedside table. He pushed the door closed with a click.

"Peter," Jean-Claude muttered thickly, as if he were speaking in his sleep.

"Not exactly." There was a second's silence and then Jean-Claude rolled over quickly to face him. He saw the thrust of an erection lift the sheet as he did so. As Jean-Claude's eyes focused, he struggled up into a sitting position on one hip, propped up on an arm. He was flushed and tousled with sleep. Now? Spring at him and drag him from the bed and beat him into the floor? He saw fear leap up into Jean-Claude's eyes, an almost ecstatic fear. He would enjoy being beaten. He took a step forward and Jean-Claude shrank back.

"What's—you—" he mumbled, his eyes staring.

"Take your time to wake up."

"I've been up. I must've gone to sleep again." He lifted his other hand and ran it through his hair.

"Waiting for Peter?" His eyes shifted to the lubricant and back.

"I don't understand. What—"

"I thought it was about time for me to take charge."

"Take charge? Does Peter know you're here?"

"I don't know. He might guess. I've come to see you."

"But why? I don't—"

"Why did the maid tell me to come right up?" He summoned up all his control. The urge to smash the boy's face was almost too great to contain, but he knew now that that would be letting him off too easily. "Don't you think it's natural for me to be interested in somebody who's been going to bed with Peter?" His stomach heaved but he had a firm grip on himself.

"But that's crazy. You don't think—"

"It's all right. You don't have to deny it. I know all about it. You met him in Nice last week."

Jean-Claude studied Charlie for a moment. He seemed reassured by what he saw and relaxed visibly. "He wanted me to. I'm in love with him," he said defensively.

"That's apt to be a pretty painful experience for you."

"I don't care. I want him with me. I want to take him away from you."

"You *are* ambitious. And what does Peter think?"

"I don't know. He's fighting it."

"I wonder why he's doing that." He felt a lessening of tension as he reconsidered his course of action. His eye was able to make a solid composition of the figure on the bed. The elements were good—the big, ruddy, copper torso curving up to heavy shoulders propped up by the column of arm, the expanse of white sheet he was sprawled on, the other white sheet that covered his legs and cut him off at the waist. The legs made an interesting pattern of the sheet. The other arm lay along them. The arch of his brows was quite magnificent. The big eyes and heavy mouth were darkly inviting. He was a fine figure of a youth, a painted statue; all the lines flowed softly into each other like Hellenistic work, faintly hermaphroditic. The smudge of hair in the middle of his chest didn't belong. "Aren't you going to ask me to sit down?" he asked.

"Oh, yes. Of course." He shifted his legs slightly.

Jean-Claude's eyes dropped to Charlie's shorts as he moved toward the bed and sat on the edge of it. He sensed a soft compliancy in the boy, which made the lubricant on the bedside table a jarring note. What had they been up to? "Tell me about it. Why do you think you can take him away from me?"

"He loves me. I know it."

"He doesn't say so?"

"No. But that's because he's fighting it. I give him things you don't." He dropped his eyes.

"Such as?"

The eyes lifted defiantly. "He likes to fuck me."

"I see," Charlie said. So that was it. This big, voluptuous youth had aroused some dormant masculine urge in Peter. It mitigated his guilt to some slight degree. "That's not surprising. You look highly fuckable."

Jean-Claude looked startled. "You mean, you—?"

"I mean just that. What was all the excitement about last night?"

"You know about it? I was losing out of my mind. Is that right? Everybody heard what you did with Peter yesterday. I wanted to make him know I would fuck him, too."

"By tearing his clothes off? I didn't like that." The murderous rage flared up in him again. Looking at the boy, feeling him melt toward him, he realized what a tenuous hold he had on reality; he could drive him insane. After that, he would take care of Peter. He forced a suggestive look into his eyes. "I thought you were interested in me when we first met."

Jean-Claude's big eyes softened. "I was. I was in love with you both at first. You were not interested in me."

"How do you know? I don't always show what I'm feeling. Peter's had you. I think it's my turn now."

"But this is incredible. Does Peter know? Do you always share each other's lovers?"

"Sure. Why not? Don't you think it's a good idea?"

"But how could I? I love Peter. He will be angry."

"That's all right. Make him jealous. That's always good when somebody is pretending not to love you."

"You're very exciting. If you think—" His free hand crept forward to Charlie's thigh and gave consent. Charlie pushed it away. He reached over and pulled the sheet from him. Jean-Claude snatched for it, but Charlie had already pushed one leg from the other and released the concealed sex. It sprang forward and lay rigid along his abdomen. Hip and buttock curved massively.

"Well, aren't you the cocky one," Charlie said. "Did I do that to you, or were you thinking of Peter?" He looked Jean-Claude in the eye.

"No. You," he murmured. Jean-Claude's eyes were yearning for him now. He saw the throb of his heart become visible ben-

64

eath his breast, his lips parting. He looked at the body and felt its lush physical appeal. There would be some perverse pleasure in it, in being where Peter had been.

He was wrenched by a tearing conflict of desires—a rage to hut and humiliate both Peter and his lover, a longing to be away from here, a stirring of the old thirst, long forgotten, to see beyond the face, to possess a stranger and discover an intimate inunguarded, satisfied eyes.

Jean-Claude swayed toward him in anticipation of a kiss and his hand moved up his thigh. Charlie pushed him away and stood slowly and pulled his shirt over his head. He kicked off his sandals. How long had it been since he had stripped for a stranger? Milly had been the last. Milly had been with him when Peter's telegram had arrived, announcing catastrophe. He stood for a moment looking down at Jean-Claude, seeing Milly, sweet Milly, funny Milly, slim and willowy, every hair removed from his body, except for 'a neatly shaped pubic patch, for the drag act he did when he could get an engagement. Charlie unfastened his shorts and let them drop to the floor. His sex stretched the silken pouch he wore against his skin.

"Come here. Let me see," Jean-Claude begged, his eyes on it.

Charlie moved back to the side of the bed. "Help yourself." He put his hands on his hips while Jean-Claude pulled the pouch down. His sex curved out heavily in front of him, partly aroused not by Jean-Claude but by associations with the past. Jean-Claude lunged across the bed and dropped his feet to the floor and took it in his mouth. Let him work for it, Charlie thought. These preliminaries were the greatest obstacle to carrying out his intentions; he still wasn't sure that he could function with Jean-Claude. He felt the stimulation of his mouth beginning to have an effect and thought of Milly insisting on seeing him with an erection before he would go to bed with him. Milly had been a bellboy in a hotel where Charlie had spent a night in sexual sport. Everything had become sex by then. Milly had appeared in response to Charlie's request for valet service. He was wearing glasses, but his velvet, almost beardless skin was stretched taut over finely modeled bones and his slim, trim body was appealing in his tight uniform. Charlie had casually let his robe fall open while giving his instructions. He was wearing nothing under it.

65

In a few minutes, Milly was back. Charlie answered his knock and he slipped swiftly into the room.

"If you'll forgive me for putting it so bluntly, sir," Milly had said without ado, "would you let me look at your cock again?" His face was impassive and his gaze level.

Charlie had burst out laughing at the unexpectedness of it and at the neat, precise manner in which he had phrased his request. "Again?" he asked.

"Yes, sir. I'm aware of the favor you were doing me just now, but it threw me off balance at the time. You might say I was blinded. If I'm correct in supposing that you were inviting me to bed, it's most important for me to see if you satisfy my extravagant requirements. It's an obsession, sir."

Charlie laughed again, amused at the stateliness of his speaking style. "I don't see how you can tell anything unless I have an erection."

"Couldn't that be managed, sir?"

(Remembering the absurdly challenging moment still excited him; he could feel things happening as Jean-Claude's mouth continued its efforts.)

"How?" he had demanded. "With me just standing here and you staring at me like an owl?"

"I'm sorry about the glasses, sir. In private, I don't wear them. I don't know whether it shows yet, but I'm getting an erection. I would be delighted if I had the same effect on you."

Charlie's eyes dropped to the tight pants. They had developed a strong jut. "You do." He pulled open his robe again and let it drop off him. "That'll give you a rough idea," he said. There was a brief silence. Charlie saw the jut of the tight trousers grow more pronounced.

"My word," the boy breathed at last. "I can't imagine why anyone would hesitate to display that. I'm nothing much in your department, but I have a very pretty ass."

"Very. I hope I pass the test."

"Oh, goodness, sir. You must forgive me. I feel like a complete idiot."

Thoughts of Milly afterward, when he had discarded the speech pattern he had invented for his job and had chatted happily in his arms, helped him now with Jean-Claude. He was being coaxed into erection. He remembered Milly's laughter at the moment of climax, laughter of joyful abandonment, and the final surge came that left him fully aroused at last. Jean-Claude released him with a gasp. "I can't any more. It's so enormous."

"Peter can," Charlie said harshly. "Never mind. We've had enough of that."

"But look," Jean-Claude held it upright against Charlie's body. "It goes up almost to your chest."

Charlie pulled his hands away and gripped it at the base and whipped it back and forth across his face. "I can beat you with it, too."

"*Aie!*" Jean-Claude cried out with delight. "It's so hard. It hurts."

"You're damn right."

"You're like a bull." Jean-Claude gazed spellbound. "I didn't know a man could be so big. It is terrifying and thrilling. Peter is not like that. Do you think I can take it all inside me?"

"I'm sure of it. You strike me as a boy who was born for cock, the bigger the better."

Jean-Claude smiled with smug satisfaction. "I think I'm finding out that you are right. But you will be gentle?"

"With you?" He looked at him coldly and saw a little shiver of anticipation run over the boy. He picked up the lubricant and held it out. "You'd better get yourself ready."

"But I have already."

"Then put some on me. Not too much. I want you to feel this." He waited while Jean-Claude open-mouthed with lust, caressed it onto him, feeling all his muscles tensing for the assault. He would annihilate him and leave him screaming for more. Jean-Claude would never know another day's peace as long as he lived. Now.

He knocked the tube out of his hand and seized his hair and flung him over. He pulled him up more onto the bed and knelt over him, straddling him, and guided his sex between his buttocks. Jean-Claude cried out as he entered him, but his body strained up to take him. Charlie thrust savagely into him, encountering the obstruction he knew and expected. His knowledge of anatomy was slight, but there was always a point that had to be passed before his sex could move freely within his partner. It was a moment for caution and restraint, but he exercised neither now. He drew back and thrust harder and Jean-

Claude cried out again. He continued the savage pressure and Jean-Claude screamed as he felt himself break through the barrier and plunge into him.

"You are so big," Jean-Claude sobbed.

"You don't have it all yet." He grappled with Jean-Claude's hips to complete the penetration.

"Bigger even than you look," Jean-Claude cried.

Charlie made another hard thrust and he felt all of his sex take possession. He rested briefly, waiting for Jean-Claude's sobs to subside. He withdrew slowly while a wail swelled in Jean-Claude's throat. He forced a long, uninterrupted entry and took possession again.

"You are a bull raping me," Jean-Claude shouted ecstatically.

Charlie liked the classical reference. He sat back on his heels, pulling the boy's hips to him. His body sprawled before him, his arms flung out in total surrender. "There. You've got it all. You like it, don't you?"

"Oh, God. You have torn me apart. You are a great steel sword. You will kill me."

"You just wish I would." He worked the hips with his hands so that Jean-Claude rode his sex, impaled on it. Charlie sat back and let himself be used. Feet beat on his back. Jean-Claude began to babble in French, reiterating the word "*amour.*" Sure. Love. Love to him was a big cock up his ass. Jean-Claude began to moan in rhythmic accompaniment to the movement of his hips. In a moment, the moans became shouts and suddenly his whole body was convulsed with an orgasm.

"Oh come! Come into me. Come!" he shouted.

Charlie flung himself down on him and drove hard into him until the boy was sobbing again and he had completed his rape with his orgasm.

He tore himself out of him and went to the bathroom he had seen through an open door. He found a shower stall. He washed himself blindly, thinking of the sobbing boy he had left on the bed. He could do anything with him now. His slave. The word aroused memories. Tony, the hustler with the Botticelli angel's face, who claimed to be the best cocksucker in town. Tony had been his first betrayal of Peter, as Milly had been his last. He hadn't attempted to keep count of how many there had been in between. Tony had never been taken in Charlie's way, but had asked for it.

68

"Jeez," he had sighed when it was over. "I wouldn't let most guys. I feel like your slave."

"How so?"

"Jesus. The way you're built. When you were inside me, Christ. If a guy can let you do that, he's got to be your slave."

And for a while he did belong to Charlie in a way. He let Charlie arrange his hair more simply. He let Charlie teach him how to dress. He suggested bringing other boys to Charlie for "some nutty sex" as a precaution against falling in love. "It's no good for a faggot to fall in love. At least, not this faggot. A hustler's got to be free. I'd get a bang out of watching you fuck other guys. We could try it all different ways."

That had been the beginning of what Charlie remembered as a sort of delirium of sex.

He stood under the shower and called Jean-Claude's name. He appeared in a moment and stood gazing at him, his eyes full of tearful awe. He stepped forward and seized Charlie and put his mouth on his. Charlie drew back and slapped his face hard. "If I want you to kiss me, I'll let you know."

"Yes, *mon amour*," he murmured. "You're so overwhelming. Next time, I won't come so quickly. I want it to go on and on. I've looked at you often, but I never imagined it could be like that. I can still feel you all inside me. It hurts. I will never want anybody but you."

Charlie smiled up at him. "Unless you find somebody bigger."

"That's not possible."

"Oh, I wouldn't be too sure about that. I've seen some that would amaze you." He lifted his fist. "How would you like something like that in you?"

Jean-Claude's lips parted. "Please, *mon amour*. I want to think only of you."

"Not Peter?"

"Oh, no. I didn't know. He was the first. I didn't know it could be like that."

Charlie pushed him under the shower and soaped the lush body thoroughly. He pulled him out and handed him a towel. Jean-Claude let himself be handled like a child. They dried themselves, Jean-Claude's eyes unwaveringly on him.

"You're wonderful to look at. You look so strong."

"I'm strong enough," Charlie said. Whips would be the next

item on the agenda. An idea occurred to him. He went to the washbasin and found a razor. "Come here."

Jean-Claude moved promptly to him. "What are you doing?"

Charlie rubbed a little soap on the straggle of hair on Jean-Claude's chest and, with a few strokes of the razor, removed it. He wiped the chest with a towel. "There. You look like a statue. Statues don't have hair. Come on." He lifted an arm and began to soap the armpit.

He tried to pull his arm away. "Not there. People will see. They'll laugh at me."

"Don't be silly. Of course they'll see. You'll start a new fashion."

He made no further protest and Charlie went to work with the razor. As he did so, he thought of Milly's hairless body, Milly, dead all these years. Millard Potowski. Killed in action. Charlie's name and address had been found among his papers, requesting that he be notified. He had often wondered what sort of performance he had chosen to give as a soldier. Whatever it had been, he must have entered into it enthusiastically, to the point of dying. When he had completed the armpits, he held both arms up and studied the effect. "Great. Now you look the way you ought to look. Your body shouldn't be all cluttered up with hair. Come here." He would put his mark on him everywhere before he left him. He sat on the edge of the bidet and pulled Jean-Claude to him. When the boy realized what he was up to, he drew back hastily. "Oh, no. Not there. You mustn't."

"It'll make your cock look much bigger. You're a big guy. You ought to look big all over."

"But I'll look ridiculous."

"Who's going to see you?" He looked into Jean-Claude's eyes. After a moment's resistance, the boy acquiesced. He stood docilely while Charlie soaped him. His sex began to lengthen under his touch. Charlie paused in his chore and stroked it erect. "There. It's easier to handle like this. I don't want to cut it off."

"I don't care as long as I have yours."

Charlie went to work with the razor. He was amazed by the effect he was creating as the blur of hair was removed. It gave a startling naked prominence to the genitalia. The soaring sex with the two spheres drawn up close against the base looked like some sort of futuristic missile, as if it was about to take off from the body. The hair had anchored it. When he was finished,

70

he sprang up and moved away to study his handiwork. The body as sexual mechanism was nakedly revealed, superb yet oddly repellent. Charlie felt a little flush of satisfaction. "You're quite a sight."

"You like me like this?"

"You're a beauty, especially with the hard-on. Let's see how long you can keep it like that."

"As long as I look at you. I want to see you hard again. It is incredible."

"Well, you—"

There was a knock on the door of the adjacent room. "*C'est toi, chérie?*" Jean-Claude called. "*Entres.*"

"*Tu es seul?*" It was Anne's voice.

"*Mais non. Tu vas voir.*" He smiled at Charlie. "Come. I want her to see you."

"Like this?" Charlie glanced at the ludicrously naked sex, unflaggingly erect.

"Of course. She will be thrilled. You mean me? She has seen me like this many times. I want to know how she likes me without hair. Come."

Charlie had never been physically modest. All right, he thought. Let's see what this will lead to. He let Jean-Claude put an arm around his shoulders and conduct him back to the bedroom. As they entered, they seemed to crowd the room with male nakedness in the presence of Anne's slight, child's figure wearing a straight floor-length dressing gown. She seemed unconcerned by it. Her devouring eyes clouded as they fixed on Charlie's.

"Oh, no. Not you. This is wrong." She shifted her eyes to her brother and took a quick breath of astonishment. "What have you done to yourself? You are obscene. *Mon pauvre* Jeannot, this is very bad."

"You mean this?" Jean-Claude asked, passing his hand across his lower abdomen. "What's wrong? He says I am a beautiful statue."

"He's wrong. Has he done this?" She turned back to Charlie, her eyes full of reproach. "I think you are not a friend to my brother. Why is Peter not here?"

"You don't understand," Jean-Claude interjected. He hugged Charlie to him. "Charlie is my lover."

"This can't be. You're in love with Peter. You must not play with love."

"This is not play. You've never seen anything like him. No one could resist him. I've never felt the way I feel with him."

Anne's eyes swept to Charlie and returned to her brother. "I think you will suffer very much for this."

Out of the mouths of babes, Charlie thought.

"Suffer!" Jean-Claude exclaimed. "He is perhaps the biggest man in the world. It is glorious suffering."

"Peter is big enough and very beautiful," Anne proclaimed.

She knows that? Charlie thought. Had they all been at it together?

"You don't know until you've seen Charlie," Jean-Claude insisted. "I will make him hard for you."

He felt Jean-Claude's hands on him and knocked them away and took a step toward Anne. "Are you really interested?" he asked.

"If Jeannot wishes it. Big is not everything. He must understand that. But of course, I am curious. I'm interested in everything about men." She spoke in her characteristically expressionless fashion.

"You've seen Peter like this?" Speaking directly to her, looking into her eyes, made him feel more keenly his nakedness and his sex was responding to it.

"Only at a distance. To me, he looked very big. But so does Jeannot. Perhaps to a girl all men look big. I wish they would be erect always. It's so thrilling."

"You're making me that way much faster than Jeannot could." He knew there was no outrage he could commit that they wouldn't have anticipated and accepted in advance. Her eyes dropped lower and his sex rose more vigorously under her examination.

"It is very thrilling. May I touch it?"

"Of course." The contact of her small hand made his body give a slight leap and his sex swelled closer to erection. She stroked it slowly and wonderingly, almost fearfully. Something about her stirred tenderness in him. She was so small and lost. Her maternal solicitude for Jean-Claude touched him. He put his hand out and touched one of the small round breasts he had

72

admired before. He had forgotten how sweet and soft a girl could be. It brought him fully erect. She gripped his sex and looked up. He saw color flood her face.

"Why do you do that? You love boys."

"It's not always all that simple." They looked into each other's eyes. Perhaps he could add a refinement to his torture of her brother. "Why don't we make love together?" he said.

"I've always dreamed of having one of Jeannot's lovers. It would make me feel even more a part of him. When will you come see him again?"

"Why not now?"

"I must prepare for you. You look as if you could give me a baby very easily. Can you come back later?"

A baby? He felt an extra little pulsing ache in his sex as she fondled it. "Of course. I have some things to do. I want Jeannot to go with me, but he can bring me back."

"You will be kind with him? He is very sensitive. He's—his spirit is delicate."

"I know what you mean."

Jean-Claude moved in close beside them and put a hand with his sister's on Charlie's sex. "You see, *chérie?* Isn't he incredible? Wait till you feel him inside you. You will be his, too. We will both be his."

"I must go now," Anne said. "If Charlie wanted you without hair, perhaps it is all right. You are both very thrilling. I will wait for you." She turned and left them.

Jean-Claude clung to his sex and looked at him with longing. "Come. You are so hard now. You will have me again."

Charlie pulled his hand away. "That was for Anne. Get dressed. We have to go."

"Where are we going?"

"I want to take the car home. You bring yours. Then we'll tell Peter what's happened."

"You're going to tell him?"

"Of course. We'll tell him together. He ought to know it's all over as far as he's concerned."

"You're going to leave him?"

Charlie's breath caught and he clenched his jaws till the spasm passed. "Come on, damn it. Do you want me or Peter?"

"You, of course."

•

"Well, then we'll have to tell him." He brushed past him and began to gather up his clothes. Anne had left him firmly aroused; he smoked a cigarette and waited for the feel of her hand on him to pass so that he could put on his shorts. He felt suddenly as disoriented as if he had survived a fit of madness. If everything that mattered in life was finished, why go on with this ugly little comedy? He pulled his clothes on. Jean-Claude had disappeared into the bathroom. He considered slipping away, but Jean-Claude's submission drove him to devise some ultimate outrage. He wanted to rub Peter's nose in the squalid mess he'd made of their lives. He called. The boy appeared in the bathroom door, fully dressed.

"Have you got your swimming things?" Charlie asked, letting his eyes slide past him. "I want to spend some time on the beach. You've got to get that bare patch sunburned like the rest of you."

"We'll go where everybody can see us together?"

"Of course."

"Oh, *mon amour*—"

"Let's get the hell out of here. Come on."

They went out into the hot day. Jean-Claude drove his car out of a shed at the side of the house and they set off, Charlie leading, back around the town and out through the vineyard to the rented villa. As he approached it, his heart began to beat so fast that he had trouble handling the car. He got out with difficulty and waited for Jean-Claude to join him and they went to the house together. Peter was waiting for them under the grapevine that covered part of the terrace.

"I see. I might have known it," he said to Charlie, without looking at Jean-Claude. "I guess I did, when Yvonne said you'd gone to town. Well?"

"Oh, we've had our moment of truth. I planned to beat the hell out of Jeannot, but it turns out you're the one who deserves the beating."

"Is that what you've come for now?"

"No. Beating's not much fun. I worked things out more interestingly. Tell him what happened, Jeannot."

"This morning? Everything?"

"Of course. Just because he's a sneak and a liar doesn't mean we have to be."

"He made love to me. It is the great experience of my life. We are all his now—you, me, even Anne."

Peter hadn't taken his eyes off Charlie. "You really have to make your points, don't you?" he said. "It couldn't be a quiet death, could it? You have to jump up and down on the corpse and cut it up into little pieces."

"I suppose you're referring to your sad little affair with Jeannot. Tell him how you feel about him now, Jeannot."

"It's very difficult. I think now I've been in love with Charlie all along from the beginning. I think I loved you because you are his. I—"

"Drop it, Jeannot," Peter said without looking at him.

Charlie could see the hurt going back deep into his eyes. He could barely force himself to look at him; tears stung his eyes and his throat ached with them. "Well, that about covers it," he said, grinding his voice out with difficulty. "If you two want a little farewell kiss, I'm going upstairs to get some things."

He left them and returned in a few minutes carrying swimming trunks and a towel and a clean shirt and shorts for later. He found Peter standing beside the door with his hands in his pockets. Jean-Claude was on the other side of the terrace and sprang into place beside him, as if for protection.

"What're you planning to do?" Peter asked in a dead voice.

"We're going to spend the day together. And the night too, probably. What do you think, Jeannot?"

"Oh, yes, *mon amour.*"

"If you go, you won't find me here when you get back." Peter said in the dead voice.

"That's the risk we take, I guess. I probably would've said the same thing last week if you'd told me your plans for Nice. Come on, Jeannot." Charlie took his arm and they left the terrace.

"Charlie," Peter cried out.

The voice cut into his heart. He gripped Jean-Claude's arm and speeded up. He dropped into the car and took a long difficult breath. "Let's go out beyond Tahiti where we don't have to wear anything," he suggested with a harsh attempt at making it sound like something he wanted to do.

They lay out on the enormous sweep of beach, naked under the sun, with their swimming trunks tucked between their legs to protect their sexes. At a distance, they could see other naked figures, groups of men and girls, couples in various combinations. Charlie waited for the sun to anesthetize him. Everything hurt deep inside him. Seeing Peter had knocked all the props out from under him, shamed him, crippled him. It was finished, nothing could ever make it right again, but he hurt in the very roots of his being.

Life was over, but he was still alive. What was he going to with all the time that was left? He had already told himself and could go on telling himself that he should forgive Peter one transgression when he himself had committed so many, but reason didn't prevail. Feelings weren't subject to will; he couldn't will himself to want Peter. The thought of Peter eagerly taking this big, deranged boy in his arms told him that he would never want him again. And how did he know that Jean-Claude was the first? It was the loss of trust that hurt the most, the discovery that the perfect truthfulness he had always believed in was an illusion. If he could manage an intrigue here, he could have done so over and over again in New York. The pain was real, stemming from an abnormal heartbeat and whatever organs pumped bile into the stomach, if that was what it was, but also from a blockage of the mind, a weight on his soul, so that he couldn't think clearly and he hurt all over, a pervasive pain, dull but almost unbearable.

He shifted about on the sand so that he came into contact with Jean-Claude. He recoiled, although he scarcely registered whose body he had touched, and went on feeling, rather than thinking, about Peter. He had never reproached him in thought or word for anything he might have done when they were apart. Fastidious. Peter was much too fastidious to be capable of whoring, but when he had been on the town during Charlie's ill-fated marriage he had made no bones about accepting expensive gifts from his lovers. He had done whatever he had done (Charlie had never known what) to have a very large sum of money settled on him by a rich benefactor. Charlie had met the benefactor and had known that Peter couldn't have been involved with him physically for pleasure, so perhaps there had been a touch of whoring, but Peter had been on his own and Charlie had felt it was none of his business.

Charlie's later exploration of the homosexual world, when he had still been successfully celibate, had been an attempt to bridge a gap in their shared experience. The bars he went to were bars he had heard Peter mention. When he found a new one, he wondered if Peter knew it. He observed the never-ending hunt for new partners; he repulsed the advances of many attractive young men. He gained his first insight into what Peter's brief life away from him had been. Even if Peter's part in the bad trouble with Hal had been less innocent than he had always believed, he would have understood. Loneliness wore down resistance. Solace was so readily at hand. All the more reason to set the highest standards and, at least when life was running its normal course, adhere to them. All the more reason why he could find no forgiveness in himself now.

When he had received Peter's distraught telegram from California, he had immediately sent Milly away even though he had just arrived to spend the night. Milly had been sweet and understanding: he had already lectured Charlie on fidelity. "I'm glad it happened with me, but it shouldn't have happened with anybody. I feel guilty for enjoying it so much."

The telegram had inevitably reminded him of something Tony had said when Charlie had asked how he had managed to escape the draft. "I told them I was a faggot. Anybody who doesn't is nuts. They catch you with a cock in your mouth and you go to prison for the rest of your life. No thanks."

Fear had clutched at his heart. The telegram seemed reassuring on this score, but he wanted to pray for the first time in his life, he wanted to do penance, anything to get Peter through safely. Tony dropped in on him the next day in the casual way he had of turning up at any hour of the day or night.

"I'm afraid I'm not going to be seeing you any more," Charlie said when they were seated in Peter's stylish living room.

"Oh? Your new kid Milly going to monopolize your time?"

"I said good-bye to him yesterday." He handed Tony the telegram and studied him as he read it. His eyes could never get their fill of his beauty. The tilted nose, the prominent cheekbones, the hollows beneath them, the full red lips, the long line of jaw punctuated by a dimple in the chin were all full of unexpected quirks and curves and angles, as if drawn by a quick nervous hand, and yet achieved perfect harmony. His rich chestnut hair lay smooth against his head, unlike the preposterous pompadour he had worn when they first met. He lifted his bold eyes to Charlie.

"Christ, honey. It's what I've always said. You know the other guy?"

"He's an old friend. An officer."

"An officer? Then it's probably all right. I know of cases. They usually try to cover it up. Two GI's is really bad. I'm sorry." He rose and went and sat on the arm of Charlie's chair. "Anyway, a guy like you wouldn't want a hustler hanging around indefinitely. We've had some wild times. I've never known anybody like you before. You've taught me a lot of things. How to speak better. How I should dress, if I had the dough. My hair." He laughed. "Maybe I'll find some rich guy to keep me. You've given me ideas. Hey, Charlie."

"Yes?"

"Nothing. I just like to say your name. You're a wonderful guy. You know what I'd like?"

"When you look at me like that, I can make a good guess. No, slave."

"OK, master." They laughed. "I won't have any trouble remembering what it's like. So that's it? No more playing around? Don't worry. I'm sure it'll work out. How about a kiss?"

"That's different. It's a crime against nature not to kiss that mouth when it's available. You didn't have to suggest it."

When Charlie released him, Tony laughed again. "It's lucky I didn't fall in love with you. Is it all right if I call in a week or so just to find out if Peter's all right?"

"Thanks, sweetheart. That would be nice."

And from that moment it had never entered his head again to make a sexual move toward anybody but Peter. He wondered what had become of Tony. After ten years, even his startling beauty must have begun to fade. He hoped he had found his rich friend.

He felt Jean-Claude's hand on him and brushed it away. How was he going to spend a whole day with this miserable boy? Maybe he couldn't, but he certainly wasn't going home. He thought of Peter's threat to leave. Let him. His rage, his lust for revenge, had become a cold painful rejection of everything they had known and made together. Except that he wouldn't leave. He couldn't; their lives were too intertwined. It would take days just to untangle their finances. Peter had put quite a lot of money in his name over the years to establish a fiction of independence. He had no intention of keeping it, but Peter would have to tell him how to give it back. He didn't understand anything about stocks and things. Luckily he had the show coming up in the fall. He could get by, probably better without Peter, who wouldn't let him do portraits and hack work, which was where the easy money was. Renounce love. Strip his life down to bare essentials. Work. His mind approved the prospect, but his pain didn't ease.

He sat up and wiped sweat out of his eyes and looked around, hoping to see somebody he knew. There was no one close enough to recognize. He saw three male figures strolling along the edge of the sea headed in his direction. He watched their approach and identified one of them as a cute American boy they had met here and there. When they were within hailing distance, Charlie lifted an arm and waved. All three waved back and the American called. Jean-Claude heard and sat up and saw them. he snatched up his trunks and wriggled into them.

"Put yours on, *mon amour*," he said.

"Why?"

"You are mine now. I don't want everybody to see you."

"You haven't acquired exclusive rights, you know. Besides, I'm covered."

"You may think so. I can see a great deal."

"Maybe somebody else would like a look."

The three had almost reached them. The American broke into a jog for the last few yards and dropped to his knees between them, arranging for a leg to almost touch Charlie's. He greeted them both, but his eyes kept darting to Charlie. He had a lively face and a trim, smooth body and his trunks had an aggressive swell. Jean-Claude knew the other two, who were Dutch, and introduced them. They all chatted of the weather and of parties they had been to or were going to.

"Where's your friend?" the American asked Charlie. "I've always seen you together before."

"Yeah. It must get monotonous."

"You're a beautiful pair. Is your friend's hair natural?"

"Sure."

"You've got a beautiful tan. It's so even all over." This was an excuse for the American's eyes to linger on his body and drop to his haphazardly covered sex. When he looked up, his eyes conveyed an open invitation. Charlie smiled into them. Christ, he thought, is this what life would be again? Sure, he could probably have a good time in bed with this boy. What then? The Dutch pair, too, perhaps? One of them, certainly, who was also eyeing him. And after that, some more experiments of the sort that Tony had arranged, that Guy had proposed yesterday? The utter desolation of it filled him with dread. He must save himself somehow. The American put a hand on his knee as if to balance himself, and the leg finally slid over and touched his. Charlie shifted slightly so that the trunks fell away from his sex. The hand tightened on his knee, and the fingers began an invisible caress. Jean-Claude, who was watching, raised an arm to make a nervous swipe at his hair.

"But look," one of the Dutchmen exclaimed, "Jeannot has shaved his armpits."

Jean-Claude dropped his arm quickly and Charlie laughed. "I did it. Isn't it sexy?"

"I've thought of doing it and didn't dare," the American said. "Do you really like it? I think I'll do mine."

"You see, Jeannot? I told you you'd start a fashion. What're you all wearing trunks for? Nobody does at this end of the beach." He plucked his own from between his legs and tossed them aside.

"You are right," the Dutchman who had been eyeing him said and promptly slipped his off.

"I don't know—" the American said.

"Go on. It's much more comfortable."

The American ducked forward and muttered, "You do things to me."

"That's very flattering. Go ahead. Nobody'll mind."

The American stood and did as he was told, turning his back to the others. His sex slanted forward stiffly. Charlie looked up at him and smiled. "Very nice," he said.

"It's not too—"

"Not at all. You're still decent. Come on, Jeannot. Everybody else is starkers. What are you waiting for?"

Jeannot's eyes burned at him. "But no, *mon amour*. You know—"

"Don't be silly. If you sit there all dressed up, you'll embarrass the rest of us."

"No. No, I—"

"Come on, men. He's hiding something from you. I happen to know what it is. You've got to see it." He glanced at the American. "Grab him." He made a pass at Jean-Claude's trunks that wasn't supposed to accomplish anything. The American crowded in close to him, letting his sex brush against him as Jean-Claude clutched at his trunks and tried to wriggle away. The Dutch pair joined in, trying to get a grip on Jean-Claude's arms. The American's hands appeared to be tugging at the trunks, but they were finding opportunities to make quick exploratory contacts with Charlie's body.

"Go on, get him," Charlie whispered. "We'll have it later."

As Jean-Claude's struggles became more frenzied, the others warmed to their task. They were all shouting and laughing. The American had got the message and was really concentrating now. When Charlie saw them all engaged, he sprang away and pulled on his trunks. He gathered up his things in one swoop and went pounding off down the beach.

"Shar—lee," Jean-Claude screamed after him. He heard shouts and laughter and then only the thud of his feet as he ran on at a fast, steady pace.

The physical exertion made him feel cleansed and free, free at least of Jean-Claude. The boy would doubtless fall in love with all three of them before the scuffle was over. His hunger for revenge was appeased; Jean-Claude was no longer any concern of his. He squinted down the beach, trying to pick out the low shack of Tahiti Beach, where the road to town ended at the sea. He had a long way to go. He couldn't run indefinitely. Would he be in time? In time for what? Peter wouldn't go anywhere. He didn't know how long he had been away, but he didn't think it could have been much more than an hour. Running and walking, he should be able to make the house in another half-hour. Say two hours in all. Just time enough for Peter to finally face what he had done and explore the extent of their loss. What would the realization of it do to him? He would survive. His grasp of life was too sunny and jaunty and assured for him to ever dream of doing himself harm, no matter how much of the assurance derived from their being together. He would suffer.

All of Charlie's protective instincts were aroused at the thought; he wanted to get to him quickly to comfort him. In a frantic moment, he might rush off in the car just for the sake of doing something. He was inclined to drive too fast. An accident. He tried to accelerate his pace but his apprehension made breathing more difficult. His chest was already heaving painfully. Goddamn Peter for all of this. What comfort could he offer? He couldn't alter the facts. And who was to comfort him? He hoped he would never feel anything for anybody ever again.

When he reached the beach installations, he turned in toward the road, looking neither to right nor left so as not to be delayed by anybody. He heard his name called once—Guy?—but didn't pause. When he reached the road, he slowed to a walk. He had to catch his breath. He forced himself to maintain a good pace, in spite of his panting. He still had several miles to go. He heard a motor and turned and saw an old Rolls Royce convertible approaching, overflowing with laughing, shouting boys and girls. It coasted up beside him and hands reached out to him, pulling him aboard. He jumped onto the runningboard and the car started forward. Hands continued to pull at him, trying to get him into the car.

"No," he shouted. "I have to get off just after the Colette house." There must have been eight of them in the Rolls, all sprawled on top of each other, all young and beautiful with the sun and high spirits. A boy put an arm around his waist. A girl held his hand. He pulled himself free. He was sick of being handled. When he saw the road through the vineyard, his heart lifted with relief and he shouted for them to stop. As soon as they had slowed sufficiently, he leaped off with a shout of thanks and went sprinting in through the vineyard. In a few moments, he caught his first glimpse of the house through the trees and, a moment later, the car, standing pretty much where he remembered leaving it so that it probably hadn't been moved. Of course Peter hadn't gone anywhere. He was just sitting there feeling quite confident of Charlie's return. He probably wasn't even aware of the havoc he had created. He would expect a few angry words and a tearful reconciliation and that would be the end of it. Only it wasn't going to be like that. Rage began to boil up in Charlie again. He should have stayed away, let him suffer, given him a bit more of his own medicine before making the final break. He would look a complete fool rushing back so soon after his defiant parting words.

He came to an abrupt halt and gave his lungs time to recover from their strain. He forced himself on as his breathing returned to normal. Anger was coursing through him and he made no effort to control it. Now that he was here, he would tell Peter what he thought of him once and for all and leave again. He should have stayed with the happy band in the Rolls instead of trudging home to a sordid little domestic scene. Married. Christ, he was sick of all of it.

The house was silent as he approached it. He mounted to the terrace and went in. Peter was nowhere about. Panic stabbed through his anger. Was he upstairs packing? Had he done something really stupid? He sprang for the stairs and raced up them. Peter was emerging from their bedroom as he reached the top. Relief struck him with such force that it took him a moment to assume the coldly hostile mask behind which he wished to hide his feelings. Peter's face had lighted up, though he didn't allow himself to smile. They confronted each other thus for a long silent moment, their eyes probing each other, Peter's full of an appeal that Charlie steeled himself against.

"I thought you were leaving," Charlie said finally, harsh and mocking.

"I thought you weren't due back till tomorrow, if then."

"Christ, you didn't really think I'd spend the night with that dismal shit, did you? An hour was bad enough."

"I know what you mean. I've thought for the last week if I could just have a day with him, I'd never want to see him again. I guess he's pretty bad."

"He's pretty bad," Charlie repeated with barely contained rage. "You've destroyed everything, for him. You had to have him no matter what it did to us. Now you decide he's pretty bad."

Peter's chin lifted defiantly. "You'd better think a little more carefully about who's destroying things. You've done something really vile, much worse than anything I could think of."

"I might have known you'd work it out that way. You're innocent and I'm to blame. Jesus Christ Almighty."

"That's not what I mean and you know it." Peter looked at him with blazingly honest eyes. "I can tell you now. All right. I really fell for him. I couldn't control it. I got a hard-on just looking at him. It was the same with him. We're not giants like you, but it's not all that easy to hide. After it had happened a couple of times, I felt as if I'd practically been to bed with him. I just wanted to get it over with and forget him. Yesterday before lunch, with you, I knew it was going to be all right. If he hadn't gone crazy last night, you'd never have known anything about it. It was all over."

"And that's all it means to you. It was just a little affair that would've been perfectly OK if I hadn't found out about it. The really bad thing is something I've done."

"Yes, it is," Peter cried, matching Charlie's anger with his own. "You didn't even want him. You had to prove you could fuck him better than I could, as if there's any doubt about that. I really hated you when you told me. It's disgusting. But I've had time to think about it and I'm glad you did it. This morning, when Yvonne told me you'd gone, I was pretty sure why and knew you'd probably find out all about it. I was so ashamed I didn't see how I could ever face you again. I thought I had to go away, or kill myself, or something. Well, that's over. And I don't hate you any more. I'm ready to accept the fact that we're both human and try to make things right again."

"That's damn decent of you," Charlie roared. "Who said anything about being human. We're a couple of faggots. We have to be goddamn supermen to get by. I though maybe we were, but no. You lie, you cheat, you go to the shit's house and play around in front of his sister and risk other people seeing you there; you lie to me over and over again, all for the sake of a big, dull body. Some superman."

All of Peter's body gathered together and squared up to him in protest. "I didn't lie," he asserted. "I agree with you about the big, dull body. When things like that are over, it's impossible to understand why it ever happened. But I never lied. Granted you made it easy by not asking many direct questions, but I knew if you trapped me I'd have to tell the truth. I was scared out of my wits, but I never really considered lying to you."

Charlie looked at him. Peter's face was grave, but composed and shone with candor. It momentarily blunted the edge of his anger. "Mnnh," he grunted and went on into the bedroom. Peter followed him. The room was in order; there was no sign of packing. His anger revived. It was just as he had expected: Peter had assumed that everything would go on as if nothing had happened. He wanted to break through his complacency; he wanted him to suffer. He became aware that his hands were trembling and he shoved them into his pockets. Peter approached and he turned and moved away.

"Please, Champ," Peter said to his back. "Can't we talk? We never have about certain things. I don't know if it will make it any better but—well, maybe you can understand. I've been thinking and thinking, trying to figure it out. I'm a lot queerer than you. We know that. I'm much more curious about boys' bodies. I've never been interested in a girl. You might never have been queer if it hadn't been for me. You've said so yourself. I have temptations that you'd never know anything about. I can resist temptation, damn it. I always have. Something broke down this time."

"It certainly did." Charlie swung around and faced him. "Can't you understand that when something so important breaks down, you can't put it together again? It's finished. Look what happened. You said you had to have him once to forget him. You had him in Nice. Why did you go on here?"

"You must know that now. You know what he wants. That's never been for me, God knows, but all of a sudden I wanted it. I had to have it. For once, somebody was really mine. I didn't want it to last, but it was all so new to me that it took me a few days to get it under control. It won't happen again."

Charlie's trembling hands were clenched into fists in his pockets. He couldn't take much more of this. "Why not? Maybe you've finally found out what you really want in bed. You don't seem to have a clue about what I want. I'm not as queer as you! What crap. Where're all the women in my life? I was married for four months. Big deal. What do you think was going on while you were away in the Army?"

Their eyes drilled into each other for an instant. Hurt sprang up in Peter's and he looked away. "Other guys?"

"I can't remember how many. Boys, boys, boys. Six or eight at a time sometimes. But there was a difference. You were away, and I was going out of my mind. Never once since. I don't let myself be curious about boys' bodies. We've had each other. The next thing, you'll tell me you've been sex-starved."

There was a beat of silence before Peter's eyes returned to Charlie's. They were unexpectedly peaceful. "Thanks. Maybe now we're getting somewhere. If I'd known that, maybe none of this would've happened. If I'd known there'd been others, I could've talked to you. Don't you understand? All my life has been you, ever since I was nineteen. Loving you, giving myself to you, taking all you've given me. I couldn't ever knowingly do anything that would change that. I need you. You're the only reason I'm alive. When something seemed to be threatening all that, I was terrified, really lost. If I'd been able to talk to you, it probably would've passed. As it was, all I could think of was to have him so everything would come clear with you again. As it turned out, I was right."

"Right?" The calm conviction with which Peter had spoken the word was the final provocation. Charlie whipped his hands out of his pockets and stepped forward and smashed one of them across Peter's face. "You little bastard. Do you think I'm going to have anything more to do with you? What's right about that?

Peter staggered slightly and supported himself on the back of a chair. He bent over it and lifted a hand to his face. For an unguarded moment, Charlie wanted to rush to him and hold him and make sure he wasn't badly hurt. Peter shook his head and straightened. His eyes glistened with tears. "It's pretty lousy of you to hit me when you know I won't hit you back."

"I'd kill you if you tried." Fury blotted out the brief spasm of tenderness. His fists were clenched, every muscle was knotted and aching with a passion for destruction. He grabbed a vase from a table near him and hurled it. Peter stepped aside and it crashed against the wall.

"Don't do that. We'll just have to pay for it."

"*You'll* have to pay for it. I'm the kept boy, remember?"

"Oh, God, don't start that again."

"Why not? Don't you want the truth? Do you think I've liked being dependent on you? I could've had a decent job, but no—I have to be a painter so we can be together like man and wife and live happily ever after. We have to break with our families because our love is too great and pure to hide. Well, I can get along on my own now, thanks to ten years of being your paid stud. There's nothing like a little whoring to launch a guy's career. Christ." He was finally attacking all that Peter cherished most in their lives and he could see it take effect. Peter's face was drawn, his eyes wide with wounded protest. He found an ashtray and sent it hurtling after the vase.

"Stop that."

"I'll stop it soon enough," he shouted. "You're not leaving, but I am. I've had enough of it. Enough of you and your lies and the dirty joke you've made of both of us. The only reason I came back was to arrange to return your goddamn money." He seized a chair and sent it crashing into Peter's legs.

"Goddamn it," Peter cried as he skipped about to extricate himself from it. He set it on its feet. The light of battle came into his eyes. "All these years you've never seemed to realize that I might let loose and beat the shit out of you. Just watch it."

"Now you're a tough guy. Jesus. Tell me about your heroic service to your country, tough guy." This was hitting below the belt, and his breath caught as he said it. He wanted to hurt him, but something in him still resisted making the break irrevocable.

Peter winced and passed a hand across his forehead. He had been prepared for Charlie's anger and, because he deserved it, he was detrmined to bow to it, to accept any punishment. When it was spent, he would do all he could to heal the inevitable wounds. "Please, Champ," he said mildly, when he had recovered his voice. "You know I don't like to think about that."

"I thought you said we could talk about anything now that we've agreed we're both cock-crazy." Charlie charged a bureau and swept everything off its top. There was a crash as china candlesticks, two ashtrays and a collection of little glass animals shattered at his feet. He turned back to Peter, appeased by the noise of destruction. "Shall we talk about this morning? What makes you think I didn't want Jean-Claude? It was very exciting being where you had been and being able to go those couple of inches farther that seemed to make all the difference to him. You're not the only one who gets a hard-on just looking at somebody. You should've seen what I did to a cute American kid just now on the beach. He was embarrassed to take his trunks off like the rest of us until I talked him into showing it. It was quite a sight. I'll probably go back and collect him when I'm finished with you. Shall I tell you about Tony and Milly and all the sailors and soldiers I've done threesomes with? Yes, with me in the middle as often as not. Have you ever tried that? You'd probably like to hear about the ones with the biggest cocks. That cute kid today might qualify, though I didn't affect him as conclusively as apparently Jean-Claude did you. I'll have to handle him a bit to make sure but he was very promising." He talked on, waiting for disgust to drive him away, soiling them both, hoping that whatever it was in him that resisted saying the final definitive word would be buried in filth and he would be free. "Well, we're both on our own now. Happy hunting. Perhaps we'll find we're sharing lovers, like Jean-Claude suggested."

"Oh, God, I can't stand this," Peter muttered. He moved nervously around the room before he faced Charlie again, and spoke in an agonized voice. "Forgive me, for God's sake. I've forgiven you for what you did today. I'm begging you to forgive me."

"Forgive you. Then what? Do you expect us to just go on the way we were before? You've killed it." He forced the words out. The brake was still operating that kept him skirting the point beyond which there could be no return.

"But you've been unfaithful to me, for God's sake," Peter cried out in a plea for truth and reason.

"Oh, I was. Hundreds of times. I hated it finally. And myself, but I was so damn lonely for you. I really believed we could make something good and decent together."

"We have. Who else do we know who has anything like it? I don't mean just queers. I mean anybody. Look at all the married couples we know."

"You could have made a pretty good case for us until a week ago. Now we're just like everybody else. *And* queers, to boot." He realized that his rage had broken. He felt nothing in its place, only a great weariness and some dead area deep inside him. He added dully, "There isn't any future. Can't you get that through your head?"

"No, I can't. I can't conceive of us not being together always."

"Chained together for life, no matter what we do to each other? That isn't my idea of the way it's been or the way it's going to be. I believe in love being exclusive. The minute you give yourself to somebody else, everything changes. You've made me want to finish with love once and for all."

Peter was immediately at his side. He had felt the softening in his anger, but the weary hopelessness that had replaced it was almost more chilling. He had to win his way through to him somehow. He put his hand tentatively on his arm. "You can't. You'd never succeed. It's too deep in both of us."

Charlie pushed him aside and strode away. "I don't want you to touch me. I'm sick of all that. How can it mean anything to me when I know you're capable of touching somebody else in the same way? When I think of both of us wallowing around with your big, sloppy boyfriend, I really want to kill you. When I see what sex can make us do, I don't want us to be together any more."

Peter's body slumped and he crossed over to a chair and dropped into it. He stared at the floor. "Then what are we going to do?"

"I don't know."

"You're not really thinking of leaving me, are you?"

"At the moment, it doesn't seem to matter much whether I go or stay. From here on, everything will just be dying. Do you want me to stick around for the end? I don't know how much fun I'll be, playing in the ruins."

"I want you to stick around, even if you're right. You know that. But it's not going to be the way you say. There aren't any ruins. Now that I'm getting used to the idea of your having played around, it makes me realize that I could actually lose you. It makes us more the same, more together. We've had our secrets. I don't want them any more." He looked up and found Charlie facing him across the room, looking down at him. "Please come here," he said. He saw conflict and hesitation in every line of Charlie's body. He offered him a faint smile. Charlie's face hardened.

"No."

Tears welled up in Peter's eyes and spilled down his cheeks; his face remained composed. "You're really punishing me. I deserve it. Punish me all you want, but please don't punish yourself any more. I can't stand it."

"It's a bit late, but thanks for the thought."

Peter rose. "Please think about how much I love you. If you'd just let us put our arms around each other for a minute, you'd know we're going to be all right."

"No."

"Well, perhaps I'd better go downstairs or somewhere. If I stay here I'll just cry or try to touch you. You know I can't be with you without wanting to touch you all the time. That's the worst punishment."

"Your eye looks a little swollen. You'd better put something on it."

"It hurts a bit. It'll be all right. I sent Yvonne away. I couldn't stand having anybody around. Should I get her back?"

"Why bother?"

Peter wiped tears from his cheeks with the palms of his hands, reluctant to go yet uneasy about staying. He had succeeded in calming Charlie, but now he seemed almost too quiet. He had never seen him like this before. There was something lethargic about him, dead but explosive, that was frightening. Should he leave him alone to let him think his way through whatever he was feeling? Should he stay and woo him? "I could do with a beer," he said, trying to create normalcy around them. "Shall I bring you one or are you coming down?"

"I don't know."

Charlie's smoky purple eyes were fixed heavily on him. They stirred a little flutter of fear around his heart. "Well, give a shout if you want anything." He started for the door.

"Wait!" Charlie saw Peter's face brighten as he turned back. Now that passions had subsided and tensions eased, he realized that, for the first time, he was seriously considering their parting. Earlier, when he had been driven by jealousy and a thirst for revenge, it had been a safety valve, the obvious thing to think of while he raged through the situation. Now the possibility was cloaked with the reality of quiet deliberation. How could they stay together? He had been right: trust had been essential. It had been the balance to his constant inner struggle against the public stigma of their relationship. Would he begin to wonder about every unaccounted hour they were apart? Would he check telephone calls for discrepancies and try to catch Peter in errors? Every day would be intolerable. Perhaps the deadness in him was the realization that their life together really was over. Had he said, without knowing it, the irrevocable word that closed all avenues of reconciliation? The desolation of a future alone was too great to be grasped. If he was still capable of wanting anything, he wanted to retain control of the situation until he had time to explore all its implications. Peter stood before him expectantly. "Take your clothes off," he said.

Peter looked startled. "What?"

"Get undressed. If anything can make me want you again, it's looking at you naked."

"Please, Champ. Do you want to make me feel like the cheap little fairy you like to say I am?"

"You know I don't mean anything I say when I'm angry. No, you may be right. Maybe sex is the only way through this. I want to see if you look any different to me now that I know you've been to bed with somebody else. If you don't, then as you say, how can anything have changed?"

Peter looked at him searchingly. "Won't you kiss me and then maybe go to bed with me naturally, the way we always do? I want you so."

"No. I've told you. I don't want to touch you. Maybe that'll change. Take your clothes off."

Peter looked at him for another hesitant moment and saw nothing recognizable in the brooding, withdrawn eyes. He dropped his own eyes as he unbuttoned his shirt and tossed it aside. He kicked off his sandals and removed the rest of his clothes without lifting his eyes again and stood submissively before him.

"You're so damn beautiful," Charlie said dispassionately, after a silence. His eyes were taking a purely esthetic delight in their study of the graceful, ruddily bronzed body. The loins were only slightly paler, a subtle gradation down to the patch of golden curls and the peculiarly pleasing proportions of the sex. It was very much in evidence and manly, but not obtrusively sexual, as he felt his own to be. His intense physical appeal was distributed throughout every inch of him, in the golden hair falling across the broad brow, along the line of the neck and the wide but not massive shoulders, in the gentle swell of the smoothly muscled breast, down the thrillingly flat abdomen, in the narrow, finely articulated hips and the long shapely legs. This body had been his alone for so long. Was he trying not to want it now? He made an effort to loosen and relax everything inside himself so that his responses would flow naturally. He felt that any hope for the future depended on this moment. He had taken Peter back after he had been one of New York's most pursued and available boys. They had had another ecstatic reunion after

Charlie had been through a similar period. Was fidelity an intellectual conception that the body didn't recognize? Was it a mistake to place so much value on it? The memories that had been recurring during the day had evoked a young, vigorous intensity that he had perhaps lost in his tranquil preoccupation with Peter. Perhaps he had cut himself off too completely from new experience. In responding to Jean-Claude, perhaps Peter was demonstrating that they could find renewal only in others. A startling thought, heavy with consequences.

When his glance returned to it, he saw that Peter's sex was growing. It never had an ungainly or misshapen moment when it passed from quiescence to erection. It filled-out evenly in a slim, straight, ever-lengthening line until its head lifted joyously. He gazed as it happened now, to him a miracle of unprovoked response, since he was not aware of the naked, longing love in his watching eyes. He raised them to Peter's. He felt his body jarred into life. "Thanks," he said.

"Thanks yourself and God bless Narcissus," Peter said in an attempt to recapture the gaiety that had always marked their intimacy. "We're built so much alike, you might just as well have been looking into that pool."

Charlie smiled faintly and shook his head. "I know all the differences. I'm just plain and solid where you're all delicacy and beauty. Go get in bed."

After a moment's hesitation, Peter turned from him and obeyed. Charlie's eyes were fixed on the exquisite curves of the shifting buttocks. Peter stretched out and his sex made a little slapping sound as it fell against his abdomen and pointed at his chest. Charlie stood without moving for another moment, studying the body spread out on the bed and waiting for him. Infidelity had broken his mastery of it. He felt a sudden, fierce lust to reassert his exclusive possession of it. Perhaps when his domination of it was once more firmly established and acknowledged, he would voluntarily abdicate—free Peter, free himself. The guidelines they had adopted for the conduct of their lives were dissolving. He felt as if he were faced with a blank canvas, blank with infinite potentialities.

He went to the side of the bed and stood over him. Peter's sex gave a little leap at his proximity. He lifted a hand to Charlie's sex where it was confined in his shorts.

92

"Oh, God, there it is, all huge and hard. Take me. Always. Always keep me yours."

Charlie looked down into his face, strained and yearning with love, and felt a little quiver of contempt (for Peter? for himself?) as he waited for the hurrying hands to remove his clothes and prepare him for the act.

When they had showered, they hitched towels around their waists and went down and fixed themselves sandwiches. They carried them and a bottle of wine out to the shade of the vines on the terrace. Peter knew that everything was still not right; there had been no gaiety in their love-making. Charlie had taken him savagely, almost as if it were the first time. It had been curiously exciting, with the startling novelty of a seduction, but lonely. Yet he was so happy that they had got beyond that major hurdle that he was bubbling with carefully restrained high spirits. In a few days, the wretched episode would have been forgotten and their life would have returned to normal.

"You know something?" Charlie said when they had begun to eat. "I want to get away from here. I've had enough of it." Just saying it gave him an enormous sense of release. The hell with its all having been planned and paid for by Peter. "I had a long talk with the Kingsleys—" He started to say "last night," but it made everything that had happened too immediate and he altered it to "—at the Graumonts'. I want to go with them."

Peter felt a slight chill at his use of the first person singular, but he knew of course that he meant them both. He wanted to ask if this decision had been influenced by the morning's events, but decided against it. "Really? Well, if you want to, I'm all for it."

"I told the Kingsleys you might have to stick around here for business."

Was he hinting that he might go alone? Peter thought of Paris and Nice and wished he had never heard of the de Belleville deal. It might fall through if he were out of touch, but he didn't care. "It's practically all sewed up. I've forgotten—how long did they say we'd be away?"

"About six weeks. Eight maybe. Practically the whole summer."

"Yes. Well, I was pretty tempted when they first mentioned it, but I thought it was out of the question because of your work."

"That's the only rub. I've got quite a lot of things pretty well started now. If we ship them back and go right home after the cruise, I think I can make it. I'll have to work like a fiend but that's all right."

Peter was glad he hadn't asked if he would go without him; better not to ask too many questions for the time being. He put his hand on Charlie's where it lay on the table. "Of course, I don't know anything about boats except for the sailing I've done with you. And I have my problem about touching you. Will we have our own cabin? Will we be able to go to bed together?"

Charlie intertwined their fingers and gave Peter's hand a squeeze. "Probably not on the boat. But Jack says that except for—I think it's the long haul from Sicily to the Gulf of Corinth, wherever that may be—he says we'll be in port almost every night. It would have to be understood that we get off and go to hotels. They're bound to want to be alone themselves."

"Yes, that's true. I forget—" He started to say "that other people have sex lives," but this put an ill-advised emphasis on sex and he ended, "well, that other people want privacy, too."

"It's a shame wasting all the rent here but Jack says that we'll spend so little on the boat that it'll all balance out in the end."

"Oh, that's just money. I want us to do what you want to do."

Charlie started to make a joke about how rich he was, but suppressed it. He had said enough about being kept. He was still feeling his way in this nerve-wrackingly unfamiliar situation. He didn't want to hurt Peter needlessly now; the time might come when he would have to deliver the big irreparable blow. He was beginning to experience long moments when it seemed as inconceivable to him as it did to Peter that they could ever part, but having seriously faced the possibility, he didn't see how his old, blind confidence could ever be restored. Even if time proved that they could survive this crisis intact, he suspected that their relationship would have to yield to adjustments. The new nagging urge to try to free himself from it remained in him. The yachting expedition had suddenly become much more than an exciting supplement to their holiday: the promise of salvation, an opportunity for trial and testing. Communal living would enforce a sort of separation on them, create space and distance between them. Perhaps this small experiment in separation would train him for a real separation if that was where they were heading. He didn't know; he knew only that there was no longer any question of an abrupt, immediate break. He said, "We can go see them this evening. Unless something turns up we haven't thought about, I think we should go."

"That's marvelous. Do you have any idea when they're planning to leave?"

"I think next week."

"Golly. So soon? I'd better check our dates and write some letters. I know we have a couple of things week after next, that dinner in Cannes for one. Well, yo, ho ho. Sailing to Greece. That's fantastic. Will you teach me how to sail?"

"Sure. We'll all have to know how to handle the boat. It's— well, exciting and peaceful at the same time. You'll love it."

"When you look like that, I wish we were leaving tomorrow."

"I'm going to see if I can't get them to start sooner. I can't afford to waste any time."

Peter rose to clear the table, but first went around behind Charlie and put his hands on his bare shoulders and kissed the top of his head. "You have forgiven me, haven't you? I'm so completely yours, it's impossible to believe that all that awful stuff really happened. I've got to know you've forgiven me."

For answer, Charlie reached up and pulled his head down and kissed him on the mouth. "I love you, baby," he said into his eyes.

For the rest of the day, they continued to treat each other as if they were both recovering from a serious illness, careful to avoid any shock or upset. Behind his courtesy, Peter sensed a distance in Charlie, a cool, speculative withdrawal with no precedent in his long experience of his shifting moods; he simply accepted it as part of the price he would have to pay for his transgression. So long as they were together, Peter didn't care how long it took to dispel the cloud that still hung over them.

At sunset, they dressed in crisp white and drove to the port to announce their decision to the Kingsleys, Charlie parked on the quaiside beyond Senequier's café, the social center of the town; he hoped to avoid a chance encounter with Jean-Claude. All the buildings along the waterfront were just beginning to emerge from the rubble the Germans had left behind them five years earlier. A great unsightly crane looked as if it had been abandoned near the entrance to the harbor. They left the car and strolled along the rank of moored yachts, sleek racing sloops, more imposing yawls and ketches and schooners, big, luxury motor cruisers, looking for the Kingsleys. They found the boat hidden beyond a miniature liner with a smokestack. The deck was deserted.

She was a sixty-foot double-ended yawl, with a black hull and teak decks, called *Cassandra*, to remind them, Jack had explained rather heavy-handedly, to pay attention to any warnings she might issue. There was nothing sleek about her, she sat solid and broad in the water. The bowsprit gave her a rakish, piratical look. Charlie had liked the look of her when he had first seen her.

Peter had paid little attention to the boat before, but now, thinking of the next six or eight weeks, he thought she looked rather small. They stood at the foot of the gangplank, and Charlie called out, "Ahoy, *Cassandra*." In a moment , Jack Kingsley's head bobbed up in the open hatch. When he saw who it was, he climbed nimbly out on deck.

"Is this the boat that's going to Greece?" Charlie asked. "Are you looking for a crew?"

Jack laughed. "Come on aboard. You make a devilishly handsome crew. And stylish too. I'm afraid the old tub can't live up to you." They all met on the narrow stern with a good deal of laughter and backslapping. "You really mean it?" Jack asked. "We've finally won you over?"

"We'd better go over the details again but I think we can work it," Charlie said. "We definitely want to. Right, Pete?"

Peter agreed, pleased at being consulted, pleased with the diminutive even though it was Charlie's usual signal that they must assume the protective coloration of the straight world and beware endearments.

"Well, this calls for drinks for all hands," Jack exclaimed. He was looking very much the seafaring man, wearing only jeans cut down to shorts, frayed around the bottoms. His body was hard and trim, with a furring of gray hair on his chest. He waved a hand around him. "Watch the varnish. She's pretty nearly ready to go. Hey, Marty."

Martha appeared in the companionway wearing a crisp, blue cotton dress and stepped out on deck beaming at them. "I don't believe it. What a glorious surprise. Are you really coming with us? "They all talked at once for a few minutes and then the three men settled into the roomy cockpit while Martha went below for drinks.

"I know neither of you will regret this," Jack said. "It certainly solves a big problem for us. You can't take just anybody on a trip like this. You two guys obviously get along well together. I'm really delighted."

"She must be beautiful under sail," Charlie said. "She's much bigger than anything I've handled."

"With all your experience, you'll probably handle her better than I do. I've read all the books, but I don't kid myself. There's no substitute for growing up with it. I've had people out on her who can turn her into a racer. Peter and I will crew for you." He slapped Peter's knee. "What say, mate?"

"Aye, aye, sir." They all laughed at nothing in particular. Martha's head appeared in the hatch with a tray bearing ice and glasses and a bottle of pastis. Charlie sprang forward to help her. She smiled her thanks up at him. While Jack poured drinks, she took Charlie's hand and looked him directly in the eye.

"I can't tell you how pleased I am. I think we're going to have a glorious time."

"I don't see how we can help it." He smiled at her, liking the look of her. He was reminded of some Dutch painter, he couldn't remember which one, but one of them had done women with Martha's very feminine but no-nonsense quality. Her heavy, fair hair, her direct blue eyes, her round cheeks, her pretty, easily smiling lips, her trim but ample body all evoked some earlier, more disciplined era. He wondered if Anne was still expecting him. Anne had reminded him of his wife—skinny little strings of girls, both of them. Martha was a full-blown woman, competent and self-contained; he felt again that he could be friends with her without fear of misunderstanding. The way she looked him in the eye and held his hand communicated only outgoing, uncomplicated good feeling.

Glasses were handed around. They all lifted them to each other. "Happy sailing," Martha said. Peter and Charlie exchanged a look that registered the felicitous moment. Jack rattled his glass.

"I hope you won't expect all these frills at sea. I understand ice is a problem in Greece. Not much yachting in those waters since the war."

"Haven't they been having a revolution or something?" Peter asked. A rich Greek client had said something to him about it.

"There was some sort of trouble, as I remember," Jack confirmed. "That was a couple of years ago."

"I should think the most important thing is to decide when we want to leave," Martha put in. "When will we be ready, darling?"

Jack scratched a graying temple. "Under a week. Say by Monday. I don't want to take up any of Charlie's painting time, but if Peter could help with some of the chores, we could make it even quicker."

"Don't worry about me," Charlie said. "I only need a day to finish up some things I want to get done. The sooner we go the better, as far as I'm concerned. Don't you agree, Pete?"

"Absolutely."

It was decided that they would leave no later than Saturday. They moved on to other matters—supplies, how expenses would be shared (the Kingsleys would be responsible for fuel, harbor charges would be split between them and so forth), the route they would follow. When questions of sailing and navigation were touched on, Peter dropped out of the conversation and observed with delight the transformation that had taken place in Charlie: his eyes were bright, his expression eager and interested, he was completely himself again. Peter was deeply grateful for the miracle; Charlie had known what he wanted and had said so without wasting time with regrets for the rented house. The house had been a mistake. If Peter had known they were going to find such a blatantly queer community, he would have chosen some other place. He could sense the potential of boredom in this nice, straight couple, but better that than the hazards he had allowed to ensnare him.

As the others continued to discuss every aspect of the trip, he began to feel that they were really going and he studied the boat with awakened eyes, looking along the deck, cluttered with unfamiliar gear, and up the tall mast with its heavy rigging. An inkling of how completely the boat would contain them and set them apart from the world crossed his consciousness. He wished that he and Charlie were going off alone, just the two of them, away from everything and everybody.

"Well, it all sounds really great," Charlie said with enthusiasm after they had had several more drinks. He looked at Peter and smiled, really smiled at him deep into his eyes as he hadn't smiled since the day before at Porquerolles. "What do you say, Pete?"

Peter burst out laughing with gratitude and happiness. "I say let's get going. I don't see how we ever thought of turning it down."

"It's definitely understood, isn't it, that eight weeks is absolutely maximum for us?" Charlie addressed the Kingsleys.

"Absolutely," Jack agreed. "You say you don't mind flying back if we decide to stay on and winter there. The same applies if we get held up for any reason and we just can't get you back here on time. Right?"

"Right." They all got to their feet as they drained their glasses. Peter eagerly agreed to come back in the morning and start learning his way around and helping out in any way he could. The Kingsleys accompanied them to the stern and stood at the top of the gangplank and waved them ashore.

"I don't believe they're queer, no matter what people say," Martha said when they were out of earshot.

Jack laughed. "Women can't ever believe any guy is queer. They can't stand the idea of a cock getting away from them."

Martha frowned as she wandered back to the cockpit and poured herself another drink. "Don't be crude. No, Peter may have had a schoolboy crush on Charlie once upon a time. They're obviously devoted to each other. It's probably just as simple as that. People have such foul imaginations."

"Are you intending to find out?" Jack asked as he took the bottle from her and poured himself another drink.

"What do you mean by that?"

"Just watch your step. That's what I mean. A small boat is no place for hanky-panky. I thought we decided we wanted them with us *because* they're queer."

"Don't be silly. We wanted them with us because we like them."

"I see. Well, they're queer, all right. I can assure you of that.

So I don't think we need really worry about any repetitions of the troubled past."

"Oh, Jack," Martha said wearily. She took several long swallows of her drink. "It's a bit odd your being so insistent about it. How can you be sure of a thing like that? Perhaps *you're* intending to find out."

Jack laughed. "I think I'd have more success than you. Unfortunately, we have no secrets from each other so it's hardly worth wasting an innuendo. However, a blow-job is a blow-job. If either of them offered to oblige, I wouldn't necessarily turn them down. Especially Peter. He's the tastiest trick I've ever seen in my life. Those eyes. He'd bring out the queer in any man."

"He's very sweet." She drained her glass.

"You prefer Charlie, of course. I know your type. He's hung. That's certainly obvious. Well, you might as well drown your dreams in drink. We've had the sense to pick two nice faggots who're nuts about each other. Let's leave it at that. We're going to have a nice quiet trip." He held the bottle over her glass and poured out a generous measure.

Preparations for departure kept Peter and Charlie very busy for the next few days. When he was with the Kingsleys, Charlie felt wholly alive and keen for adventure. Alone with Peter, he was still aware at times of a deadness in himself. He didn't know what it was. Something was gone, something was broken. Whether it was something that time would restore, repair, heal, he couldn't tell, but it filled him with curiosity. Life was taking on more interest than it had had for a long time. When his curiosity flagged, he fell into long moments of deep depression from which he felt nothing could rouse him. Peter could, with his sweetness, his bright vitality, his evident determination to pretend that nothing was wrong. Charlie would find himself laughing with the same delight he had always felt with him. Still, he was looking forward to being on the boat where he felt he would be able to arrive at a cool assessment of the future.

Peter immediately became Jack's preferred and adept helper. He learned much more quickly and competently than Charlie about the workings of the motor. He was able to shinny up the mast to fix a block that had got jammed. Charlie had always liked being with him in a healthy, outdoor atmosphere, playing tennis with him, swimming, playing an occasional Saturday afternoon game of touch football with neighbors. It seemed to mitigate the onus of the forbidden bond that held them. He was pleased that Jack and Peter got along so well together.

Jack's preparations converted what at first had seemed a casual cruise into a serious and complex undertaking. Charlie's experience had been confined to off-shore racing with an occasional brief cruise along the New England coast. He was fascinated by the navigational equipment that he didn't know how to use. He was amazed at all the facilities available to yachtsmen, the detailed charts with their depth markings, the Mediterranean pilot book with its careful descriptions of the lights and shelter and holding ground of every port they planned to visit. He found it extraordinary that the governments of the world permitted yachtsmen to buy duty-free liquor and fuel and cigarettes. If he could believe his eyes, a bottle of the best Scotch would cost one dollar and five cents on board.

After three days, they had developed into a well-meshed team and the boat was ready to sail. There was no authorized dealer in duty-free stores at St. Tropez, so Jack planned to put in at Antibes before really getting under way. There were people in Cannes that Peter felt he ought to see on business. As a consequence, they were to make this first short stage of the trip independently the next day, Charlie and Peter by car, the Kingsleys alone on the boat. They would regroup in Antibes the day after.

"Be sure to bring lots of sweaters," Jack said as they were having a farewell drink.

"Really? Why?" Peter asked.

"It can get chilly at night. I suppose you don't have any wet-weather gear. It doesn't matter. We can share out what we've got on board."

"Jack will never get over crossing the Atlantic," Martha said, smiling at Charlie.

Charlie smiled in return. "Who can blame him? I don't think I'd want to try it."

"Really?" Martha looked at him with the pleasure of discovering an unexpected ally. "Jack thought I was an awful coward for not going with him."

They made elaborate farewells that would have been appropriate to a permanent separation; a special tie of comradeship had grown up between them in these few days. Martha kissed Charlie and Peter on both cheeks in the French fashion, a sweet and sexless embrace. They shook hands and patted each other and exchanged assurances that they'd meet in Antibes day after tomorrow.

Leaving the boat, Charlie and Peter encountered Guy de Sainval. He greeted them with elegant cordiality.

"I've been looking for you two everywhere. What *have* you been up to? I've called you more times than I care to admit. If you turn into recluses, there will be no point in my staying here."

They told him about their imminent voyage on *Cassandra*.

"That's the American couple? But how can you? They have no crew. I rather enjoy the yachting life myself, but only with an army of divine stewards at my beck and call. How brave and Spartan of you. And you're leaving so soon? How lucky I found you. Madeleine is having a party for me tonight. I was determined to have you."

Charlie and Peter glanced at each other and made simultaneous sounds of polite refusal.

"But you must. It's in honor of Harry leaving me again. I think this makes the eighth time. He'll be back, but we must celebrate while we can. Everybody you know will be there. We will make it a farewell party for you. I've even invited some very disreputable young men to make sure Jeannot would come. He's gone quite mad. I hear he arranged an absolutely spell-binding orgy last night." Guy looked at Peter. "Only a few days ago the mere mention of your name would have brought him running. I think fidelity is your exclusivity."

"I'm sorry, Guy," Charlie cut in hastily. "We just haven't time for parties. We're getting away first thing in the morning."

"But this is impossible." Guy put his hand on Charlie's arm. "You were to be my campaign for the summer. The *bouillabaisse* was only the preliminary to an absolutely dazzling series of maneuvers. Why should Jeannot be the only one to benefit from your divine visitation?" He flashed them a wicked smile. "Oh, yes, I'm afraid Jeannot and *la petite soeur* Anne have been talking. It cheered me up enormously. The thought of having both of you, since that's apparently the form your fidelity takes, made me quite giddy."

"Don't believe everything you hear," Charlie said coolly, managing a slight smile and revealing nothing of the anger that shook him.

Guy lifted a silencing hand to him. "Oh, but I want to. Some of the details about you—too delectable, though they didn't come as a complete surprise. Tomorrow morning? I shall have my bags packed. I don't think Greece sounds like my sort of country, but there must be some place where the pastures are greener—or the men more like you two."

"I hope you find it. We've got to run along." Charlie held out his hand and Guy shook it. "Thanks again for the other day. *Au revoir*."

"*Au revoir*. You may well say it. We'll meet again. I'm sure of it."

Charlie had pulled his hand away and started on to the car before Peter could complete his farewells. He hurried after, cursing Guy and filled with dismay. They got into the car in silence.

"Jesus." Charlie muttered before starting it. "Pleased with yourself?"

"Sure. I feel like shooting myself again. I'm sorry. Thank God, you're getting us away from here."

Charlie was thinking the same thing. What he had done with the French boy had been vile, but he couldn't exonerate Peter from creating the situation that had incited him. Thank God for the boat. Once on board he would find every means to test the strength of the bonds that held him. If he found a weakness anywhere, he would break free once and for all.

Their departure for Cannes the next morning was silent and furtive; they were like criminals fleeing the scene of the crime. Once away and on the road, their spirits lifted. They both felt the past slipping away behind them. Charlie dropped a hand from the wheel and took one of Peter's. "God, we're out of it," he said. "I never want to get involved with a bunch of queers again."

"Me too, darling. I'm going to have to start practicing not calling you that."

"My baby. I'll be thinking it even if I can't say it." They squeezed each other's hands.

They found their way down to the squalid little port of Antibes at noon the next day, after arranging to store their car and three suitcases of excess clothing. *Cassandra* looked much bigger amid a scattering of fishing boats. Their reunion with the Kingsleys was as excessive as their parting. They felt like the only four people on earth. Charlie and Peter eased their suitcases down the steep companionway that rose from the galley. Now that the boat had become home, they both looked around them as if they had never seen it before, taking possession of it. The galley was quite roomy, compactly fitted, and the same area contained a chart desk where Jack's navigational equipment was stored. From there, they entered the saloon cabin, which was fitted out like a living room. Bright covers and cushions turned the bunks they would use into divans. There were bookshelves, and curtains at the portholes, and brass lamps and a table fixed in the middle, which folded out into a dining table. Forward was the head, with a deep closet opposite. Beyond that was the fo'c'sle cabin for Jack and Martha.

They all gathered in the saloon amid luggage. Martha had drinks ready. It was very hot. The Kingsleys reported on their trip of the day before, which had been uneventful.

"We got all the stores on this morning," Jack announced. "What I'm planning is to pull out of here about sunset after an early supper. That should get us to Corsica sometime in the morning. About noon, maybe. I don't like to put into strange harbors at night. The run should take us about sixteen hours, depending on the wind."

He had drawn up a schedule of watches, which he now produced. Peter was to be on from eight to midnight, Charlie from midnight to four, Jack the bleak hours from four to eight in the morning. Charlie saw the sense of it. He would be around to keep an eye out when Peter, the least experienced of them, took over in the early part of the night. When Peter relieved Jack at eight, Martha would be there to lend a hand if need be.

"Unless we find a better arrangement, we can stick to these hours for the whole trip," Jack said, his weathered, rugged features bent over the sheet of paper. "During the day, it doesn't matter so much, so long as Charlie and I get our sleep. In theory, we three will spell each other at four-hour intervals. I haven't given Martha a regular watch because she'll be doing the cooking, and I'll expect her to help out whenever she's needed during the day. Is that OK with everybody?"

"It's pretty soft for us," Peter said to Martha.

"He apparently thinks we need our beauty sleep. I'm not complaining."

"I think it's fine," Charlie said to their captain. "It's damn decent of you to take the worst bit."

"The dawn watch? I love it. Our whole way of living is going to change now, anyway. You'll see. No more of those stylish nine-thirty dinners you've been going to."

"Thank God," Charlie said.

"You want to come look at the charts?" Jack and Charlie rose and moved toward the galley-chart room.

"I'll get our stuff stowed away," Peter said as they left. He turned to Martha. "Show me where to put everything."

Charlie and Jack leaned over the chart showing Corsica and part of the French coast around Antibes, while Jack did something fascinating with what looked like two rulers fastened together by swiveled bars. He moved them, snapping together and parting, across the chart to the printed face of a compass. "All this is old stuff to you, naturally. That's our course."

"Yeah," Charlie said, reluctant to admit his ignorance. He had never used a chart.

Jack twirled a pair of dividers that moved like a man on stilts across the chart from Antibes to the northern tip of Corsica. "Sixteen hours, if we're lucky. We do five, six, seven knots with decent winds. It takes a gale to move us any faster. I hope we don't have too many of those. Have you ever used a mileage log?"

"No," Charlie said. He didn't even know what Jack was talking about.

Jack indicated a tubular object with a little propeller at the end of it hanging over his desk. A long cord was attached to it, coiled up neatly, at the other end of which was a clocklike instrument with a little window with numerals in it that obviously clicked around, like a speedometer. Jack tapped the face with a finger. "Always make a note of the mileage reading and the time and the new compass reading whenever you change course. I mean, if the wind shifts or anything. That way, I'll be able to plot our course pretty accurately. Excuse me if I'm telling you stuff you know."

"No, I've always sailed by dead reckoning. Time, compass and this thing. I should be able to manage that." He felt physically comfortable with Jack. If their shoulders touched, it was because they were crowded for space and they had to touch. After the past weeks, it was a relief to feel nothing equivocal in the movements of another man's body.

"I'll explain it to Peter, too," Jack said, "but he'll probably be explaining it to *me* before I get through. It's amazing how quick that guy is around a boat."

"He's quick, all right. I think he's going to love it."

They returned to the saloon and Martha left them to prepare lunch. Peter was emptying a suitcase into a locker above one of the bunks.

"I'm just shoving everything in together," he announced cheerfully.

Martha served them a lunch of salad and cold meats and fruit. Peter and Charlie ate with the care of weight-watchers, the Kingsleys with less restraint.

"You'll have to do better than that," Jack said. "We agreed to divide the food-and-wine bill by four. You're cheating yourselves."

"It's the price we pay for being able to go on wearing our old clothes," Peter said. "You're obviously one of those people who can eat all they want and never put on a pound."

"He's infuriating," Martha said, looking at Charlie. "I'm always planning to get rid of five pounds, but he sets such a bad example. Don't let him undermine you. You both have such beautiful figures."

"Thank you, ma'am," Charlie said with a smile. "If I say the same about you, it'll sound as if I'm just being polite. But it's true. You've got the kind of body I like to draw. Really marvelous." He said it sincerely but impersonally, and she accepted it in the same spirit with a flattered smile that wasn't in the least flirtatious.

They sat about and chatted for some time after lunch. Peter volunteered to help Martha clean up the dishes. Eventually, Jack went off to clear papers with the port authorities. Martha went forward to her cabin and closed the door. Peter and Charlie smiled at each other and gave a quick glance around and exchanged a brief kiss.

"Well, I guess we're going to Greece," Peter said.

"Who would've ever guessed it?"

106

"We have a fabulous life. It's going to be better than ever now. We've left all that behind us, haven't we?"

"I think so. I want to."

"So do I, except to go on being so horribly sorry I let it happen."

"I know you are, baby." Changing the subject, he said, "We might as well take the car back to that garage and leave it."

When they returned on foot, Jack was on board. He roamed restlessly about the boat, communicating a sense of imminent departure. He disappeared for some time into the cramped engine room behind the companionway. He reappeared on deck forward where they heard him thumping at something. They went up to join him and see if they could be useful. He was checking the dinghy where it was lashed to the roof of the cabin housing. There was some shade on the deck now from the gentle rise of the town. Jack took Peter forward to the mainmast, where he began to explain the rigging and the routine for raising sail. Charlie glanced down the hatch and saw Martha's head. He perched on the top step of the companionway and she looked up at him with a smile.

"I suppose you'll feel you're back in the nursery, having dinner at this hour. I do," she said, removing things from cupboards. "Do you want a martini?"

"I don't think so. Too strong."

"We always have them. A bad habit we've brought with us from New York."

She set about her preparations. Jack and Peter came back and joined him in the cockpit.

"It looks as if we're going to have a beautiful night," Jack said. "The barometer's dropped a bit, but that doesn't seem to mean anything around here. We have one beautiful day after another and the barometer goes on rising and falling as if that's what it's being paid for."

Martha handed up an iced shaker and glasses. "Is Peter going to have a martini?" she asked.

"No. We'll have whisky. I'll come down there and do it if you'll show me where things are." Charlie let himself down the companionway and stood beside her. She showed him the icebox and where the bottles were stowed. He chipped ice and put it in glasses. He pumped water into a small pitcher. He found a bottle of whisky. He brushed against her a good deal; he hoped she didn't think he was doing it on purpose. He put everything out on the deck at the top of the companionway and joined the others in the cockpit.

He poured drinks for Peter and himself and they drank and talked together as the sun lowered in the sky. Martha joined them and Jack gave her a martini and refilled his own glass. The Kingsleys' martinis went quickly. They had had three when Charlie and Peter were starting their second whisky. Charlie had observed that they were steady drinkers, but he had expected this evening to be different. It wasn't wise to try to handle a boat drunk at night, and they were definitely getting drunk. They were beginning to make little mistakes with their words, and Martha's laughter was becoming rather unrestrained. Charlie and Peter glanced at each other and lifted their eyebrows. Martha filled Jack's glass once more and emptied the shaker into hers, waiting for the last drop.

"Well, I'd better see about food," she said. She pulled herself up and, balancing her brimming glass with exaggerated care, she maneuvered herself down the companionway with great skill. Charlie silently congratulated her but wondered if she could do it so well when she had finished the contents of the glass.

The meal was hearty, soup and a beef stew that Martha insisted she had prepared herself that morning, although nobody expressed any doubt, and they elected to eat it on deck in the fading afternoon light. They washed it down generously with wine. When they had had coffee, Charlie went below and helped Martha with the dishes. She swayed a bit at the sink but considering her intake, she managed very well.

When he went back up on deck, Jack rose. Charlie watched him closely. He looked a bit unsteady, but he braced himself with a hand on the boom above his head. "All set below?" he asked. Charlie nodded. "Well, we might as well get the gangplank in." He managed the cluttered after-area without stumbling and went firmly down the gangplank. Charlie obviously had been needlessly alarmed by Jack's drinking; he knew he couldn't take that much himself. Jack looked competent as he untied one of the stern lines and threw it aboard. He untied the other and threw one end of it to Peter who caught it and gathered it in so that it remained looped around the bollard.

He ran nimbly up the gangplank and lifted it on its davits after him. He uncoupled it from the deck and all three of them eased it in along the gunwale and lashed it down. "So long, land," he said. He clapped Peter on the shoulder. "Come on, mate. Let's get the anchor up." He bent over to a panel behind the wheel and turned a key and pushed a button. The engine rumbled into life. He turned to Charlie. "You stay on the wheel. You can play that line out and pull it aboard when we're clear." He led Peter forward and they started heaving on a hand windlass with a great clatter of chain. Charlie was impressed. It had all been done quickly and expeditiously. He couldn't really grasp that they were almost off. Martha appeared in the hatch and he grinned at her from behind the wheel.

"We're leaving?" she called above the rumble of motor and the clatter of chain. He saluted the land with a gesture of farewell. They were moving slowly out into the middle of the harbor, the line playing out behind. When he came to the end of it, he flung it astern and pulled it rapidly on board, making sure to keep it clear of the propeller.

He was briefly seized by a sense of total unreality as he told himself that he was on a boat, cut off from land, with two near-strangers. How had it happened? Then he was caught up once more in the excitement of departure. Jack and Peter seemed to have encountered a snag with the anchor. The chain was silent. Jack was moving out along the bowsprit pulling at something. Peter heaved at the windlass some more and the chain gave a final rattle. Jack waved a signal astern. Martha, who had come out on deck and was watching, came back to Charlie and pulled a lever and adjusted the throttle and they moved forward under power. Martha stood beside the wheel while Charlie gave a wide berth to the end of the breakwater and headed for the open sea. As soon as they reached it, they were caught in a heavy swell. In another few minutes they were out in full sunlight again but the sun was low, just above the jagged outline of the Estérels. There was a pleasant southerly breeze. Charlie checked the compass mounted on the steering column and the wind-direction pennant at the top of the mast. Their course would take them on a nice easy reach if the breeze held.

"Let's get the sails up," Jack called. He was still standing forward with Peter.

Charlie glanced over his shoulder back to shore. They had plenty of sea room. He looked at Martha and nodded; she leaned over and cut back the throttle as he eased the bow into the wind. He held it there as they rolled and heaved on the swell. Peter ran back, pulling off stops as he came, as if he had been doing it all his life. He looked at Charlie and winked. He ran forward and he and Jack began hauling up the mainsail. As it opened and fell about them, Charlie had to fend it off, struggling to hold the boat in position against the swell. He didn't know what had become of Martha. Gear banged and clattered about him. As the sail rose slowly, he eased off on the mainsheet and the great boom began to swing heavily, perilously close to his head. The sail was gaff-rigged and it took them another minute to get it set. Charlie rocked with the movement of the boat, clinging to the wheel. Jack and Peter seized another halyard and broke out a big jib that was carried on the mainstay out at the end of the bowsprit. It dipped toward the water but they got it up quickly and Martha materialized from somewhere and began to grapple with its sheet. Jack and Peter came running aft as he swung the wheel to port and grabbed the mainsheet. He handed it to Peter as the pitching bow fell off. He held it steady and eased it up as the sails took the breeze. Martha bent over and cut the motor. The bow bit into the water, the boat leveled and surged forward, the sea hissed along the hull. The momentary chaos was replaced by a deep, singing peace. Charlie looked at Peter and laughed joyfully. He was trembling with excitement.

"How about that?" he demanded into Peter's shining eyes.

"Wow! It's something. It must be nice to be the captain. The crew has to really work."

"Aren't you going to give us the mizzen?" Charlie asked Jack with a glance at the mast behind him.

"I don't particularly like to use it at night. It's just one more thing to bother about if conditions change."

Charlie shrugged. "I wonder where this damn swell is coming from."

"That's the Med for you," Jack said. "You get conditions from all over all mixed up together. It never makes any sense."

"How about breaking out a bottle of wine? I feel like celebrating." Even before the words were out, Charlie wondered if he should have made the suggestion. He glanced at Jack, telling himself that here was a man who knew his job. With a green crew, he had performed admirably. Perhaps he could drink a whole bottle of gin before dinner without showing it.

"I'll get it," Peter volunteered.

Jack and Martha were neatly coiling the sheets so that they could be easily freed.

"You might ease up on the main," Charlie suggested. "This is your course. It's almost on a quarter." Jack did as he was told until the sail developed a slight luff. "Back in just a bit. There. That's fine."

"Jib all right?"

Charlie nodded. Jack looked around him and snapped his fingers and went below. Peter came back with an open bottle of wine and three glasses. Jack followed with the mileage log. He took it to the stern and threw it overboard and played out the line and attached the clock mechanism to the aft stay. He checked his watch and leaned over Charlie for a glance at the compass and went below again.

"Jack doesn't want any wine," Peter explained.

"None for me," Martha said. "I may have a nightcap later." She was sitting rather huddled up on the cockpit bench gazing out at the setting sun. She seemed suddenly silent and preoccupied. They were out far enough now so that the sun had escaped the mountains and was sinking directly into the sea.

Peter filled two glasses and they looked at each other and silently toasted themselves. Charlie had settled into the cushioned seat behind the wheel. There was just room for Peter to squeeze in beside him.

"You want to see how it feels?" Charlie asked. He took both glasses and moved over so Peter could take the wheel. As soon as he did so, they veered up into the wind. Charlie laughed and got them back on course with his foot.

Peter held the wheel intently for a few minutes. "I see," he said finally. "You have to pay attention all the time. I'm still not quite sure which way to turn the wheel to get the compass marking in the right place."

"Just think of it as being opposites. If you turn the wheel up this way, the compass reading falls off that way. I guess that's right. It gets to be an automatic reflex. You'll get used to it."

"I'd better practice tomorrow. Hell, this is my watch coming up now, isn't it?"

"Don't be silly. I'll take it tonight. You can stay with me and see how it goes." They touched secretly as Charlie handed Peter his glass and eased himself back behind the wheel. He glanced around once more. The land mass behind them, the vast panorama of coastal towns backed by foothills rising to the distant peaks of the lower Alps, was already misty in the fading light. The sun was just touching the rim of the sea, a hotly blazing red sphere. He remembered "Red sun at night, sailors' delight."

The breeze was freshening, which surprised him. He would have expected it to die out as evening came. The wheel was developing quite a pull. The light changed abruptly from day to dusk. He scanned the horizon, looking for weather indications. Everything was gray, a gray sky meeting the darker gray of the sea. He was looking forward to the imminent night; sailing under the stars with this breeze would be marvelous, despite the troublesome swell.

Jack came up on deck and joined them. "How's she going?" he inquired with evident pride of ownership.

"Great. I'm getting the feel of it. If it weren't for this damn swell, I think I could really make her zoom. The wind's picking up."

"The barometer's fallen quite a bit," Jack said with a touch of anxiety in his voice. "Not that that necessarily means anything."

Martha snapped out of her reverie. "What did you say? Do you think we should go back?"

"Now don't start that," Jack said sharply.

Charlie was astonished to realize that she meant it. She knew they were planning to be at sea for days on end—at least during the crossing from Sicily to the Gulf of Corinth—with no possibility of going back anywhere. They wouldn't get very far if she wanted to return already.

"What is it? What's the matter?" Peter asked, looking puzzled.

"Nothing," Charlie assured him. "Jack thinks we might have some bad weather, that's all."

"It looks fine to me."

Charlie continued to study the sea and sky. There were no clouds anywhere and the sea heaved in the swell that rolled away all around them. He slowly became aware of an odd smudge of darkness ahead of them. He realized that he had noticed it some time ago, but now it seemed to be intensifying. It had no

112

shape or dimension, a black smudge he couldn't relate to anything he had ever seen before. It looked unnatural, as if there were something wrong with his vision. He blinked, but it was still there. He looked away and let his eyes travel slowly along the horizon toward it to see if he could tell where and how it began. It had no definition. It was just there, getting darker now. Their course was taking them straight for it. "Do you notice anything funny up ahead," he asked Jack.

Jack straightened and peered forward. "You mean where it's getting dark? That's just night coming, isn't it?"

"I suppose so, but I've never seen it come in just one place before."

"I see what you mean."

Charlie watched as it continued to blacken and begin to swell a bit. He heard something that sounded like the approach of a thousand beating wings and glanced up in alarm. They were smacked over hard by a great gust of wind. Charlie immediately eased the wheel to right them, but the gust had already passed on. Then he saw what he'd been looking for, the darker gray and white of turbulent water ahead, and he welcomed it as something familiar, a relief from the eerie, black nothing that had been threatening them.

"We're getting into something," he said. He checked the mainsheet to make sure it was on a slip knot for immediate release.

"You think so?" Jack asked. "Hell. I guess maybe we'd better get the goddamn jib in. Come on, mate."

Before he and Peter had even started forward, they were in it. The wind whistled in the shrouds and knocked them down again, but this time it wasn't a solitary gust but a new condition to contend with. The turbulent sea was rushing at them with startling rapidity. Jack grabbed Peter's arm and they both lunged forward.

"I'm not going to be able to help much," Charlie shouted, grappling with the wheel. "I can't hold her up in the wind in this swell. Don't you want the motor?"

"We're sailors, boy, not tourists," Jack bawled.

The drink talking? It seemed foolhardy to Charlie to attempt any work on the deck without all the help at their command. The threat of unmanageable seas was clear and immediate. "Definitely no motor?" he shouted questioningly.

"Hell, no. Let go the jib sheet."

"Not yet," he ordered Martha quickly. She stared at him as if she didn't know who he was, but didn't move. His heart was in his mouth as he watched the two struggling forward, lurching and clinging to the rail. Hang on, for Christ's sake, he prayed to Peter. He didn't see how they were going to get the jib down without dropping it into the water. He was carrying as much luff in the sails as he could without killing their way entirely.

When they reached the mast, Charlie nodded to Martha. "Go ahead. Let go the jib sheet."

She scrambled to do his bidding. The canvas leaped free and cracked back in a murderous assault on Peter and Jack. Jack grabbed it and struggled forward with it. Charlie was thankful to see that he was leaving Peter at the mast to handle the halyard. Jack straddled the bowsprit and battled with the flailing canvas as the jib came down slowly.

The strain on the wheel eased briefly. They were almost into the rushing white-capped sea. Charlie lifted and braced himself to meet it. The first big wave ran in and hit them. The bowsprit rose chillingly and pointed at the sky and fell with a crash and plowed into the water. Jack disappeared under churning sea. The bow scooped up gallons of water as the bowsprit sprang clear, Jack still straddling it, and sent a flood hurtling back along the deck. Charlie's heart pounded up with terror as he saw Peter make a spring for the bowsprit and join Jack where he was wrestling with the jib. The bow fell and they both disappeared under the foaming sea. Martha leaned over the deck and vomited. That'll get some of the booze out of you, Charlie thought savagely. He was beginning to get the feel of the boat under these challenging circumstances. She was reassuringly tough; with the jib down, she staggered painfully, but he could sail her. The mainsail probably should have been reefed, but it was too late for that now. Martha attempted to struggle to her feet and fell back. She repeated the attempt. On the third try, she succeeded and went skittering across the deck.

"Close the hatch cover," he shouted as she lowered herself down the companionway. He didn't watch to see if she obeyed. All of his will was directed at the two up forward, urging them to finish with the jib and get back. Let the damn thing go if need be. His heart stopped every time Peter was plunged into the sea. He was so preoccupied with Peter's safety that he didn't notice how quickly it was getting dark. At last, he saw him staggering up from the bowsprit as the bow shook itself out of the water and come pitching and careening back along the deck. His golden hair was plastered to his head, his dripping clothes clung to his body. He looked naked and beautiful.

"Go below," Charlie shouted at him.

In answer, Peter crashed into the cockpit and was flung against the leeward bulwark and vomited over the side. He was trembling from head to foot. Charlie lunged forward and grabbed him by the wrist and pulled him to him. Peter fell on his knees against him.

"Go below," Charlie shouted. "Get dry. Put blankets over you. Stay there."

Peter looked up at him with an exhausted but jaunty smile. "I've got to stay with you."

"Don't be a damn fool. Nobody can do anything now. I'll get you if I need you."

"Promise?"

Charlie nodded and gave him a little push. He scuttled across the deck almost on his hands and knees and crashed against the hatchway door and dropped down the companionway. Charlie drew a deep breath of relief, and then remembered Jack. He looked forward and saw him slumped down on the deck halfway aft, vomiting in his turn over the side. Drunken bastard, Charlie thought. "Get back here," he yelled.

Jack crawled back and collapsed into the cockpit. "Jib's secured," he called brokenly.

"Go rest," Charlie shouted. "Turn on the running lights. Come back when you're feeling better."

Only when he was alone did Charlie fully register how dark it was. He lifted himself cautiously and peered ahead. His skin crawled and he went cold all over.

His first thought was that he was sailing into the gates of hell. The dark smudge had become a seething black mass that was about to engulf them. He looked behind him. There was still some gray light back there. His hands were trembling on the wheel. Should he turn back? He would never be able to get the boat about alone. Would the motor help? Perhaps, but when he thought of the moment when they would have to take the seas broadside, he quailed. He tried to reason with himself. It was only weather. As a kid, he had been through what everybody had agreed was pretty rough stuff. This was the sunny, blue Mediterranean; if they hit some freak disturbance, it was bound to pass over quickly. So long as it didn't take them with it.

Charlie gripped the wheel and braced himself in his seat. He gritted his teeth to summon up every ounce of courage in him and looked again. It was like looking into a bubbling cauldron of tar. It writhed and bulged. He was struggling to suppress a shout of terror when he was in it. It was like having his head plunged into a bottle of ink. The boat rose like an elevator and came crashing down. A ton of water fell on him. The sea swirled around his knees. Were they sinking? He had to get to Peter. Suddenly a great jagged fork of lightning came crackling at him and he ducked as his ears were split by an explosion of thunder. Sea streamed away around him. He found that only his feet were still sloshing about in water. He remembered Jack telling him it was a self-bailing cockpit.

He glanced at the small glow of the lighted binnacle and saw they were heading almost fifty degrees south of their course. Should he check the mileage and make a note of the time? His teeth were chattering and he clamped them shut. He felt the boat rising under him again, still rising until it felt as if it was leaving the water, and then falling sickeningly away until it settled with a crash. Another mountain of water fell over him. There was a succession of small shocks as if they were grinding into a rock. He heard chaos break out below, things falling and smashing and banging against each other. The whole boat shuddered beneath him and then gathered itself together and surged forward. He couldn't see anything. He was steering by the feel of the wind against his face and by those moments when he could gauge clearly the stress of the wheel. Lightning glared and crackled again and there was another detonation of thunder. In the brief, blinding light, he saw that the mast and sail were still there. He took a fresh grip on the wheel and squared his shoulders and cursed the elements. He didn't have time to be terrified any more. All his muscles were tensed, his mind intent on countering the terrible battering of the sea and wind. His greatest fear was that the wind would be knocked out of the sail. If the great boom began to swing, it could take the mast with it. He was so intent on his labored manipulations of the wheel that he didn't see Peter until he tumbled down beside him. He was wearing some sort of coat with his bare legs sticking out from under it.

"Christ, what's happening?" he shouted into Charlie's ear.

"Plenty," Charlie answered in the same way. "I'm glad to see you. It's lonely up here.'

Peter put his arm around him and leaned against his soaked back. "It's taken me about fifteen minutes to get here," he shouted. "We going to be all right?"

"Pray, baby. I'm doing my best. Is that shit Jack going to give me a hand?"

"Martha says he's sick. Can't I help?"

Charlie's words were drowned as another wall of water fell on them. "Go below, baby," he shouted when he could speak again. "You're taking my mind off my job. Be careful, for God's sake. Tell Jack sweet dreams."

"I want to stay. You might need me."

"All I need is somebody to take the wheel. I can't let you do that. Go below."

"I wish I knew more about it."

"Don't worry. I'm OK. If anything really bad happens, get up here as fast as you can. Thanks for coming. I'd hug you if I could let go this fucking wheel."

Peter slipped off his coat. The wind grabbed at it, but he helped Charlie shoot one arm into it, and then the other. Charlie realized it was one of their smart city raincoats, soaked through. Peter was naked except for shorts.

"I'll be back," he shouted.

Charlie watched his pale form teeter across the deck and disappear. Although he was shaking all over, he wasn't really cold. The sodden coat was some protection against the wind. He felt a glow of gratitude for Peter. Somebody was still functioning on this damned boat. He was beginning to respond automatically to its wild careening. He was finding ways to correct to some slight degree the worst of the heaving and pitching. Water rushed at him from every direction. Swirling down the decks, tumbling into the cockpit, falling on him from above and behind. He thought it might be raining but couldn't be sure. His eyes were beginning to make out dim shapes, the shape of the sail, the shape of the cabin housing. The noise was stupefying: the roar of the sea, the crack and rattle of the rigging, the strange thumps and crashes from below.

Charlie's eye was caught by something white quite high above him moving toward him. It couldn't be, his mind protested. Not a wave up there. His blood froze. His mind went blank with terror. The boat was seized by chaos: it rose, it crashed, it shuddered to a halt, it lurched free, it shook itself and crashed again. Charlie's hands were locked to the wheel and he was slumped over it, his eyes closed, unable to breathe as he was pummeled and submerged by water. God keep Peter; it was his only coherent thought. He was simply a pair of clutching hands. All the rest of him had surrendered to the cataclysm that had fallen on him. Slowly, he became aware that he was still there. He could breathe again. The boat was still under him. They were plowing on. A new noise had been added to the din, a spasmodic, giant hammering somewhere forward. He shook water out of his eyes, waiting for his vision to clear from the stinging salt. He was still alive, or passed over into an eternity of furious sea. There was a splintering flash of lightning and this time there was a beat before the explosion of thunder. Peter was beside him again, wearing another coat.

"Was that really bad?" he called.

"If we get anything worse, we've had it. What's going on down there?"

"It's a shambles. A great pile of water came down the hatch. I was up to my knees. It's run off somewhere."

"What are the fucking Kingsleys doing?"

"Not that, I'll bet. I guess they're sick." He was cut off by the great hammering. "What the hell is that?"

"I don't know." Charlie strained his eyes forward and noticed that the shape of the cabin housing had changed. There was a bulge along the side that hadn't been there before. "The goddamn dinghy. It's come loose!"

"Should I do something about it?"

"Christ, no! Let it go."

"I was scared shitless down there. I'm going to stay with you."

"Maybe you better. All I could think about was you when all that was going on."

"If we're going to drown, I'd like us to do it together."

It was such a comfort having Peter beside him that Charlie began to feel some slight, grim pleasure in his battle. Nothing changed, except that the interval between lightning and thunder lengthened by a second or two. The boat continued its wild gyrations. The sea continued to fall on them unrelentingly. Peter had his arm around his waist and was clinging to him.

"Is this what it's been like up here?" he shouted.

"This and worse."

"You're fantastic. I'd have given up long ago."

"If we get through it, I'm going to drink a whole bottle of whisky."

Charlie had lost all sense of time. The constant battering was working his nerves into knots. He began to worry about things outside the immediate stresses of the storm. He wondered about bigger boats; there must be liners in and out of Corsica. He could discern a faint glow where the running lights should be. He assumed they must be bright enough from forward but would any lights be really visible in this sea? He couldn't alter his course much no matter what turned up in his path. He began to imagine them being cut in two after his endless struggle to keep them afloat.

"For God's sake, tell me if you see anything out there!" he shouted at Peter. They leaned their heads together.

"I can't tell what's water and what's sky," Peter called against his ear.

"That's the trouble. Not sick any more?"

"I'm getting used to it. Have you been through things like this before?"

"God, no. Don't worry. We're going to make it."

Peter hugged him. Charlie's eyes stung with the salt and were beginning to ache from the strain of staring into the black frenzy of the night. He kept seeing dark forms in front of him that dissolved when he blinked. He didn't know how long he had been clinging to the wheel. An hour? Five hours? As the possibility of survival emerged and became a coherent hope, his nerves knotted even tighter. Could he hold out? He had to, even if it took all night. Aside from the lives depending on him, it was a struggle he had committed all of himself to, a challenge he had accepted. Another hour—another five?—passed in grim repetition of all they'd already been through, the pitching and tossing,

119

the sickening falls. Charlie didn't know when he became aware that water was no longer falling on them in breath-stopping masses, but was being flung at them in solid sheets of spray. This was doubtless an improvement. Sometime later, he realized that it was costing him less effort to hold himself braced in his seat. He looked up at the sky and let out a whoop of joy and triumph. Peter started up from a doze.

"What? What is it?" he exclaimed.

"Look up there," Charlie shouted. "There's a star."

"That's good, isn't it?"

"Oh, God. 'Good!' It's the most wonderful thing I've ever seen in my life. Oh, my holy Christ! We're getting out of it. Oh, my baby, the goddamn thing must be almost over."

Little by little, the signs turned more favorable. The air around them ceased to tear at them with screaming frenzy and settled into a full-throated roar of wind. The sea was still enormous, but the rise and fall of the boat was less extreme; the elevator sensation passed. More stars appeared. Eventually, Charlie cautiously eased the sheet and worked his way back on course. Since he judged that they could have made very little progress in these harrowing hours, he made no attempt to compensate for them. They might make a landfall a few miles farther south than Jack expected. What difference did it make? They were alive and the boat held solid beneath them.

After another passage of unmarked time, they were sailing under a sky full of stars. The sea remained rough and the wind strong, but these were reasonable conditions and the boat was obviously made for them. She skudded along, heeling only slightly, taking on very little water.

Charlie took a deep breath and squared his shoulders. He felt the strain in his muscles slowly relax. He had forgotten it was possible for his body to move easily. "God, baby, go get us a bottle of whisky," he exclaimed. He still had to speak loudly, but he didn't have to shout. "Don't bother with glasses. They'll just slop it around. I want it inside me. Put on a dry sweater and bring me one. And check the time, will you?"

Peter kissed him on the side of the face and went off. He returned with the things Charlie had requested. Charlie took a thirsty pull on the bottle before quickly shedding his coat and shirt and wriggling into the sweater, using his feet to hold the wheel.

"God! More whisky. What time is it?"

"About ten after two."

"You're kidding. Is that all? I feel as if it had been a week."

"I know. Normally, we'd just be thinking about going to bed. It's unbelievable. Still, you've been on since a little after seven. That's seven hours. I don't see how you did it."

"There were moments when I didn't think I could." The whisky was untangling Charlie's nerves. He felt a surge of pride in his achievement. Damn few men could have managed it, beginning with the male passenger below.

"I wish I could take over for you now. You must be really bushed."

"No, I feel wonderful. This is the way I love it. Feel the way we're roaring along. Look at that sky. It's beautiful."

Peter laughed. "You're a regular old sea dog. I've never seen you like this."

"I love it and I'm good at it, damn it. An hour ago, I swore I'd never get on a boat again if we got through the night. Listen, I think there's a flashlight hanging over the chart table. Get it and check the dinghy, will you? We might as well see if we can do anything about it, since it's still with us. But be careful. We're still bouncing around."

"I don't mind this. This is fine." He went off and Charlie saw a beam of light playing along the side of the cabin before he returned. "I think it's all right," he reported. "It's wedged in against the rail and one line seems to be more or less holding it."

"God, Jack doesn't even know how to lash a dinghy. I'm going to have to go over everything carefully tomorrow and see what else needs attention." He took the light and flashed it at the mileage log behind him. Thirteen miles. It figured. Maybe eight or nine miles the first hour-and-a-half and straight up-and-down ever since. Corsica was still a long way off. Jack might not like to go into strange ports at night, but Charlie had no qualms about it. This wind would have to hold if they hoped to get in before sundown tomorrow. Today, he corrected himself.

He urged Peter to stretch out on the bench beside him, since he didn't want to go back below, and he was soon asleep. The whisky lulled Charlie so that whole blocks of time seemed to spin off into shapeless reveries. It seemed quite soon when he noticed a lightening of the sky. Dawn coming already? It must be after four. He considered asking Peter to go down and wake Jack and decided against it. He didn't want him up here. Let him make a thorough louse-up right at the beginning. Him and his schedule of watches. If they had been depending on him to get them through, they'd all be at the bottom of the sea. Faggots to the rescue. He and Peter could handle the boat without anybody's help. He reached out and stroked the golden head, white now in the growing light. The hair was almost dry and curled softly over his ears. Peter laughed in his sleep. My lover, Charlie thought, my mate. The only person he had cared for deeply and passionately in all his life. Devoted, loyal, true—and capable of treachery. He could think it now without a pang. He felt more complete in himself than he ever had before, assured and self-sufficient. If he could conquer the elements, he could surely conquer himself. Was this the way it happened—the slow loosening of bonds without pain? He looked up at the sail and wondered if he could ease up more on the sheet.

The sky was growing brighter in the east. At last, a rim of gold appeared on the horizon and then the sun rose rapidly as if it were on runners. Within minutes, he was in a sparkling world of blue sea and tumbling whitecaps. No land was visible. Charlie's chest felt as if it would burst with gratitude and joy. He had longed so for this day; its coming was a vast release from terror and fatigue. He felt wonderful. He leaned forward and touched Peter's head again, tugging gently at his hair. Peter opened his eyes and saw him and smiled. Then his eyes rolled around, and he sat up quickly.

"Hey. Look at us." He sprang to his feet, revealing an erection. He looked down at himself and laughed and adjusted it in his tight jeans. "Dreaming of you. God, what a day. There's nothing anywhere."

"Nope. We're at sea."

"Can't I take it now? You must be dead. Don't you want to pee?"

"I'm about to burst." He moved over and Peter sat behind the wheel. "There's nothing to it now. Just hold her on course." Charlie rose stiffly and stretched himself all over. He got up onto the stern and released what seemed to be several gallons of water. The shorts he had been caught in the evening before were still wet, but he could feel the sun burning into him. They'd be dry soon enough. He returned to Peter's side. "Do you think you can get the jib up alone?" he asked.

"Sure. There's nothing to it. Getting it down is the problem."

Charlie laughed. "I hope it won't be like that again. You might as well take that sweater off. You'll get a bit wet."

Peter handed over the wheel and threw off his sweater. Charlie's eyes followed the graceful body as he ran up along the deck. "Bring the sheet back first," he called after him in reminder. He realized that the leeward deck would have to be cleared of the dinghy before they could get the jib up. He hoped Peter could manage that alone. He wanted to get the boat really operating before anybody came up from below. The night had given him a proprietary right. He didn't want to relinquish the wheel to anybody but Peter, under his supervision, although he supposed he would have to sleep sooner or later. Peter moved about in the bow for some time. Eventually he led the sheet back along the leeward deck and climbed over the dinghy. His T-shirt was wet and clinging to him.

"Things are sort of a mess up there," he reported. "I'll have to get that thing out of the way, won't I?"

"Yes, if you can."

"Well, my bowknots might not be very nautical but I can certainly tie it up for the time being." He returned to the dinghy and grappled with it. He managed to ease it back up onto the roof and tie it on.

"Great," Charlie called. "Let's have the jib. We've got to make it snappy." He got hold of the end of the sheet and as soon as Peter was at the mast and had gripped the halyard, he turned the wheel and they went pitching up close to the wind. "Get it up fast," he shouted. As soon as the canvas was at the top of the stay, whipping in the wind, he fell off again and hauled in on the sheet, steadying the wheel with his knee. The rope was pulling hard; it made him realize how close to total exhaustion he was. "Get back here," he shouted angrily.

Peter looked back and then dropped what he was doing and came running to him. "I was just coiling the line," he explained.

"I'm sorry, baby. Take this damn thing. It's pulling my arms out." As Peter grabbed it, Charlie let the wheel take its normal course and they pitched up into the wind again. "There. Get it in. OK. Tie it off with the slipknot Jack showed you." When

Peter was done, he eased the bow off, the added canvas took the wind, the bow fell and lifted and they leaped forward with a great surge. Charlie laughed exultantly, his exhaustion forgotten. "Now we're going somewhere, by God!"

Peter fixed them coffee, which they both laced liberally with whisky. Charlie let Peter take the wheel again, sitting beside him and giving him pointers. As the sun's heat intensified, they both stripped to the waist. Charlie slipped his arm around Peter's back and under his armpit and put his hand on his chest, stroking the puckered nipples and feeling the muscles working. Peter giggled.

"Sailing is sexy," he said.

The sun was quite high in the sky when the first of the pair Charlie had begun to think of disdainfully as "the passengers" appeared in the hatch. Martha looked haggard and disheveled in the bright morning light. Charlie's hand was still on Peter's breast. He let it drop, but deliberately, without haste, and left his arm where it was. Martha climbed on up onto the deck and lurched aft and slumped beside them on the windward bench. She looked around with stricken eyes. "Aren't we getting to Corsica?" she asked.

"We're getting there. We weren't exactly speeding last night."

She shuddered and straightened and hugged herself. She looked at him with something like awe in her eyes. "You got us through it," she said.

"Peter helped."

"Ha!" Peter exclaimed. "Some help. I slept up here for a few hours."

"You were here to help if I needed you."

Peter noted the steel in his voice and remained uneasily silent. Was he going to give the Kingsleys a rough time? Martha had apparently caught his point. "Jack was terribly sick," she said defensively.

"It could happen to any of us, I guess. Still, if your boat's sinking, I should think you'd want to try to do something about it."

"What could I do?" she pleaded. The awe was still in her eyes. "You saved our lives."

"I'm not talking about you. But never mind. I had a lovely time. Thank God for Peter." He lifted his arm and ran his hand over Peter's shoulders and gripped his neck with a little squeeze and left it there.

Peter concentrated on the compass. His cheeks were burning and his heart had begun to beat trippingly. Charlie was in a dangerous mood. He trembled for Jack, but Charlie had the right to throw his weight around after what he had been through.

"It's so rough still," Martha said piteously. "Are we running into another storm?"

Charlie laughed. "Good lord, look around you. It's a beautiful day. Where would a storm come from?"

"Is it normal for there to be this much wind?"

"I don't know. All I know is, we're really moving."

"It's terrifying. After last night, I know I can't go on. I'd just be a burden. I'll leave you in Corsica and you three can go on without me."

"Oh, no." Charlie smiled and shook his head firmly. She was part of his command; he wasn't going to tolerate desertions. The next they knew, Jack would want to go back. He hadn't saved their boat for them for that. "Last night was a freak. You're not going to be a burden. You're going to do your share with the rest of us."

"But I hate it. I always have. I can't reason with Jack about it." Her eyes filled with tears. "That's why I wanted so much to have people I like with us this time."

Charlie looked her in the eye and let his expression soften. "Well, here we all are. Pull yourself together. Be the nice, sensible girl you've always been. After all, you sold *us* on this trip."

"I don't know. I'll try. After last night, I know you can do anything. That makes it a little less terrifying." She looked across at him adoringly. Now I'm a father figure, Charlie thought.

"Well, how about—" he began.

"Don't tell Jack what I said," she interrupted in a low aside. She had apparently caught movement out of the corner of her eye, for now Jack emerged from the hatch. He braced himself against the opening and looked around him. Charlie removed his hand from Peter's neck.

"Who put the jib up?" he demanded testily.

"Peter did," Charlie replied. He found Jack looking unexpectedly well and remembered that he'd had a nice long rest.

"We're carrying an awful lot of sail for so much wind."

"Don't be ridiculous. We're sailing beautifully."

"That's easy for you to say, but Peter and I have to get it down if we run into trouble."

"I can, Jack," Charlie said evenly. "I want Peter on the wheel as much as possible today. I think we'll all agree after last night that the more of us who can handle the thing alone the better. That OK with you, Pete?"

"Sure. I'm beginning to really enjoy it." He held his breath, waiting to see if Charlie would let Jack off so easily. He was taking over; if he didn't push it too far, there wasn't much Jack could do about it.

"There's one thing I think we all feel," Jack said, settling on one of the cockpit benches and speaking in a man-to-man fashion. "Judging from what was going on below, you must've done an absolutely superhuman job last night. You get all the medals. I'm sorry I was so knocked out. I don't know what hit me."

"A man can't help it if he's sick. The worst of it happened during my watch, or Peter's anyway," Charlie said magnanimously. "Would you mind checking the lashing of the dinghy? It broke loose last night. We almost lost it. Let me know if you need any help." Charlie's command was established. He ran his thumb unnoticed back and forth along Peter's side at a ticklish spot as Jack went off to do his bidding. Peter leaned over the compass, suppressing laughter. Charlie turned to Martha. "I was going to ask you, can you rustle us up some food? I don't care whether it's breakfast, lunch or dinner. I could eat all three."

She smiled at him adoringly and left. Charlie and Peter remained together at the wheel. After securing the dinghy, Jack checked the mileage and questioned Charlie about the timing of the events of the night and went off to do his notations and calculations. Charlie slipped his arm around Peter again and caressed his chest and abdomen and held him close against himself. He had come through the night, tempered by terror, feeling reckless and impatient of weakness or incompetence of any sort. If either he or Peter had behaved like Jack, he could imagine the Kingsleys saying, What can you expect of queers? He hoped he had shown them what they could expect: a sense of duty, some courage, and tenacity. In the Kingsleys' eyes, he had nothing to be ashamed of. He had earned the right to hold Peter if he wanted to. They had endured the night together; Peter had stuck by his side. He could feel all of Peter's body responding to his hand now. Why shouldn't he express the sense of deep, indivisible comradeship that he felt for him? He dropped his head behind Peter and kissed his back and put his other hand on him and pulled him back against his naked chest. Peter made little murmuring sounds of pleasure.

Charlie didn't shift his position when Martha reappeared, although he stopped the caressing movement of his fingers. When she reached the cockpit carrying plates, he removed his hands from Peter and took the plates, meeting her eye and smiling up at her. "Here, baby. Go ahead and eat," Charlie directed, offering a plate to Peter. "I can manage the wheel with my feet."

Peter couldn't believe his ears as he relinquished the wheel and took the food. Martha sat on the bench beside them. The preparation of food seemed to have rescued her from the odd disintegration that had begun almost as soon as they had left port the evening before. She had arranged her hair and put on lipstick and was once more the pretty, comfortable woman they knew. Only, the way she looked at Charlie was new; it told him he could do no wrong.

The plates contained ham-and-egg sandwiches on slabs of French bread and hamburgers, sensible food under the circumstances, easy to eat. They pushed it into their mouths, laughing a great deal at their piggishness. When they had finished, they licked their fingers and groaned with pleasure and exclaimed about how good it had been.

"You're so wonderful t o be with," Martha said, looking at Charlie. "You always seem to be having such fun together."

Charlie ran his hand through Peter's hair and gripped it and rocked his head back and forth.

"What do you expect with a nut like this? God, you're absolutely solid with salt." He leaned toward him and, holding the back of his head with one hand, licked the forefinger of the other and began to wipe salt delicately from Peter's eyelashes. "Your goddamn furry eyelashes." He glanced at Martha. "Have you noticed them? They're amazing."

"I know. I've been green with envy," Martha said, her eyes not wavering from Charlie.

Peter's blushes came and went, happily concealed, he was sure, by his tan. He had longed so for everything to return to normal between them; he had dreaded any new or unexpected shift in Charlie's moods, but this was so thrilling that he succumbed to it without making any attempt to understand it. He supposed that to Martha there might seem nothing sexual about it but he knew that Charlie was putting their relationship on display in a way that was a defiance of everything he knew of his nature. Even "baby" might seem innocuous enough to her, but it was Charlie's most secretly intimate term of endearment and he had said it aloud in front of a third person. Had it been a slip of the tongue? No. Charlie didn't make slips of the tongue, and the way he was putting his hands on him made it clear that he had wanted to say it. Peter had resumed control of the wheel and he was glad that he had something to hold onto so that he couldn't be tempted to respond in kind. God knows what they might end up doing.

"Scoot forward just a bit," Charlie said. "If I could get a leg up here behind you I could sort of stretch out a little." Peter edged forward and Charlie put his leg up on the cushion. He put his hands on Peter's waist and pulled him back close in between his open legs so that Peter could feel his sex begin to stir behind him. "There. How's that?" Charlie demanded with a tremor of laughter in his voice.

"Great," Peter managed, hoping the gasp couldn't be heard in it. He gripped the wheel, waiting for his heart to calm down. Charlie laid a hand on his shoulder and began to instruct him further in the handling of the boat. He put Martha to work trimming sheets as he had Peter head into the wind and fall off and taught him how to come about. There was too much wind to attempt to jibe. When Charlie leaned forward to check the compass, Peter could feel the aroused sex shifting about until it was thrust up hard against the small of his back. The sides of their heads brushed against each other. Charlie had obviously decided to drive him mad with desire. When something was said that gave him an excuse to laugh, Peter released his pent-up, enthralled excitement in peals of laughter. Charlie joined in. Martha sat back and watched them with an approving smile.

"You really are marvelous together," she said. "I've never seen two more attractive men."

Late in the morning, when he was confident that Peter was capable of handling the boat under stable conditions, Charlie decided that he ought to get some rest.

"Just stay on the wheel," he told Peter when he had sent Martha forward on a manufactured errand. "If you get hungry, let Martha bring food up to you. If there's any change in the weather, shout for me. I want to show them that we can manage this by ourselves."

"By ourselves!" Peter murmured. "If only we were. I suppose you know I'm apt to tear your clothes off at any moment."

Charlie chuckled and rose and let his fingers stray along Peter's shoulder for a moment, and then went below. He picked his way through the debris in the cabin and dropped onto a bunk and slept.

When he awoke, after performing a summary toilet in the cramped head and putting on fresh shorts, he climbed up and stood in the hatch and looked around. A long, green, wooded island ahead of them pierced him with a thrill of incredulous delight. Corsica. They had found it. Land looked solid and hospitable. The sea was calmer and the wind had dropped a bit. They were still moving along smartly. He looked aft where the three were gathered in the cockpit. Peter and Martha greeted him with happy smiles. Jack seemed to come to attention slightly, as if he wanted to look his most alert and competent. Charlie moved around behind the wheel and touched Peter's shoulder.

"I'll take it now," he said. "You need some sleep, too."

"Actually, it's my watch coming up," Jack said.

"I'll let you take it in a while. I want to check everything on deck."

"I figure we'll be in before six if the wind doesn't poop out. I wouldn't want to come in here at night."

"Don't worry about it, Jack. We've got the pilot instructions. According to the chart, there's a big open bay at Calvi with plenty of anchorage. There's nothing to it. How about getting the mizzen up?"

"Do you think it's worth the bother?"

"If you want to get in before dark." He looked at Peter and winked. "Go on below and get some sleep."

"You're indestructible," Martha said to Charlie. "You've had barely three hours."

They sailed into the bay at Calvi not long after five o'clock. The still water was a shock to all of them; their bodies had become forcefully conditioned to the pitch of the sea. They brought the three sails down and Charlie switched on the motor and headed into the quai. When they were close enough, he cut the motor back and glided into position to drop anchor.

"Let her go," he called to Peter and Jack in the bow. The

harsh rattle of chain rang out over the peaceful water. The stern swung around. Charlie put the motor into reverse. His maneuvering with the unfamiliar motor was less skillful than his sailing; he engaged in a good deal of backing and filling, cursing to himself.

Jack had come back and was standing beside him. "I'd better take over," he said.

Charlie cursed him silently. "I have to get the hang of it, Jack," he said reasonably. Loungers had gathered on the quai. When they were within reach, Martha and Peter threw stern lines to them. Jack was once more in the bow playing out chain. As they were pulled in, Charlie cut the motor. In the stunning silence, his body was caught by a deep, shuddering breath. He felt safe. He hadn't known it was possible to feel so safe. He looked across the still water at the wide sweep of the bay and the towering peak that rose above it, still bearing traces of snow on its summit, and felt totally enclosed and protected. He could understand Martha's reluctance to leave harbor. Yet there was the big sense of achievement, too. He had done something important. He wanted more of the same. He couldn't imagine nature having anything worse in store for them; he wanted to explore and extend the satisfactions of his command. He stirred himself and looked astern. Peter had leaped ashore and was securing their lines. Charlie unlashed the gangplank and hoisted it aft and eased it over to Peter and coupled it to the deck. When Peter came aboard, they all went to work furling the heavy sails. It was hard work and they were sweating when it was done.

"I could use a drink," Jack said.

Naturally, Charlie thought. "I could, too," he agreed. "Then we'll run along."

"You're going ashore?"

"Of course. There must be a hotel here."

"There's still a lot of work to do. Everything's a mess below."

"Now, come on, Jack. You haven't had what could be called a strenuous time of it so far. You can surely stow things below."

"As you wish." Martha produced glasses and ice and whisky and brought up the shaker of martinis. When they'd had one drink, Peter and Charlie went below to gather up their toilet kit and fresh shirts and trousers.

"Listen," Peter said when they were out of earshot. "Maybe

we should stay with them tonight. It's our first stop. They seemed to expect it."

"Hell, no. It was clearly understood that we'd go ashore when we were in port. I've had enough of them for the moment. I want to be with you."

Peter couldn't argue with that. They climbed back up on deck and said goodnight to the Kingsleys and left them, Martha looking lonely, Jack resentful.

There wasn't much to the town. There was a row of low buildings across the street from the quai. There was long, white building across the bay that looked like a grand hotel, but they didn't want to go that far. They found a restaurant with rooms above it and went up to wash and change for dinner.

"God. A bed," Charlie exclaimed when they were alone in the room. "I feel as if I hadn't seen one for days. Don't let me go anywhere near it or I'll never get up."

"Is something going on in your head? I mean, I can hardly walk straight."

"Sure. I'm really reeling. The motion of the ocean."

"It's normal? I thought there was something wrong with me."

Charlie smiled and went to him and took him in his arms and held him close. "There's nothing wrong with you, baby. God, you were good last night." He kissed him on the ear.

"I wish I'd been able to do something."

"You did plenty. I don't think I could've got through it if you hadn't been there."

"Don't worry. I'll always be there."

Charlie released him with a hug and stood with his arm around his shoulder as he opened the toilet case and sorted out their things. It had never occurred to Peter that he would welcome a shift in the whole pattern and feeling of their being together but this was turning into one of the memorable days of his life. He wanted to tell Charlie what it had felt like being held in front of Martha but he didn't want to spoil it by making him self-conscious and decided to wait and see if Charlie would give him a clue as to why he had done it. It had been sexless, in a way, except when he had pulled him in close between his legs. The thrill of it was still with him as he warned himself to let Charlie take all the initiative in this new public display of physical intimacy. Until he understood it, there was a danger of making the wrong move.

Feminine passivity was not alien to him. As he had insisted to himself and Charlie, Jeannot had been only an aberration. He was quite aware of the broad feminine streak in his nature and was inclined to take an amused and tolerant view of it. He didn't see how it could hurt anybody but himself. There was scope enough for his masculinity in the management of their lives; he had been the breadwinner, he was making a successful career in a fiercely competitive field, he knew how money worked and enjoyed using his knowledge, he responded to the hunt. He had been tough with Charlie about his work, insisting that he devote all his time to it, had constituted himself the guardian of his talent and had had the satisfaction of watching him slowly win substantial recognition.

On the other hand, he had felt no male compunctions about dropping the de Belleville deal just when he was on the point of pulling it off. His man had called and he had followed, even though there were things in the collection—some superb bronzes, some startling antique glass—that he was particularly well-placed to dispose of for a profit he had calculated might go as high as fifty thousand dollars. He didn't think the deal would fall through, even in his absence, but he couldn't imagine having any deep regrets if it did. He had always had a cheerful and sanguine view of life, despite not having had a particularly happy childhood (a bigoted but ineffectual father, a series of dreary military schools). Everything that happened after was what counted. Charlie had seduced him and revealed to him the true nature of his sexual appetites just at an age when they might have emerged under less happy circumstances to eternally torment him. His optimism had been put to a test only twice; once when Charlie had rejected him in favor of marriage, but that had been for only a few months and had given him an opportunity for a doubtless necessary and beneficial sexual education; the second time was so bound up with the obliterated memory that it too had been obliterated, though while it was going on he had felt that it would destroy him. Charlie had saved him; his man, his husband, Charlie who seemed to be, inexplicably, hard on the heels of the worst crisis they had ever been through, on the verge of publicly acknowledging what Peter had always regarded as a truer marriage than that of most people he knew.

Charlie's arm was still around him as he reluctantly finished laying out their toilet articles. It gave him another hug and then they broke apart to wash and dress. When they were ready to go down to dinner, Charlie touched his hair caressingly and gave him a tender kiss on the mouth. "You're looking absolutely sublime," he said.

Peter flashed him a dazzling smile. "You sure know how to turn a fella's head."

Charlie's arm was around his shoulder once again as they went down to dinner. After they had eaten, and drunk two bottles of wine, Charlie slumped over the table in mock collapse. He pulled himself up with a smile.

"I'm really feeling the let-down. It's probably not even nine yet, but I think I'm going to have to go to bed."

"You've had only three hours sleep since yesterday morning. That's—my God, it's over thirty-six hours. I'm dead too."

"OK, mate. Let's see if I can get out of this chair." The brooding look that had become familiar to Peter in the last week returned unexpectedly and dismayingly to Charlie's eyes. "That's what you are, isn't it? My mate?" he asked with curious intensity.

"I'll say."

"I'm counting on you. Especially in the next few days. I'll never trust Jack after last night. I want you to learn how to handle the boat as well as I do. The hell with watches. I want us to stay on the wheel as much as possible. We can sleep together in the cockpit and spell each other. We'll give the passengers a hell of a cruise."

Peter didn't understand why he laid such stress on it, but he felt a thrill of response. They were in league together. A whole new dimension in their relationship was opening up before them.

They climbed up to their room and threw off their clothes and fell into bed. Peter rolled over on his side and Charlie put his arms around him and pulled him close until they fitted together like pieces in a puzzle, Peter's back to Charlie's front. Peter wriggled his hips back until Charlie's powerful, inert sex was pressed against his buttocks.

"I'm asleep already, my baby," Charlie murmured.

"My Charlie. Darling. Dearest. Me too.' They slept, too exhausted to profit further from their night of privacy.

At a conference the next morning, during which Jack seemed to have recovered his aplomb, it was agreed to spend a quiet day while some necessary repairs were made below to locker fastenings and other odds and ends and leave again in the evening. Bonifacio was at the southern tip of the island if they needed a port of refuge; otherwise, they would sail between Corsica and Sardinia and take an easterly course for Capri. When these details were settled, Charlie stood at the rail and studied the sky. Martha moved in close beside him.

"What about those clouds?" she asked. "What do they mean?"

There was a bank of fluffy, white clouds low in the west. Charlie chuckled. "I haven't the slightest idea. They're very pretty."

"Aren't you really ever frightened? Not even last night? I mean, the night before?"

"Good God, I was scared out of my wits. But there's always the law of averages. That won't happen to us again."

Their hands brushed against each other at their sides. She held his and entwined his fingers in hers. "I really wouldn't go on if it weren't for you and Peter. I don't understand it, but you make the boat feel much safer than it ever has before."

"I'm glad." He gave her hand a squeeze and drew his away. "You'll see. It's going to be great."

"Maybe you can make it seem that way. You don't know how much I hate it. It's Jack's toy. Now that we've committed so much money to it and rearranged our lives around it, I don't see how I'm ever going to get away."

"It sounds like a problem."

"It is, but probably not a very interesting one. It may explain why it means so much to me to be with two people who seem to enjoy everything they do together. It must be wonderful to have a friendship like that."

"It is." Was she trying to pump him? He didn't think so. She spoke straightforwardly and seemed to choose her words to say exactly what she meant. "I certainly want you to enjoy it all with us," Charlie said. "I can't do anything about the weather but I promise not to go out if it looks at all tricky. How's that? Just let me know if there's anything we can do to make it better for you."

She looked at him with clear blue eyes in which the light of adoration still shone. "You're a very nice man." She put her hand briefly on his arm and moved away.

Even Charlie felt little tremors of apprehension around his heart as they made preparations to weigh anchor that evening. It was too beautiful; he would never again trust the Mediterranean's smiling face.

The night turned out as perfect as he had hoped the first one would be, with just enough favorable breeze to keep them moving. Jack went to bed soon after they were out of port, having consumed his usual quantity of pre-dinner martinis. Martha sat on in the cockpit for a while, alone on a bench, while Peter and Charlie shared the seat behind the wheel. Charlie's big, square hand was planted firmly on Peter's body. As much as he loved it, Peter continued to wonder about it. He was wearing a black sweater and the hand was very visible even in the dark. It didn't do anything much, just moved about on his chest and sometimes massaged his neck and shoulders. Peter was in charge of the wheel and Charlie pointed out falling stars to Martha with his free hand. When she left them, he put both hands on Peter, moved him forward slightly, got his leg up on the cushion again and pulled him close. Peter briefly dropped his head back against Charlie's.

"Oh, God, hold me like this always," he murmured. He took a hand off the wheel and felt behind him for the bulky bunched-up sex. "Am I allowed to unfasten your pants?"

"Better not, baby. It's too risky. Besides, you're supposed to be concentrating on sailing."

"Teacher's being a big help."

Charlie ran his hands over Peter's thighs and covered his crotch with them and pulled him closer. "That makes two of us. Let's just stay like this. It feels good."

"Good? It's my idea of heaven. The sky and the sound we make moving through the water and the breeze and you holding me. Like you said, peaceful and thrilling. I'm so damn happy I want to cry."

As the night wore on, Charlie insisted that Peter should get some sleep and he did so, stretched out on the bench beside Charlie, a hand flung out on his knee. When Jack appeared at four, reporting for his watch for the first time, Charlie passed on his navigational information and let him take over. He roused Peter and they both went below. He didn't intend to stay away long. He was back on deck soon after dawn urging Jack not to waste time by putting in at Bonifacio. Because the weather was fine there was no argument, and they passed through the Strait and headed for Capri more than two hundred miles away.

Normal time was suspended. Their time was governed by the demands of the boat and the rhythm of their alternating watches. They ate ravenously when they were hungry and slept at odd hours when they had no duties to perform. The weather remained fine, so that Martha was smiling and apparently content. The winds were variable and never strong, so they didn't make very good time. When the wind was against them, Jack plotted a course, proceeding from the compass reading they were able to follow close-hauled and giving them mileage indications when they were to come about. With no preconditioning, Peter had no difficulty following Jack's method. Charlie, trained to racing tactics based on tacking whenever it was possible to take advantage of the slightest shift in wind, found it confining and couldn't resist going about, with all its attendant labor of retrimming sheets, when he felt that enough could be gained to justify it. He kept scrupulous hour and mileage notations so that Jack couldn't complain. The latter prided himself on being able to point out their exact position on his beautifully kept charts. Peter's long runs and Charlie's zig-zags showed up like something from a Madison Avenue product-performance report.

Martha and Charlie and Peter spent the days in the briefest swimming costumes, turning a deep, ruddy mahogany. Martha's body was lovely, all curves and smooth, glowing skin. During particularly calm hours, Charlie took to sketching her as she lay about the deck. The bits of bikini spoiled the line; he wished he could do her without them. Her little-girl adoration had perhaps acquired an element of desire; he didn't know for sure. He frequently caught her eyes on his body. She would look up and meet his eyes unwaveringly, a little smile on her lips. It was so open and relaxed that it didn't bother him. After all, he looked at her body a lot too, without wanting it. Whatever the nature of her feeling for him, it made her an admirable companion. She laughed at his jokes. She took his side in any discussion. She didn't make the mistake of trying to monopolize his attention. She included Peter in their conversations. Only Jack led a life slightly apart. He spent a lot of time with his charts. He slept more than the rest of them. Once, he came up on deck in his frayed shorts and did something very professional-looking with his sextant. Charlie supposed it was good that at least one of them cared where they were.

When Charlie turned over the wheel to Jack early on the third morning, he had begun to spot lights ahead of them, whether land or boats he couldn't tell. He came back on deck a few hours later and found that they were sailing among islands. Jack was looking pleased with himself.

"Right where you expected them to be?" Charlie asked amiably.

"Yep. That one up there is Ischia. Capri's ahead of us somewhere. We should be in by midafternoon."

Jack's prediction proved reasonably accurate. They were tied up and shipshape in the crowded port of Capri by drink time. The fringes of the main town were visible far above them. Peter and Charlie had packed a bag with their finest summer finery and were eager to be off. Neither of them had been to Capri before. They had a duty drink with the Kingsleys and rose to go.

"You're going up to town?" Jack asked.

"Of course."

"It must be nice to be a tourist."

"Aren't you going?"

"Somebody has to watch the boat. I understand the people here will strip you down to your spars if you give them the chance."

"Are you suggesting we should take turns or something?" Charlie demanded.

"No, no, no. We agreed you'd go ashore in the evening. Strictly speaking, we agreed you'd stay in hotels at night. It might be reasonable for us to go up and have dinner and let you go up later."

Charlie wondered if he had a point, but Martha relieved him of a decision.

"No, darling," she said soothingly to Jack. "Don't let's bother this evening. As I remember, it's terribly crowded and touristy. We might have a look around in the morning if the boys come back early enough." She looked at Charlie and he gave her a gratified smile.

"Fine. We'll be back by nine if that's all right."

They left it at that and Peter and Charlie found a taxi and went looping up the steep road to town.

"I was worried there for a minute," Peter said. "I guess he could have made a case."

"Balls. There's harbor police on duty. He was just trying it on to see how we would take it. Bully for good old Martha."

"It helps for her to be in love with you."

"You think she is?"

"Think it? She's obviously mad for you. It takes one to know one. I know exactly how she feels."

Charlie put his hand on his knee and they laughed together. They were deposited at a big square on the edge of a cliff. A street led off it into what was apparently the town. They were barely out of the taxi before a horde of small boys in uniforms bearing the names of hotels swarmed over them, shouting and snatching at their suitcase. They laughed as they tried to ward off the attack.

"Do we have any idea what hotel we want to go to?" Charlie asked.

"Let them fight it out. The winner gets us."

The driver of the taxi was gesticulating at them and shouting something. Charlie gave him a dollar. The driver did a conjuring trick with it and continued to shout and gesticulate. As if he had been waiting for them, Guy de Sainval appeared before them. With a few authoritative words, he stilled the din. He looked at them and smiled.

"The fates favor us. I've never seen anything so beautiful in my life. What have you done to yourselves?" He turned to Peter. "I obviously haven't been paying enough attention to you. You're superb."

They pumped his hand and greeted him as if he were a long-lost friend. They both felt that they hadn't seen him for weeks. "What are you doing here?" they asked in unison.

"Harry didn't come back. My friends thought I should console myself. I came yesterday and may stay the rest of my life. Wait till you see the beauties. One understands poor old Tiberius so well. But you two? Speaking of gods, why aren't you in Greece?"

"We're getting there. We've only been out less than a week."

"Tell us what hotel we should stay at," Peter said.

138

Guy looked at him for a moment, cocking his aristocratic bird's face from side to side. "Divine words issuing from a divine head. Why not stay at mine? At least, I'll have you under the same roof. That's a start." He surveyed the jostling boys and snapped his fingers at one who apparently had the right label. He sprang forward and seized the bag from Charlie and raced off with it as if he were afraid the others might wrestle it from him. Guy clapped his hands together and pointed them at Charlie. "How extraordinary. I was talking about you last night with an old friend of yours. Heaven knows how your name came up. I won't say more, except that you've apparently always had impeccable taste."

"What are you talking about?"

"One of the beauties, my dear. Perhaps *the* beauty. I'm speaking of resident fauna, of course. I don't include exotica like you. Apollo rising from the sea. It's distracting to be confronted by two of you, especially since Apollo never went near the sea, as far as I know. That was that other one. That dreadful Poseidon."

Guy was leading them into the town. They crossed a square so enclosed that it felt like a room. It was crowded with chairs and tables, occupied for the most part by young men wearing bizarre and colorful clothing—shirts of net, golden sandals, curiously slashed and laced trousers. Here and there were undigested lumps of Germanic-looking tourists in sensible shoes and hats and summer suits. Heads turned as they passed, conversations in a dozen languages were interrupted.

"I think I'm going to be an even greater success than I am already," Guy said. "People will be battering at my door to be introduced to you."

They passed through twisting streets lined with shops overflowing with leather goods and fruit and tourist trinkets. They came to an unassuming glass door flush with the street and entered. An opulent hotel opened out before them, backed by a garden. They were welcomed by the management with a great repetition of "*Oui, monsieur le comte*" and "*Non, monsieur le comte*" for Guy.

"*Eh bien*," Guy said when they had registered. "We're going to a party at Dino's in a little while. Dino di Lorenzo. Do you know him?"

"I know who he is," Peter said.

"Ah, yes, of course. He has one or two good pictures. Very rich. He might be useful for you to know. His food and drink are exquisite. You'll be wooed by the most beautiful boys this side of the heavenly choir. They're frightfully expensive but that's of no interest to you two."

"Do you know if an American called Peggy Guggenheim's here?" Peter asked. "I think she usually spends some time here."

"I've heard of her. She has a friend here—you know, the one that takes care of Norman Douglas—he should know. He'll probably be at Dino's tonight. Will eight-thirty suit you? We'll meet down here. And don't think for a minute that the drinks that will soon be brought you are gifts of the management. It's from me." He turned to Charlie. "Be prepared for a surprise. Your friend will be there, of course."

They thanked him and were escorted to their room by a pretty little bellboy. Charlie thought briefly of Milly. Once alone, Peter gave Charlie a kiss and laughed and shook his head.

"Where are we? It's incredible. We must be dreaming. We did sail in here on a yacht, didn't we? And now look at us. Golly, you were so right. There's something about sailing and the sun and sea, and wearing old clothes or nothing, and then suddenly finding yourself in a place like this, that really hits you. It's nothing like traveling in the usual way."

Their windows gave onto a vista of villas and terraced gardens falling away to the sea. The sun was setting into it. Charlie looked and found nothing new in it and turned away. "I knew you'd love it, baby," he said.

There was a knock on the door and a table was rolled in bearing a bottle of whisky, a bottle of champagne in an ice bucket and a bowl of caviar on ice.

"You wish me to open both, *signori?*" the waiter asked. They assented and he did so and left. Peter led Charlie to the table.

"Really, Guy is too much," he said. "He even remembered that I like champagne at parties. And caviar! What should we do to thank him?"

"Sell him another of my pictures." They laughed together as they poured themselves drinks.

"Are you sure you want to go to this party?" Peter asked. The thought of a horde of beautiful boys made him a trifle nervous. If they were singled out for attentions, it would be difficult to feign total indifference. Charlie had admitted to susceptibilities Peter had never suspected existed. He didn't know how he would take it now if he caught him showing even a casual interest in a beauty. All in all, he would prefer for both of them to avoid temptation rather than resist it. "You know what it'll be like. You've always hated queer parties."

"That's because everybody's usually so hideously unattractive." Charlie smiled at him across his glass. "I'm perfectly happy looking at beauties. Since we're queer, it's about time we got some fun out of it."

Peter laughed with astonishment. Charlie had never so cheerfully and unabashedly put himself on an equal footing with their kind. Was there an element of danger in the openness he had always longed for? "I wonder who this mysterious friend of yours is. Guy made a point of him being *your* friend. It must be a long time since you've seen him."

"I can't imagine. Somebody from Princeton? I don't remember anybody at Princeton who would qualify as *the* beauty of Capri." There were so few possibilities that Charlie had already made a guess at who it must be. He saw no reason to tell Peter until he knew.

"Probably one of those dozens of lovers you had while I was away," Peter said boldly, testing Charlie's new permissiveness. Charlie's lovers were so firmly in the past that they should be able to joke about them but they had never had anything of the sort to joke about before. He had an apprehensive moment waiting to see how Charlie would respond.

"Could be," he said casually. "There were some beauties among them."

"I'll bet there were." Peter grinned, feeling a new total ease in their intimacy. All Charlie's guards were falling at last. If there was danger in it, it was a danger accompanied by the promise of rich rewards. "Thank God they were all so long ago. They must be positively decrepit by now." He uttered a peal of exuberant laughter as he threw off restraint and refilled his glass.

He made substantial inroads on the bottle of champagne while they prepared to meet Guy. His hilarity grew and was contagious. They were laughing so much that they had difficulty getting dressed. They both wore rough silk suits with bright, open-necked silk shirts. There were golden streaks in Charlie's hair that almost matched Peter's white-gold head. Their skin took the sun in the same way so that they were equally dark. The similarity between them had become startling.

"I'm not going to go on telling you how beautiful you are," Guy said when they appeared in the lobby. "It accomplishes nothing for me and simply makes you more pleased with each other."

Charlie put his arm around Peter's shoulder as they thanked him again for his gift.

"I thought you were sending us drinks," Charlie said. "I didn't know it was going to be the whole bar. Peter's drunk. It'll be your fault if he disgraces us."

"I'm going to. I'm going to elope with Guy. You never buy me caviar."

"Come then. We'll go to the party first and elope after."

They set off away from the town down a stepped walk that wandered through gardens and villas. Palms and cypresses were silhouetted against the dark luminous sky. In time, they came to an ornate gate and turned into a vine-clad colonnade. Party sounds accompanied them and grew louder as they approached. They came out onto a wide, brightly lighted terrace with columns framing the sea. The company was mostly male, with a few exquisitely turned-out women scattered about, like part of the decor. Drinks were offered them as they were introduced to their host. Guy was immediately surrounded by friends. He performed introductions, interests shifted, Peter was soon the laughing center of a group of his own. As it should be, Charlie thought. He was glad for him to be on his own. He had established his claim to him on the boat; Peter wouldn't forget his insistent hands.

Charlie remained beside Guy. He found the standard of beauty extraordinarily high but all the young men looked as if they'd been cut out of a pattern—dark, liquid-eyed, ruby-lipped, pearly-toothed. Their speech followed a pattern, too, with all the same words given an exaggerated emphasis so that he felt hemmed in by imminent hysteria.

"Come. We must find him, your friend," Guy said, leading Charlie away. They crossed the terrace, constantly intercepted by dark ruby-lipped youths whom Guy introduced. Charlie wondered how he could tell them apart. Their liquid eyes lingered in Charlie's when he smiled at them politely. They entered a vast living room, whose French doors gave onto the terrace. Charlie was introduced to a stylish woman. They moved on. Charlie saw him.

His back was turned, but he recognized him instantly. He had guessed right. He touched Guy's arm and nodded in his direction. Guy peered and then smiled in affirmation.

Charlie approached him from behind. When he was close he stopped and said his name. Tony whirled and stared. He was little changed, but his features were fined-down and leanly sculptured. The cheekbones were more prominent, the hollows beneath them deeper, the long line of his jaw was stripped of all excess flesh. The mouth was still a provocation. His hair swept back from his brow very much as Charlie had arranged it long ago. His body looked refined and elegant in his smartly tailored white jacket.

"I don't believe it," Tony murmured.

They smiled as they moved toward each other. Tony lifted his head and his lips parted expectantly. Holding his drink carefully to avoid spilling it, Charlie put his other arm around him and their mouths met. They exchanged a long, consuming kiss. Charlie became aware of a hush falling around them. Let the fancy faggots stare. Was Peter watching? He would explain it later. There were a number of things he was just beginning to understand that he would explain to Peter. Their lips clung to each other another moment and then they drew apart.

"That mouth," Charlie murmured, looking at it.

"Did I ever tell you about yours?" Tony asked. "It's really you, all right. The one and only. I was talking about you just last night."

"I know. Guy told me, but wouldn't tell who it was. I guessed it was you."

"Really? How?"

"He said it was *the* beauty of Capri. I couldn't think of anybody else who would fill the bill." They laughed and Charlie drank his drink, which he had somehow managed not to spill. Tony didn't have a glass. Charlie was amazed at the transformation of his voice and accent. The roughness was gone. There was a trill in his *r* and some of his vowels had acquired a foreign shape. If he were meeting him for the first time, he wouldn't have been sure he was an American.

"I was crushed when I heard you'd left St. Tropez," Tony said.

"We're going to be there later in the season. To have missed you by so little would've been more than I could bear."

"We?"

Tony smiled slyly. "Haven't you heard?" He laughed and pronounced the name of the king of a minor European country whose throne had been a wartime casualty and who was frequently mentioned in international gossip columns.

"You're with *him*?" Charlie asked, astounded.

"I'm a queen. Who would've suspected it? How long are you going to be here? I was just leaving. His Majesty is having some trouble with his arthritis."

"We're here on a yacht. We leave sometime tomorrow."

"Oh, no," Tony protested. "I've got to talk to you. You're still with Peter, aren't you? That's marvelous. It must be some sort of a record. I suppose you couldn't come with me now for a little while?"

"Why not?"

"Would you? That would be heaven. It's very near. I have to go see that His Majesty is fed properly. We could have a gossip and come back."

"Let's go," Charlie said promptly. He looked for Peter as they made their way through the crowd to the terrace. He didn't see him. It didn't matter. It was time for them to stop keeping such close tabs on each other. He encountered Guy.

"Tell Peter when you see him that I've gone with Tony. I'll be back later."

"Fidelity. Fidelity. I never knew the word had so many meanings."

Charlie laughed. "Just say that I'm with an old friend—not that I'm in bed with an old friend." He caught up with Tony. They strolled back up toward the town and in a few minutes turned in at a gate. A policeman was standing in front of it and gave them a spirited salute as they passed.

"I'm stunned," Charlie said. "Little old Tony. You've really made it."

"Thanks to you. You gave me ideas. I've been over here since the war ended. It's hustlers' paradise. Well, that's over. Unless a *reigning* monarch proposes, I think I've gone as far as I want to go."

They walked up through a garden to broad steps that mounted

144

to a lavishly furnished terrace. At the top, Tony stopped. "We might as well stay out here. I'll go check in with His Majesty. I promised to tell him who was there. I'll send somebody out with drinks." Tony went on into an ornate living room. Charlie could see servants moving about inside. He had the curious sense of a "presence" locked away somewhere within. Tony stopped and spoke to a liveried manservant and gestured toward the terrace. The man came out and asked Charlie what he wanted to drink.

Tony was soon back. He stood in the doorway and looked at Charlie for a long moment. "Charlie. Remember what just saying your name used to do to me? You're more magnificent than ever." He resumed his gutter voice, "I'll let ya fuck me, if that's watcha want." They both laughed. Tony's face sobered. "Some joke. If you knew how often I've thought of it and wished it could've happened just once more. I know I shouldn't rush things, but is there any chance? Would you be even faintly interested?"

"What would His Majesty say?"

"Oh, I'm allowed a private life. We're terribly civilized about that sort of thing over here."

"Well then, much as I hate to, I'll have to say no. I'll bet you don't hear that word often."

"I guess that kiss gave me ideas. I thought I felt things happening."

"You did. God knows what might've happened if we hadn't been in public. But hell, kiddo, all that ended for me the day we said goodbye."

"Peter? Still, you're here. Won't he think things?"

"Maybe. I admit I'm setting a bit of a precedent."

"Tongues will wag. I can assure you of that. I'm not known here for my conversation." Tony laughed and went to the table where the servant had left drinks and poured himself a glass of soda. "His Majesty will be furious. A rebuff to the king's consort. I'll have to spread the word that we spent an hour of bliss. Oh, Charlie. I've thought of you so much always. I've wanted you to know how your little hustler was making out. I can't believe it's really you. How about having a quiet dinner here? That party's going to go on all night. I should stick around here long enough to tuck His Majesty in."

Charlie accepted and Tony summoned a servant and gave orders.

"Are you off the booze?" Charlie inquired.

"I'm hitting thirty, sweetheart. Sacrifices must be made if I'm to go on living the good life. We mustn't have any little sags or creases. His Majesty can't throw me out. I've seen to that. But I must think of my idle hours. I don't want to get used to hearing that word you just said."

They dined in a small library off the living room, Tony having explained that the dining room was too big for intimacy. He told Charlie the story of his life in Europe, which was largely the story of being handed from one rich man to another on an ascending social scale, culminating in a king. They returned to the terrace for brandy. On the way, Tony showed him an array of silver-framed, signed photographs of familiar crowned heads. "It's amazing to think that I'm related to them all by bed. Not bad, for a hustler."

The memory of the tough, little streetboy was difficult to keep in focus in the face of this smooth, stylish beauty, but Charlie was glad he had come. He had always made much of his distaste for the homosexual world but it had brought him Tony, their lives had touched, he had contributed largely to what Tony was now. It wasn't a bad creation. He would be the butt of ugly jokes by right-thinking people, but if he were a woman, he would be deemed a success. He was a whore, but a whore in the accepted tradition of royal mistresses. Charlie couldn't see that his being a man should make all that much difference. What was happening to his precious standards? In any case, none of this would have been of any interest to Peter. It was right and reasonable that they should expand their lives beyond the limits of their preoccupation with each other. He rose and took a turn around the terrace. "Are you planning to go back to the party?"

"Oh, I suppose I'll pop in and see what new combinations have developed during the evening. His Majesty will be interested to hear. Besides, I want to meet Peter. Guy says he's adorable and looks like you, except that he's beautiful and you're handsome. That's the way he put it. I guess that's why we girls go for you."

"I haven't been getting much sleep lately. I think I'll skip it. Get somebody to introduce you to Peter. Tell him I've gone back to the hotel." Let Peter have the whole evening on his own. It would be good for him, no matter what happened.

Tony rose and stood in front of him. Charlie put his hands on his shoulders and studied the exquisite mouth. Tony pulled him to him and lifted his head and their mouths met again and opened to each other. Tony's body swayed against him and his hands roamed over his back. He pulled his mouth away breathlessly and dropped his forehead onto Charlie's shoulder. Charlie ran his hand through his hair and held his head.

"Sure," he said gently. "It could happen again, but it's not going to. You don't really mind, do you?"

Tony shook his head and lifted it and smiled up at him. "I'll go back to the party and find a trick and the beast in me will be appeased. If I'm very lucky, it'll be a little bit like you. Every now and then, it has been."

Charlie looked at his mouth and ran a forefinger over it. "One of nature's masterpieces. I hope I see it again. We'll keep in touch, won't we? We can send Christmas cards, at least. I'm really glad for you."

They gave each other a little hug and smiled and broke apart. Charlie started down the steps.

"Charlie." Charlie stopped and turned back. "I've always wanted to tell you. I really was in love with you for a little while. The only time I let that happen to me. But I had it. I'll never forget it."

"Take care, kiddo." He went on down through the garden and out the gate. The policeman saluted as he left. He found the hotel without much difficulty and was surprised to learn that their room key had already been taken. He went up and found the light on and Peter lying in one of the beds with his back turned.

"You're here already." Charlie spoke quietly in case he was asleep.

Peter rolled over and lay on his back. There was a brief silence. "Why did you do it?" he asked in an expressionless voice.

"Do what?"

"Kiss that boy. The rest of it."

"You saw that? Because I wanted to."

"He *is* a beauty. What else did you want to do?"

"I wanted to talk to him." Charlie started to undress slowly. "I was planning to go back and join you, but I changed my mind and came home. He was going to tell you."

"That's all?"

"All? I can talk to a guy, even a beauty, without going to bed with him, if that's what you mean. Maybe you're right. Maybe I'm not very curious about boys' bodies, although it's hardly pertinent in this case. I satisfied my curiosity about him a good many years ago. He was ready to relive the past. I refused."

"Oh, Christ. You kiss a guy passionately in front of a whole crowd of people and then go running off with him and I'm supposed to believe you just wanted a little chat."

"Oh? Does it matter what we believe about the things we tell each other? We know inside what we've done."

"I see. The Chinese water torture." Peter's voice grew more positive as he went on. "I cheated on you once. I never will again, no matter what happens. You know it matters for us to believe each other."

"I've thought a lot of things matter that maybe don't. I'm finding out."

"Is it part of finding out to do whatever we want to do, regardless of the other's feelings?"

"What's wrong with that? Isn't that pretty much how it's always been? Have you been suppressing all sorts of hidden desires out of consideration for me? Aside from the ones you've told me about, of course."

Peter's intimations of danger had materialized with shocking rapidity. It wasn't so much what Charlie was saying as his brutally detached manner that hurt, especially after the last few days when surely they had been drawing closer, their beings more intimately intertwined than ever before. Was he able to hold him in front of Martha simply because he felt removed, detached, no longer deeply stirred by him? He was frightened and lost. "Everything's been so wonderful between us for the last week," he asserted to reassure himself. "Why do you want to ruin it?"

Charlie had taken off his clothes. Peter's eyes ran over the athlete's body as he went to the other bed and stretched out on it. "I'm tired of the kid-glove treatment. You're mine. You gave yourself to somebody else. I won't let that happen again."

"Is that why you hold me all the time?"

"Perhaps. Mostly, I hold you because I like to. It's finally occurred to me that there's no reason on earth why I shouldn't. I'm trying to find out if we can make everything work right for both of us. Come here."

"Why?"

"Because I want you to."

"I'm not sure I want to."

"Oh, come on. Of course you do. It doesn't matter. I'll come there." He rose and crossed to Peter's bed and dropped down beside him and took him in his arms and kissed him. Peter's mouth opened to his and their tongues met and played together.

Charlie pulled his head back and looked him in the eye. "I just kissed Tony like that. Some of his saliva is probably still in my mouth. Now it's in yours. Does that disgust you?"

Peter's eyes widened with shock. "Yes," he breathed.

"Didn't you ever kiss Jean-Claude and let me kiss you afterward? People are great germ carriers. Didn't you do things with your body and then offer it to me? Perhaps you let me kiss your cock after you'd been fucking him. Did you?"

Peter tore himself from him and clawed his way upright to the edge of the bed and covered his face with his hands. His shoulders heaved and a strangled cry broke from him. "Go on," he gasped. "Make me feel so foul and dirty that I'll never be able to let you touch me again."

Charlie swung himself up beside him and grasped his wrists and pulled his hands away. "No. I still want you. That's the thing that sometimes comes close to disgusting me. I thought I wouldn't, remember, but there's no question about that now. Let's face ourselves, for Christ's sake. You started something that isn't going to end that quickly. Maybe it'll never end. I thought of leaving you, not for long and mostly when I was angry, but seriously for a little while. I don't want to leave you, goddamn it, but I don't want to stay with you if it means going on hiding everything we really are. I kissed Tony because I wanted to, but Christ, the hypocrisy—all those faggots eyeing each other and waiting to pounce. Well, I pounced. I didn't happen to want him, but that's aside from the point. Maybe it'll happen with somebody I do want. What'll I do then? I don't know, but I'm prepared to find out, just the way you did. I'm so goddamn sick of pretending. I'm sure you are too. I know you've always wished I wasn't so fucking buttoned up. Well, here I am, unbuttoned. You can damn well take the consequences."

Peter sat slumped over, his eyes closed, waiting to recover from this sudden expulsion from his fool's paradise. He had thought the wounds had healed, but Charlie had bared them, still raw and bleeding. He straightened and opened his eyes and looked levelly at Charlie. "I'm ready to face anything if we do it together."

"We can't always do things together. That's another thing. We've been suffocating. We've been living our great dream of love and all the time it turns out you've been fighting temptations. I don't know what you should've done because there's a lot I'm just beginning to understand, but there's something wrong somewhere. We've survived so far because we've been young and goddamn beautiful and nuts about each other. Yes. Narcissus. But we're not going to be young much longer and things are going to change. I don't know how, but I'm certainly going to think about it. *And* do something about it, if it seems necessary. So I hold you in front of Martha and go off with Tony tonight. Straws in the wind. In case you've noticed I don't hold you in front of Jack; it's not because I'm shy. It's just because he'd probably think he ought to make a crack, and I'd beat the shit out of him and that would be the end of the trip. I do know one thing, now that Jean-Claude is over the dam. I feel so much for you, it goes so deep, it's so complete and a part of me that if we never went to bed together again, it wouldn't change. It's good to know, but it's a problem because I don't want it to block out everything else. We need air, baby. So. Do you want me to kiss you the way I really feel it?"

Tears had welled up in Peter's eyes. He took a long difficult breath and smiled. "God, you certainly put a guy through the wringer. I don't know whether I'm in or out from one minute to the next. Yes, I always want you to kiss me. The rest can wait till later."

"Yes, later." Charlie put his hand on Peter's hair and drew him to him. Their mouths met and their teeth clashed in their hunger for each other. Their hands moved slowly over each other until they both were having trouble breathing. They drew apart.

"Let me—" Peter whispered.

"Yes. Go on. Quickly." Charlie took a deep breath, his eyes melting into Peter's. "I want to make love to you. God, what an expression. As if you manufactured it. I want to drown myself in you."

The next day, *Cassandra* crossed the bay to Naples to take

on water and fresh food. Charlie and Peter found that it was like a homecoming being back on board. Charlie felt a sort of family feeling even for Jack. Martha wanted to know all about their evening ashore. They told her about the meeting with Guy and about the party, making it sound quite proper and suburban. They lay overnight in an ugly corner of the noisy port and left the next day for the Straits of Messina. It was another long run of over two hundred miles. Charlie welcomed the deliverance from land. He was in charge once more, with nothing more complicated to decide than whether to let out or take in the sails.

They slipped back into the familiar rhythm of their days. The winds remained light; Greece still seemed a long way off. Charlie and Peter had brought copies of Homer and Herodotus and Thucydides and they began to find time to read. To Charlie, the *Iliad* was particularly adapted to the rhythm of the sea. The voyage acquired a new poetic depth that gripped him when he was awake and beat in his ears when he slept.

They were in well-traveled shipping lanes now so they had to learn a new skill of judging other boats' courses and staying well clear of them. It wasn't always easy, especially at night. With no landmarks to aid, speed was often tricky to estimate. One day, when Jack was blithely steering on a collision course with a large steamer, Charlie had almost to wrest the wheel away from him before he could convince him of his error.

With Homer drumming in his ears and the responsibility for the boat resting ever more firmly in his hands, he found himself rarely sleeping more than a couple of hours at a time. The dawn hours just after his watch were definitely devoted to sleep, but he sometimes interrupted them, too, with a turn on deck. He went up early one morning only an hour or so after Jack had relieved him. The first thing he saw in the half-light before sunrise was the hulk of a freighter passing startlingly close across their stern. "Jesus," he muttered and looked back at the wheel for Jack. He wasn't there.

He sprang out from the hatch and saw him. He had made himself a nest of clothing and blankets on the deck just aft of the seat and was sound asleep. Charlie went charging aft, roaring. "Goddamn son of a bitch! Wake up, you stupid bastard. Of all the fucking asinine—"

Jack sat up dazedly. "What's the matter? What seems to be the trouble?"

"You're asleep, that's the trouble, you stupid shit."

"Now, take it easy." Jack shook coverings off himself and slid down onto the seat behind the wheel. "I may have dozed off for a minute—"

"Dozed off? You've made yourself a fucking bed. Christ Almighty! I sometimes think you want to sink your goddamn boat."

"What's all the shouting about? There's practically no wind. She can sail herself in—"

"What about that?" Charlie shouted, pointing at the tanker. "She can sail herself right into that. Is that what you want?" Charlie saw that Jack had lashed the wheel. He tore the rope off and shook it in Jack's face. "If anything's tied up around here, it ought to be you."

"I saw that freighter an hour ago. He could see us. That's what we have lights for. Do you think he's going to try to ram us?"

"It's stupid idiocy to go to sleep on the wheel. You have four hours a day when you're supposed to be good for something. If that's too much for you, let me know. I'm running the goddamn boat, anyway."

"Because you want to. I like to see a man doing a job well that he likes doing. I wouldn't want to depend on you for navigation."

"Oh, Christ. You head south, you head east, you head south again. Some navigation."

"Why are you such a bastard, Charlie?" Jack asked conversationally. "I know you're really a good guy. Why are you such a bastard on the surface?"

Charlie studied him briefly. The skull looked strong, as did the regular weathered features, but he saw a slack weakness around the mouth and despised him for it. Charlie turned from him and scanned the horizon. The sun was just about to do its spectacular run up the sky. He dropped onto one of the benches and stretched his legs out in front of him. "There's a breeze coming in from the northeast. You'd better be ready to get the boom over. I'll help you with the sheets. From now on, I'll stay up here till sunup. You can take over then. Peter will be able to sleep a little later."

"I'd like you to answer my question. Why do you always want

to act the bastard? What makes you think you can get away with it?"

Charlie sized him up with a flick of his eyes. Sinewy. Tough-looking. He hadn't yet come within that category of "older men" with whom Charlie would consider it unfair to fight.

"The fact is that I *can* get away with it," he said coolly.

"What makes you want to? That's the question that interests me. You know, sometimes you don't seem quite human to me. At the beginning I actually thought you might make a pass at me. I could understand that. That would be human."

"What in hell are you talking about?" Charlie demanded. All his muscles stiffened, but he remained in his relaxed lounging position.

"You seemed to like me when we met up in St. Tropez. I know about you, of course. I thought you might make a pass at me and I would've understood. I wouldn't have minded. I don't go for that sort of thing myself, but I understand. It's a perfectly natural human thing that happens."

The fact that Jack might actually be trying, in his misguided way, to have a heart-to-heart talk was the only thing that kept Charlie from hitting him. "Whether or not I'm a cocksucker is my business," he said evenly. "But I'll tell you one thing. If I were, you'd be the last man on earth I'd come anywhere near."

"Really? I thought for guys like you, a cock was a cock. I have an idea Peter might be interested. We're real buddies."

"You son of a bitch. Are you trying to suggest you want it? Are *you* making some sort of a pass?"

"That would be putting it a bit strongly. After all, Marty is damn good at it. I don't have to look for it. Still, a change every now and then never did anybody any harm."

"Christ! I ought to throw you overboard and get it over with," Charlie said, barely keeping his voice under control and not allowing his body to stir. If he let himself go, he was afraid he *would* throw him overboard.

"You see? You won't let up, will you? I'm trying to tell you I understand. I thought we could be friends."

"You haven't said one word so far that suggests you understand anything about me. And I'm not looking for friends."

"Suit yourself. But all this he-man stuff, running the boat and everything. You do it damn well. But don't you think you're overcompensating a bit? You're going to knock yourself out."

Charlie's hands were clenched into fists. His teeth ground together. Don't do it, he warned himself. Fighting on a boat was too dangerous. He sprang up and came to rest against the hatch door. The release of movement left him trembling all over. He took several deep breaths until he was sure he could speak. He looked astern. "We'll get the breeze in a couple of minutes," he said. "You can handle the fucking sheets yourself."

He lay in his bunk, still trembling with rage. He could save their goddamn lives, but all that really mattered to Jack was that he was queer. He couldn't resist rubbing his nose in it. He thought of Martha. He could have her anytime he wanted; he was sure of that now. He ought to goddamn well fuck her and tell Jack about it afterward. The shit. An incompetent drunk. All rolled up in his nest like a goddamn baby. He punched his pillow with his clenched fist. Would he be able to go on with the trip after this? Hell, yes. He would simply extend and consolidate his control until Jack was consigned exclusively to his charts. His thoughts returned to Martha. It had become increasingly obvious that she wanted him, though she remained so easy and open and undemanding that he still hadn't had a moment of feeling crowded or hemmed-in by her. She was his faithful lieutenant, almost as dependable as Peter. She had none of the predatory quality he associated with women. She was the most attractive female he had been on such intimate terms with. Her body was beautiful, her face sweet and appealing, her eyes adoring. He had the impression that making love with her would be a soothing, opulent celebration of physical pleasure. Something to think about. He had never known such selfless love. It commanded attention, reminding him of what he had said to Peter about needing air. It would put Jack in his place; he would have nothing left but technical title to the boat.

She was there, just a few feet away beyond the bulkhead. He was strongly tempted to go to her now. They would be as private as if they were locked in a hotel room. Jack couldn't leave the deck. Peter was asleep. In any case, Peter wouldn't mind. It had always been understood between them that Charlie might want a girl. He hadn't so far, but it could happen. He imagined the welcome she would give him and tugged at the silken pouch he wore and adjusted the sheet to cover himself and give his sex room to expand. It did so as he thought of how often he had caught her eyes looking at him there.

Neither he nor Peter ever stripped for bed on board. They both always woke up with erections. Their brief underpants offered meager concealment. Their sheets often slipped off them. Martha came and went while they were sleeping; it was very likely that she had seen them both in all their glory. If so, it hadn't satisfied her curiosity. Her eyes were always on him, sometimes searching out his own, more often on his mouth as he spoke or roaming his body and settling on his crotch. Yes, it could happen. He wished he thought Jack would really care.

Shortly after noon, they sighted Stromboli. It was easily identifiable: a plume of black smoke rose into the sky above its high peak. Within an hour, the morning's breeze had died entirely. They lay in a flat, leaden sea, the rigging creaking slightly, as motionless as if the boat had been set in cement.

They lay thus the rest of the day, with Stromboli smoking in the distance off their starboard bow. One of the rare areas of agreement between Charlie and Jack concerned the dubious practice of swimming off the boat unless it was anchored, but it was stiflingly hot and they threw a ladder over the side and swam frequently, keeping within easy reach of the boat.

They lay motionless all night. There was a faint glow in the sky where Stromboli was. By midmorning the next day, it seemed to all of them as if no breeze would ever stir again. They were fixed for all eternity in this flat seascape, the black hull set in an expanse of leaden sea with Stromboli daubed in on the horizon. Charlie rigged an awning over part of the cockpit with a spare jib. He waited till they were gathered for lunch before raising the question that was on all their minds.

"How long are we willing to go on sitting here?" he asked.

"We don't seem to have much choice," Jack said.

"I think we should set a limit on it. Tonight. Tomorrow morning at the latest." Charlie addressed Peter and Martha. He had adopted a policy of addressing Jack directly as little as possible.

"And then what do we do?" Jack asked.

"Turn on the motor, for God's sake. It's there for a purpose."

"That's out of the question," Jack asserted. "I have to keep the fuel for getting in and out of ports and any real emergencies that might turn up."

"How much fuel do you have on board?" he asked Martha.

"I don't know exactly," Jack said. "That is, I use the motor so little that I've never figured out how much running time I get on a gallon."

"All the marine engines I've ever heard of never use much more than a gallon an hour. The Straits of Messina are about fifty miles away. I checked the charts. What do you do on the motor? Six or seven knots? Let's say seven or eight hours on motor—maximum. You've certainly got eight gallons of fuel on board."

"Of course we have," Martha put in. "The tank's enormous."

"That's not the point," Jack objected. "The point is we've got to conserve fuel for when we really need it. I've heard it's very difficult to get in the Greek islands."

"We're nowhere near the Greek islands yet, and never will be, at this rate," Charlie pointed out. "You can get fuel in Catania. The pilot book says so."

"Charlie's right, darling," Martha said. "We'll all go mad if we sit here another day."

"Oh, I know you can all out-vote me. Charlie's our household god. If he says turn the motor on, we turn the motor on. This is one thing I'm not putting to a vote."

"Don't be silly, Jack," Peter said. "We all know you're the captain when it gets right down to it. Hell, it's your boat. I don't know anything about it, but you wouldn't want to sit here for a week, would you?"

"It's not a question of what I want. This is a sailboat, not a motor yacht. You do what the wind permits. Anybody can get to Greece on an engine."

"God, the mystique of the sea," Charlie said with heavy irony, raising his eyebrows at Peter.

"You don't understand what Charlie's saying," Martha said to Jack, looking at Charlie. "He just wants to put a limit to how long we wait. We could all relax and stop holding our breath for the slightest puff of wind."

Charlie looked into her eyes and nodded almost imperceptibly. Somehow, their eyes made more of it than he had intended; he had committed himself. Her lips parted and her eyes dropped and he guessed that she was blushing, though it didn't show through her tan. There was still the question of whether he really wanted it.

"You're wasting your time," Jack said with finality. "This is one time we're going to do it my way. I've got perfectly sound reasons. No motor."

Charlie sprang to his feet and ran forward to the bow and dived into the sea. He struck out for Stromboli. He wanted to get as far away from the boat and Jack as possible. It was intolerable to be subject to his whim. He swam with a fast vigorous stroke and moved rapidly away. He continued to swim after he heard Peter calling him. He went on when his lungs were straining for air. He was going slower but he pushed himself on with arms and legs that were beginning to ache. He was a good swimmer, and he swam until his chest was heaving for air. He stopped and gulped air in great, rattling gasps. He could barely move his arms and legs enough to keep himself afloat. He shook his head feebly to clear his eyes and looked back.

He was shocked to see how far he had traveled. The boat looked very small in the distance. He was too far away to see any movement on it. Would he be able to make his way back? Of course. Don't panic. Just lie out and float until you've got your breath back. He did so while his chest heaved and gasped for air.

The sea felt infinitely vast and deep around him. He was touched by a tremor of fear. His mind conjured up pictures of Homeric monsters beneath him. He fought himself into a vertical position.

His breath began to come in sobs. He felt too small. It was unnatural and horrifying. As long as he kept moving in relationship to the boat, proportion was partially restored. Away from it. Toward it. The trick was not to care. If he could force himself on a little farther, his body would rebel, he wouldn't be able to keep his head above water, it would be over quickly. He would be scarcely aware of its happening.

He experienced a great loosening of inner tensions. Death. Nothing. Why go on searching? What difference did any of it make? Let it all go. He had thought of doing away with himself once or twice in the past but always with terror and despair. This was quite different; this was a total yielding to the appeal of nullity, a great easing of all strain. Why go on pushing and prodding at Peter's life? Why fight Jack? How could he consider, even half-heartedly, a further involvement with Martha? It was all so unimportant. He became aware of his aching body and his gasping lungs. It was too much trouble to go back. Wait here until he could move more easily. Push on just a moment longer than he had before. And then oblivion. It felt so restful that he forgot to move his arms and legs and his head went under. He came up coughing and choking. If he stayed out here much longer, he wouldn't have to make the decision. He shook water out of his eyes. As he did so, he caught a glint of gold in the sea somewhere between him and the boat.

The peace that had been lulling him was instantly shattered. Peter mustn't know he had overextended himself. He mustn't know what he had been thinking. Above all, he mustn't come this far. Charlie wasn't sure that either of them could make it back. He summoned what strength he had left and forced his body into a slow breast stroke and headed for the boat. He should have known that Peter would come after him, just as he would come after Peter. If they were to drown, they would drown together. He would never leave Peter behind. When they met, Charlie shook his head to show that he couldn't speak or stop. Peter looked drawn and tired. He circled round and adopted a breast stroke, too.

"You're crazy to go so far," he called.

Charlie didn't attempt to answer. The boat still looked very far away, appallingly far away now that he wanted to return to it. Only his determination for Peter not to guess that he was in trouble drove him on. He could no longer feel his body moving. It had to move. He had to make it back to the boat. The last five minutes were a numbing trial of endurance. He could no longer see. When he bumped into the boat he fumbled for the ladder. Peter guided him to it and helped him hook his arms over a rung. He hung on it with his head bowed and waited for his senses to resume their function and air to heal his tortured lungs. He felt Peter trying to help him up the ladder and shook his head again. He heard voices, but didn't know what they were saying.

At last, he heard Jack ask good-naturedly, "What were you trying to prove this time, Johnny Weissmuller? Did you think I'd turn the motor on to come rescue you? I know you can take care of yourself."

Charlie felt laughter struggling up in his wracked body. The joke would have been on Jack if he'd drowned. As the owner of a boat with a missing passenger, he would probably have been tied up for weeks in the next port of call. He managed to pull himself up the ladder and fell onto his back on deck, his body still heaving, a smile on his open mouth.

"I always thought I was as good a swimmer as you, but Jesus," Peter said from nearby. "What was the idea?"

"I wanted—a change of scenery," Charlie managed to get out slowly between his panting. Martha knelt beside him and lifted his head and put a cushion under it. Her hands lingered on his shoulders.

"He's completely exhausted," she said sharply, presumably to Jack. "I told you you should've at least put the dinghy over."

"I knew he wouldn't attempt anything he couldn't manage," Jack replied.

Charlie lay on the deck without moving, still touched by death's appeal. His brief flirtation with it left him curious. Did he want to die? He didn't think so, yet the answer didn't come as clearly and immediately as he would have expected it to half an hour ago. That moment of numb drifting peace had altered his perspective, added a scrap of knowledge to the sum of what he was learning about himself. He felt, oddly, better-equipped for life, as if he had discovered a new resource in himself, a new option. There was no need to have been so deeply hurt by Peter's disloyalty. Love needn't be the bondage he had made of it. There was an ultimate freedom.

A breeze rescued them from the doldrums that evening. It was favorably northerly, and by luck they entered the Straits of Messina the next morning when the current was right for them to go straight through. This required the help of the motor, which gave Jack an opportunity to point out that this was the sort of thing he was saving fuel for. The sea swirled around them oddly. Homer's Scylla and Charybdis. It required no great effort of imagination to see how the myth was born. They put into Catania, not for fuel, but for water and ice and fresh food. Early one morning, they sailed out into the rising sun and set their course for Greece, which lay across four hundred miles of open sea.

They encountered some days of ideal sailing weather with brisk breezes and only light, choppy seas. They spent most of one day rolling helplessly in a heavy swell with only a light breeze to steady them. The great boom swung ominously above them, sometimes crashing out to the limits of the sheet with a great yank that shook the whole boat. The motor was obviously called for, but Charlie didn't suggest it. If Jack wanted to lose his mast, that was his business. They would probably survive. And if they didn't, worse things could happen to them.

One night, a storm flashed and rumbled away to the south of them, reviving uneasy memories of their first night out, but it stayed away. Martha remained on deck quite late, sitting close to Charlie and Peter, watching, clutching for Charlie's hand when there was a particularly bright flash.

Charlie laughed at her. "You know perfectly well the storm's nowhere near unless the lightning and thunder come practically at the same moment."

"Yes, but if the lightning's brighter, that means it's getting closer, doesn't it?"

"Not necessarily. It has to do with clouds and things. Come on, Pete. Don't you know any meteorological lore? We mustn't let Martha be frightened."

Peter laughed in the dark. "With me, it's easy. If Charlie says the storm's not coming. I believe him. You gotta have faith."

"I know," Martha agreed. "What would we do without him? I'm not really frightened any more." She clung to Charlie's hand and he left it in her keeping.

Because he had ceased to discourage her, she had quickly fallen into the habit of touching him frequently, a hand on his arm when he passed, a hand on his shoulder or back when they were moving about each other. Only when the hand became discreetly caressing did he look her in the eye with an admonishing glance to tell her to stop it. Their eyes spoke openly of the situation she had created, hers hopeful and submissive, his noncommittal since the slight significant nod he had offered her several days ago. He was growing increasingly fond of her and found her enormously pleasing physically but he wasn't going to let her entice him into a meaningless little sexual encounter. Nothing would happen unless it became essential to some grand design that seemed to be vaguely taking shape somewhere just beneath his consciousness. She might play a part in it; at times, he hoped she would, though he couldn't imagine how she could.

He was wedded to the sea. Sea and sky offered few exciting

forms; but the fine, constantly shifting gradation of grays and blues was a challenge to his eye. His intent study of them sharpened his sensibilities and developed in him an acute weather sense. He knew from the changing colors around him that conditions would alter some time before the event. A milky-gray sea with curious deeper-gray shadows beneath it, seas streaked with blue on paler blue, the run of indigo at the horizon all had their meaning for him. Sunrises and sunsets were fascinatingly spectacular, great color organs in full voice, but it was the delicate shading of gray to blue to deep-midnight hues that excited him endlessly and told him most.

Peter was amazed at the varied satisfactions Charlie derived from the sea and their journey on it. For Peter, as he grew more expert, there was the simple joy of sailing and the more intense joy he found in the harmony between them when they handled the sails and the helm together. He was vastly impressed when Charlie predicted a shift in the wind that took place an hour later. When he told stories from Thucydides about the doomed Athenians in the pits of Syracuse or pointed out with awed excitement that Odysseus must have passed this way on his long voyage home to Ithaca, which lay somewhere ahead of them to the north, Peter felt the extra dimension that he was finding in the trip and was excited for him. It had turned into a big experience for him and they were sharing it. Another imperishable link forged for the future.

Except for Jack, who doubtless knew, none of them bothered to remember what day it was or how long they had been out. On the morning of the fifth or sixth day, Charlie was on the wheel when the sun rose out of distant, jagged peaks. For an instant, he thought it might be a cloud formation and then he knew it was land. He leaped to his feet, his heart pounding with excitement. Jack had told him to expect it, but the reality of Greece, the distant blue mountains in the dazzling morning light, was a thrill nothing could have prepared him for. He leaned over and ruffled Peter's hair.

"Wake up, baby. Look!" he cried triumphantly.

Peter immediately sat up. When he saw Charlie standing, he stood, too, and looked forward. "My God. Is that it? We've really made it?" He turned a radiant face to Charlie.

161

"Unless it turns out to be Africa or something. I guess we can hand it to Jack's navigation. Isn't it fabulous? My God. Greece." As the sun climbed the sky, the land mass acquired dimension. It rose in tiers behind what appeared to be twin headlands much closer to them. He knew from the charts that two islands guarded the entrance to the Gulf of Corinth. If these were the islands, Jack had really done his job. When he emerged for his watch, Charlie greeted him with an exultant smile, all differences forgotten for the moment.

"How about that?" Charlie demanded, waving ahead.

Jack looked. "Would you mind hanging on there for another few minutes?" He went below and returned with binoculars and the pilot book. The book had profile sketches of the entrance to the gulf. Jack scanned the land with the binoculars and checked the book.

"Bang on it?" Charlie asked with pride in Jack's achievement.

Jack turned back with a satisfied smile. "That's Cephalonia and the other's Zante. We go between them."

"Fantastic. Right on the nose. You couldn't have done better if we'd had road signs."

They all laughed together. Jack took the wheel, but Peter and Charlie didn't go below. They sat together in the bow and watched Greece take shape before them.

At dawn the next morning, they motored into Patras, their first Greek port, and tied up to Greek soil. They were all on deck for the event. Martha broke out the American flag astern.

"Just a week from Sicily. Not bad," Jack said, when he had cut the motor.

A week was no measure of time to the rest of them. It was a moment or an eternity. Charlie felt as if they had been journeying back in time, so that for him it was like entering a new and mythical world. As the sun rose, a crowd of children and young men gathered at the foot of the gangplank and stared silently at them. They were having some breakfast coffee when a group of officials, some uniformed, some not, mounted the gangplank, saluting and bowing and speaking volubly a language they presumed was Greek. Jack took them below. They had had official visits in Italy, and Jack had mentioned something about an officer coming aboard at Calvi, but this conference lasted almost two hours, while the three on deck sat and paced and wondered what it was all about.

"The port is pretty hideous, but I want to go ashore," Charlie said. "The town might be worth seeing. I suppose we ought to wait for the crowd below."

"I think you have to," Martha said. "Passports and all."

The boarding party finally emerged, beaming and dropping bits of English. "How do you do?" one said to each of them as he left.

Jack shook hands with all of them at the gangplank and dropped back into the cockpit. "They were all very nice. But slow! God!" he explained. "They looked at all the papers at least sixteen times. I had to keep turning them right side up for them. It seems we're the first American yacht to put in here since the war." They all felt pleased with themselves and vaguely historical.

Charlie and Peter pulled on trousers and shirts and waved to the Kingsleys and walked down the gangplank. They stepped off it and stood on Greek soil. A youth moved out of the crowd that still lingered there and confronted them. "You want," he informed them.

"Money. Bank," Charlie said, showing traveler's checks.

The youth took Charlie's hand and led him off. Charlie was briefly startled but, once adjusted to it, found it rather sweet. "I've got myself a new boyfriend," he murmured. They laughed. They both felt slightly drunk, their heads reeling with the motion of the boat. They crossed broken ground to the road that ran around the port. They skirted a huddle of mean-looking buildings and climbed steps up to busy streets. They saw other men holding hands as they strolled.

"Do you suppose it means anything?" Peter wondered.

"God knows. Maybe Socrates didn't die in vain."

They came to a forlorn-looking square. There were a great many cafés with a great many shabby men sitting at tables. Women passed, some with scarves over their mouths and noses; none were sitting at the cafés. There was a great din of talk but little other noise. Loaded donkeys padded by in the street. They noticed older men with great, baggy trousers and thick woolen cloths wound around their waists. They came to a building with indecipherable gilt letters on a glass door and their guide said, "Bank."

Charlie thanked him and started to reach for a tip, but the youth held the door open and entered with them. Was he going to wait till they'd changed some money and try to rob them? He led them to a counter and they found themselves launched on an endless transaction. Six men gathered behind the counter, passing the checks and Charlie's passport from hand to hand. They discussed them at length. They went in search of forms and put them down and forgot where they were. People came in off the street and joined in the discussion. In the midst of it, coffee was served them with glasses of iced water and plates with little dabs of something sweet on them. When it was all over and Charlie had recovered his passport and uncashed checks with a handful of *drachma,* they all shook hands and beamed at each other. The Greeks repeated "Amerika" and "Amerikani" a good deal. Charlie and Peter tried to thank them, and their guide led them out. "You want," he told them again.

"Hotel," Peter said. "The best. Very good." The youth nodded and led them around the square.

"Apparently there is one," Peter said.

"There better be. How long has it been?" Charlie took his hand and held it as they walked. "If it's a national custom, we might as well take advantage of it."

"How about that? Ten years, and we're finally holding hands in the street." He laughed with delight and squeezed Charlie's hand.

They went a little way up a side street and the youth started into what was obviously an old-fashioned but adequate-looking hotel. "Fine," Peter said. "Later." He mimed carrying bags. "Boat now." The youth seemed to understand. They started back to the port. They had seen nothing beautiful; on the contrary, a pall of commonplace ugliness hung over the whole place, but it had begun to exert a spell on them. In the midst of the confusion at the bank, the coffee had been a touchingly thoughtful gesture. Beneath the picturesque touches of donkeys and baggy trousers and muffled women, there was the peace of time. They held hands, reveling in the general indifference. When they came within sight of the boat, they dropped them. At the foot of the gangplank, Charlie took some Greek coins out of his pocket and offered them to the youth. He drew back with consternation.

"No, no, no," he protested.

Charlie wondered if the coins were worthless. He tried one of the bills. The youth's protests redoubled. "I seem to have made a *faux pas*," he muttered to Peter. He turned to the youth and pointed at the boat. "Do you want to go on board? See. The boat."

The youth broke into a happy grin. He spoke harshly to the children who were still gathered there and made gestures of shooing them away and marched proudly up the gangplank.

When the boy was gone, Jack proposed moving on later in the day. It was still only ten in the morning. "There's an old Venetian port just across the gulf that sounds pretty good in the pilot book. We could all use a decent night's sleep. This place looks as if it would be noisy in the morning. All these fishing boats around. It's pretty hot and dusty, too."

"We'd like to have a night in a hotel," Peter said.

"That's what I mean. Those customs guys promised to get water to us before noon. We could have lunch and go on across. It's less than fifteen miles."

Martha wanted to go ashore to shop for fruit and vegetables. She looked at Charlie as she proposed it. Charlie urged Peter to go with her on the valid grounds that he had had no sleep since the day before. Now that they would be stopping frequently and would be more independent of the boat, he intended to take care not to let himself get caught with her alone until he knew better what he might make of it.

They followed Jack's program and sailed across the gulf at its narrowest point to a tiny, picturesque port with remains of Venetian fortifications. The water hadn't been provided till midafternoon, so the sun was setting when they had finished furling the sails. A knot of children formed at the foot of the gangplank. A sailor drifted up and asked for their papers and took them away. Martha rolled the flag on its pole and stowed it. They had drinks. A few lights came on in the austere little whitewashed square that faced the port. There was a statue of a military-looking personage in the middle of it. It was almost dark when Peter stood up.

"We better go look for a hotel," he said.

"The town's a good deal smaller than I expected it to be," Jack said.

The same thought had occurred to both Peter and Charlie. They agreed to come back and pick up their things when they had found a hotel; neither of them had much hope of success. As they were crossing the square, three youths emerged from the shadows and joined them.

"Hotel," Peter said. The three conferred and then nodded and pointed and one of them took Peter's hand. They continued across the square. "Here we go again. My Greek's getting pretty good."

"At least, there seems to be a hotel. I was beginning to have my doubts."

"Me too."

A street ran along the back of the square parallel to the shore. There were lights here, but there was nothing suggesting a hotel. They passed several dimly lighted bare-looking shops and turned into a side street leading farther into the town. They made several more turns. All the buildings were whitewashed and loomed palely in the dark. The streets were immaculate. They came to another small square with trees set about in it. Bright lights spilled from a big room with wide doors open onto it. Unpainted wooden tables and chairs were set about within and in front under a grape arbor. Voices were singing. Their escort delivered them to a gnarled old man, who struggled to his feet as they entered.

"Hotel?" Peter said hopefully.

"You American? Me American too. From Cairo, Illynoise. Where you from?" The old man held their hands and fell back into his chair, urging them down beside him. They sat. Their escort disappeared. Other old men scattered about the room edged their chairs closer and surrounded them. The old man from Cairo called for ouzo. The singing was coming from two men in the back of the room who gazed at each other intently as they produced an odd, wailing dirge. They were singing *at* each other. A copper tankard was set on the table and plates of olives and sliced tomatoes. The old man poured a clear liquid into small glasses with a trembling hand. "You like ouzo? Greek drink. Good." He speared a slice of tomato and held it in front of Peter's mouth. Peter ate it. He repeated the offering with Charlie. He clinked his glass against theirs and they all drank. Peter and Charlie had never had ouzo before. It tasted strong and sweet. The old man let loose a barrage of questions while the onlookers sat and nodded at their friend's dazzling command of English. Where you from? Got kids? Womans? What you do here?

This seemed an appropriate opening for the business at hand. "We're looking for a hotel," Peter explained.

"No. No hotel here. Was hotel. Closed. Go bust. You want room? Sleep?"

"Yes. That's the idea."

"Me got good room. Four beds. Three left."

"How do you mean, three left?"

"One good man sleep already. You take two beds. One left."

Charlie and Peter looked at each other with dismay. "I'm afraid that's not what we want," Charlie said.

"You Americans. Want room, bath. Me know." He chortled. "Not like that here. Never mind. You take two beds. Sleep. Sleep good."

"Thanks a lot, but I don't think we'll bother. What we really wanted was a bath to get cleaned up." Charlie looked at Peter and leaned his head toward the door. They didn't find it easy to extricate themselves. The old man insisted that they finish the ouzo. They got slightly drunk while the old man told them about his shop in Cairo and fed them tomatoes. He had been back in Greece for twenty years, through the war and the civil war that was recently ended. Very bad. Troubles still. Government no good.

They finally managed to get to their feet. Charlie pulled out money to pay for the drinks. The old man refused indignantly. There was a rumble of protest from the others.

Charlie hastily put his money away. Money was apparently a dirty word here; so far, they hadn't spent a *drachma*. They thanked the old man and nodded and smiled at the others and made their escape.

"Damn Jack," Peter said as they went out. "*I* could kill him this time. I was looking forward so to tonight."

"I know. There was no reason to leave Patras."

"Still, I like it here. Everybody's so damn nice." Peter started across the square.

"We came this way," Charlie said pointing off to the right.

"I know. But let's go back a different way. I want to see the rest of the town. It's amazing how whitewash lights up in the dark."

"You go ahead, baby. You like to prowl around on your own. I'm really bushed. I'll tell Martha we want something to eat. Don't get lost."

"I'll just work my way back to the port. You're sure you know the way back?"

"If I don't, I'm sure half the town will turn out to show me."

"OK. I'll race you." They touched and parted.

Peter crossed the square and wandered down a narrow street that turned frequently, but seemed to be headed in the general direction of the sea. Most of this part of the town appeared to be abandoned. There were many fallen roofs and broken walls. They made interesting shapes in the night. He heard footsteps near him and then there was a rush of movement and he was suddenly surrounded by dark forms. Charlie was right. Greece seemed to specialize in escorts. A light was shined in his face and quickly doused. Men spoke together in lowered voices. Were they soldiers? The police?

"I was just going—" he began.

The sound of his voice seemed to bring them to a decision. They moved in close to him and prodded him in the direction from which he had come. There was no menace in the way they handled him, only a sort of rough impatience. He tried to stop to explain that he wanted to go back to the port, but they hustled him on. He hadn't figured out yet how many they were. Three? Four? They turned off into a street he had noticed on his way that seemed to lead out of town. They passed more ruined houses. There began to be gaps between them. Eventually, they turned into one of these and he stumbled over stones. He was so busy trying to watch his footing that he didn't see anything else until he heard a key turn in a lock and he was pushed through a door. The door closed behind them and the flashlight snapped on. Its beam wandered and focused on a lamp on a table. Surely not the police. A match was struck and the lamp was lighted. They all began to talk at once and moved around the room, settling into it. They were wearing a sort of uniform in that they were all dressed in shabby trousers and black sweaters with round necks. Inappropriate for the season. There were only three of them.

The room was dirty and dilapidated and looked unused, with a big table in the middle and some chairs, several stripped beds against the walls with boards instead of springs and kitchen equipment at one end. Peter's eye was caught by two guns propped against the wall. He had been too astonished to really wonder what they wanted with him. Now he began to wonder very much. He hoped they wouldn't keep him long enough for Charlie to start worrying about him. They paid no attention to him for several minutes as they talked among themselves. He had time to sort them out. He guessed they were younger than they looked, probably a good deal younger than he. One was very good-looking in a dark, dangerous way. His fiery eyes slanted slightly, giving him an oriental look. His hard, flat cheeks made the mouth bold and voracious. The other two were quite nondescript, dark and lean and harmless-looking. They had a military air about them, as if they were camping out here during a lull in a battle, but they seemed wild and undisciplined at the same time.

The good-looking one went to the end of the room and returned with a straw-covered jug and some thick glasses, which he put on the table. He poured pale liquid into a glass and drank it. He approached Peter with a friendly smile. Peter was taller than all three of them, which gave him confidence. Everybody had been so friendly and helpful here: there was nothing to worry about. Language was the problem. He wondered if he would ever find out what they wanted. The good-looking one said a word, which Peter didn't understand; then he said "Dollari" and rubbed his thumb and forefinger together. The Greek continued to smile in an almost ingratiating way. Had they simply wanted to rob him? What a stupid waste of time.

"I don't have any," he said. He turned the pockets of his trousers inside out. He remembered his hip pocket and turned it inside out too. He was wearing a skintight sailor's jersey, which could conceal nothing. He held his arms out and shrugged.

The good-looking one took his arm and led him to a chair and smiled at him again. Peter smiled back and sat. Perhaps he had misunderstood. Perhaps they hadn't wanted money. The good-looking one sat beside him and filled a glass from the jug. The others dropped into chairs across from them. The good-looking one filled another glass and handed it to Peter. He pointed at himself.

"Yanni," he said. He pointed at the two across the table. "Costa. Stavros." He pointed at himself again and repeated "Yanni" and then pointed at Peter.

Peter gathered that they were introducing themselves. "Peter," he said.

"Peet—" Yanni stumbled over the name and then his face lighted with comprehension as he pronounced, "Petros." He lifted a glass and clinked it against Peter's. "Petros. Yanni." He gestured to Peter to drink.

He did so. The liquid was sharp and pungent and tasted of pine, like alcoholic bath essence. He tried not to make a face as he choked it down. He supposed it was the Greek wine he had heard of called retsina. He looked at Yanni and said the word questioningly.

Its effect was sensational. Yanni laughed boisterously and repeated it, nodding. He put his arm around Peter's shoulders and hugged him. He spoke to the others, repeating the word several more times. He dropped his hand to Peter's knee and left it there while he refilled their glasses and said once more, "retsina." There was more to this than hearty camaraderie. Peter was quick to detect the caress in the hand. He had suspected it before when the Greek had held his arm. Now there was no doubt of it: Yanni was as queer as they come. Perhaps all the hand-holding did mean something; perhaps he and Charlie had found their country. Peter looked into flashing eyes and smiled his recognition. The hand caressed his knee. He was aware of time passing, but with this familiar element added to the situation he felt more in control. He wasn't going to let it turn into a party, as seemed the rule in Greece, but he could afford a few more minutes to see if the mystery would be elucidated. Meanwhile, it wasn't disagreeable to have the caressing hand on his knee; Yanni was damned attractive. His body looked powerful and well-formed under the shabby clothes, as were his hands. His mouth had the excitingly hungry look.

The three had entered into lively conversation, during which Yanni kept looking at Peter and laughing slyly. Peter began to wonder if they knew why they had brought him here.

After a few minutes, he put his glass down with a little thump and interrupted firmly. "I have to go." He pointed at himself, he pointed at his watch, he pointed at the door. Yanni leaned toward him and gripped his hand and twisted his wrist to see the watch better. He removed the hand from his knee and put it on his arm and openly caressed it. He spoke, touching the watch and pointing at himself. Peter shrugged uncomprehendingly. Had he never seen a watch before? He lifted Peter's hand and unfastened the watchstrap and handed the watch across the table. Peter yanked his hand away and made a grab for it, but it was gone. That was that. They had brought him here to rob him and he had nothing else for them to rob. He stood up. At a word from Yanni, the other two were immediately upon him and forced him back into his chair. Yanni swung his chair around and faced him. The Greek eased himself back and slid his hips forward and put his hands on his thighs. The thick fabric of his trousers made a great bulge between his legs. He ran his fingers back and forth over it and said something and they all laughed.

Peter was getting angry. He cursed himself for having smiled so amiably; it had obviously been interpreted as giving consent to whatever Yanni had in mind. He wasn't smiling now. Yanni continued the tease with his crotch, looking at Peter expectantly as if he were bound to react to it. If he was so self-confident, why didn't he send the others away? Peter had no fears about handling him alone. He sensed suddenly that whatever they had planned for him, they were all in it together, although he had detected no caress in the others' hands. A gang-rape? Alarm sharpened his anger. His eyes shifted as he tried to settle on the best means of escape. Yanni spoke again and Peter was seized and flung to his knees between his legs. Yanni tangled his fingers in his hair and jerked his head back. Peter's mouth dropped open. Yanni's was immediately on it, his tongue thrusting into it. Peter clamped his teeth together hard on it. He was released with a shout of pain. He snaked through three pairs of legs and scrambled to his feet and turned to face them, his fists ready. Yanni was almost on him, glowering with rage. He made a grab for him as if he wanted to take him in his arms. Peter sidestepped and swung his fist. He was off balance and it was a glancing blow, but Yanni staggered back with a surprised look in his face. Then the other two were on him.

He flung them off and struck out at them, but they crowded in on him, shouting and laughing, so that he had no room to maneuver. He felt a sort of idiot innocence in them; it was a sadistic schoolboy prank. Since they clung to his arms, he brought his knees into play, trying to get them in the crotch. He thought of making a break for one of the guns, but the thought went as quickly as it came. This wasn't a movie. He didn't want to kill anybody or get killed.

Yanni returned to the fray. He flung himself on Peter's back and put an arm around his neck and got a lock on it. His hips ground up against his buttocks. Peter could feel the sex against him. They pulled and pushed and dragged him toward a bed against the wall, while Yanni's hand fumbled at his crotch, apparently baffled by the pouch that held him all bunched together. None of it made any sense unless they were convinced that he was willing and was just putting up a token resistance, like a girl. Perhaps Yanni had boasted of what an easy conquest he would be and the other two still believed him. Otherwise, what did they think they could do with him on a bed? Thinking of Jeannot, he expected them to start pulling his clothes off and the forbidden memory came rushing in on him. A beefy, sneering face from long ago filled his mind's eye. He went wild with rage; his body heaved and lunged and twisted in a frenzy of resistance. Yanni was no threat to his self-respect because they were linked by shared tastes, but they would have to knock him out before he'd let himself be stripped in front of the other two. Their grip was hard on him as they swayed with him toward the bed. Yanni hooked a leg around his and he lost his footing and they surged forward almost to the edge of it. He could feel their balance going and they all crashed to the floor. An elbow smashed into his eye as they went and his head reeled until he was brought up hard on the floor. They were a sweating, panting mass of tangled bodies. His face was crushed against somebody's chest. One hand was trapped under a leg. He was reminded of schoolboy grapplings, tests of strength, with their constant threat of ending in disgrace for him. He had always had a tendency to get an erection at any close physical contact with other boys. He hadn't known what it meant until he met Charlie. Unlike Charlie, he had always shunned the experiences that this tendency might have led him into.

There was no risk of his getting an erection now, even though a hand had found the pouch again. He couldn't imagine what he had done to encourage such persistence. The chest rolled off his face. He wrenched his hand free and twisted his body clear of other entanglements and for a moment felt no hands on him as he sprang to his feet. Yanni came up with him, reaching for the top of his trousers. He knocked the hands away, stepped back, tripped on something, swung at him. It was another glancing blow, but it momentarily removed Yanni from his immediate vicinity. The other two were up now and lunged at him. He squared off, took aim and drove his fist with all his weight behind it into an approaching chin. He felt the shock all the way up his arm. There was a gratifying crack and his assailant crumpled to the floor. He turned quickly and brought his knee up hard into the other's crotch. There was a shriek of pain and the Greek staggered back and fell onto one of the plank beds writhing in agony. Maybe this *was* a movie. Bodies were disposed picturesquely around the room. Only the one he had found attractive remained in the field. Peter was breathing hard and his eye felt as if it were swelling shut, but he was spoiling for battle. He watched warily as Yanni approached, smiling ingratiatingly again. He stopped a few feet away and spoke, pointing at himself and then at Peter.

Still propositioning him? Peter pointed at the door. "I'm going. Understood?"

Yanni pointed at himself and Peter and then at the door and spoke again.

Did he want them to go together? Peter shook his head. "I'm clearing out. Goodbye," he said as he started to turn away. He just had time to register the murderous look that sprang up into the fierce eyes before Yanni sprang forward and smashed his fist into Peter's mouth. "You son of a bitch," he muttered as he regained his balance. He shook his head and went at the Greek with his fists. It was quickly evident that Yanni knew nothing about defense. He met Peter's attack by swinging at him in return, leaving himself wide open. Peter methodically pounded his face with his fists, backing him across the room until his hands hurt and his arms ached. At last, Yanni fell to his knees with his arms around Peter's hips and swayed forward and buried his face in his crotch. Peter's sex swelled with triumph. He had beaten the Greek into submission; his body was his by right of conquest. He realized that the thrill of cruelty coursing through him was an aspect of desire. He wanted to go on hurting him. His sex grew against the battered face that was pressed to it.

"Christ, I should fuck you till you couldn't see straight," he said hoarsely. His chest was still heaving. He thought of Charlie, worried and waiting for him. He pulled the Greek's arms from him roughly and flung him to the floor. He lay on his stomach, shaken by silent sobs. Peter lingered over him another moment while his sex subsided. Cruelty was replaced by pity. Poor bastard, he thought, he must be really hard up if he was ready to go through all this for it. It was tough for faggots everywhere.

He turned and rushed to the door. He had some difficulty with the big key that projected from it, but after turning it back and forth in a screeching lock, he got the door open and was away. He stumbled over rough terrain and found the road and set off at a fast pace. He hoped Charlie hadn't worked himself into a state about him. The fight had dislocated his sense of time, but he didn't think the whole thing had taken much more than half-an-hour. That wasn't too long; Charlie was probably just beginning to worry now. Walking jarred his wounds and made his head throb, but he didn't slow down. The vision of his left eye was dim, and it was swollen almost closed now. His mouth was more painful. He supposed some teeth had been smashed through it. His lips were stiff and felt enormous on one side. He kept them parted to ease the pain. He would probably have trouble speaking by the time he got back to the boat. That would be a nuisance because he was bursting to tell Charlie all about it.

The memory that he had successfully isolated in some mental limbo all these years, the memory that had stirred during the fight, crowded his mind once more and for the first time since the event, he didn't resist it. After ten years, his honor had been vindicated. The three Greeks had been an adequate substitute for the sergeant. He had almost forgiven Hal years ago. Silly son of a bitch.

He had known from the beginning that his commanding officer had been on the make for him, although nothing overt had been said or done. When Hal returned from a leave and told him about meeting Charlie, it all came out into the open.

"I told him I'd do anything to get you," Hal said with a smile when he had summoned Peter to his office on some pretext to tell him about the meeting.

"What did he say?"

"He said I'd never succeed."

Peter laughed fondly. 'That's my Charlie. I'm glad he knows that."

Months passed and it became a sort of joke between them.

Whenever Peter had a weekend leave, Hal would send for him on his return and quiz him.

"Have you been a good boy? You haven't succumbed to temptation?"

"That's what's so amazing. I'm never tempted. I meet guys who would normally bowl me over and nothing happens. Like you, for instance, captain honey." Peter smiled into the fascinating green eyes.

"I wonder how Charlie's doing."

"I don't wonder. I know. It's the same for both of us. I guess we were born for each other."

As the months passed, Peter longed for Charlie to move to San Francisco where they could be together at least for weekends. They had agreed before he was inducted that it would be easier for both of them to make it a clean separation, rather than subject themselves to the strains and frustrations of brief, irregular meetings. He still thought their decision valid, but being able to talk about him with Hal made a single-minded acceptance of military routine more difficult. He had been destined for West Point from birth and had always hated the prospect so that he hadn't hesitated to resign his appointment in order to live with Charlie, but with the country at war he was proud to be in uniform. He was doing his duty and sharing his generation's experience. He wished he would be shipped overseas so there could be no more question of having Charlie near him.

He was killing a Saturday night as best he could on a weekend pass in San Francisco when he ran into Hal in a flagrantly queer bar. Peter noticed immediately that his captain had had a lot to drink.

"I've been looking for you," Hal said. "So this is the sort of place you frequent."

"Sure. I love joints like this. They're so crazy. You up for the weekend, too?"

"No. I told you. I was looking for you. I'm OD in the morning. I was having a drink or two with my fellow officers and gentlemen when I suddenly couldn't stand not knowing what you were doing. It's getting bad, soldier." He drained his drink and rattled the ice in his glass for another.

Even drunk, he didn't lose his aristocratic look. Peter found his voice thrilling, deep and melodious, with haunting, dark resonances in it. "You're planning to drive back tonight? You'd better take it easy on the booze."

"It's a little late to worry about that. I'm properly potted. Do you expect me to really believe that you're not out cruising?"

"No. Honestly. I had dinner with a damn nice couple I've met here—guys, I mean. They don't do the bars. I've been wandering around waiting to get sleepy."

"Well, here I am. I'm not bad, as pickups go."

"I'll say, captain honey. You shouldn't waste your time on me. Why don't you circulate? There're some very pretty numbers around."

Hal had been given a fresh drink. He drained off half of it in one gulp and stood looking at Peter, swaying slightly. "No. I'll tell you what. If you'll help me find my car, I'll buzz on back. I just wanted to show myself. I suddenly got a funny feeling that tonight was the night you'd change your mind. I wanted to be available, in case. You can't say I've pursued you up until now."

"No. It wouldn't have got you anywhere, but I appreciate it. OK. I'm ready to go. Let's have that old, crisp, military bearing. The streets are crawling with MPs."

Hal finished his drink in another gulp. They put money on the bar and collected change and left. Hal walked straight but with great deliberation. He didn't seem to know where the car was or particularly care. They walked back and forth slowly and finally turned into a side street and found it. Hal offered to drive Peter to his hotel and got in behind the wheel. After Peter had seated himself beside him, nothing happened. Peter looked at him. He was sitting very straight, but his eyes were closed.

"Oh, for God's sake." Peter shook his arm and he came to with a start. "You can't do a two-hour drive in this condition."

"Maybe better have a little snooze. Sleep it off in the car."

"You're nuts. MPs don't like officers sleeping in cars. If they found you, they'd wake you up and you'd have to drive."

"Got an extra bed?"

"Yes, but—" Peter hesitated but he couldn't see anything really wrong with it and there was no alternative. Hal was too drunk to be left on his own. "All right. You can come with me. But listen. I can take care of myself if somebody makes a pass at me but I like you too much to go through all that. No nonsense. Promise?"

176

"Scout's honor."

"OK. Let me drive." He got out and went around the car and found Hal still struggling to get out from under the wheel. He gave him a helpful push and got in. He was staying in a modest hotel near the Crystal Palace Market; he couldn't afford anything grand. He had turned over the income from his investments to Charlie so that he could concentrate on his painting without having to find a job.

He drove to the hotel and parked. Hal's eyes were closed again. He nudged him with his elbow. "Hey. Pfc. Martin reporting, sir."

"Just dropped off for a moment, soldier," Hal rumbled.

"I can't for the life of me remember my goddamn room number. You wait here. I'll be right back. Are you listening? I'll go up first and you can follow me."

Hal nodded and Peter left him and went into the hotel. He gave his name and collected his key. Servicemen were coming and going. He and Hal wouldn't be conspicuous. He started back for the door and caught sight of Hal standing rigidly in a corner of the lobby. He went to him and muttered his room number and turned directly to the elevator. He had been in the room only long enough to turn on some lights when Hal knocked. He let him in and Hal immediately gathered him into his arms. It was nice to be held and Peter ran his hands over his back and gave him a hug before pulling away.

"All right. Enough of that. You better get to bed. You're going to have to get up at dawn."

Peter felt all his nerves tighten as Hal began to remove his beautifully cut jacket. He liked him. He was wonderful looking. He wanted to see his body. Was that all he would want? He had issued his invitation with the certainty that he was impregnable, but he knew suddenly that he was facing a test. He wouldn't let anything happen even if he had to lock himself in the bathroom, but he didn't want the clear, constant, obsessive preoccupation with Charlie to be broken. He wanted desperately not to feel the slightest quiver of desire for anybody. It would somehow tarnish the resplendent glow of his love.

He undressed slowly as he watched Hal casually drop his clothes. He seemed much less drunk than he had a few minutes before. His shirt was off. Socks and shoes lay on the floor. He

177

rose and with a swift movement of long legs stood naked in front of Peter.

"No passes. Right?" Hal said, moving toward him.

Peter's eyes slid past him, gathering an impression of startling beauty. Trust Charlie. He removed his trousers, but left his brief underpants on. Hal stopped a few feet from him and smiled.

"Isn't this marvelous? You must know how often I've imagined it. You're just as gorgeous as I thought you'd be, which is hard to believe. Aren't you going to take that sexy little thing off?"

"No. I don't think Charlie would want me to." Peter's nerves were steadying. A deep, ecstatic contentment was spreading through him. He really did want only Charlie. In a moment he would be able to look at Hal without a qualm.

"Don't be silly. Dozens of guys see you naked every day. What's wrong with me?"

To prove to himself that this was, in fact, no different than the shower-room exposure of the barracks, he peeled off the bit of silken stuff and tossed it away. "It's been damn near a year since I've been alone in a bedroom with a beautiful guy and look at me. Nothing. How's that for true love?"

"Beautiful. Darling Peter. I don't suppose it's a great surprise for you to see what you do to me."

Peter looked into the green eyes and laughed. "I'm not letting myself look, but I'm getting a pretty vivid picture out of the corner of my eye. It's very flattering, but I told you you shouldn't waste all that on me. We'd better cover you up. Go to bed." He squeezed his arm as he passed him and went into the bathroom. When he returned, Hal was lying uncovered on the bed. His erect sex was lifted tautly above his belly.

"Wow," Peter exclaimed, confident now that he was invulnerable to temptation. "It's a crying shame nobody's getting any fun out of that. You and Charlie must have had a high old time together."

"Did he tell you about us?"

"Sure. He said you taught him the works when he was a freshman. You sure did a good job of it. He's fabulous." Peter pulled back the covers of the other bed and lay down under them.

"Did he say that? How amazing. I thought he was the most experienced kid I'd ever been to bed with."

"Oh, well, that's Charlie. He always likes to pretend he's one step ahead of everybody else."

"That stupendous cock. He's certainly one step ahead of everybody there. Is it really as big as I remember?"

"It's big, all right, but if truth must be told, I've had bigger. Never better. For somebody who likes being fucked as much as I do, that's saying something."

Hal swung his feet to the floor and rose and dropped down on the edge of Peter's bed. Peter was immediately upright and sitting on the opposite side, poised for flight.

"Now come on, honey. None of that. You promised. Go back where you belong."

"Can't we just lie here and talk?"

"Lie here, my Aunt Matilda! What do you think I'm made of, for God's sakes? One of the most attractive guys I've ever known, waving that thing in my face. I'd love to hold it and make things happen. I could do that without getting a hard-on myself. There wouldn't be anything unfaithful about it. It would be because I like you and you have a gorgeous cock, but I'm not going to. I want to go back to Charlie exactly the way I left him, no new experiences, no little secret thrills, nothing. It's probably hard to understand what it's like being so in love with somebody."

"Is it all right if I just sit here for a little while?"

"If you put something over that."

Hal leaned across to the other bed and pulled the pillow to him and put it on his lap. Peter lay down again. Hal put his hand on the side of his face and stroked it. "If I can't have anything else, I'd love to see you with a hard-on," he said. "Isn't there anything we can do about that?"

Peter laughed. "Stick around till morning. All the guys in the barracks wake up that way. We compare them. It's very military." Feeling the warmth of companionship, soothed by the gentle hand, Peter was aware more poignantly than ever of the depth of his longing for Charlie. He didn't see how he was going to get through another year of this. Another two? Tears welled up behind his closed lids. He took a deep breath that caught in his chest.

"You two are really torturing yourselves," Hal said. "I told Charlie. It's a sweet idea, but it can't work. If you go on like this, something's going to snap."

"Did you try to take him to bed when you saw him in New York?"

"Sure."

"I'm almost sorry you didn't succeed." Peter giggled. "If you had, maybe I would've been able to do something with you. Our teacher." His mind slid down into a pocket of sleep and swooped up again. "What?" he asked dazedly.

"I said, have you ever tried it the other way around?"

"Fucked a guy? No. Oh, technically, Charlie once. But it was so sudden and unexpected that it doesn't really count. When it comes to sex, I'm one of the girls. There's never been any doubt about that."

"Wouldn't you like to try it so you know what it's like?"

"Not really. Have you?" Peter felt himself spinning into another hollow of sleep.

"As a matter of fact, no."

Peter put his hand on Hal's and pressed it comfortingly against his face. "We both want a man called Charlie," he mumbled. "Don't let's confuse ourselves."

Hal said something, but Peter didn't hear him. He felt as if he were falling. He plunged and plunged again and was asleep.

He was awakened by light in his eyes. He blinked and saw the back of Hal's head on the pillow. As the fog of sleep cleared, he realized that he was lying on his side up close against Hal's back and his erect sex was held between Hal's thighs. Simultaneously, he became aware of movement in the room and he struggled up in sudden alarm. As he did so, Hal rolled over and reached out for him blindly and tried to take his sex in his mouth.

"For Christ's sake," Peter cried in warning.

They scrambled up together, Hal still reaching for him as if to bring him back to bed until his hands suddenly fell away. They stood naked and erect, confronting two MPs. The soldiers advanced on them.

"Well, a couple of lilies," one of them said. He was a big man with a beefy neck and a sneer on his thin lips. He struck their subsiding erections lightly with his club. "What a shame. We're interrupting something. They make a real pretty pair, wouldn't you say, Ed?"

"Watch your step, sergeant," Hal said, managing an astonishing note of authority. He gave his name and rank.

"I see, sir. Sorry I didn't notice your insignia." The sergeant turned to Peter, the sneer more pronounced on his face. "You a general, sis?" Peter identified himself, although his heart was beating so fast that he could hardly get it out. The sergeant nodded. "A commissioned officer and an enlisted man. You're in real trouble. Your men love you, do they, captain?"

Peter saw his shorts on the floor and made a dash for them. The sergeant stepped nimbly after him and ran his club between his legs as he bent for them. Peter sprang up and the sergeant guffawed.

"How's that for size, sis?"

Peter took a step toward him. His fists were ready to strike. Their eyes clashed and the sneer was replaced by the glint of battle. A warning sounded in Peter's mind. They might still talk their way out of it. Hitting the sergeant wouldn't help. Maybe Hal would know what to do; he had got them into this mess. He wouldn't mind socking him, too. He backed away to the chair where he had left his neatly folded uniform. It was some gratification to note that the sergeant kept his distance.

He and Hal put on their clothes in silence without looking at each other. When they were dressed, the sergeant approached Peter once more and prodded him with his club. "OK, sis. We'll see you get back to your base. Your girl friend here—oh, sorry, sir. You'll be hearing from the provost marshal's office."

"For God's sake, aren't you going to say anything, captain?" Peter pleaded. "We haven't done anything."

"I have the impression that I'd be wasting my time with the sergeant. I'll straighten it out when I get back to the base." Hal was looking sober again and very dashing in his uniform. He addressed the sergeant with the condescension of one accustomed to command. "If you think you have to put in a report, you might get a few things straight. Private Martin and I are old friends. We knew each other before we were in the service, so it's not a question of fraternization. We had a few drinks together, and I decided it wouldn't be wise to drive back so I came here for a little sleep. That's all there is to it."

"I see, sir. I don't guess I have to mention your sneaking past the desk clerk without registering. But how about this being nude in the same bed together and you having his prick in your mouth? How do you want me to put that in the report? Sir."

"He didn't, damn it," Peter burst out. "We were both asleep until you walked in. What happens when you're waked up suddenly? We were both just sort of falling over each other trying to get up."

"Well, maybe my eyesight is failing. Maybe I should put in for retirement." The sneer was firmly fixed on the thin lips. "I sure thought I saw the both of you in the same bed."

"Nobody says you didn't, goddamn it," Peter maintained stoutly. He still wanted to hit the sergeant, but the fact that he was willing to talk was hopeful. "We were both drunk. I went to sleep as soon as we came in. I don't know what happened after that. Maybe he didn't notice there was another bed. Tell them, sir."

"I don't see any particular need to argue it out with the sergeant. However—as Private Martin says, he went to sleep while we were talking. I turned out the light and stumbled around and got into the first bed I came to. Once I was in it, it didn't seem worth the trouble to move. We've slept in the same bed before, when there wasn't another available."

"Of course," Peter confirmed with conviction.

"Well, you tell your story, sis, and I'll tell mine. The court-martial will decide."

Peter's blood froze. His thoughts had been skirting the possibility; to hear the words spoken made him want to cry out with fear and outraged innocence. "Why do you want to talk like that? You're just making trouble for nothing. Why can't you just let it go?"

"Because you're a fucking little pansy, that's why," the sergeant roared. "It sticks out all over you." Peter's feet shifted and his fist lifted again, but the sergeant was prepared for him. He put his club against his chest and shoved. "You try any tricks and you'll get this across the side of your head, and then some. Those fancy little panties you wear. That yellow hair. Your shitty long prick. Decent men don't have pricks like that. Both of you. Excuse me, sir. I don't say all pansies should be shot—waste of ammunition—but there ought to be a place where they're put away so they can't have anything to do with real men. Get a move on, Nelly."

Peter's spirit recoiled. He had rarely been exposed to the world's derision and hostility, and the sergeant's contempt cut into him and brought him close to tears. He struggled against about his sexual tastes in order to bolster the truth about the them, he struggled against the mindless condemnation that suddenly threatened to crush him. "Just a minute," he said with desperate determination. "If you want to make a case out of this, you ought to have some evidence. Why don't you check the towels and bedclothes? If there was any sex going on here, there should be traces."

"You want me to have your stomach pumped out to see how much of his come you've swallowed? Get going."

When he was returned to the base the next morning, after spending the rest of the night on a bench in an MP post, he found that his belongings had already been searched and his letters from Charlie seized. That such deeply personal and precious possessions should be subjected to uncomprehending or hostile scrutiny numbed him at first with despair. None of this must touch Charlie.

There had been a sort of passionate innocence in his enthralled submission to his first lover that had colored all their brief life together. Everything about Charlie represented beauty to him—his body, his face, his nature, his talent, his upright manliness—there was beauty in all of him. Going through the day with him, eating with him, laughing with him, discussing serious matters, walking around town or in the country together, playing, working, it was all wholesome and happy and beautiful. He had grown up well aware of the taboo against homosexuality, but he had never been able to grasp that it could apply to them. It was directed against the habitués of queer bars, the effeminate men who tried to seduce schoolboys, the boys who wore makeup and were out for anything in pants. Even when he had been briefly, to some extent, a part of that world, when Charlie had rejected him and got married, it had never really touched him. He had been promiscuous, but he had gone to bed only with young men who attracted him and who wanted him. There had been nothing dirty about it. He had accepted gifts but they had been given freely and with gratitude. His one act of exhibitionistic masturbation in front of a rich man who afterward became his friend and benefactor had been performed when he was so drunk that it had seemed to have a kind of sexless purity. They had been wretched months, but nothing about them had induced guilt or shame.

For the first time in his life, he had been determined to lie night before and to protect Hal, but he couldn't lie his way around the letters. In a way, he wasn't sorry. It would have been a denial of his love. If he admitted his true nature, his insistence on his innocence the night before would surely be more convincing.

He was summoned to his first interview with a psychiatrist later in the day. The psychiatrist was a neat, efficient-looking, dark, youngish man with thick-rimmed spectacles. His manner was neutral, and he put his questions about the incident at the hotel dryly. He wanted to know more about his friendship with Hal. Peter tread warily. Now that Charlie's letters had entered the case, it wouldn't help Hal to suggest that they had been intimate.

"Didn't Captain Bohlen state that you've shared a bed before?"

"Yes. I'm a bit vague about that. I remember a house party a couple of years ago where the guys had to double up to make room for the girls. There were a lot of us. I don't remember much about it."

"You admit being naked together?"

"Yes."

"You deny that Captain Bohlen committed fellatio with you?"

"What's that?"

The psychiatrist hesitated, looking exasperated. "In the vernacular, cocksucking."

"I absolutely deny it. I was half-asleep and trying to get out of bed. So was Captain Bohlen. We were falling around on top of each other. Maybe my cock looked as if it was near his mouth for a second, but that's all. Do you think we're out of our minds? The MPs were already in the room."

"You mean you would've been prepared for him to commit such an act if you'd been alone with him?"

"I don't mean anything of the sort. He's never given the slightest sign that he'd be interested in that kind of thing. If he had, I wouldn't have let him."

"You wouldn't?" There was a silence as the psychiatrist opened a drawer and put the packet of Charlie's letters on the desk between them.

Peter looked him in the eye. "All right. You know why I wouldn't."

The psychiatrist's manner grew more sympathetic as he questioned Peter about Charlie. As his confidence was won, Peter tried to explain that the very fact of Charlie's existence made his sex life of no more than academic interest to anybody. "I wouldn't touch another guy with a ten-foot pole," he exclaimed fervently.

"Well, it's up to the legal department to decide how to handle the case. I can only advise on the psychological issues. They may want to make it a criminal case and try for a prison sentence."

"Prison," Peter repeated, falling deeper into a state of shock.

"I don't want to alarm you unnecessarily. I'll draw up a statement based on what you've told me. In essence, you're an avowed homosexual. That's grounds for immediate separation from the service."

"But I don't want separation," Peter insisted, rousing himself. "I'm in love with somebody. What difference does it make to the Army if it's a man or a girl?"

"Oh, come now. Surely, even you recognize that there are social issues involved. We've found that homosexuals don't make a satisfactory adjustment to the military environment."

"That's a lot of crap. Is it my fault if Captain Bohlen got drunk and got into the wrong bed? He says himself that's the way it happened. What about my record?" He reiterated his innocence with Hal, he continued to insist that Charlie was irrelevant to the case and that the Army had no legal right to introduce him into it. Neither now nor at any time later did Peter see in the episode an opportunity for a quick release and an early return to Charlie. He had made his commitment; he must honor it if he were to continue to cherish his love and demand respect for it.

He was one of the most popular men in his company. He had performed his duties well and scrupulously. He had prided himself on both counts. Nobody had the right to cast doubt on his ability to conduct himself properly in an admittedly alien atmosphere.

"Well, we don't have to decide anything right now," the psychiatrist concluded. "I'll draw up a statement for you to sign. We'll have another talk in a day or two."

"Shouldn't I have a lawyer?"

"We'll see about that when the time comes."

It was quickly apparent that the story had become public property. Everywhere Peter went, he felt space developing around him. In the shower rooms, the washbasins on either side of him were vacated when he took up his position in front of one. The frequently obscene horseplay under the showers was suspended at his appearance. The men who had been openly flirting with him went out of their way to avoid him. Only the laughing stock of the base, an undisguisedly effeminate, chinless youth was an exception. "Don't let them get you down, doll," he said when he encountered Peter the next day. "You've hit it lucky. You've had that luscious captain and you'll soon be back in civilian drag. What more could a girl want?"

It wasn't a great comfort, but he valued the intention. He went through two days of numb despair, shaken occasionally by spasms of terror as the word "prison" passed through his mind. His second interview with the psychiatrist was shorter and the man's manner had hardened.

"Let me make the position clear. I have a statement here for you to sign. You'll go through the formality of a court-martial and will be dishonorably discharged. You're being let off lightly because we find it lowers morale to have the officers' prestige damaged by a case like this. Captain Bohlen will be allowed to resign his commission. If you were both charged with unnatural acts, his only defense would be drunkenness and his bewilderment at the practiced advances of an experienced homosexual. The sergeant who arrested you has put in his report that he had the impression that you were trying to force your penis into Captain Bohlen's mouth and he was fighting you off. Even if he were acquitted, his usefulness to the Army would be seriously compromised. Drunkenness is never an excuse for an officer. You would probably receive a stiff prison sentence, and the whole thing would leave a nasty taste in a great many mouths. If you really feel the sense of duty you profess, I advise you to sign."

Peter glanced over the statement with eyes that refused to focus. He gathered that it was an admission of a past record of confirmed homosexuality. There was something about having enticed an officer into bed for the purpose of sexual gratification. It wasn't clear to him whether he was supposed to have succeeded.

186

"There's no catch to this?" he asked. His mouth was so dry that it could barely form the words. "You're not getting me to sign and then throw the book at me?"

"I assure you that everybody involved in this is anxious to get it over with as quickly and quietly as possible."

"Can I have my letters back?"

"They'll be returned to you with your discharge, naturally."

He gripped a pen in unfeeling fingers and scribbled his signature and sat back, feeling as if the world as he knew it had ended.

In the few days that preceded his court-martial, the numbness passed and he went a little mad with rage. He waited, hypersensitively alert, for the slightest affront. If anybody had said a derogatory word, he would have felt the full force of Peter's unbalanced physical frustration. He wanted to beat everybody and anybody. In the void that had been created around him there was nobody to strike out at. Everywhere he went, he was on a constant lookout for the sergeant. There was no doubt what he would do if he found him. He would leap at him and kill him with his bare hands, or be killed in the attempt.

When the day came for his cout-martial, he dressed carefully. In immaculate uniform, shaved, scrubbed, his golden hair tamed and neatly arranged, he looked like a romanticized, idealized version of the All-American boy. He knew it, which gave him a certain mad satisfaction. The court took time only to describe him in loathsome terms, which he had never dreamed could be applied to himself. He was a pervert, a sodomite, an unrepentent sexual deviate. He felt as if the filth of the world were being flung at him. He squared his shoulders and lifted his golden head and smiled slightly. He was aware all through the proceedings that the eyes of one of the officer-judges were constantly, insinuatingly, attempting to make contact with his. The world was a cesspool, but he wasn't fit to inhabit it. He was a disgrace to his uniform, a disgrace to his country, everything he had believed in was vile.

Only Charlie's angry, loving loyalty, expressed in his letters, had kept him on an even keel. When they were finally reunited, if Charlie had expressed the slightest doubt about the facts of the case, he would have been swept up in the torrent of Peter's rage against mankind; his almost apologetic solicitude had made him a rock of faith to which Peter had clung.

Now, hurrying through the dangerous night past luminous whitewashed houses, paying for his haste with increasing pain, gladly suffered to spare Charlie a needless moment of anxiety, Peter was amazed at how successfully he had suppresses his memory of that black period. He knew more or less the way it had happened and remembered the worst parts, but there were big gaps in the sequence of events and none of it had the power to hurt him now. The threat that had seemed about to crush him then had failed to materialize; he had rarely been made to feel an outcast in the years that followed.

When he had found himself at last with Charlie once more, his first thought had been to arm himself for survival. His income was barely enough for both of them to live on. He wouldn't hear of Charlie looking for a job again. His painting, which had developed excitingly during his year alone, was an integral part of Peter's vision of making the most of their lives by defying convention. Hs was newly determined never to apply for a job himself; he wouldn't submit to being questioned about his military record or draft status. He augmented their income from capital while he resumed his study of the stock market. Money might be a protection against society's condemnation. He had already been startlingly successful with his investments and now he took to spending some time every day at his broker's, listening to advice and picking up tips.

Charlie's grandmother, who was the only member of his family he cared about deeply and who had banished him because of his liaison with Peter, died suddenly and left Charlie a token ten thousand dollars out of the large fortune that had previously been destined for him. Peter assumed management of the inheritance as a challenge; he couldn't hope to make Charlie as rich as he would have been if he had renounced their love, but he could make a stab at it. He took risks, but he was gambling for high stakes. He was lucky and he was shrewd, and by the time the war ended he had built up a modest fortune. All along, he had been taking courses at Columbia with the aim of becoming an art dealer; now he was in a position to launch himself. He had learned that nobody worried about his sex life when self-interest was involved, although on a couple of occasions people had attempted to use it as a sort of blackmail to gain an advantage over him. He had seen to it that they regretted it. With the opportunity to erect barriers around their relationship that money provided, his bitterness passed and he slowly recovered his old, easy, cheerful responses to life. If the experience had left a hardness in him, it was the hardness that everyone who makes demands of life must acquire: in his case, a hard proprietary determination to protect and defend his love, buried beneath his soft, adoring submission to his lover.

After hurrying through dark streets for what seemed like hours, he came to a cross street with a few lights along it. It looked familiar. Wasn't the port just beyond? His spirits rose and he put on another little burst of speed. In another few minutes, he came rushing out into the square that fronted the port. The boat was there. He stopped to catch his breath. Charlie must have been watching for him; he called Peter's name.

"Come here," he called back and waited. Charlie came running down the gangplank to him. Peter grabbed his arm as his eyes widened at the first sight of his face and led him off into shadow at the side of the square.

"For God's sake, what's happened to you?" Charlie demanded, his voice rough with anxiety. "I've been worried sick."

"I know. I'm sorry." Peter stopped as soon as they were in deep shadow. "Is my face a mess?"

"Jesus! Poor darling baby. Tell me."

"You should see the other guys." Peter laughed through almost immobile lips. He told his story, having difficulty forming some of the words.

"If they just wanted to rob you, why did they take you to that house?" Charlie demanded when he had finished. "It doesn't make any sense."

"I know. That's what I kept wondering. I think sex must've been part of it right from the beginning. I get the impression that it's accepted here in a casual sort of way. You know, just horsing around with an orgasm thrown in. They seemed to take it for granted that I'd play along with it. The bastards. It wasn't like that with the one called Yanni. He really wanted the works. Maybe he had to let his pals have their fun before he took over."

"Then why beat you up, for God's sake?"

"They didn't." Peter laughed painfully. "I beat them up. They didn't seem to know what to do when I fought back. The eye was an accident. The Yanni one didn't get me in the mouth until

I'd let him have a couple of good ones. It was amazing how he just sort of folded up at my feet."

Charlie caught the satisfaction in the way he said it. "Christ Almighty, I'll kill them. Where are they? Do you know where you were?"

"I could get pretty near it. Everything looked alike in the dark. I'm not sure."

"We've got to find the police. Do you think you ought to see a doctor?"

"What kind of a doctor would we find around here? Anyway it's only a black eye and a split lip. Maybe Martha has some stuff on board. Don't tell the Kingsleys about the sex part. They'll think it happened just because I'm queer."

"They damn well better not." Charlie took his hands. He felt something odd about them and lifted them to the light. "My God. They're all swollen."

"Sure. Battling Pete. I wish you could've seen me. I was really something when I got going."

Charlie put an arm around him and hugged him. "You're something all right, mate. God, I was glad to see you. I didn't see how you could get run over around here, but I imagined everything else. Come on. We'll get you fixed up and then we'll go to the police."

"Don't bother. I took care of them. I don't think they'll try messing around with pretty foreigners again."

"You're suddenly driving everybody crazy. I shouldn't be so used to you. You've probably just come into full bloom, and I haven't even noticed it."

They laughed while Peter thought of Jeannot again. He was glad his face was messed up. Charlie couldn't suspect him of being acquiescent this time. "I guess I just look like a pushover," he said. "Goldilocks. It's just as well I went to all those military schools. God knows, they left the mind untouched, but I do know how to hit people."

They reached the foot of the gangplank with their arms around each other. Martha appeared at the head of it as Peter started up. When he came nearer, she gasped and put her hands to her face.

"Oh, my poor darling," she moaned. "What happened? Come here. We've got to do something about you."

190

Charlie was behind him pushing him up the gangplank with his hands on his hips. When they stepped out onto the narrow afterdeck, he stayed beside him with a hand on his shoulder and lifted Peter's arm in the gesture of victory.

"Three thugs jumped him. He beat the hell out of them. Isn't he fantastic?" Pride rang in Charlie's voice. "Wait'll you see his hands."

"But it must hurt," Martha exclaimed. "I've got things that should help. We'll take care of you first and then I want to hear all about it."

"Here. Just sit here, baby." Charlie guided him to one of the cockpit benches and seated him. "I'll get you a good stiff drink while Martha attends to the first aid."

They went below, leaving Peter in a daze of exhilaration and delight. Charlie had used the endearment in public again. It was more healing than anything Martha could do for him; he was no longer aware of pain. He sprawled back on the bench and felt like a conquering hero. Charlie returned with a whisky and a bundle that turned out to be crushed ice wrapped in a dish-cloth.

"Martha says to put this on your eye. Take a good swallow of this first." Charlie sat beside him while he took a long gulp of the strong drink. Peter applied the icepack and rested the hand holding the glass on Charlie's thigh. It was the first act of public physical intimacy with Charlie that he had initiated, and he left his hand where it was when Martha appeared with a basin.

"Finish your drink and then bathe your hands in this," she said.

Charlie held his hand for a moment as if to indicate that he liked having it there and then lifted it to Peter's mouth and rested it lightly on his wrist while Peter drained the glass. He took the glass and slid his arm around him.

"I'll hold that on your eye." He cradled Peter's head in the crook of his arm and held the icepack while Martha put the basin on his lap. Peter immersed his hands in warm liquid that smelled medicinal. Martha sat on the other side of him and began to swab his mouth gently with a warm cloth. He was a knight attended by squires.

"It must have bled a lot," Martha said tenderly. "It's already beginning to form a scab. I'll put some penicillin on it and then we'll have to let nature take its course. He won't be able to eat the sausages I've got for you."

"Soup would be good, wouldn't it?" Charlie suggested. "How about soft-boiled eggs? We could spoon 'em into him."

Peter sensed a solidarity between them, which, through Charlie, included him. There was something parental in their treatment of him, soothing and cozy. It struck him as appropriate that Jack shouldn't be with them. H e was probably asleep already.

"Darling Peter," Martha said, giving his mouth a final dab. "I can't bear to see that beautiful mouth all swollen. I'll open a can of something. Clear bouillon is probably best. He shouldn't move his mouth any more than necessary. Make him give his hands a good soaking." She rose and left them.

"Everything's beginning to feel much better," Peter said. "Thanks, darling. You're being so damn nice to me."

"Why shouldn't we be?"

Peter had intended his thanks for Charlie but he wasn't surprised that he spoke for Martha, as well. They had ministered to him as a couple. "She's really sweet, isn't she?"

"She is. She's come through damn well."

"Talk about driving people crazy. You're doing all right."

Charlie chuckled. "Whatever she feels, she'd never be a nuisance. I've never known a girl like her."

"You tempted?"

"Maybe. Every now and then, when she makes it so obvious what she wants. You wouldn't mind, would you?"

"Not really, so long as you don't leave me out in the cold."

Charlie put a hand on his arm and stroked it. "Don't worry. I doubt if anything will happen, but if it did, it wouldn't have anything to do with us."

"That's silly. Anything you do has everything to do with us, but I know what you mean. I'm hardly the one to talk."

"*That's* silly. It's all forgotten, baby. We're off on a whole new phase."

"What—" New phases could be dangerous, but it was thrilling to hear the note of total forgiveness in his voice. It carried them a step beyond their talk in Capri. He longed to hear more about the new phase, but Martha was coming up the companionway.

As she approached, she saw Charlie's arm encircling Peter's

shoulders so that he could hold the ice on his eye. She saw his other hand moving idly, caressingly, along Peter's arm. They were so beautiful together. She was filled with tenderness for them. Charlie's gentle, loving care of his friend sometimes made her knees feel as if they would give way. His touching him and holding him so openly in front of her admitted her to an enchanted circle of love. She put the food she was carrying on the other bench.

"Now then." She took the basin and emptied it over the side and handed Peter a towel. "Did that seem to help?"

Peter flexed his fingers. "A lot. Thanks, lovey."

"I'll heat another batch for later." She held out a plate of food and a bowl of soup to them. Peter took the icepack from Charlie and they drew apart. All of Martha's attention was for Peter. She sat beside him. "I just warmed up the bouillon. I didn't want your mouth to get burned."

"It's perfect. You're a dream."

"The eggs will be ready in a minute."

"Wine, too, please ma'am," Charlie said.

"Oh, of course. I'll get it. I don't want Peter to talk, but you've got to tell me what happened."

They spent another hour or two on deck, with Peter very much the center of attention. They discussed a truncated version of the incident. Martha came and went with salves and healing baths. Charlie and Peter got a bit drunk on wine. They all went below together.

Martha snapped off the deck light. "Jack said we didn't have to show a riding light here".

"Save the batteries," Peter and Charlie chorused, and they all laughed. Martha kissed them both on the cheek in the roomy saloon cabin and wished them goodnight and went forward. Charlie stripped down to his shorts.

"I hope you're not going to be hot in that jersey, baby. We can't get it over your head without hurting you."

"No. It'll be all right." Peter pulled off his pants and went to the head and returned and stretched out on his bunk. Charlie turned off the one dim light and went and knelt beside him. He kissed him on the forehead and on the uninjured eye and on the side of his face.

"I want so badly to kiss you," Peter whispered.

"Soon, slugger," Charlie said softly, not bothering to whisper. "I want a lot more than that." He felt Peter's hand on him, lifting his sex out of its pouch and holding it as it lengthened and hardened. It was a bold initiative of the sort that Peter had never taken; Charlie smiled to himself. He moved his hand down under the sheet to Peter's already rigid sex as his own rose against the side of the bunk. He nuzzled Peter's ear. "I don't mind if they find us like this, but I don't particularly want to show them the works. Squeeze over." He lifted himself onto the bunk and gathered Peter into his arms and covered them with the sheet. Peter pulled him close and they lay together. Their sexes straining against each other.

"Oh God," Peter whispered, his heart racing. "I can't believe it. I've wanted you here for weeks and haven't even dared think it."

Charlie worked the jersey up under his armpits and kissed his nipples. He hunched down and kissed his sex, while Peter thrashed about in his arms and tugged at his hair.

"No. Don't, darling," he whispered. "Please. We mustn't."

Charlie straightened and they lay together again. "I don't care who sees us," Charlie murmured, "but I guess you're right."

"Anyway, I want it all. Stay here with me." There was an uncharacteristic imperative in the urgent whisper.

Charlie smiled again in the dark and stroked his hair. "Anything you say, baby. Go to sleep, sweet love. You've had a rough evening."

"I'll say. I really beat the shit out of those guys." His sex gave a little leap as he said it and he ran his hand over Charlie's buttocks and pulled him closer. Charlie was still smiling as he kissed his forehead again and continued to stroke his hair. Something seemed to fall into place in the grand design he was nurturing on the edge of his consciousness.

Charlie woke up at dawn and extricated himself carefully without waking Peter and went to his own bunk. It wasn't likely that either of the Kingsleys had come through yet, but it didn't matter. A captain's rights were extensive, including sleeping with the crew. He pulled the sheet over himself and slept another hour.

They were all up early. Jack was facetious about Peter's ruined face as they gathered in the cockpit for coffee.

"You look like a real sailor now, Peter boy. Shore leaves. Bar-room brawls. It's a wonder you didn't bring a wench on board with you."

"Oh, I did. She was a shy maiden. I hustled her ashore before you could get your hands on her."

"Wise lad." Jack laughed. "You know, the funny thing is I actually thought for a minute you had somebody in your bunk with you when I came above during the night."

"Who says I didn't? You have to be pretty spry to keep up with the slugger."

Charlie glanced at Martha and found her eyes on him and winked. Peter took his arm and pulled him down onto the seat beside him.

"Isn't my beauty blinding? I just took a good look at myself. Have you ever seen anything like the colors?" His eye was in fact an astonishing variety of somber purples and maroons, but considerably less swollen. He could speak more easily. His hands were stiff, but not very painful; he couldn't handle the lines but the wheel wouldn't be too difficult for him. He was nominated helmsman of the day. They were soon out and Charlie and Jack had the sails up and they were headed into the rising sun.

After all the days in open sea, Charlie expected this landlocked sail to be a let-down, but he had not yet learned to reckon with these waters. The Gulf of Corinth opened out majestically as they advanced into it, contained by high distant peaks that still bore traces of snow. No land was visible ahead of them. Within an hour, a southwesterly wind had risen and continued to stiffen all through the morning. A heavy sea began to roll in behind them. They were getting the wind very nearly on their beam, ideal for sailing, and Charlie trimmed the sheets for maximum speed. The sea was coming from a slightly different quarter, lifting them and sending them hurtling into deepening troughs, but Peter skillfully held *Cassandra* steady, and they were taking on very little water. Charlie went careening aft and dropped beside Peter at the wheel. They beamed at each other.

"How about this for racing?" Charlie demanded. "It's the best yet."

"It's like riding a bucking bronco."

"You're doing beautifully, baby. Let me take over for a while. Give your hands a rest."

"I don't need to, but help yourself."

They shifted on the seat and Charlie took the wheel. Peter put his arm around him and held him as he had been held by Charlie so often in the last couple of weeks. He felt very daring for a moment, but there was none of the stiffening in Charlie that he was accustomed to when he made a move toward him in public.

"How about us last night?" Peter laughed without letting his lips move. "I guess Jack saw us."

"Sure. So what?"

"You're making me so damn proud." He could talk about it now. Charlie's altered behavior no longer seemed a fluke, an erratic aftermath to Jean-Claude but a new, fixed pattern he could count on. They could talk about it and make it their own. "You know I've always wanted it like this, people taking us for what we are—a couple, lovers—married, goddamn it."

"It's about time you have it the way you want it. Just wait— Good God! Hold onto your hat. Here comes a big one."

Peter had time to glance astern at what appeared to be a wall of water rising above them and then they were lifted giddily and held for a breathtaking moment before they rushed like a surf-board down the side of the wave. Charlie spun the wheel one way and then the other to hold his course. Their downward plunge stopped with a jolt and the bow lifted, scooping up sea and sending it hurtling back along the deck. There was a crash below.

"Is this going to be as bad as the first night?" Peter asked.

Charlie looked around at the crystalline sky and the sparkling, white-capped sea and shook his head. "This isn't a storm. It's just a good blow. It's amazing the sea can get so big in here. The wind's actually letting up a bit."

Jack came struggling up the companionway and stood braced against the cabin housing. "Hadn't we better get some of this sail down?" he called.

"Are you nuts? We're really moving."

"I don't like heeling this much."

"Boats are meant to heel, Jack. Do you want to turn on the motor?"

"At the rate we're going, we'll be at the canal just after dark."

"Anything wrong with that?"

"I've heard it's difficult to spot. You know I don't like being in against unfamiliar land at night."

"I've checked the pilot book. Lights will make it easier to find. The wind's not going to hold much longer, anyway."

"If you say so."

Jack lingered a little longer and then went below again. Peter realized that he was still holding Charlie.

Martha brought them food, looking worried. "Is everything all right?" she asked.

"Everything's perfect, except that it's not going to last much longer," Charlie assured her.

Her expression immediately cleared. Relieved of anxiety, she realized what had caused the little wave of distaste she had felt when she had joined them: for the first time, Peter had been holding Charlie. It struck her as inappropriate; it diminished Charlie's masculinity. She was glad the food gave Peter something else to do with his hands. She sat with them, wearing the bikini that always made Charlie want to undress her so that he could really study her body. Peter made them laugh at his efforts to eat without hurting his mouth.

The sun was moving down in the west when, as Charlie had expected, the wind began to die. Low-lying land was dimly visible ahead. The sea remained heavy so that they rolled and tossed as progress ceased. Jack came up for a turn on the wheel and Charlie sent Peter below for a nap.

"I suppose you know where we are," he said to Jack.

Jack checked the mileage log and looked ahead. "About fifteen miles west of the canal."

"So near and yet so far. Listen Jack, just once, couldn't we use the goddamn engine? This almost qualifies as getting into harbor. A couple of hours on the motor would get us there. Otherwise, we won't get through till morning. It's going to be hell wallowing around out here."

"The sea's bound to calm down soon. Just hold your horses. I've been planning to go through in the morning all along."

"Jesus! We have to waste twelve hours just so you can follow your plan?"

"That's about it. I know it's hard for you to accept, but this is my boat and when it comes to the motor we do things my way."

"Even when it's the wrong way. God! Wanting to shorten sail the one time we're really zooming."

"I didn't insist, but there are certain things I will insist about. While we're on the subject, I won't have the boat turned into a male brothel. Stay out of Peter's bunk."

"Brothel?" Charlie repeated calmly. "Do you think we pay each other? What's the matter, Jack? You jealous? Why don't you offer Peter money? I'd love to see what's left of you afterward."

"Just remember. I've warned you."

"I see. Well then, let me tell you this. I'll sleep with Peter whenever I damn well please. I've given it some thought and I've decided that whatever Peter and I do together can't hurt anybody else."

"Good lord, man, haven't you any sense of decency?"

"Does it really upset you so to see two guys sleeping together? Maybe you should see a doctor."

"What if I'd come through when you weren't sleeping?"

"Do you think we'd let you see us making love? It's too good for any audience."

"Don't you care what Martha thinks of you?"

"Why don't you ask her what she thinks of us? OK? If you get us to hotels in the evening the way you said you would, it won't be a problem. The bunk's too narrow to make it a habit, anyway, but any time I want to sleep with my mate, I will. Understood?"

"Christ! You really think you're God, don't you?"

"No, just a guy who's learning to get along in the world. You're the one who made a big thing about my being queer. Well, now you've seen me in bed with Peter. God forbid you shouldn't be able to fit all the little pegs into all the little holes in your mind."

"I think we've had about enough of this conversation."

"Fine. I accept your apology for the brothel bit. If you're not going to be a good sport and turn on the motor, I might as well get some sleep. Alone, in case you're consumed by curiosity." He smiled cheerfully and rose and careened across the deck to the campionway.

They were all on deck at daybreak for their passage, under power, through the long, straight, awesome ditch of the canal. By noon, they were tying up in Turkolimino, the yacht harbor near Piraeus. Jack's navigation had paid off; they had sailed right up to the entrance to the canal even though it was still invisible when they were only a couple of miles from it; they found the small yacht harbor before Charlie had been able to pick out the great port of Piraeus in the jumble of steep, built-up coastline. He had expected the Acropolis to be a conspicuous landmark. He could find no trace of it.

They were still furling the sails and making the deck shipshape when they received a ceremonial visit from officials who seemed little interested in the ship's papers but wished to underline the fact that they were the first American yacht in Greek waters since the war. A delegate from the Royal Yacht Club appeared to offer them free use of the club's facilities during their stay. Jack was beaming. Because the formalities were short, nothing prevented Charlie and Peter from ducking below to dress, put some clothes in a bag and gather up a considerable accumulation of laundry. When they returned to the deck, Martha and Jack were waiting in the cockpit with drinks. They all drank and congratulated themselves on their successful voyage. They were to have two days of independent sight-seeing before setting off into the Aegean. Martha looked at Charlie so longingly that he agreed to come down to the boat at noon the next day and perhaps go on an excursion with the Kingsleys. Peter unabashedly took his hand.

"Come on, Champ. I'm going to spend all afternoon in a tub."

After extensive farewells, Charlie and Peter went ashore and found a battered taxi and told the driver to take them to Athens. Saying the word made a tingle run down Charlie's spine. He crouched forward at the window, buffeted by blasts of hot air as they clattered over a corrugated road, and continued his search for the Acropolis. When he saw it at last, the Parthenon lying parched and serene on a low hill, he experienced a shock of recognition, as if he had known it always. He sat back and gripped Peter's hand.

"My God!" he exclaimed. "There it is. This trip's really making sense."

"I'll say. We're home. These people knew what life was all about. Men loved each other and women had children. If things were like that nowadays, even I might be straight." He still couldn't move his lips when he laughed.

199

As soon as they were alone in a big old-fashioned room in the Grande Bretagne, Peter began to shed his clothes.

"I'm going to spend an hour in the bathroom. Let's order some lunch up here. After that—well, guess what. How marvelous of you to ask for a double bed."

Charlie hadn't exactly asked. The clerk had offered them the choice of twin beds or a double and Charlie had said that a double would do. When he was naked, Peter darted over to him and gave him a quick hug.

"Damn my mouth. Consider yourself kissed," he said and went frisking on into the bathroom. Charlie called down for cold lobster and a salad and cold white wine. He went to a long shuttered window and peered out. The Parthenon was there under a blazing sun, the ruin of it looking as if it had been planned with great precision. They were in Athens and they were approaching a moment that he felt he had been preparing for, unconsciously at first, ever since St. Tropez.

An electric fan on the bureau stirred the still air. He stood in its draft and thoughtfully began to remove his clothes. He had closely observed Peter's every move for the last two days and he had sensed in him a new, hardy self-assertiveness that he related to the episode with Jean-Claude. That hadn't been an isolated phenomenon, but the expression of a healthy, emerging need. The fight had solidified it. Something in Peter was struggling free of the domination he had sought from Charlie all these years. The way Peter had told him to order lunch was a detail, but symptomatic. A few weeks ago he would have asked if they could have it in the room. Charlie knew he could use his body to widen Peter's freedom, and perhaps his own. He didn't know where this was leading, but he felt sure that it would pave the way for even more crucial developments. Now that the moment was near, he looked forward to it with more excitement than he had expected. He chuckled to himself. What would he be up to next?

He put on a dressing gown and, when the knock on the door came, admitted their lunch. He was tempted to join Peter in the bathroom, but resisted it. Things might happen and he didn't want his plan disrupted. He twirled the wine in the ice bucket and waited.

Peter came out eventually, wearing a towel around his waist.

His hair was darkened by water and slicked down. His eye and mouth were no longer disfiguring but curiously provocative, a blemish that underlined his beauty.

"I'm just about the cleanest friend you'll ever have," he announced. "Hey. Lunch. Lobster. Marvelous."

Charlie went to him and removed the towel and kissed his neck and ran his hands over his cool skin. "I won't be long," he said.

"No, don't be, beautiful. I feel as if it's been months."

Charlie shaved and took a quick shower and returned, wearing his dressing gown. Peter was stretched out on the bed wearing his. He sprang up.

"Bed is sublime. That poor lobster doesn't know how close he's come to being completely ignored."

They sat at table and ate and laughed together. Peter's eyes flirted as if they'd just met. Charlie had stopped thinking about his plan; he quite simply wanted him, in exactly the way he had been intending to have him. No wonder everybody's been tearing him to pieces, he thought.

"We're not going to order coffee, are we?" Peter asked when they had picked the lobster clean.

"Not unless we let the waiter serve us in bed."

Peter flashed him a lopsided smile. "I'm about ten times more in love with you than I've ever been. I didn't think it was possible. I'll go get ready."

Charlie put a hand over his. "No. I will. It's my turn, baby."

"What do you mean?"

"Just that. I want you that way."

"You what?" Peter looked thunderstruck.

"Of course. Upside down and sideways. I've been thinking about it for days."

"But I couldn't!" Peter expostulated.

"Why couldn't you? You have before."

"Once. A hundred years ago when I didn't know what I was doing."

"You could with Jean-Claude."

Peter's expression immediately became guarded. Perhaps the punishment wasn't over, after all. "Why do you bring him up?"

Charlie laughed. "It's all right, baby. Honest. We can talk about it. We don't have to pretend it didn't happen."

"I don't want to pretend anything if you understand I hate myself for it."

"You shouldn't. I'll bet you could have with that Greek you beat up, too."

Peter stared at him. "You're spooky. How do you know that? It was sort of a sadistic thing, only for a second, but you're right. I could have, if I'd really wanted to, if you see what I mean."

"Sure. So what's wrong with me?"

"But you're different. You're you. I'm dying for you to have me the way you always do. It doesn't make sense any other way." Peter's heart was beating fast. He couldn't believe that Charlie really meant it. They hadn't had time to talk about the "new phase." Was this what he had meant? He felt danger as acutely as if he were in a runaway car. "Please, my darling. Please take me. I want you so much."

"Same here. It's taken me ten years, for God's sake. I want to be had by a prizefighter." He rose and went around behind Peter and put his hands inside his dressing gown and ran them over his chest and down over his abdomen. Peter shifted slightly in his chair and his sex sprang up from between his legs. Charlie held it with both hands and laughed. "What a fraud. What do you mean, you couldn't?"

"It's not that. I mean—well, I'll probably come before I even get started."

"Then we'll start all over again."

Peter dropped his head back against Charlie and held his arms in place around him with his hands while he tried to assimilate this overwhelming proposal. Could it be as uncomplicated as Charlie was making it sound? A simple desire? Whatever the dangers, he was amazed at his growing urge to perform the act. He wanted to take him. He imagined bearing down into him, compelling the submission of his body, and his heart raced faster. "Oh, God, I'm so excited I can hardly breathe. You really mean it? Do you think I'm long enough to do it the way you do it with me?"

"Did you do it that way with Jean-Claude?"

"Of course not. I just—you know, in the time-honored fashion."

"That's the way I want it. I want you to fuck me, baby, and not think about my cock or anything else. Really take me for yourself. I'll be better than your French boyfriend."

"Jesus! Don't, darling. I'm about to come right now."

"Hold everything." He released Peter and grabbed the table and gave it a shove toward the door. He pushed it into the hall and locked the door and went to the bathroom. When he returned, he was naked. His sex was heavy and extended, not yet erect. Peter had put the chairs back against the wall and was pulling the covers off the bed. Charlie's eyes followed the curve of his buttocks and his sex began to lift. Peter turned and waited beside the bed, watching the approach of the jutting, heavily swinging, hardening flesh. He reached for it and completed its erection with his hands.

"Oh, God, I can't stand not having it. We're not making any sense."

Charlie had some lubricant in his hand and applied it. "We've carried on enough about my cock," he said. "Yours is sensational. You want me, don't you baby?

"*Want* you. Christ! You're driving me crazy. I've never felt anything like it."

Charlie laughed. "That's wonderful. Come on. Rape me. I'm going to be the best fuck you've ever had." He dropped onto the bed, pulling Peter after him by his sex. He lay on his side with his back turned and waited for Peter to move in against him. He guided the sex to him and moved his hips to take it. Peter cried out as he began his entry.

"I told you. Oh Christ! I'm going to come."

"No you're not, baby. Take a deep breath. Now. Just let me have it. Don't worry about hurting me. I can take you." There was a moment of difficulty, but Charlie worked his hips to get them through it and Peter lunged into him. His breath caught at the unfamiliar pain.

Peter's chest was heaving and his breath was coming in harsh gasps. "I'm inside you. Oh, Christ. Is it all right?"

"I'll say. You're in charge now. Take me, baby."

"Will I ever!" He rolled Charlie over onto his stomach and bit his shoulders as he lifted himself to his knees astride Charlie's thighs. He straightened and pulled Charlie's hips to him so that his sex shot deeper into him. Charlie felt the strong grip in his hands and thrilled to it.

"Yes, baby! Christ, you're fantastic." He propped his forehead on his crossed arms and surrendered himself to the hard shaft of flesh that was beginning to drive into him. The pain passed and he was gripped by the excitement in this reversal of roles. Peter's excitement fed his own. He was taking possession of his body exultantly, using it demandingly for his pleasure. He shuddered with delight as Peter grasped his shoulders and slowly rode into him until he felt that there was no area in him that hadn't been invaded. He cried out with joy as Peter completed the penetration with a final thrust that locked him between straining thighs. This was a man, reveling in his male prowess. Charlie felt a deep identification with him that went beyond union and became unity. He was so stirred by the power in him that he felt himself approaching orgasm.

"Christ Almighty," he cried incredulously. "You're making me come."

"Oh, God. Yes. Me too." Peter's hands were all over him and then his fingers dug into his hips as he drove into him with long, unsparing strokes. Charlie's hips lifted to receive him and their bodies moved in frenzied harmony. They laughed and shouted as the tension built up between them.

"Christ, yes. You're incredible," Charlie gasped. "I didn't know. Oh, please—" He broke off with a great strangled shout as his body was shaken by the spasms of his orgasm.

Peter flung his arms around him and clung to his back and shouted, and shouted again, and Charlie knew that he was streaming into him. He fell out flat, Peter still clinging to his back, and their bodies leaped and jerked together in the aftermath of orgasm. They lay still at last. Peter made a move to withdraw, but Charlie held him.

"No. Stay. I like you there."

"Really?" Peter's voice was shallow and spent. "I'll never understand you. I can't believe it. You really wanted me to, didn't you?"

Charlie chuckled. "That's the impression I hoped to give."

A spurt of laughter broke from Peter. It made his sex leap up. "How marvelous. Next time, I won't huff and puff so much and be so awkward."

"Christ. If that was awkward, you must be something when you're in form. I wonder who else you've been practicing with."

Peter's laughter rang with delight. "Am I really good? Next time, we won't come so quickly. I wanted it to go on and on."

204

"Jesus. You do—on and on inside me. What a cock. It feels a mile long." He worked obscure muscles and they both laughed.

Peter pressed himself against his back. His sex stirred again. "Imagine what yours feels like. Mmm. See what happens just thinking about it."

"Oh, Slugger baby. I'm stunned by you. I didn't know I could feel so much a part of you." His hand found Peter's head and he twined his hair around his fingers.

"Darling. Darling. Charlie darling," Peter crooned. "Feel what you do to me. I didn't know it was possible so soon after. Do you really want me to again?"

"As if I could stop you. It's a mile long again. What a guy. Go on. Make me feel a part of you some more."

Their discovery of unfamiliar aspects of each other stamped Athens with magic. They strolled about it later hand-in-hand, arm-in-arm, arms around shoulders, oblivious to the admiring stares of the populace, seeing wonder and beauty everywhere in the shabby little town. Although they were almost exactly the same height, Peter had never felt as tall as Charlie. Now he towered and looked into his eyes from a giddy height. He handled him with the possessive confidence that had hitherto been Charlie's prerogative. When they repeated the act of love that night, Peter was still thrilled by his ability to perform it so successfully, but it confirmed his suspicion that he could feel natural and complete only when their positions were reversed. Something in the core of him yearned to be possessed. He felt like a child with a new toy. The novelty of it was breathtaking and he wanted more, but he knew the time would come when he would want to resume their accustomed roles. Just thinking about it brought the peace he had always known in Charlie's arms.

Charlie was fascinated by the dislocation he was causing in their relationship; the satisfaction of it for him was not only sexual but creative. He was providing a whole new base for Peter's personality. He had never been effeminate in manner, but there had been a softness that was overlaid now by a new aggressive little swagger. Charlie was introducing him to his masculinity. It brought them closer and yet placed a distance between them, the distance of independence. For the first time, he felt in Peter a readiness to face the world on his own. Therein lay the freedom he had been thinking about. It opened up all sorts of possibilities, which could be included in his grand design.

They slept late the next morning and they were so eager for each other, so absorbed in each other that Charlie forgot his promise to Martha, and they didn't return to the boat until late in the afternoon. By then, all that they had crowded into their time ashore made them feel as if they had been away so long that they wouldn't have been surprised to find it gone. It was there, and Martha was so uncomplicatedly delighted to see them that Charlie didn't feel guilty for having failed to keep their appointment.

She immediately noticed the change in them. She felt it first in Peter. There was a light in his eyes when he looked at her, a firmness in his touch when they embraced that made her aware for the first time of his sexual attraction. He was so stunning physically that she was surprised she hadn't felt it before. It couldn't intrude on her passion for Charlie, but Peter made her feel feminine now instead of merely maternal. She no longer found it distasteful when he put his hand on Charlie's shoulder. They both struck her as superbly male.

When they had greeted each other and kissed chastely and all talked at once for several minutes, Martha went below to get drinks. Jack came out on deck looking more a country-club type than the sea dog they had become accustomed to. He was wearing slacks and a sports shirt. He greeted Peter expansively and was cordial to Charlie. He surveyed Peter's face.

"That's clearing up nicely, sport. The girls will be swooning over you again in another couple of days. We're celebrities. A couple of reporters have been down. Everybody's being very helpful at the club. We've been invited to dinner tonight by the Prime Minister, or the ex-Prime Minister. I'm afraid I'm not up on Greek politics."

Martha brought the drinks and they settled down in the cockpit. They discussed their sight-seeing—apparently they had all been at the Acropolis within an hour of each other the afternoon before—and moved on to plans for departure the following morning. Martha began to be aware that there was something different about Charlie but she couldn't quite place it. Was there a new decisiveness in his eye when he looked at her or was she just imagining it? Its possible significance made her light-headed and she drank her drink faster than she knew was good for her.

"I've been getting some very interesting pointers from the characters here," Jack said. "It seems there's a very fine temple at Aegina, but it's away from the regular port, above a fairly deserted bay. There probably isn't much in the way of accommodations for you guys."

"Aegina? That's pretty much where the Peloponnesian wars started," Charlie said with interest. "Is that near here?"

"Sure. It's just off to the south. You can see it. It seems we came past Salamis, too, yesterday morning, but I was so busy finding this place I didn't notice. We're right where everything started. Well, anyway, the other possibility is an island called Poros we can make in a day's run. They say it has a good hotel. It's up to you to decide if we skip Aegina."

Charlie glanced at Peter and started to speak, but Peter was ahead of him. "I'll tell you what I think, Jack," he said. "We've had a long sail and it was great, but I'd like to start doing the way you said—putting in every night and going to hotels. At least, for the next couple of weeks. Maybe later, when we're getting closer to the end of our trip, we'll want to skip around more. What do you say, Champ?" Peter put his hand on his knee and looked at him hopefully.

"Right, Slugger," Charlie said with a smile. "We can always take a look at Aegina on the way back."

"Well, that's settled," Jack said with no sign of displeasure. "We can throw the watch schedule overboard. We'll be running a cruise boat from now on."

"How heavenly," Martha said delightedly, pouring a second drink before Peter and Charlie were halfway through their first. "That's the way I really like it. We've been hearing about so many marvelous places to see."

They parted soon after for their last night in Athens. Charlie laughed when they had moved off from the boat. "You might as well have told him we like to sleep together."

"Well, we do. Did you mind?"

"Of course not. As a matter of fact, I *have* told him."

"Really?"

"He told me to stay out of your bunk. I said he mustn't expect the impossible, or words to that effect."

"We're getting pretty sassy. Do you think the gods will slap us down?"

"If I know the gods they're on our side. If a seagull starts making passes at you, look out. It'll be Zeus in disguise. You know, in my madder moments, I wonder if it's possible that Jack has his eye on you."

"Please. Spare me your gruesome fantasies. Not possibly. I'd know it if he did." They joked and laughed together and found a taxi to take them back to the Grande Bretagne.

They were off early the next morning, all sails hanging limply, on a flat and hazy sea. Jack gave them a course that would carry them past the western tip of Aegina. They drifted. Every now and then, the wake from a freighter rocked them wildly. Charlie studied the land around them, but couldn't make heads or tails of it. There were islands everywhere and hazy promontories and land masses that were part of the mainland. It was hard to tell them apart. They drifted while Charlie reduced his vision of the past to its real visible scale. Here, great empires had risen and fallen, navies had clashed, armies had marched, momentous events that in Charlie's mind required huge canvases to reenact had all taken place within spitting distance of each other. Just over his right shoulder, the majestic power of Persia had been challenged and defeated at Salamis, making way for the rise of Athens and the creation of a state that still existed. The hazy finger of land ahead of them that was Aegina had been important enough to decide the fate of generations of Greeks. It made antiquity seem very cozy. The scale was human. It must have been marvelous, he thought, to have the known world so near at hand. No wonder men became leaders and heroes when they were younger than he was now, and rushed happily to their death before they were forty. Death. There must have been much to be said for a quick, strenuous life when the world and its wonders were so intimately available. He felt a yearning to stretch experience, to live and die intensely, regardless of consequences.

A land breeze whispered in from behind them and they began to drift with more purpose. He remembered that they had taken on ice and called to Martha and Peter who were sunning themselves forward. When they sat up, he made a gesture of drinking and left the wheel untended while he ran below to get cold beer for all of them. Jack was sitting at his chart table busily doing something with his papers. When he returned to the deck, Peter and Martha were sitting in the cockpit. He took the beer back to them. When he handed Martha her glass, their fingers touched and they exchanged a glance, his eyes affectionate and amused, hers undisguisedly adoring. He took a sip of the beer and moaned. "God! How have we managed without this? Ambrosia."

He studied the top of her bikini where the swelling, pale flesh of her breasts met the rich suntan of her shoulders, and wanted to tell her to go forward and get tan all over. He didn't, but it bothered him esthetically. He couldn't help thinking how much prettier she would be naked without white patches. Not that it was any concern of his. Unless. Perhaps. The intensity of her adoration demanded a place in his grand design.

They drank more beer and got quite giddy under the sun. When Martha brought them an early lunch, they were lying off Aegina and the breeze was beginning to shift around to the south. When it steadied at last, it was moderate and Charlie knew they would be lucky if it lasted the afternoon, but he optimistically trimmed the sheets for a real sail. Peter eased the helm up close to the wind. Jack came above and gave them some landmarks to beat their way toward. They didn't appear to be approaching an island but a long, unbroken line of mainland coast. Peter was learning to sail Charlie's way, in small-boat-racing style, and they had a lively afternoon tacking into the unreliable wind. As they worked their way in closer to land, the wind shifted more to the west and freshened and for almost an hour they had a brisk run for the saddle of a mountain Jack had pointed out to them. It ended abruptly in total calm. Jack came above again.

"You want me to take over for a while?" he asked.

"There's no real need to, Jack," Charlie said. "We've had it. I guess we'll spend the night here."

Jack looked around him. "No. That's Poros there. You're headed straight for the narrows."

"That's an island? I'll be damned. I couldn't imagine what we were doing over here, but this is where you said to come."

"Absolutely. It's right up against the mainland. I guess it won't look like an island till we get inside. We'll use the motor. After

all, we're running a cruise boat now. Have to satisfy the cus-
tomers. I said you'd sleep in a hotel tonight and you will. It's
only about five miles."

Charlie and Peter clapped each other on the back and cheered.
"By God, he's not Captain Bligh, after all," Charlie said. "Good
old Jack."

"You two handled the boat damn well. With that wind, I never
thought we'd get this far."

They got the heavy sails down and motored toward what they
could see now was a narrow passage between two low spits of
land. They passed through and entered a long lagoon. Olive
groves climbed the hills that enclosed it. Jack swung the bow
to the east and they found themselves headed for a distant town
of white cubes piled up on a low hill surmounted by a bell tower.
It gleamed with a rosy radiance in the lowering sun. Across a
narrow inlet there were more scattered buildings.

"God. How superb," Peter exclaimed.

"Troezen," Charlie murmured. "That's what I remember about
Poros. I read it in some guidebook. Phaedra. Hippolytus. It all
happened up in the hills near here."

"It's the most beautiful place I've ever seen in my life," Martha
said. They were all three standing near the hatch gazing forward,
Charlie in the middle. He put his arms around their waists and
gave Peter a special little hug. "Do you suppose this is what
Greece is going to be like? I'll never leave." He looked at Peter,
pleased to see that the discoloration of his eye was scarcely
noticeable now and his mouth, though still a bit lumpy, looked
well enough to kiss.

The town was not as distant as it had at first looked. They
were soon tied up at a quai below the bell tower and the crowd
they were beginning to expect had gathered at the foot of the
gangplank. A great stillness emanated from the land, broken by
the occasional rattle of an ancient car from the mainland across
the narrow sea passage. There was a whitewashed hotel only
a few yards away on the other side of the quai; Peter and Charlie
had already learned to recognize the letters that made up the
word for "hotel" even though they didn't know how to pronounce
them.

"Are you going to stay there?" Martha asked hopefully.

"It's certainly a hotel and it looks open," Peter said. "I want
to go exploring."

"Uh-oh, here we go again." Charlie laughed. "You'd better stick with your bodyguard this time."

They had a drink with the Kingsleys and went ashore as the sun was setting, carrying a small bag, having made no definite plans for departure. They were immediately surrounded by young men who talked volubly at them. "Hotel," Charlie and Peter kept repeating. The welcoming committee pointed at the nearby hotel and shook their heads and wagged their fingers. They pointed across the lagoon to what appeared to be a big, old-fashioned mansion set apart in extensive gardens. They nodded and beamed and made a gesture with their hands with all the fingers gathered together and pointing upwards that somehow suggested well-being or completion. Since the spokesman for the group was very good-looking, with sleek, dark hair and a flashing white smile, Charlie and Peter were inclined to take his word for it. He took Charlie's hand and jerked his head toward the water and looked at him questioningly. Charlie shrugged and smiled. They all moved down the quai to a small boat. The handsome one stopped in front of Charlie.

"Costa," he said after a few preliminary remarks, pointing at himself. He pointed at Charlie, letting the tip of his finger brush against his chest.

Charlie said his own name, but Costa didn't seem satisfied with it. He let his finger rest on his chest and spoke very deliberately. Charlie tried variations. "Carlos?" he suggested. Costa's expression cleared and his smile flashed. He flattened his hand and gently patted his chest. He turned to Peter who was ready with "Petros." This elicited a murmur of approval from the group and a number of pats on the back as the two names were repeated. Costa helped them into the stern of the little boat, two more young men jumped in forward, and they went chugging off in the direction of what Peter and Charlie assumed was a hotel.

"It does seem awfully easy to get abducted here," Charlie said.

"He's dreamy looking, the bossy one."

"Not bad at all. Available too, I should think."

"Oh, sure. You see what I mean? I think they're all available. They just don't think there's anything special about it."

When they reached their destination, Charlie produced money but Costa shrank from it and indignantly tossed his head back in the Greek negative. Their escort of three accompanied them up through terraced gardens to what looked like a big shabbily luxurious private house. There was a flurry of maids when they entered a dark foyer. A stately looking old woman appeared in front of them. She spoke to Costa and the three young Greeks withdrew. Charlie smiled at Costa and called "thank you" as they went.

"How nice to have you here. I am Mrs. Voulganis," the woman said in perfect English. "You've come on a yacht? How exciting. Does that mean the tourists will come again? I turned my house into a hotel just when everything stopped. You wish to be together or do you want separate rooms?"

A maid showed them into a big high-ceilinged room with an enormous double bed. Shuttered French windows gave onto a balcony and the garden and sea beyond. The bath was down the hall but there was no one else in the hotel. Everything was immaculate. They congratulated themselves on having accepted Costa's suggestion while they put their things away. It was getting dark, so they bathed quickly and went to ask Mrs. Voulganis where they should have dinner.

"I no longer serve meals. Of course, if you stay and let me know in the morning, I could have dinner prepared for you tomorrow. But surely Costa will show you where to go."

"Costa?"

"The young man who brought you. He's waiting for you."

Charlie and Peter exchanged an astonished glance. "Does he work for you or should we pay him?" Charlie asked.

"Oh, he'd never dream of taking money from you. Your being here will be a big event for all the young men. I'm sure you'll have a very delightful evening."

Charlie and Peter hurried down through the garden to the boat. Costa saw them coming and stood and flicked a cigarette into the sea. The other two were lolling in the stern with their arms around each other. Costa held Charlie's arm as they stepped aboard and continued to hold it as he spoke to him animatedly. He said "Petros" several times and pointed across the water. Peter and Charlie glanced at each other and smiled helplessly. Costa started the motor. Night fell as they chugged back toward the town. The bell tower was lighted and lights were strung out along the quai.

"Maybe we're going to find me a boyfriend," Peter said. "The rest of you seem to be paired off."

Charlie laughed and put his arm around him. They slipped around the bow of *Cassandra* and continued along into the passage between island and mainland. Other small boats were plying back and forth.

Costa cut the motor and they drifted in and tied up across from a vegetable shop spilling over with tomatoes and lemons. They scrambled ashore and Costa once more fell into step beside Charlie and took his hand and led the way along the front.

They rounded a corner into a square and entered a big, bare room very like the one where the man from Cairo, Illinois, had introduced them to ouzo. Groups of men were sitting about at tables. They sat at an empty one, Charlie and Peter together, Costa at Charlie's side.

Costa called out to a big man in a dirty white apron. Other youths entered, as if they had been following them, and sat with them. Names were pronounced that neither Peter nor Charlie attempted to keep straight. They weren't better-looking than any other group of young men; of the ten or twelve who had soon gathered around the table, only a couple could compete with Costa. Several were very homely indeed, but they all had the advantage of being deeply tanned, of having white teeth and sturdy bodies. The way they all pressed in against each other, leaning on each other's shoulders, taking each other's hands, made an attractive ensemble and created a feeling of warm, young camaraderie.

Food was put on the table—sliced tomatoes and cucumbers and lumps of white cheese and sections of octopus in oil—and metal tankards of wine. They all began to feed each other, holding out bits on forks. Costa filled two small glasses for Peter and Charlie and clinked his own with theirs. They drank. Peter knew what to expect, but he saw Charlie gag and he burst out laughing. He put his arm around his shoulder and encountered Costa's. They both held Charlie.

"It's all right when you get used to it," Peter reassured him.

"You mean you're actually supposed to drink it?" He did so and shuddered.

Scratchy music suddenly filled the room, a strange, wailing minor plaint. A boy from another table rose and began a solo in a clear space at one end of the room. Nobody paid any particular attention to him except Charlie and Peter, who were fascinated by the slow ritual of the dance. The boy held his arms out from his sides as he circled with small, precise steps, communicating a sense of deep concentration. He did low knee bends and slapped the floor, he leaped into the air and performed acrobatic turns and slapped his feet. There were scattered shouts of "*oopa*" from around the room and applause when the music ended.

More food was brought. Tankards were emptied and replenished. More records were put on the old wind-up phonograph in the back of the room. More youths danced. A pair from their table performed a duet. They weaved about together without touching, circling each other until one leaped savagely feet first at the other and locked his legs around his hips. He held his body out horizontally, his arms above his head, in an attitude of surrender while the other swung him proudly, as primitive as Pan, in the final measures of the dance. There was a keyed-up tingle of excitement in the laughter and applause that followed.

Four or five young men rose and began to gather at the end of the room. Peter felt a hand on his shoulder. He looked up and his gaze moved over a pretty mouth with a slight pout in it, a shapely nose, straight brows above big, dark eyes. The boy spoke to him and said "Petros." He was very young, no more than seventeen or eighteen. A cheap, flimsy shirt barely covered a smooth, brown, boyish chest. Charlie became aware of someone behind him and looked up, too.

"Trust you," he said. "You got the beauty."

"All things come to him who waits."

"He wants you to dance. Go on. He's an angel."

The boy was holding out his hand. Peter glanced at it as he took it, a good sinewy hand with long fingers. He rose, finding that he was several inches taller than the boy, and they went together to where the dancers had arranged themselves in a row linked together with handkerchiefs in their hands. The boy produced a frayed bit of cloth and Peter held the end of it and fell into place at the end of the line. The music started and the row moved into the dance. The steps were neat and brisk and Peter followed as the row moved away from him, making no attempt to dance but watching feet. The dancers reversed, putting Peter in the lead. He let the boy take over and walked along with him. The row moved forward and stamped their heels on the floor and did a knee bend in unison. The steps looked childishly simple and Peter began to perform them while the boy smiled and nodded at him, but something in the rhythm eluded him. Just as he thought he was getting it, the dancers took a step that ran counter to his instincts and he found himself stumbling awkwardly after them. The boy hooked their forefingers together around the handkerchief and exerted pressure. Peter glanced up and their eyes met and Peter stumbled again at the impact of the boy's look of invitation and desire. The music ended and Peter laughed and shook his head.

The boy took his hand and they returned to the table. "You'd be amazed how difficult it is," he said to Charlie as he sat.

"You didn't disgrace us too badly."

The boy had found a chair and was squeezing in on the other side of Peter. He took Peter's hand and lifted his arm and placed it around his shoulders. "Petros," he said. He pointed to himself. "Dimitri."

"Dimitri." Peter held his glass out to him. He took it and drank and lifted the glass to Peter's lips and tilted it. He spoke, pointing back and forth at them, and ended with a questioning look that was still filled with desire.

Peter smiled at him. "If you're saying what I think you're saying, the answer is probably no, but don't go away."

Dimitri lay a hand on his thigh and leaned against him. Peter let his fingers stray lightly over his shoulder. He turned to Charlie. "I seem to have a boyfriend, after all."

"So it would appear. Give him a hug for me."

"This is all so crazy. How did we get here? Shouldn't we be looking for the Kingsleys to decide about tomorrow?"

"The hell with them. We're seeing Greece. Besides, I'm getting drunk. This stuff is something. I feel as if I had a forest fire in my stomach."

Dimitri was pressing on Peter's thigh. He turned back to him. The boy pointed at a plate in front of him and said a word. He looked at Peter expectantly and repeated it. Peter imitated the sound and Dimitri smiled and nodded excitedly. He straightened and pointed to other objects on the table and said words, which Peter attempted to reproduce. It was a Greek lesson. He learned that the table was something like "trapeze" and that the word for chair was impossible to pronounce.

The others became aware of the game and quickly took it up.

Soon, they were all reaching across the table tugging at Charlie's and Peter's hands to get their attention, shouting words at them. Peter was laughing helplessly. Dimitri pointed to his mouth and said a word. He touched Peter's lips with his fingertips and waited for him to repeat it. When he did, Dimitri darted his head forward and kissed him on the mouth. It was a chaste kiss with closed lips and only a hint of tongue between them. The others all laughed and cheered as Peter felt himself blushing. He gave the boy's shoulder a little hug to acknowledge it.

They drank a great deal more wine, Peter and Dimitri sharing a glass. There was a momentary lull when Peter thought the party was breaking up and then they were all outside. Charlie and Peter tried to press money on Costa and were indignantly rebuffed. "Philos, philos," he kept repeating. He put his arms around them both and pulled them to him in turn and kissed them on the cheek. They all crowded back into his boat. In the scramble to get aboard, Peter was separated from Charlie. He didn't think he had allowed it to happen on purpose. He was pulled down between two youths who put their arms around him. Dimitri sat on the floorboards and shouldered his way in between his knees and looped his arms around his legs. He dropped his head back onto his crotch and moved it secretly to and fro against him. It was impossible for Peter to conceal the effect it had and he was drunk enough to feel that it didn't matter. The boy laughed softly and turned his head and rubbed his cheek against him. Under cover of the darkness, Peter stroked his hair. The boy made a little murmuring sound and hitched himself in closer and lifted his head so that Peter's sex was freed to lift along his belly. Dimitri settled his head beside it. Somebody began to sing and the others joined in a slow, sad song with thrilling stops and great soaring climaxes. The singing drowned the noise of the motor as they headed out across the still lagoon.

Peter was seized with a heart-bursting euphoria. Charlie was near. The splendor of the star-filled sky brought tears to his eyes. The boy had aroused him but he didn't want to carry it any further. He toyed with his face with a hand. Dimitri ran his tongue over it and nibbled his fingers in a way that made Peter giggle. It was like playing with a puppy. He moved his other hand over the boy's brow and down his nose and stroked his beardless cheeks with the backs of his fingers and held his chin and ran the tips of his fingers down his long neck. Dimitri's grip on his legs tightened and he bit his thumb. Peter stroked his soft lips; the mouth opened and he touched teeth and tongue. Dimitri ran his tongue between his fingers and darted it over the palm of his hand. Peter squeezed his shoulders with his thighs and slipped a hand inside his shirt and played with his nipples and learned the feel of his hairless chest. They both laughed at their game.

The boat seemed to be going a long way. Eventually, he saw that they were headed in toward land. Another boat emerged out of the night with a half-a-dozen dark figures in it and they ran in together, all of them calling back and forth to each other across the water. Peter could see a stand of tall cane just back from what appeared to be a strip of sandy shore. Costa cut the motor, and they all began to stir from the langorous positions into which they had fallen, disentangling themselves from each other and sitting up. Peter eased Dimitri's shoulders out from between his legs. The boat bumped on a soft bottom and two boys were immediately over the side, beaching her. Peter and Dimitri stood with the others, crowded close to each other so that the boy was able to touch Peter's sex discreetly. It responded to the pressure. Charlie appeared beside them.

"God knows what we're up to, but I don't have the impression they're going to murder us. They could rob us of all we have and we'd still have had our money's worth. Wasn't that beautiful?"

"Sublime. I'm drunk and loving it."

"How's your sweetheart?"

"Still clinging."

"Attaboy."

The group had started leaping ashore. The other boat pulled in beside them. Charlie touched his hand and moved forward. Peter and Dimitri followed. They were among the last ashore and when they entered a narrow path through the high cane they were alone. The path led out of the cane into an olive grove. He could hear the others moving through it ahead, bursting into snatches of song. Dimitri jostled up against him and Peter put his arms out to steady him. The boy melted into him and their open mouths were on each other, their tongues meeting. Dimitri's fingers clutched at Peter's hair and his mouth became devouring. Peter's hands were on his buttocks. They quivered under his touch and muscles rippled in provocation. Their invitation was undeniably exciting; briefly, it seemed to him as if Charlie were urging him on. Dimitri released his head and slipped his hands down between their waists. Peter wondered what he was doing and then realized that the boy was dropping his trousers. He was preparing to give himself here in the field. Peter's heart pounded at this tribute to his virility, but he found Dimitri's hands and gripped them and drew his head back.

"That's about enough of that," he said with shaken laughter. It was still a thrilling novelty to find that he was wanted in that way and that he was quite capable of satisfying the desire, but Charlie firmly blocked temptation once more. He didn't need or want anybody else. He knew the feel of the young body; his curiosity was appeased. He took a step back. He could see Dimitri's eyes, wide and glazed with longing in the dark. He ruffled his hair affectionately and waited for him to fasten his trousers and took his arm and hurried him along the path. He could still hear snatches of song ahead of them. He walked fast, pushing Dimitri along beside him. They had almost caught up when he saw lights ahead and they were once more part of the group as they rounded a low building. They came out into an area of hard-packed earth covered by a shaggy cane roof. Light came from a hissing lamp suspended from the caning. He took a long look at the boy he had held in his arms. Dimitri's eyes swam into his. Peter wished for a moment that they were back in the olive grove. He took his hand as they all reassembled around a table, their numbers swelled by the occupants of the second boat. Water rushed by in a ditch at the edge of the covered area. Peter could see that there was some sort of cultivation just beyond the range of the light. A cypress rose against the sky. He felt remote from the world he knew, but this simpler world was beginning to acquire reality. He leaned across the table to Charlie, who was still in Costa's charge.

"I guess we came here just for the sake of going somewhere. I suppose that makes sense."

Charlie glanced at Dimitri and smiled. "I know why he came here. He looks as if he'd follow you to the ends of the earth."

More food and wine was put in front of them. Time ceased.

218

They sang and drank and ate. Eventually, they were all on their feet wandering down through the olive grove again. The sky was paling; the stars no longer sparkled with jeweled brilliance. Charlie found himself in the lead with Costa and some of the occupants of the other boat. One of them had been flirting with him for the last hour. He looked almost as young as Peter's boy, but unlike Dimitri he had an assured and arrogant air. When they came out through the tall cane onto the strip of beach, the boy took his arm and urged him toward the second boat. Charlie pulled away, but a thought struck him. Peter and Dimitri were apparently lagging. He yanked the boat's line off a rock where it had been looped and made gestures of departure. The boy smiled knowingly and said something to the others climbing into the boat. There was a burst of laughter. Charlie walked into the water and began to push the boat off the beach. The boy joined him and the boat was clear. As he clambered aboard, Charlie felt a wrench deep within him, but it was right to remove himself from the scene. The motor started and they began to move off. What was the point of thinking about freedom and independence if they never had an opportunity to exercise it? Peter had a clear field now to make what he would of the young Greek's wide-eyed infatuation.

The boy whose name he didn't know sat beside him. He talked and laughed. He spread his legs and stroked his crotch, displaying himself. Charlie didn't bother to look. He noticed that they weren't headed directly toward the lights of the town but off to one side where the hotel was. Apparently everybody knew all about them. The run back seemed much shorter than it had going out. They were soon drifting in toward the cement landing block in front of the hotel. Charlie rose and the boy rose with him. Charlie pushed him down and indicated that he was to stay. When the boat was in close enough, he called *"efharrystow,"* which was as close as he could come to "thank you," to the group in general and jumped ashore. The boy jumped after him and the boat pulled away, Charlie crossed to the steps leading up to the hotel. The boy followed. When Charlie stopped, he put a hand on Charlie's hip and started to slide it around behind. Charlie brushed it away.

"Petros. *Philos mou,*" he said. "Not you."

"*Avrio?*" the boy asked with his knowing smile.

Charlie had learned that "*avrio*" meant "tomorrow." "Sure. *Avario.*"

The boy spoke at length, with gestures. Arranging a rendezvous? Charlie smiled and nodded and said "*kali nikta*" and continued up to the hotel. He felt lonely and virtuous. He tried to keep his thoughts off Peter and his sweet young conquest. His mind circled the enigma of Martha. She had figured quite definitely and interestingly in his thoughts in Athens, but he was less sure now whether anything would come of it. He felt a pleasant, lustful warmth toward her, but this didn't alter the comfortable feeling he had always had with her, nor could thoughts of her erase from his mind the image of Peter and the Greek boy naked together, Peter taking him as the boy obviously yearned to be taken. Dimitri wouldn't have clung to him so tenaciously if he hadn't felt in him a promise of satisfaction. Perhaps Peter had committed himself in some way right at the start. He had to stop thinking about him. He had freely given him scope to make his own decision. That was the way it had to be from now on if they weren't to suffocate in their preoccupation with each other. He had created more air around them.

He had undressed and washed and brushed his teeth when he heard the popping of a motor approaching across the water. He heard it cut back to idle and voices calling, Peter's among them. A thrill of relief ran through him. He had gambled and won. In another few minutes Peter came hurrying into the room.

"There you are," he exclaimed. "Thank God! What happened to you?"

"I was enticed into the other boat by one of my suitors and we took off."

Peter laughed. "That young one who was eyeing you at the end? Isn't it amazing? You can't say they're all queer. It doesn't mean anything. Even we aren't queer here. They're all expecting it and ready for it, some of them maybe more than others."

"Your boy readier than any, it seemed to me."

"I'll say. At least, that's the way he was acting all night, but he didn't seem surprised or particularly upset when I left him just now."

"You're not sorry?"

"About what?"

"Not staying with him and having him. I mean, I assume you didn't."

"Of course, I didn't. Are you crazy? Do you think I want every kid who smiles at me?"

"I don't know," Charlie said unconcernedly, glowing with inner triumph. He stretched out naked on the bed. "You must've considered it at one point or another."

Peter began to undress. What new tack was Charlie taking now? Instinct told him that it was somehow connected with their sexual experiments. He felt as if Charlie were cutting him loose, urging him on, offering him a freedom he didn't want. He thought of the kiss he had exchanged with Dimitri in parting a few minutes ago. He had been too anxious to find Charlie to do more than hold his hand on the way back, but as they arrived he had turned to him and Dimitri's mouth had opened to his in a devouring way. As Peter jumped ashore, he had heard laughter and saw the boy gathered into somebody else's arms. A satisfactory ending. Easy come, easy go. Nothing had dimmed the clear, urgent longing he felt for Charlie now. "The *idea* of having him was exciting. I don't deny that," he said, looking at Charlie levelly. "I had plenty of chance to, God knows. For some peculiar reason, I happen to prefer you. Do I have to say it?"

"I just don't want us to get in each other's way when things are happening to us. We've got a long life ahead of us."

"I'd want to get in your way if anything like that were happening to you." The simplicity of it, it seemed to him, made it worth saying. He knew Charlie's tendency to intellectualize their relationship to a point where it had no connection with their simple wants and needs. He added facetiously, "What's wrong with helping each other overcome the temptations of the flesh?"

"Like standing there all gorgeous and naked in front of me?" They looked at each other and laughed. "If you still feel like fucking somebody, I have a suggestion to make."

"No, darling. Please. The other way around. Make me yours. I need it."

"There's no law against doing it both ways. You first. I want what your boy didn't get." He watched the quick lift of Peter's sex as he approached the bed.

They slept late and dressed hurriedly and gulped down some coffee, feeling like naughty children for not having reported back to the Kingsleys sooner. As it turned out, they needn't have worried. They found Martha and Jack looking relaxed and content.

"It's been dead calm so far," Jack said. "Something seems to be stirring now. Do you want another night here or shall we go on if we get a bit of breeze?"

Charlie questioned Peter with his eyes. Peter shook his head. "We had a fabulous night. We'll tell you all about it. I don't see much sense in doing it again. Let's go." He was thinking primarily of Dimitri. He didn't want to go on teasing the boy. If they stayed, they would surely see him again.

"Right you are. There's an island called Hydra that people say is worth seeing. It's only a couple of hours away. Let's have some lunch and see if it looks as if we can make it for tonight."

Charlie looked at the sky and felt the air against his skin. "I don't think we'll get anything much, Jack. Maybe enough to get us part of the way."

"Well, that's all right. It's close enough so I don't mind falling back on the motor if we have to."

"We're getting to be regular tourists," Charlie said to Martha with a laugh.

"You must tell me about your night. We saw you go by with swarms of young men."

"The segregation of the sexes. It's amazing. I haven't seen a single pretty girl. You're a lovely novelty."

Martha laughed and looked prettily flustered as she put a hand on his arm.

They reached Hydra in early evening after having spent most of the afternoon wondering if they were going in the right direction. Even Jack began to question his chart readings. The island had been partly visible from the time they left Poros and when they cleared a point of the Peloponnesus, all of it was stretched out before them, a long, high barrier of land with no sign of a town. They could see only a few big white buildings on high ground, which they identified as monasteries. They had a southwesterly breeze again so they couldn't follow the southwesterly course Jack had given them but fell off toward the eastern end of the island. They had a rather lethargic sail while Charlie and Peter and Martha chatted about Poros and drank cold beer in the cockpit.

"Why don't you go forward and get some sun all over?" Charlie suggested impulsively to Martha. He had finally said it. If he was ever to know her naked body, he wanted it without the white patches. "It's silly to have all those strap marks. We'll give you fair warning if we have to come up for anything."

"What a good idea," she said. They looked at each other and he let his eyes be held. Hers were full of questions, primarily searching for the answer to whether she had finally stirred him physically. He allowed his eyes to answer with a cautious affirmative. He had taken another step toward what was becoming perhaps an inevitable confrontation. A joyful acquiescence lighted her face as she rose obediently and did as she was told.

As the afternoon waned, Jack turned on the motor and headed them for where he insisted the town must be. "We're bound to be to the east of it," he asserted, as if to convince himself. "We'll just follow the coast and we can't miss it."

Slowly, it revealed itself, first in a big house set on a high promontory, then in what appeared to be a ruined fort and small light-tower on a headland opposite. They rounded a point and within minutes the whole town was before them, a perfect amphitheater descending in tiers to the still circle of the small harbor. The upper tiers were streaked with ochre and showed other signs of ruin; only the lower town was whitewashed and looked intact. There were a few unexpected Italianate stone mansions down around the port. They motored in and were enclosed by the twin promontories and moored against the quai in the middle of town. Bulky, gaily painted caïques were tied up here and there.

"This really is turning into an adventure," Charlie said as he and Peter were preparing to go ashore. "Coming into port in the evening, not knowing what to expect."

"Every place is so different. Poros already seems long ago."

When they went up on deck, their welcoming committee was still gathered at the foot of the gangplank, a knot of children and young men. Jack and Martha were having their martinis.

"Aren't you going to have a drink?" she asked.

"We'll go check the hotel situation and come back," Charlie said. They descended the gangplank and welcoming youths fell into step around them. They were led to an old man sitting in front of a café who spoke atrocious English. He plied them with ouzo and told them about his life in the United States while the youths stood around and watched. At last, the old man spoke peremptorily in Greek and they were all allowed to proceed to the hotel, again a big, converted private house a few dozen yards behind the huddle of buildings around the port and set under a vast magnolia tree. The town rose steeply around it. When they had washed, they found the youths waiting for them under the magnolia tree. They had been joined by a weedy figure with a droopy moustache who introduced himself as Will Barstowe. He was very English. When Charlie and Peter said their names, he was visibly impressed.

"Of course. I know of you. Mutual friends, I dare say. How extraordinary. I'm a painter too, after a fashion." He released a torrent of Greek and the youths dispersed. "I told them they could come stare at you later. The town will be *en fête* tonight."

They wandered back toward the port, dropping conversational bits of information about themselves. It turned out that Barstowe had been living in Poros for some time and was in Hydra only for a visit. Costa was his friend. The way he said it left no doubt as to his meaning.

"Tell us about everything," Peter demanded, fascinated by this congenial world they were discovering. "How does it work? I mean, where do the children come from?"

"Oh, they all get married. Costa's wife has already been picked out for him. I'll doubtless help them set up housekeeping. Some of them continue their amorous romps with boys afterward, some of them don't. Nobody pays any attention. It's all pretty much as it was in classical days, I should think. Do you know if there was a lovely lad called Dimitri with you last night?"

Charlie laughed. "He was, indeed. He fell in love with Peter."

"I'm not surprised. I've watched him develop. He's just begun to join in manly sport. I rather suspect he might turn out to be queer in the way we mean. Very few of them are. Quite utterly dreary in bed, actually."

Reminded of his amorous assault in the Gulf of Corinth, Peter told Will Barstowe the story, still seeking enlightenment.

"Ah, yes. Well, you see, the civil war left behind a certain number of dissidents," the Englishman explained. "A few still roam the more remote districts. They're usually armed. Their Marxist principles are easily adapted to simple banditry. And most Greeks regard male foreigners as fair game, in any event. I'm afraid rather a lot of us have been more than cooperative. They were probably most astonished when you resisted. A bit

of robbery. A bit of buggery. It keeps the revolutionary spirit
alive."

They all laughed and Charlie and Peter invited him to the
boat for drinks and introduced him to the Kingsleys. He was
full of local lore about the days when Hydra had been a great
sea power during the Napoleonic wars. He entertained them
while they sat in the cockpit and watched laden donkeys tiptoe
past the gangplank on dainty feet.

"I know!" Peter exclaimed suddenly. "The quiet. I haven't
heard a car since we've been here."

"Good heavens, no. No roads, you know. Nothing but steps.
No electricity worth speaking of. It'll come on in a while and
stay on till midnight. No telephones. A boat comes from Athens
from time to time with mail. This is real Greece. Ah. Just as
I expected. The foreign colony will now make a subtle play to
be invited on board."

"Invite them, by all means," Jack said.

The foreign colony was embryonic, at best: a young Hungarian
woman with an Italian lover who had recently bought a house,
an English couple who were renting one for the summer. Their
subtle play consisted of pausing at the gangplank and waving
at Will Barstowe.

They were invited aboard. The foursome on the boat became,
for the first time since they had been together, social entities
instead of a working team. Martha kept a hand on Charlie's arm
and referred all questions about the trip to him. Jack flirted with
the Hungarian. Peter charmed everybody. When the sun had set
and a few dim lights had come on along the port, they all went
ashore and a few paces up a side street to where some tables
had been set out on the cobbles. They were served some very
bad food and worse retsina. Peter paid. In time, the foreign colony drifted off, except for Will Barstowe.

"I'll tell you what," Jack said. "That English couple asked us
for drinks tomorrow. I've got some odds and ends I want to get
done on the motor. Why don't we stay here another day and
then really get cracking?"

They left it at that and the Kingsleys went back to the boat.
Barstowe led Peter and Charlie up another side street to a big
bare *taverna* that already looked familiar to them. The clientele
was similar to the night before except that there were many fewer

of them and none to compare to Costa or Dimitri. The atmosphere of male camaraderie was the same, as were the sexual undertones. Their entrance caused a stir and they quickly had a group around their table. With Barstowe as an interpreter, they were able to really learn some Greek. Peter was becoming adept at stringing words together and completing the meaning with his hands. Boys danced what appeared to be the same dances. They drank too much retsina and slept late again the next morning.

When they returned to the port, they felt as if they had been living there for days. The town was so small and so sparsely populated that they kept waving and smiling at people from the night before, both local youths and foreign colony. It was like living in a large open-air club. Martha joined them and took Charlie's hand and suggested a swim. Peter fetched their trunks and towels from the boat and they started around the port. Will Barstowe joined them and told them where to go. He pointed out a great, crumbling stone pile of a house on the opposite arm of the harbor and told them it was for sale for two hundred dollars. Peter wanted to buy it on the spot.

Charlie laughed. "What in the world would we do with it?"

"What difference does it make? I want it."

"We've just started our cruise. We may find houses all over the place. We can't buy them all."

"I love it here. Two hundred dollars, for God's sake."

Barstowe settled the question by pointing out that the owner was in Athens and the sale could hardly be completed by next morning.

"All right. At the end of the trip. If we haven't found anything else. Promise?"

"Promise," Charlie agreed. Barstowe wrote down the owner's name and address.

A northerly wind was rising, whipping up the sea outside. They swam off rocks. They ate. They slept. They climbed steep steps to have drinks with the English couple and sat on a magnificent terrace overlooking the town and the sea. Peter kept talking about the great pile of masonry on the other side of the port. "The sunset must be glorious from over there," he said. And, "It's not as high as this house. Not so much of a climb."

Charlie was aware that Martha was always at his side. He felt quite differently about her on land than on the boat; she seemed much more a part of real life. From this perspective, he was struck by how completely she had cut herself off from Jack since the start of the trip. All her points of reference were to Charlie. She was making them a couple. He was sure it must be noticeable to everyone. It was very agreeable to turn to this sweet, pretty young woman and find her eyes on him, ready to agree with him, eager to show him off in his best light to anyone they were talking to. The pleasant warmth she stirred in him became at times a surge of genuine desire. If the looks she gave him meant anything, she would probably make him a memorable bed partner.

He and Peter wandered around town after dinner with Will Barstowe and parted from him like old friends and went to bed early. They were up not long after dawn. The northerly wind was already picking up when they went down to the boat.

"Looks as if we're going to get a blow," Jack said as they came aboard.

"Yeah. We'll get the old tub moving," Charlie agreed with an eager light in his eye. A group of idlers gathered as they pulled in the gangplank and they all smiled and waved back and forth as they motored out of the port. The sea pitched them about as they struggled with the sails. Peter came running aft and helped Charlie trim the sheets as the bow lifted and bit into the sea. They looked back and had one last glimpse of the great amphitheater shining in the morning sun.

"We've got to come back here," Peter said.

"It's beautiful, isn't it? Maybe we'll have time at the end."

The wind grew stronger and rolled up big seas as they progressed. It was on the quarter, which gave them a clear reach to their destination, Mykonos, with a stopover in Siros that night. With all sails set, Charlie and Peter pushed the boat like a racer, heeling over and sending spray flying across the deck. They made good speed. By midday, they were approaching the islands of Kea and Kithnos, which formed a sort of portal to the Cyclades and between which they would pass. They had accomplished a bit better than half the day's run to Siros. The sea was piling higher, battering them and knocking them over on their side.

"What happens if it gets worse?" Peter asked. He had to raise his voice to carry over the roar of the wind and the crash of sea.

"It's beginning to kill our way. I've been thinking of getting the jib down, but then we'd really stop. The pilot book says there's a current running against us between these islands. You see those rollers? I wonder."

"Is it dangerous?"

"Good lord, no. It's a goddamn bore. This nutty sea. You don't know what it's going to do from one minute to the next. You better get the master of the charts." The land ahead of them was beginning to have an appeal even for Charlie.

Peter scuttled across the deck to the companionway, one knee crooked oddly to compensate for the slant of the deck. Jack appeared with Peter following. They careened into the cockpit.

"We're going to have a hell of a time getting through here," Charlie shouted. "Is there any shelter on this side?"

Jack pointed to the southern tip of Kithnos. "It looks good. I didn't want to butt in. There won't be any hotels."

"Don't let's get an obsession about hotels. I'm ready to pack it in." He turned to Peter. "OK, Slugger. Let's ease the sheets. We're going to fly. Keep clear, Jack." Charlie pulled the helm over and they fell off the wind as he and Peter played out the sheets. *Cassandra* rose and raced in a long slide down the slope of a wave. Charlie grappled with the wheel. "Hell and damn. Whenever I give in, I always wish I hadn't. We probably could've battled our way through."

Peter laughed. "You kill me when you turn into an old salt."

Martha appeared, looking radiant, and joined them in the cockpit. "We're going in? I wasn't frightened. Honestly. I never am with you. But I can't pretend I enjoyed the last hour. Shall I fix you some food?"

"If you think you can on this roller-coaster. We won't be in for an hour or more."

Cassandra lifted and went scudding down the side of another wave. "This is rather fun after what we've been doing. I think I can manage." She waited for her moment and made a dash for the companionway. Jack was standing in it with a chart, gazing at the coast ahead. Charlie noticed how she seemed to shrink as she squeezed around him to go below. Jack turned and nodded.

"You're about on it," he called. "It shouldn't be difficult to find."

It wasn't. They sailed into a deep, wooded, deserted bay, pass-

228

ing in a matter of moments from the wild turbulence outside into still waters. The sudden peace of it was paralyzing. Charlie turned the motor on briefly to get into shallower water. The anchor chain rattled. Silence enfolded them. Charlie stretched to ease his tense muscles and became aware of the nervous hum of cicadas. A good land sound. They all joined in getting the sails down and furled. Peter jumped overboard.

"Ohhh," he groaned when he surfaced. "It's bliss. Everybody in."

"We can still get to Mykonos tomorrow," Charlie said to Jack. "There's nothing special about Siros, is there?"

"Not that I know of. We can give it a miss and go right on. It was very sporting of you to put in and not attempt the impossible. It shows consideration for the rest of us, even though you'd like to do it differently. I admire that."

"Thanks, Jack." Charlie felt sorry for him. He had become so completely irrelevant. He wondered why he had been so bothered by him at the start. Charlie hung the swimming steps over the side and jumped in after Peter. Martha joined them.

As the afternoon wore on, Charlie began to find the boat cramped and confining. When they were at sea, handling the wheel and the sheets, there seemed to be plenty of room, but now Martha filled every corner of it. It made him restless. He avoided her eye and her touch. There was something explosive in all four of them being crowded together like this. He would have to study their itinerary more closely and make sure that they didn't leave port unless they were sure they could get to a hotel at the end of the day.

They were off at dawn in a quiet sea, but with a breeze rippling over it that Charlie knew was going to build. By midmorning conditions were the same as they had been the day before, and later, when they had Siros off their starboard beam, their progress had virtually come to a halt in the heavy sea.

Jack was frowning when he came above. "This isn't much fun," he said as he fell into the cockpit. "I'm getting bloody bored with this *meltemi* or whatever it's called."

Charlie shrugged. "I couldn't agree with you more. Maybe we'll never get to Mykonos. Do you want to put in at Siros, after all?"

"I think you made the right decision yesterday. Things are about the same today."

"You make your point clear," Charlie laughed. Siros was a big town and there would be hotels. "All right. I'll put her on a broader reach for another half-hour and then I'll jibe her over. I want to show Peter how to do it. Come back if you want to see some fun."

"It doesn't seem ideal for sailing lessons, but I'm sure you know what you're doing." Jack staggered to the companionway and went below.

Peter eased the sheets as Charlie adjusted the helm for a more southerly course. The movement of the boat smoothed. They picked up speed. The town of Siros slowly came into view: two humps on a camel's back, densely packed with white cubes of houses, stark without majesty. When Charlie judged that they could make the port on a comfortable starboard reach, he squeezed Peter's knee.

"OK, baby. Let's do this right. Make sure your lines are clear. That whacking, great boom will be coming at us and swinging over to the other side. When it starts in, take up on the sheet like mad so you control it every second. Once it's over, you can let the sheet run, but not too fast. Keep control of it, baby. We don't want to strip Jack's decks for him."

Peter saw the light of excitement in Charlie's eyes and laughed excitedly in response. "Nobody knows how to control a sheet like I do. All set."

"Right. Let's go." He pulled the bow slowly off the wind. The boat pitched and rolled as the sea took her. The mainsail flapped warningly and the boom started its swing. Charlie released the starboard jib sheet and lunged for the one to port and simultaneously shouted, "Now. Get her in fast."

The boat dipped breathtakingly as Charlie hauled in on the jib sheet and the boom swung in amidships. Peter had the sheet taut as it continued its swing with a crack of blocks, almost yanking Peter off his feet. He played the line off without releasing it. The bow swooped giddily and Charlie wrestled with the wheel to steady her. When they were able to look, Siros was off their starboard bow. They sat back and laughed.

"Wow. That thing's got a kick in it," Peter exclaimed. "Was that all right, captain?"

"Just about perfect, mate."

Jack came above. "I didn't want to get in your way. It seemed to go very smoothly, considering. I must admit my heart was in my mouth."

"I almost spat mine out at one point," Charlie said. "This sure feels like a hell of a lot of boat when you're doing tricks with it."

When the time came, they grappled the sails down and motored into a busy commercial port and moored stern-in to a crowded quai. Peter and Charlie decided to have lunch ashore and they left the Kingsleys after promising to check in later. They went reeling down the quai, unable to control their legs after two days of rough seas. They didn't get far before they were picked up by a smiling young man who reminded them of Costa. He had a taxi. He insisted that they get into it and drove them a block to a citified but charming square with stylishly pruned trees in it. He indicated a hotel of heavy nineteenth-century grandeur. They discussed having a swim as they pulled out money for the short ride. Their driver heard and understood and stretched out a hand to them and pointed at himself and repeated "*bagno*" several times. They gathered he wanted to take them somewhere.

"*Ecky fie?*" Peter asked, persuaded that he was speaking Greek. After a moment's bafflement, the driver grasped his meaning. He beamed as he made gestures at his mouth for eating and patted his stomach. They went in and took a room and returned with their swimming things. They drove up through the town over the saddle between the two humps and down through a pastoral scene of timeless beauty to the other side of the island. The driver accomplished the trip twisted around in his seat addressing his passengers, who understood only snatches of what he was saying. Occasionally he glanced at the road.

He pulled up at a small whitewashed building at the edge of a long, deserted, sandy beach. They all got out of the car and the driver escorted them around under a grape arbor and introduced them to the proprietor and his family. When they offered the driver money, he was able to postpone the ugly moment of payment by indicating that he would come back for them later.

They had a simple meal, under the arbor, of tiny fish they

could eat whole and eggs and salad. Small children stared at them and the proprietor shooed them away from time to time. They drank a good deal of retsina and drifted into a state of dazed euphoria unaware that the Greeks had invented the word.

They swam and lay out under the sun and dozed. They drank more retsina and swam again and lay side-by-side on the sand as the sun lowered toward the sea. Peter had been aware of Charlie's eyes on him insistently all afternoon. It thrilled him to be the prolonged, uninterrupted center of his attention. He felt for his hand and held it. Charlie rolled over against him and propped himself up and kissed him gently on the lips.

"Golly," Peter murmured into his eyes. "Right out in public. I must be an exhibitionist at heart. I hope the gods are sitting upon Mount Olympus watching us."

"It's exciting, isn't it?" There was a curious melancholy in his voice. He ran a finger over Peter's lips. "Come on, baby. I suppose we've got to get dressed. That crazy taxi will be along any minute."

They were dropped off at the hotel and they bathed and dressed for the evening. Their driver was waiting for them in the square and they indicated that they would be back. They strolled down to the port to see the Kingsleys. Charlie was struck by how stirred up the water was. All the boats were rolling at their moorings. Men were shouting at each other and hauling on lines. Two sizable fishing boats were on the verge of disaster, hopelessly entangled and crashing against each other while men ran about their decks to no apparent purpose. The sun had dropped behind the humps and a sinister yellowish-gray light bathed the scene. Charlie's pace quickened and Peter matched it. As they got farther along the quai, the wind hit them with angry force. Ahead of them, *Cassandra* was rolling with the others, her great mast describing a slow arc against the darkening sky. Charlie and Peter hurried down the gangplank and found the Kingsleys forlornly drinking martinis in the cockpit. Martha brightened and rose.

"Oh, good. I hoped you'd come. I'll get you drinks."

"This is a lousy harbor," Jack growled.

It took Charlie only a minute to see that they were in trouble. He took a glass from Martha as he watched the bow fall off to starboard, rising and falling with the swell. A furious gust slammed against his back and his breath caught as they continued to swing in, just clearing the boat next to them. He was about to cry out in warning when the swing was arrested and reversed and they straightened slowly, bucking against the anchor like a crazed horse against a bridle.

"Jesus," he exclaimed in momentary relief. "Have you been riding like this long? You must be dragging the goddamn anchor."

"I've tried taking up on the chain. It's lousy holding ground. The pilot book says so."

"You've probably pulled the anchor in beside us. Are you going to just sit there?" He ran forward and saw the chain running slackly into the water. He ran back. "We've got to get another anchor out, for Christ's sakes."

"That means putting the dinghy over," Jack objected.

"You're damn right it does. Come on, baby, let's get cracking. Get your spare ready, Jack. Make sure it has plenty of line on it." He peeled off his fresh shirt. Peter was blushing as he did the same. Charlie had never used the endearment in front of Jack. Charlie sprang forward with Peter at his heels and they struggled to get the dinghy onto its davits. It was hard work on the rolling boat. Charlie tried to keep an anxious eye on the bow. If the anchor dragged another few feet, one of the strong gusts could smash Cassandra on the quai. He cursed Jack for calmly drinking martinis in the face of this evident peril. They pushed and pulled and lifted and got the dinghy into place. There was a small, rusty derelict cargo boat close beside them to port, but there was room to lower it. Jack joined them.

"The anchor's ready. There's a good fifty meters of line on it."

"OK. Lower away." They dropped the dinghy overboard and Peter jumped into it without waiting to be told and unfastened the tackle. "This is going to be a sweat, baby. Take the anchor out as far as you can and dump her. You'll have to work well to windward of us. And hurry, for God's sake. It's getting dark." Charlie led the dinghy forward and Jack lay on his stomach and lowered the anchor into the stern. Jack had lashed the end of the line to a bollard forward. He dropped the neat coil onto the anchor and Peter began to row away. It was obviously a hard pull. The wind kept pushing him off to starboard of them. He turned into it and tugged on the oars. He was only a gray blur on the black sea when they saw the dinghy turn and start back in. Charlie sprang forward to where the line was secured and began to take up on it, jerking it in to settle the anchor. He had taken in only half-a-dozen meters when it seemed to hold. He took in a few more meters to straighten the bow and watched it fall off to starboard and held his breath again. It pitched and halted and the reverse swing began much sooner than it had before. He released a satisfied sigh and prayed that it would hold. He went back to the davits to wait for Peter. When the dinghy came bumping in alongside, he dropped the blocks down and Peter refastened the tackle and climbed up over the side. He was breathing heavily.

"Whew. That was tough going," he panted.

Charlie put his arm around his naked shoulders and hugged him. "Good going. Hey, Jack," he called. Then to Peter, "Go on back and have a drink."

Jack appeared and he and Charlie got the dinghy back on board and lashed to the cabin roof. Charlie stood and watched the swing of the bow again. It was dark now, but he picked out a building silhouetted against the sky on the other side of the port as a landmark when the swing was arrested. He went aft to the others, who were all standing in the cockpit. Martha handed him his drink.

"Are we all right?" she asked anxiously.

"So far, so good. You'd better run back to the hotel and get our things, Slugger. Hurry. I don't know how long we'll be able to stay here."

Peter tossed back his drink and snatched up his shirt and was off. In the light of the deck lamp, Charlie could see the terror start up in Martha's eyes.

"Do you mean we—" she began.

He took her arm and caressed the inside of it secretly with his fingers. He looked into her eyes. "You're not going to be frightened. Right? Good girl."

With a convulsive movement of her arm, she pressed his hand against her breast. He continued his caress. Her lips parted and the corners lifted in a little smile. "Yes. All right. I'll do my best."

"What is all this?" Jack demanded testily. "What do you mean, you don't know how long we'll be able to stay?"

"Just that. We're all right for the moment. I hope to God the anchor holds. But what if it doesn't? We could turn the motor on and run on the stern lines, but I don't think much of the idea. Not for all night."

"Are you considering going *out* in this?"

Charlie drained his glass and handed it to Martha for more. "Of course. We'd better reef the mainsail all the way down just in case."

"It's absolutely out of the question."

Charlie looked at Jack and shrugged. "In that case, Peter and I will go back to the hotel. It's your boat. If you want to smash her up here in the port, help yourself."

"No. No, of course not. I appreciate your rallying 'round. Mightn't it help putting a line to this wreck beside us?"

"I wouldn't risk it, Jack. If we drag its anchor, it'll be on top of us and then we've really had it."

"I certainly don't like the idea of going out."

Martha handed Charlie a replenished glass and he gulped down half of it to steady his own nerves. "I'm not crazy about it, either. Still, if we were caught out in it, we'd get through. How about rustling up some food, old gal? I have a feeling this is going to be a long night." He watched the bow plunging toward the landmark he had selected. It stopped more or less where he hoped it would. Perhaps they had dragged a little. He couldn't be sure. "Let's get to work on that sail," he said as he finished his drink in a second gulp.

They were struggling with the sail when Peter returned. The wind kept clutching it and tearing it out of their hands.

"Hey. Help," Charlie called when he saw Peter.

"What's going on? Are we really leaving? I thought we were supposed to be safe in port." He pulled off his shirt again and joined them on the roof of the cabin.

"I don't know whether we're safe or not. Here. Hold this down."

With Peter's help, the job went quicker. Charlie kept an eye on the bow. From this altered angle, lying along the boom, his landmark was no longer dependable, but he was almost sure they were dragging again. As soon as the sail was reefed, he dropped to the deck and checked. It wasn't as bad as he had feared. The bow plunged a little beyond his landmark and held. They were still safe for a while.

"Better get the gangplank in," he said. "We may want to let out on the stern lines."

When that chore was done, they gathered in the cockpit where Martha was guarding a plate of sandwiches. She managed to pour them more drinks. Charlie began to pay more attention to the hulk on their port side. The gap between them was definitely narrowing. In the bad gusts, it loomed toward them, leaving not even room to launch the dinghy, but he was aware, too, that the gusts were coming less frequently. If they could hang on here till dawn, they would probably have a few hours of relative calm, as they had had this morning.

"Why don't you two try to get some sleep?" he suggested to the Kingsleys when they had eaten and had several more drinks. He had been watching the bow slide farther past his landmark and he didn't want them around if he had to act. "You better make sure everything is well stowed away below."

"Good idea," Jack agreed. "Come on, Marty."

Martha squeezed Charlie's arm as she passed him and they went below. He dropped into the cockpit and sat beside Peter and kissed him lingeringly on the mouth.

"I guess that'll have to do," he said, drawing away. "We're always being cheated of our nights of bliss and rapture."

"I'll say. What's up now?"

"We've been dragging anchor for the last hour. But I think the wind is calming down. The longer we wait the better." He unfastened his fly and stood and slipped off his trousers. "Here take these fancy pants down and get me something I can work in. Bring those wet-weather windbreakers, too."

"Damn. I thought you were going to do a striptease." Peter gathered up their clothes and went below. Charlie stood watching the bow as it started its swing to starboard. It went bucking past his landmark and continued on. It hesitated long enough for him to hope that it was holding and then continued sickeningly on until they were menaced by the quai. His muscles tensed and a chill ran down his spine. He sprang for the wheel and switched the motor on. He brought the bow back into line while the stern lines squeaked with the strain. He had to make a hasty adjustment of the helm to keep from heading on over into the derelict to port. Peter returned wearing jeans and carrying things for both of them.

"Just dump it," Charlie said. "I can't let go of the wheel. We haven't got any anchor at all. They're probably both under us. Go see if you can get the regular one up easily."

Peter ran forward and worked the windlass for what seemed, to Charlie's straining nerves, a long time. Eventually, he came running back.

"It's up," he reported. "Shall I get the other one up?"

"The stern lines first. We're getting out of here." He put the motor momentarily into reverse to make Peter's job easier.

Jack appeared in the hatch. "Need any help?" he called.

Charlie glanced behind him. Peter had one stern line in and was pulling the other out of the ring it had been looped through. "Get on the anchor," he called. The stern began to swing around as it was freed. "The anchor. Quick," he snapped to Peter. The wind was pushing them down fast on the boats anchored to starboard of them. His heart was beating rapidly. He saw Peter and Jack hauling in on the anchor. He tried to jockey the boat clear of hazards while he waited tensely. At last, Peter straightened and waved an all-clear signal. He took a long breath and expelled it as he moved the boat slowly out into the middle of the harbor.

"Get the main up when you're set up there," he called. He had an opportunity now to look around him at the weather. The sky was clear and brilliant. The wind was still strong, but steady and probably dropping. The sea was going to be bad, but it didn't frighten him; he had complete confidence in the boat and in his ability to handle her. He saw Jack and Peter moving around the mast and he swung the boat into the wind as the sail came up. Reefed down, it was only a scrap of cloth. He hauled the sheet in as close as he could get it. Jack came aft.

"If you'll hold on here for a minute, I want to take a last look at the chart," Charlie said. "We won't be going anywhere except up and down." He hurried below and was back quickly and pulled on pants and a windbreaker. "OK, Jack, you might as well go below. There's no point in all of us getting wet."

Peter came running aft and dropped into the cockpit as Jack left. The boat was picking up speed and they were approaching the open sea. He could see whitecaps rolling past the entrance to the harbor. He cut the motor and braced himself to meet them. The boat swept past the breakwater and stopped with a crash.

He could feel it shudder in its depths. He felt a great craving to return to the dubious safety of the port, but he clenched his teeth, gripped the wheel and eased them closer into the wind. The bow lifted and plowed into the sea. Water poured over them, but he could feel the scrap of sail take the wind and pull them forward. After a few minutes, when he had got used to the movement and the pull of the wheel, he glanced back. They were already a comfortable distance from land.

"Christ, you're brave," Peter shouted. "Coming out here of your own free will."

"Think of the first night. Thank your stars it won't be like that." Another wall of water fell on them. "Happy cruising in the Aegean."

Peter lurched up and fell into the seat beside him and put an arm around him. "What fun," he said into his ear. "I don't know why we all go on loving you."

Charlie thought of Martha. His impulsively caressing fingers had been a declaration. She must be very confident of him now. "Go below, baby," he said. "We're just going to slop around for a while."

"I like being drowned."

"You're a nut. Get some sleep. I may need you later."

"If you say so. My ardor is getting a bit damp."

They laughed and kissed briefly and Peter left.

The sea calmed slowly as the wind died. In the hour before dawn there was almost total calm, but as the sky lightened he could feel the wind picking up again. He was able to leave the wheel and run forward and get the jib up. Even with the reduced mainsail, he could feel them beginning to make some speed. He set an easterly course for Mykonos. When the sun rose, he saw that he had worked his way back to the northern tip of Siros and was six or eight miles off it. The others emerged one by one. Peter was first. He came prancing aft and flopped down beside Charlie.

"You're a fair sight. Do you want me to lick the salt off you? Is it going to be a decent day for a change?"

"Not a prayer. Just like yesterday. I don't think we'll ever get to Mykonos. Who decided we wanted to go there, anyway?"

By mid-morning, the sea was rolling down on them again, knocking them over and slowing their progress.

Jack came up frowning as if the weather were a problem he was trying to solve. He zig-zagged aft and sat beside Charlie.

"The chart shows a cove at the tip of Delos," he said. "It looks beautifully sheltered."

"But Mykonos is right there in front of us. We can make it in a few more hours."

"A few more hours of this? Martha's had a hellish time. She's being a very good sport about it."

"Is there a hotel at Delos?"

"I thought you didn't want hotels to become an obsession."

Charlie shrugged. "You're right. This is a goddamn bore." He released the sheets resignedly and leaned on the wheel and headed in the direction Jack indicated. They roller-coastered down toward Delos.

The cove was lovely and deserted and as sheltered as Jack had hoped. The sea rolled past its entrance, but immediately within it the water was as smooth as glass. The anchor chain rattled and the paralysis of peace descended again. When they had the sails down, they all sat around drinking cold beer. The Kingsleys had providentially brought on more ice at Siros. Peter was excited about Delos being the birthplace of Apollo and he and Jack discussed walking over to visit the site. Charlie found his thoughts drifting and his eyes dropping shut. He pulled himself up with an effort.

"If we're going on an expedition, I'd better have a snooze before lunch. It's been over thirty hours." He went below and threw himself on his bunk without taking his clothes off.

He awoke feeling drugged. He heard dishes clattering in the galley as he tried to rouse himself. He struggled out of the bunk and went to the door. Martha was putting things away in cupboards. She smiled at him—absently? nervously? He was still too dazed with sleep to take much account of her mood.

"Well, you're human after all," she said. "I thought you were going to sleep all day."

"I feel as if I'd been knocked out."

"You'd better have some coffee. We've had lunch without you. We all agreed you needed the rest." She poured a cup of coffee and handed it to him. He took it and started for the companionway. She made a little move to arrest him. "Jack and Peter have gone ashore."

Slowly, it got through to him: alone at last. He took a long swallow of the hot coffee and his head began to clear. "That so? Gone to see the sights?" he asked, feeling his way cautiously as he aroused himself to focus all his sensibilities on her.

"If there's a hotel, they may be locked in a room by now, for all I know." She spoke deliberately, as if she had rehearsed the words.

It was so uncharacteristic of her that he was touched by it. He could see now that she was in a tangle of nerves. "Ah. Sex rears its tousled little head. Do you really think that's a possibility?"

"I don't know." She looked momentarily confused, as if she had expected some other reaction. "I mean—Jack's straight, of course, but he's crazy about Peter. If that's the way it works out, he'd probably go along."

"I see. Peter's queer. Queers are mad for anything in pants. I know that's what Jack thinks."

"He's an attractive man."

"Is he? I doubt it. Not in that way."

"What about you? Are you as queer as everybody says?"

He threw his head back and laughed. "Now come on, sweetie. Relax. Is that any way to talk to a friend? This isn't you at all. Maybe we'd better start all over again. If you want to know if I'm queer, just ask." He was fully awake now. He looked into her eyes and saw all her defenses collapse, her plan of attack, if that was what it was, crumble. All that was left was the undemanding, little-girl adoration he knew so well. Their moment had come at last. He was moved by her and welcomed it, feeling desire respond to desire.

"Are you?" she asked in a small voice.

"I thought I'd made it pretty obvious that I'm in love with Peter."

"Oh, I understand that. I love to see you together. You're so sweet to each other. But the other. I mean—do you—"

He finished his coffee and put the cup down on the counter. He leaned against the door. "People who are in love with each other usually have sex together, if that's what you're getting at," he said kindly. He watched as she reached behind her and unfastened the bikini top and dropped it.

"Then that doesn't mean anything to you?" she asked, still worshiping him with her eyes.

It meant a great deal to him. He put his hands in his pockets and shifted his sex so that it would be less cramped. He knew her body well, but the full, firm curve of her breasts was more exciting naked than he had expected. She hadn't the vanity to pose in any way, or "present" them. She simply stood and offered herself to his gaze. He was glad he had told her to get some sun on them. The mark of the bikini was still there, but not pronounced enough to mar the line. Her nipples were not big, which pleased him. They gave a lift to the heavy rounded forms. His hands wanted to feel the tender flesh. He looked into her eyes again. "Lovely, I've often wanted to draw them. But are you sure this is a good idea? I don't mind Peter knowing, but I don't particularly want him to catch us in the act. What about Jack?"

"You mean you want me?" Her eyes pleaded with him.

"What did you expect? Why did you take that thing off? Oh, I see. You mean because I'm queer? There *is* that."

"You're not. I've never believed it."

He smiled. "Sweetie, if I'm not queer, we can drop the word from the language." It excited him further to speak frankly to her. "I guess the question should be, do you want me, now that I've told you?"

"What difference does it make, if you want me?"

"Probably a lot. We can talk about that later. You still haven't told me about Jack."

"They just left about fifteen minutes ago, so we don't have to worry." She unfastened her shorts and let them fall. "I wouldn't care if he found me like this."

His eyes roamed over her nakedness. It touched him deeply. Her body seemed to yearn toward him. Her pubic hair was blonde and didn't distract from the lovely flow of hip and thigh. The curve of her belly balanced the twin curves of her breasts. She was voluptuously, luxuriously a woman. "The female form divine," he said almost to himself, "It *is* divine." He was so absorbed by her that he forgot for a moment that he was involved now personally. Then the inappropriateness of his clothing struck him. He was bursting to match her womanliness with his manhood. "It takes two to play this game," he said with a little laugh. He peeled off his tight jersey and tossed it behind him into the saloon. He unbuttoned his jeans and his sex sprang up into full erection as it was freed. He lifted his bare feet and stepped out of jeans and undershorts and straightened before her. "Adam and

Eve," he said, feeling as if they were made to be naked together.

Her lips had parted. Her eyes were wide on him. "Oh, no," she murmured.

"It is a bit much. You must've known what to expect by now."

"I've looked, of course. I couldn't help it. I didn't know a man could be so magnificent."

"You're gorgeous. Is that all we're going to do—just look?"

She approached him slowly, her eyes on his sex. It moved slightly, straining upward as if to meet her. Her knees were weak with the longing that had been born in her as she had come to know his body. Only in the last few weeks had she become aware of the extent to which she had been impoverished by her brother, and his adolescent violation of her. Charlie had instilled in her for the first time a desire, an obsessive craving to be entered by a man. Gazing day after day at the massive instrument gathered between his legs, watching its size and shape alter when he lay in the sun or emerged from the sea, stealing breathless glimpses of the great column lifting the sheet when he slept, she had felt increasingly a terrible emptiness in her, an aching sickness of emptiness that only he could fill.

She had been only nine when her fourteen-year-old brother had first taken her; for the next year, he had brought his friends to her and allowed them to use her. She had grown up thinking of boys as tiresomely similar and of the sexual act as an awkward and sometimes painful prodding of her body. When she had married Jack and he had introduced her to the pleasures they could find with their mouths, she had felt as if she had discovered the source of physical love.

Charlie had been a revelation. She had fallen in love with her eyes but he had quickly fixed himself in the center of her emotions. He was a god, with a god's beauty and strength and understanding. Only he would have had the kindness to help her through her rude and blundering opening about Jack and Peter. She had thought she would have to goad him into responding to her, but he had seemed to anticipate every move she had made and now his godlike sex rose before her in overwhelming evidence of his desire.

She couldn't take her eyes off it, though it thrilled her so deeply that her vision seemed blurred. It gave an impression of great weight so that its upward curve, springing out from its thick base, was implicit with devastating power.

242

He reached out for her, but she dropped down in front of him and felt the heat of his sex on her lips and tongue. It tasted salty and she filled her mouth with it. She moaned and her head swam as she realized that his body was at last hers. She heard him gasp and his hips swayed as she ran her tongue back to its base and took his tightly gathered testicles in her mouth. She drew back and gazed at the soaring head, shining and ripe, and stretched her jaws to clamp her teeth gently on the rigid, heavily-veined flesh. Her head reeled again when she thought of having it inside her. She didn't care how much it might hurt her; it would fill her tormenting emptiness.

"You'd better come back up here unless this is the way you want me," he said after a moment. He was amazed at what she was doing and at the skill she displayed. He had always thought of her lying back and receiving him, ample and placid and fe-male. He held her shoulders as she rose, her hand on his sex, and pulled her closer. He looked into her ecstatic eyes and smiled. "This is pretty marvelous, isn't it?"

"You're so beautiful. I adore you. There's so much of you to adore."

He chuckled. "It's a question of proper care and feeding. You do amazing things with your mouth." He shaped her breasts with his hands and took her mouth in his. He held her breasts and swayed her body lightly against his so that their nipples caressed each other. Their kiss grew deeper. He drew back and took a long breath. "Everything we do seems to make me want to come. I'm sort of planning to have you. Any preparations? Are you wearing something?"

"No. Don't think about that." She still held his sex as they went into the saloon and stretched out on the bunk he'd just vacated. When he lifted himself over her, she put her hands on his shoulders and urged him downward in his turn.

"No. Not that," he said.

"Oh, no. Of course not. I'm sorry, my precious."

He laughed softly. "It's all right. Don't worry about it. I've never really wanted to, that's all. I don't particularly like to suck cock either. I guess I'm not very oral."

She ran her hands from his shoulders down to his sex. "Come into me. That's all I want. I've dreamed of it for so long."

"You know what you're doing? It's a bit risky."

"Oh, yes. Please. Nothing else matters." She spread her legs and lifted her hips to him and held his sex while he inserted it and moved slowly into her. He smiled down at her, watching her body writhe and lift to take him. She was moaning and making little sobbing sounds as she savored every inch of him. He held back to prolong her pleasure, proud of her response. She flung her legs around his hips and grappled him to her. He allowed himself to complete his entry with a lunge.

"Oh, God! You," she cried. Her eyes were wide and staring. "I've never felt such bliss. You've taken me. My precious lover. You're mine. I can't believe it."

"Does it feel good?"

"Like an invading army." She laughed and choked. "I can't wait for the looting and raping to begin." He drew back slowly and drove hard into her. She uttered a cry that was nearly a scream. "You're so far inside me," she gasped. "Nobody's ever been there before. You're going to give me a baby. I know it."

"You want that?" he asked as a thrill ran through him. The exultation in her voice was contagious. Stray thoughts that had been drifting through his head for the last few weeks seemed to take form and fit together. Suddenly, it all made sense. He knew now the part she was destined to play. Joy was racing through his body and deep into hers.

"I want it, my precious. Now that you're here I know that's what I've been dreaming of."

"How marvelous." He opened his mouth on her breast and played with her hard nipple with his tongue. Her body leaped under him. He remained propped up on his knees and elbows so that she could lift and lower herself on him, drawing him all the way into her, swiveling her hips and moving him around inside her. She was moaning again and making her sobbing sounds. He had never performed the act with procreation as an end; his wife hadn't wanted children. All his awareness seemed to be concentrated in his sex, as if all of him were inside her, mighty with life. He existed only to plant himself in her. "Are we doing it the way you like it?" he asked with his mouth against a breast. "I want you to come. Then I'll make you a baby."

"Can you wait? My glorious lover. Go on as long as you can. I've never had anything like it. There's so much of you inside me. All you. I can never get enough of you." She spoke between gasps as she worked him all through her. Her hands roamed over him. He lifted his head to watch her body working. The simplicity of their coupling delighted him. Male and female, like a plug in a socket. He was plugged into her, but the current would flow from him. His loins felt heavy with it. She lowered herself and grasped the base of his shaft and rotated her hips around the portion that was still within her. She gripped him hard, using him, while her other hand fondled his testicles. She uttered a series of ecstatic cries.

"Oh, yes, sweetheart. Do that," he urged. "You look as if you were stirring the soup."

She laughed wildly. "Oh, God, I'm going to come. Almost. Soon." She redoubled the efforts of her writhing body. Her hands felt his taut abdomen and moved up over his chest. She flung her arms around him and held her body to him while her hips strained up to take all of him into her. She dropped back and gripped his sex again and stirred it into her. He nuzzled her breasts, making them leap and quiver under his lips. She was moaning and crying out rhythmically now as her body writhed under him.

"Now!" she cried. "Take me! Do it. Come with me." Her legs dropped from him. He took a grip on her shoulders and drew back and began to drive into her. She gripped his buttocks and pulled him in hard at the end of each long stroke. His breath was coming fast. She shouted and laughed and sobbed and he felt all her body dissolving under him. He drove into her and drove again and came shouting after her as he felt himself burst and rush pounding into her.

They lay together trembling as their excitement subsided and their breathing became normal.

"Well," he said finally. His head was turned from her, his chin against her shoulder. "There's nothing wrong with that. You're really not going to wash me out of you?"

"No, never. It wouldn't do any good anyway. You're so far up inside me."

"Then let's stay like this for a while. You made me feel so damn potent just now. If we play our cards right, we can do it again just to make sure."

"I want to stay like this forever. You still feel huge." Her hands began to stray over his back and shoulders.

"Why haven't you had a baby with Jack?" He lifted his head

and propped himself on his elbows so he could look into her face. It was so prettily put together. Her smooth brown skin had wonderful peachy highlights.

"We've had all the tests. He's sterile. We usually do it with our mouths."

"You're wonderful at that. But you like it this way?"

"Oh, God, with you. I've never known anything like it."

"How do you mean?"

"A man inside me, making me come. It's never happened before."

"That's not possible."

"I told you, with Jack it's usually with the mouth. There haven't been many others, except long ago when it didn't count. I don't even know if men are generally built like you."

"You mean my cock? You can say it."

"Yes, your beautiful great cock."

He laughed. "Feel that? I guess it likes attention."

"Doesn't it get plenty? Are many men so big?" She ran her hands down over his buttocks and pressed him to her.

"It's bigger than average, but it's not all that unique." Thoughts were fitting together again. He had been preparing Peter for something. His grand design was grander than he had realized. He needed more time to sort it out. He went on, "Peter's is almost as big and *really* beautiful. Haven't you noticed?"

"I suppose I should say no, but yes, I have. He's lovely-looking, but you're such a man. I can't imagine why I thought you'd want me to do it with my mouth."

"Because I'm a faggot?"

"You're not a faggot."

He smiled into her eyes. "You've got to learn to say that without making it sound like a dread disease. Sex is fabulous with you, but I've always known it would be with a girl I felt really in touch with. You mustn't let that confuse you. When you say I'm yours, it just can't be. I'm a taker. Goodness, this is turning into very conversational sex. I like it. Sex between a man and a women is more a sharing, I guess, giving and taking. You share everything with another man much more than you could with a woman, but I guess the sex part is more solitary. Selfish, probably. It's more masculine really, if you look at it that way. I'm a very butch faggot, but a faggot all the same." He laughed.

"Stop calling yourself that."

"You started it. No. I'm sorry. You said 'queer'."

"Please don't. I'm in love with you. You know that."

"Yes. That's something nobody can ever do anything about, but I'm sorry. I don't want you to be hurt. I'm in love with Peter. I always have been and always will be. Till madness do us part."

"Madness?"

"I sometimes think I may be losing my mind," he said thoughtfully. "Some pretty mad thoughts are racing around in my head right now."

"Tell me."

"Not yet. I'm not being a tease. There's a lot I don't understand yet about this."

"I don't mind waiting, my precious." She slipped her hand down and found his testicles and cradled them. She felt more intimate with him than she ever had with any other being. Even while he was defining the limits of his response to her, she could feel love and goodness flowing from him. Perhaps he felt more for her than he realized. She could wait indefinitely while she helped him free himself from Peter's hold.

Her hand tickled his balls and his body jerked in response. "Go on, do that some more. I'm getting a whopping great hard-on again. Can you feel it?"

"It's felt as if you had a hard-on all along. I can feel it moving. It's heavenly."

"God, yes. It's fascinating getting a hard-on and talking and thinking about giving you another baby all at the same time. I love giving you babies. We'll make it twins. If it really happens, what's Jack supposed to think?"

"I don't know. Maybe I'd better let him do it properly in the next week or two. He'll think it's a miracle."

"No. Don't do that yet. Give me some time. We'll talk about it. I don't want him to fuck you while this is going on. Do you understand?"

She looked into his eyes with gratitude. "Yes, my precious lover."

"I mean it. Maybe Jack should know I'm the father. You want me to make you pregnant. You're in love with me. Let's wait and see how it should be for all of us. It's pretty tremendous. We've got to know what's good for the baby, too."

"Who wants to decide anything now? All I can think about is your great cock. Oh, God. The invading army."

"Mmmm. Everything is really operating now." He propped himself up with his knees and withdrew slowly to the edge of her entrance and thrust purposefully into her. She cried out and her body shuddered under him. He looked into her eyes and saw the passion lighting up in them. He swallowed hard. "Christ, don't you think I'd like to love you and have children with you?" he cried with sudden unexpected anguish.

"Fuck me, my great lover," she soothed him. "That's all I want. Yes. Oh, yes. Make me come again. Oh, God, you're the only one."

They were waiting in the cockpit, dressed and having drinks when they saw Jack and Peter appear late in the afternoon over the low ridge that enclosed the cove. They went forward and waved as the two ashore carried the dinghy down to the still water and launched it from the arc of beach.

"I feel as if it must show all over me," Martha murmured, as the dinghy approached. "I'm so blissfully happy."

"Just don't try to hide it by being off-hand with me," Charlie warned. "That would be the biggest giveaway of all."

Jack and Peter were talking at once when they came aboard, telling about the ancient ruined city, the mosaics, the fragments of statuary and carved stone lying about in the open, the remains of the Apollonian cult, including a monumental marble phallus, complete with balls.

"We saw only one guard the entire time we were there," Peter said. "It's fantastic, like a great outdoor museum. I could make a fortune if most of it weren't too heavy to lift. Still, I've got my eye on a couple of things. You've both got to come tomorrow. This is the most exciting place yet."

"The seas are bigger than ever," Jack said. "It's lucky we put in here. We couldn't have found a better place to sit it out."

They talked about Delos during the evening and got out guide-books to read up on it. When Jack and Martha went to bed, Charlie and Peter lingered a while on deck, drinking wine and talking.

"It's mad. Cocks in every direction." Peter laughed. "I can't wait for you to see it. Aside from all that, it's so beautiful, the way the hill goes down to the sea. There's a magnificent view of the islands."

Sitting side-by-side, with Peter's arm around his shoulder, Charlie longed to tell him what had happened, but he knew he must wait until they could get away from the boat for a day or two. The atmosphere was dense enough without Peter being involved. And he would be involved. He wanted him to be involved. There were already things he had resolved to speak to Martha about. He leaned to Peter's mouth and nibbled his lips gently with teeth and tongue.

"The way you kiss me these days," Peter said with a giggle. "You may yet seduce me."

Charlie had never loved him so tenderly nor been so stirred by him as thoughts of possible developments ran through his head. He put his hand on his golden hair. "Better go to bed, baby. I really have to catch up on my sleep."

When Peter came to wake him in the morning, he had been aware of all their comings and goings for some time. He pretended to be asleep and groaned when Peter tugged his foot. "So soon?"

"It's after eight. We're ready to go. Come on, Champ."

"You all go ahead. I need another hour. I'll swim ashore and join you."

"OK. When you go up the beach, you'll find a path. Just stay on it till you get to the site. A little farther along you'll see some walls with two huge statues sticking out of them. You can't miss it. I'll wait for you around there somewhere. Just call."

Charlie lay in his bunk, listening to the sounds of departure. He was sure Martha would find an excuse to stay on board. He heard the dinghy bumping against the side. He heard the splash of oars. He waited a few moments and then leaped up and shed his shorts and performed his morning toilet. He poured himself a cup of coffee from the pot that was still hot on the stove and mounted the companionway naked. He looked around him. The wind was still blowing. The dinghy was beached. There was nobody in sight on shore. He moved out onto the deck and looked up along it. She was lying out naked, with towels and cushions around her, her hands covering her nipples. He carried his cup forward and joined her. She sat up and grabbed at a towel and slowly pushed it aside as she gazed up at him.

"The birthplace of Apollo. How gorgeous of you to come to me naked. I was afraid I'd dreamed we're lovers. Was sleeping just an excuse?"

He nodded. "I thought you'd stay. What did you say?"

"I said if you were going to join them, somebody should stay with the boat. Jack always goes for that." Her eyes strayed over him and returned to his sex. "I can really look at you, at last. Even like that, you can tell it must get enormous. I've dreamed so often of your being naked with me in the sun so that I could see all of you."

"Isn't it marvelous? It feels wonderful being like this together. I'm ready to get enormous for you." He put the cup down on the cabin roof. She was immediately crouched before him, arousing him with her mouth. He laughed as he lifted and hardened. When he was fully erect, she sat back on her haunches and looked up at him.

"How it soars. It's sublime from this angle. So powerful. It must make you feel so proud. That monumental phallus they were talking about. What do we want with a statue?"

He dropped to his knees in front of her and she held his sex upright against himself while he stroked her breasts with the tips of his fingers. They were lost for a rapt moment in contemplation of each other's bodies.

"I'm trying to decide what to do next," he said with a grin. "Come on. Sit down." He sat with his legs out in front of him around her. He lifted her legs over his thighs and moved in close to her. He ran his hands up her thighs and over the full curve of her belly.

"That's where I'm supposed to lose five pounds," she said.

"I like it. It's a bit Rubens, but not too much." She held his testicles in both hands and exerted a slight pressure so that his sex stood straight between them, swaying slightly. "Well, what shall we do with it?"

"Like this." She lay her fingers along it lightly and pulled it down to her. "It's so hard. Does it hurt for me to force it down like this?"

"It feels marvelous. Go ahead."

250

They both watched as she tipped forward, lifting herself on his thighs, and inserted the head and gripped the shaft and moved it around within her. They took quick simultaneous breaths.

"You're stirring the soup again." They laughed together.

"That's where it makes me come."

"You mean, there's all that left-over cock doing nobody any good?"

"Oh, no. I'm just discovering all it's good for. It's for holding like this and for coming way up inside me. I feel sorry for women who haven't had anything like this."

"Can you really come like that?"

"I could."

"Do it. I want to see."

"You really want me to? You don't think it's shameless of me? Letting you watch and all?"

"What's wrong with being shameless? It's exciting to see you doing things with my cock." He put his arms around her shoulders and leaned his head against hers as she gripped his sex and began to move it firmly within her. Her breath quickened.

"Oh, yes," she gasped. "This is what I've always wanted and not known it. Holding a great hard cock and doing this with it. Oh, God. Just this much of you feels huge inside me. Let me do this."

"I sure will. I'll be ready to come with you."

"Not yet. Wait. Please."

"Don't worry. I'm doing fine."

She continued the movement while he stroked her back and breasts and thighs. She was panting and moaning. "Oh, yes. Yes," she cried at last. She let go of his sex and gripped his waist and pulled herself to him, taking all of him into her. He put his hands behind him and propped himself on his arms and threw his head back and lifted his hips. He gave a shout as he felt himself exploding deep within her. She made incoherent sounds of satisfaction as she fell against his chest, her arms clinging to him as she bore down on his sex, driving it deeper into her as he rocked with the spasm of his orgasm. After a few minutes, he eased her back so that she was sitting on the deck once more.

"We do have fun," he said with a chuckle.

"Was it good for you?"

"God, yes, considering we made it up on the spur of the moment." His sex slowly slipped from her and lay on the deck. He reached for a towel and started to wipe it. She took the towel and did it for him.

"I hope you don't expect me to be ladylike and hide how crazy I am for this. I still can't believe you're letting me hold it, that it's all swollen like this for me, that it's getting softer because it's just filled me with you. I want to sit so I don't lose what you've just given me." She tossed the towel aside and lifted her legs from his thighs and folded them under her and sat between his outspread legs. One hand continued to caress his sex, keeping it extended and partially erect.

"I'm going to have to go pretty soon," he said. "I've been thinking a lot. There's so much we have to talk about."

"Are you going to tell me you're queer again? It's not very convincing after the way you make love to me."

"Oh, I'm probably bisexual. I think most people are if they're relaxed about it. That's one of the things I want you to understand. About me and Peter. Under different circumstances I suppose I might have had an affair with him and then gone on and had a family and all the rest of it. That's the way I thought it was going to be when it started. We had to make so many sacrifices to have it the way we both wanted it. Complete and good. The most important person in my life was my grandmother before Peter. This can't be very interesting for you, but it's important. When we decided we really wanted to live together, that was the end of her. Disinherited and the lot. His family. My family. Friends we had to cut because they wouldn't understand. The lying and deception to make it easier for people we had to work with. When you're an outcast, you hang on to whatever good you have in life. Talk about bonds of steel. Even if we didn't love being together, we'd probably hang on just to convince ourselves that it had all been worth it. My life in a nutshell. I want you to tell me about you. What about being married to Jack?"

"What about it?"

"I'm serious. I want to know. You've been together about as long as Peter and I. It must mean something to you."

"No. Nothing. Not for a long time. When he bought this boat,

I told him I couldn't go on living with him. He doesn't care. I've stayed on the way people do, waiting for something to happen that would force me to decide. I'm glad I did. I've been marvelously happy with you on board, so it's not just the boat. When you go, I'll hate it more than ever. I'll go, too. Home probably. To my parents in Rhode Island, maybe, if I'm pregnant. I know I am. Money's no problem, thank heavens."

"Then what?"

"A divorce, of course. I've never known how to do anything, so I doubt if I'll get a job. I'll jog along. With a baby, I'll be happier than I have been for years."

She was so utterly undemanding. It was the quality in her that made him feel that almost anything was possible. "You're sure you know what you're saying? It might be pretty important. It's really finished with Jack? Regardless of this, you've been planning to clear out?"

"Of course. Couldn't you tell? If we didn't have to get through this cruise together, I'd tell him today. As you say, I don't particularly want him to catch us in the act, but I'm not even sure of that. I'd like him to see what a man should look like." His sex responded in her hand and she began to stroke it more insistently. She knew her worship of it was the only hold she had over him, but he was opening out the situation much sooner than she had dared hope. His interest in her future, the hint that he wanted her to be free, it was all leading up to something. She chose her words carefully so as not to frighten him off.

"You've always been so sweet to me, much more than men who've said they love me. Will you want to know the baby?"

"God, yes. I've always wanted one, but my wife wouldn't hear of it. Peter would adore a baby of mine. He's always wanted me to have one, but it's got to be his, too. I want it to be ours." As he spoke, his sex surged out in her hand and hardened more. He laughed. "That's what we get for being naked. No secrets. Now you know how exciting that sounds to me."

"I don't understand. What's exciting?"

"I want Peter to have you. Now. Soon. So we won't know who the father is."

She stared at him, immediate shock banishing thought. "You really *are* mad," she said.

"No. Don't you understand? We're practically the same person.

I'd be much more yours when you've had him. He's part of me. He'd make you more mine. I want him to make you pregnant with me."

She became aware that his sex was standing erect in her hand. She watched it lift imperiously as she ran her fingers over it and knew that it commanded her. "It's too late," she said. "All night, I could feel you growing inside me. I can tell something's happened. You've made me too completely yours. I can't even imagine anybody else."

"But that's what I'm telling you. It won't be anybody else. It'll be all three of us together. He'd never do it unless I'm there. You'll see. It really will be complete. As soon as we get to Mykonos, we'll arrange something. We can't do anything on the boat. I can't even talk to Peter while we're all cooped up together. When will you know?"

"About the baby? My period's due in eight or nine days. I'll know before that. Things begin to happen to me. They won't this time."

"That's plenty of time for Peter."

"Why do you think he'll want it? He's never given the slightest sign of it."

"He's never had a girl. I think he's beginning to want one, without even knowing it. You'll make him love it and you'll love it, too. He's so beautiful. I love the way his body works. I can't wait to see him with you."

She knew she had no choice. She could only evaluate the risks and be prepared to seize whatever advantages were offered her. Sharing herself with Peter might dissolve whatever slight possessiveness he might feel for her, permit him to disassociate himself from her completely. Yet she couldn't understand his giving her his lover unless he too wanted to be free. If he wished to use her as the instrument to break the bond between them, she would willingly submit. He would be free for her. "Do you think you'll still have sex with Peter after all this?" she asked, careful to make it sound as if it was of no great matter to her.

"Of course," he said for the record, but he wasn't sure of anything. He had always stubbornly insisted to himself that their "unnatural" love was perfectly natural, but it seemed to him at last that the label was applicable, not to the feeling they had for each other but to the acts with which they expressed it. They

254

were endlessly repetitious, leading to nothing. Martha had introduced him to the reproductive rhythm of life, with all its shifts, its promises, its surprises. Her menstrual period had suddenly become a matter of intense interest to him. "I don't know what's going to happen," he said, putting his hand on hers as it moved up and down on his sex. "None of us do. First, we've got to know if you're pregnant. I wish the child didn't have to have Jack's name. Maybe you should come live near us. Who knows? I'm thinking of lots of possibilities. Can you feel what it's doing to me? We'd better stop this. We don't have time for more. I told Peter an hour."

He dropped his hand but hers gripped him more purposefully. "Let me do it like this. I want to see what it looks like when you come."

"Really? Good lord. If you go on like that, it'll only take a second." His head fell back and he closed his eyes and she took possession of him. This sterile act had significance when performed by the mother of his child. Her interest was legitimate. There was no reason why she shouldn't become part of their lives. Some arrangement could be worked out. One of them might even marry her and they could have more children. A child wholly Peter's. The thought of it brought him immediately to orgasm. His hips lurched up from the deck with the spasms and he felt himself jetting into the air. She continued to stroke him until he began to subside and then he felt the towel on him again. He lifted his head and looked at her.

"You're magnificent, like an erupting volcano," she said. "I know what happens now when you're inside me. No wonder I'm pregnant. It comes shooting out of you. I won't do it again. It's such a waste. But I have to see everything about you."

"My bag of tricks is pretty limited. That's about it." He leaned forward and kissed her lightly on the lips. "Off to join the archaeologists. No more of this till Mykonos. We've got to keep Jack out of it till you know. After that, it's up to you." He rose and left her.

He found Jack and Peter digging about near the statues Peter had mentioned. Their eyes glittered with acquisitiveness.

"Look what I've found already," Peter said, holding out an exquisitely carved bird's head, a swan or a goose or a wild duck.

"I know it's awful to take things like this. It might be the missing link that'll give the key to a whole epoch, and all that. But if I don't take it, somebody else will. I don't see why they don't do something about it. Look what Jack's found."

Jack had dug clear a portion of a carved slab with a frieze of animals. It was too big to move. "Trust an art dealer to find something he can put in his pocket," he said.

Peter conducted Charlie all over the wide hillside site with a proprietary air. Charlie felt the magic in it. The wind roared among the ruined walls. The great seas crashed against nearby islands. The light lay in the air like gold. It was all luminous and windswept and as old as time. He had to make an effort to speak above a whisper. Peter led him down to the row of eerie lions and the great smashed phallus. Vanished gods. He felt the melancholy of loss. He reached out and took Peter's hand. After a moment, Peter started to pull away.

"Hey, this is Greece," Charlie said, holding him. "This is Delos. Men can hold hands here."

"I was thinking of Jack."

"Who cares about Jack?" They strolled on hand-in-hand.

Charlie took Peter's hand again when the three of them were returning to the boat for lunch. It amused him that Jack was probably thinking "Faggot!" about the man who had just fucked his wife.

Later in the afternoon, Jack proposed that they should all show Martha the site. Charlie glanced meaningfully at Peter and said he would stay on board.

"I might as well stay with Charlie," Peter said.

They watched the couple walk up the beach and drop from sight on the other side of the ridge. They looked into each other's eyes and smiled.

"Were you thinking what I was?" Peter asked.

"What else? Listen, baby, I know you're having a good time here, but is it all right if we try to get away tonight? Time is passing. We've been out almost a month."

"Is that all? It seems more like a year. Sure, let's go. I thought we were waiting for the wind to die."

"That might take a year. If we get that lull before dawn, we can make it to Mykonos in no time. We still have a lot to see."

"Fine with me. Now about that other matter I had in mind."

"A quick swim and then let's get at it, mate."

They dropped their shorts on the deck and dived over the side. Charlie wanted to keep their sex life constant so that when he told Peter about Martha he wouldn't think that she had intruded on them in any way. He couldn't take Peter as he had taken Martha, but after his wholly masculine experience with her the thought of reverting to the feminine role he had recently assumed with Peter intrigued and excited him. Peculiar, certainly. Mad, perhaps? He hoped it would all emerge into the coherent plan that seemed at times within his grasp.

When he suggested over drinks that they should make another try for Mykonos early the next morning, Martha's eyes widened and she glanced quickly at Peter before her regard returned questioningly to Charlie. Had he told Peter? He shook his head slightly. They all agreed to his suggestion.

He and Peter stayed on deck through the night, sleeping fitfully while Charlie kept an eye on the weather. He watched as the pattern he had already noted repeated itself. The quiet hour before dawn came. He leaned over and gently roused Peter.

"OK, baby. Thank God, Jack agreed to let us use the motor till we get around Delos. Get the anchor up. Let's go."

An hour after sunrise, they were tied up in the port of Mykonos and the wind was renewing its relentless attack.

"We'll clear off and leave you in peace," Charlie said when all four were finishing breakfast together.

"Don't you want to go sight-seeing later?" Martha asked, her increasingly possessive eyes on his.

"How long are we going to stay here?" he asked in reply.

"Let's decide that tomorrow," Jack suggested. "This is probably the last civilized place we'll hit before Crete, where we can get ice and restaurant meals and all that sort of thing. Let's see what the bloody wind does."

"Come back when you've found a hotel," Martha said.

"I may get some sleep," Charlie told her. He wanted to hold her off for a bit, work her up, make her long for him *and* Peter. "We'll be around."

Mykonos turned out to be the most touristic place they'd been to. The hotel was new and modern and charmingly set under pine trees above the harbor. Charlie asked for a double bed and when he saw it, his mind was filled with images of Peter and Martha in it. He was deeply excited by the prospect, but he postponed speaking to Peter about it. He wanted another day of the status quo to prove to him that nothing had changed between them.

When they went the next morning to check in at the boat, they found Jack doing something greasy to the generator in the engine room.

"Thank heavens. You've come to rescue me," Martha greeted them. He looked into her eyes and saw the urgency of her desire in them. "He'll be down there for hours. Will you take me up to those windmills? I'm fascinated by them."

The island was dotted with windmills, but Martha pointed out a row of three just above and behind the town. One of them wasn't operating; the other two had their sails out and were spinning as merrily as toys reefed down in the persistent gale.

"We've been meaning to have a look at them. I suspect they're run by motors," Charlie said. "You want to go now? Come on."

She called down to Jack and they walked back along the quai and through the town and found a road leading up to them. There was a string of donkeys outside one of them and they went to its open door. Their ears were assailed by a great din. A man and a boy were busy inside. When the man saw the three blond foreigners, he motioned them in. They entered and stood beside a great stone wheel whirling in a stone base. Grain was being fed into it on one side and ground flour was spewing into a sack on the other. There was other gear, apparently for lowering and raising the wheel and braking it. Everything was made of stone and carved wood and leather thongs and rope. It looked as if it could have been assembled thousands of years ago; they all gazed at it with wonder. The man singled out Peter as his interlocutor and within a moment the two were having a lively conversation with their hands, pointing at various parts of the mechanism and making explanatory gestures.

Martha touched Charlie's hand and moved her eyes to a stairway leading up to a hole in the plank ceiling. She moved toward it and he followed her and they mounted it. It led up to a cramped loft with a steeply pitched roof, so that there was room to stand only in the middle near the spinning central shaft, pro-

pelled by an axle that was geared into it and ran out to the
long spokes to which the sails were fixed. Again, it was all of
wood and leather and rope. Charlie was reminded of the night
of the storm. The whole building vibrated with the flailing arms
of the wheel and the straining sails. There was an impression
of rushing, dangerous movement. Everything was spinning and
whirling. The loft was filled with a deafening clatter. Charlie
remained in the stairway, his feet and calves showing in the room
below. When Martha saw that he had stopped, she crouched
in front of him so that their heads were on a level.

"I had to talk to you," she said. Her voice was covered by
the noise of the working machinery, but he could hear her with
surprising clarity. "I've been thinking about Peter. I understand
what you mean. Do you still want us together?"

"I haven't been able to think about anything else. Has Jack
said any more about when we leave?"

"I know he's not planning to leave today."

"Good. You've got to come to the hotel. Can you manage that?"

"I've already told him I'd like a night in a hotel to rest and
soak in a tub before we go off on more island-hopping."

"Smart girl. He won't want to come with you?"

"Never. He won't leave the boat."

"Good. Come tonight. We're in 316. Try to get a room near
us."

"What does Peter say?"

"I haven't said anything to him yet. I will this evening."

"What if he doesn't want to?"

"He will. When do you think you'll come?"

"Jack will expect me to spend the evening with him. About
eleven. I'm doing it because you want it and I understand what
you mean about being the same person. I couldn't if I felt I were
being unfaithful to you. You know that, don't you? You'll have
me too?"

"Of course. Both of us. That's the point."

"I think such unladylike thoughts about you. I haven't stopped
wanting you for a second. I've almost told Jack several times."

"Unless we decide to cut the trip short, you can't. Wait till
tonight and we—" He felt the stair sag under him. He looked
down and saw Peter coming up. He smiled down at him and
waited until he was on the step below him. He put his hand

on his shoulder. "Martha's coming down. There's no room for two. She's hypnotized by all the things going round." He turned back to Martha. "Come on. Peter wants to come up." He gave Peter's shoulder a little caress as he slipped past him and went down. In a moment, Martha joined him and they smiled and nodded to the miller and went out. They found a wall out of earshot and protected from the wind, but within view of the door and sat and waited for Peter.

"What were you about to say?" she asked. "Wait till tonight and we'll what?"

"Know better what happens next. I want so for Peter to like it. I'd like him to find a girl of his own. Even marry her. It wouldn't change anything between us. Nothing can. We'll always be together even if we don't necessarily live in the same house."

"Did you mean it when you said you'd like me to live near you?"

"Of course. It all depends on Peter. He'll make you pregnant tonight if I haven't."

"But you have. I know it. I can feel you growing in me."

He smiled fondly at her. "I guess you really want it. Well, so do I. I'd love to watch a kid grow up. A boy, naturally. If we wanted him to have a brother, I suppose we could even get married."

"I should think you'd stop feeling like an outcast if you were married."

"Would you marry me, sweetie?" He laughed incredulously. "That's what's so marvelous about all this. We don't have to rush into anything. We're not breaking up a happy home. I wouldn't do anything to make Peter unhappy. There's no great drama."

"Except that I'm in love with you."

Charlie sobered, but she didn't make him feel guilty or defensive. Most women would have made the declaration sound like blackmail. "I know, sweetheart. I must sound sometimes as if I thought you were a machine for making babies. If I didn't like you so damn much, I never would've let this happen. You don't give me the feeling you're sorry."

"How could I be? I'm with you and I'm in love with you. I've had your magnificent body. Your magnificent cock. Let's face it, I'd do almost anything for it. Has it been getting hard the way it did when we were talking the day before yesterday?"

"It is now. Wow." He burst into laughter. "I can't wait for tonight. Just come to our room as soon as you can."

"Will you—"

Peter appeared at the door with the miller and they shook hands and gesticulated at each other and parted. Charlie rose and met Peter as he approached and linked his arm in his. Peter looked at him with pleased expectancy, but Charlie led him wordlessly to Martha and stood in front of her.

"You see what I mean?" he asked.

"Yes. About everything."

"What have you two been up to?" Peter asked, looking as if he had missed a joke.

"I've been telling Martha how much I love you."

Peter was struck dumb. "What a—" he blurted and could say no more. He felt Charlie's arm holding him close. He saw Martha's pretty face smiling up at him.

"He doesn't have to say it. It's plain enough," she said.

Peter recovered his voice and uttered a peal of incredulous laughter. "For God's sake. What is this? All right. *I* love *him*. That must be pretty plain, too."

"It is." She rose and took his other arm. "Darling Peter."

Charlie moved around beside her and they escorted her back to the boat. Peter sensed that something had happened between them, but he couldn't imagine what could have provoked Charlie to such frankness. They had a drink on board and talked of getting away the following night during the lull. Martha remarked casually that she might have a night in a hotel. She paid a great deal of attention to Peter, which he found flattering after the weeks of concentration on Charlie. Puzzling, too. When they left the Kingsleys to have lunch ashore, Peter queried him about the conversation at the windmill, but Charlie spoke as if it had had no particular significance.

"I felt like saying it. I don't want to keep it secret any more."

"I wish I'd been there. When it comes to you and love, I have a word or two to say myself."

Without making a point of it, Charlie arranged that they have dinner a little earlier than usual and when they were finished suggested that they go back to the hotel. "We have things to talk about," he said.

"I thought so." Peter had been aware of a recklessness in him, a mounting restlessness that included him in an air of odd hilarity. Charlie was laughing a lot. The evening promised to be cheerful. "Is it more about what you and Martha were talking about?"

"Right," Charlie said with a laugh.

When they were in the room, Charlie told Peter to undress and did so himself. They stretched out on the double bed together and Charlie propped himself on an elbow. "I like to see all of you when we talk." He ran a finger along the muscles of his chest and down to his navel and pressed. "Room service," he said, in reference to an old joke of theirs. They laughed and Peter reached out for his sex. "Well then," Charlie began. "First of all, it's happened. Martha and me. Like I said it might."

Peter drew his hand away from his sex and lay very still. There was a moment's silence. "I see," he said finally. "Are you sure you have to tell me about it?"

"Of course. That's it. She's coming here in a little while."

"Where?"

"Here. To the room. That's what I have to talk to you about."

Peter sat upright and threw his legs over the side of the bed. "This is beginning to sound familiar. You married the girl the last time I had to stay away and leave you alone. What am I supposed to do this time? Take a walk around the block or go get another room?"

Charlie reached out for him and laughed as he tried to pull him back beside him. "Come here, damn it. Don't be silly, baby. Will you listen to me? You're not going anywhere." He could feel Peter giving in to him. He hurried on. "We did it—like that. You know. Without taking any of the usual precautions. She may be pregnant. I want you to have her. If she has a baby, I want it to be as much yours as it is mine."

Peter gazed at him a long moment with unguarded, devoted eyes. "You really mean that, don't you? You're incredible. That's the most wonderful thing ever." He passed his hand across his forehead and shook his head slightly. "I couldn't, darling. Don't you understand? I just don't feel like that about girls. I could never get it up."

Charlie pulled him down beside him. "Of course you can, baby. We'll be together. You have this beautiful cock that's made for fucking. I should know. I'll do it, too. We'll both be inside her. We'll be together. You've always said you'd have a girl if

I was with you." He felt Peter's sex swell in his hand. "There. You see? You can't deny you think it's sexy."

"I do when you say it. I know if she were here, nothing would happen. I can't stand the way females are made there, all open and—nothing. I won't be able to. How do you think that'll make me feel with Martha?"

"But think about what I'm saying. We can have a baby together. It'll be ours."

Peter looked into his eyes wonderingly. "Is that the way it works? You mean it'll be a sort of mixture of both of us?"

"Not exactly. We did it day before yesterday. No, the day before that. Anyway, that's only two nights between. Nobody can possibly tell who the father is when it happens so close together."

"I see." He laughed briefly. "There wouldn't be any doubt in my mind. What does Martha think?"

"About you having her? All women find you attractive, baby, and then some. She thinks she's in love with me. No, that's not right. I guess she really is. She wants a baby. Jack can't give her one and they're all washed up anyway. She understands why I want you to do it with her. That's what we were talking about this morning. She hasn't had much of this kind of sex. She's crazy for it. You'll see. She'll make it really good for you."

"This kind of sex?"

"Old-fashioned fucking. She's used to sucking cock and having Jack go down on her."

"I'll be damned. Our Martha's a cocksucker?" Peter's body shook with laughter. "Welcome to the club. I don't know, darling. I feel so damn self-conscious. She must think we're nuts."

"I told her that I'm in love with you and that we'll always be together. That's not nuts."

"If you keep on saying things like that, I could fuck a mountain goat. I never thought we'd be going in for threesomes in our old age. I'm not sure how I feel about the idea. I admit that seeing you with her would be exciting, but I don't think I'd like it more than once. This couldn't happen with a boy, could it, darling?"

"Certainly not. You're the only boy I want. That gets truer every day."

"Then that's all right. I guess I'm not much for kooky sex. OK. Let's say she has our child. Then what?"

"I don't know. We'll just have to wait and see."

"There're no commitments you haven't told me about?"

"Absolutely not. She knows I'm in love with you, not with her. It's all perfectly clear and straight. We haven't had a chance to talk about it in a big way. I couldn't have until you were part of it, anyway. Any talking, from now on, we'll do together."

"You're quite a sublime person." He stretched all his body and wriggled in closer to Charlie. "I'd like you to kiss me rather a lot before our privacy is invaded." He sat up suddenly. "No. No. No. I just can't do it. I'll go out if you want. I can't be a part of something that risks coming between us."

"How can it come between us? I've done it. I want you to do it. It'll be part of what we have together." Charlie's voice hardened. "I mean it, baby. Aside from anything else, I want you to have a girl. It's something you've got to try."

Peter fell back with a sigh. "All right. I'll make a fool of myself, if that's what you want. You'll see. Nothing will happen. Look at me. I feel as if I'd never get another erection as long as I live. When is she supposed to come?"

"Soon. Half an hour, maybe."

"Let's order some wine. Getting a little drunk might help."

Ordering wine on the house phone and waiting and calling again and getting the wine without the glasses and sending back for them with some ice took the better part of a quarter of an hour. They had had time to drink only a glass when there was a knock on the door. Charlie rolled over and started to get up.

"Put something on," Peter muttered urgently. He pulled the sheet over himself.

Charlie laughed. "You don't have to get dressed to fuck, silly." He rose and stood behind the door and opened it. Martha slipped in wearing a long dressing gown and he closed the door behind her.

Peter's heart leaped up in his chest. He saw them smile intimately at each other. He saw Charlie take the robe as Martha dropped it. They stood together stunningly naked, superbly matched, an idealization of male and female. He noted with satisfaction that being near her didn't give Charlie an immediate erection. Peter found her breasts beautiful, full and tender-looking. He couldn't look below them. The involuntary glimpse he had caught left him with an impression of something incomplete and deformed. She looked maimed. Charlie said something

264

that Peter didn't hear and then sprang for the bed and fell on him. His hands were on all his ticklish places.

"Since when have you been shy about letting people see you?" Charlie demanded, laughing and grappling his body around sideways on the bed. Peter's feet dropped to the floor as he laughed helplessly and tried to escape the tickling hands. He felt Charlie's rigid sex beating against him as he lifted himself and darted about above him, kissing his neck and chest and shoulders. He, not Martha, had given Charlie an erection. Charlie was indulging in these glorious intimacies in front of her. He howled with laughter as his own sex reared up with pride and gratitude. Charlie tugged at the tangled sheet and tore it off him.

"Look what he's hiding from us," he cried.

Peter felt soft flesh brushing against his thighs and then practiced hands and tongue and lips took his sex. His body contracted in a great leap. "Oh, Christ!" he cried.

Charlie was sprawled beside him, cradling his head on his arm. "You're being raped, baby," he said excitedly. "You're beautiful. Let her do it until you're almost ready to come. Don't think about anything but coming inside her. When you know what it's like, you can do it your way later." He lowered his mouth to Peter's and ran his tongue teasingly over his lips.

Peter gasped and shook his head. "No. Oh, Christ! Now, quickly."

"Really?" Charlie laughed triumphantly and seized him and pulled him back all the way onto the bed. Somehow Martha was beside him and then blindly he was on top of her. He felt hands all over his body. He felt his sex engulfed in deep, sliding warmth and he uttered a hoarse shout as he was shaken by an immediate orgasm.

Charlie slipped his hand down between Peter's buttocks. He could feel the throb of his ejaculation. He lifted himself to his knees and stroked his buttocks and the small of his back and ran his hands up to his neck and down across his broad shoulders. This beautiful body had fulfilled its function at last. He felt a great, satisfied tenderness for it. His sex lifted rigidly as he thought of entering Peter now as he lay with Martha, having them both through him. Perhaps some other time. Peter was a man and inviolable now.

After another moment, Peter stirred, "God. Some performance," he said. "I felt like a prize bull with everybody standing around helping." He lifted his head and looked into Martha's eyes for the first time. "Fancy meeting you here," he said jauntily. They all laughed and as the contagion of it gripped them, Peter rolled away from her and lay on his back, convulsed. Still laughing, Charlie moved into position between her knees and Martha's laughter died. He dropped forward over her and propped himself on his arms and moved his knees back until she could lower his sex and direct it into her. Peter's laughter choked in his throat as he saw him make his first thrust. The way she held his sex with both hands, the way he moved his body in response to hers suggested a knowledgeable intimacy that made Peter feel they had performed this act many times. Charlie's powerful body arched over her, his muscles tensed as he lowered himself slowly to brush her breasts with his chest and straightened his arms again. She was beginning to moan and cry out. Their movements became more agitated. In the way her body lifted to it Peter could sense her devouring hunger for the shaft of flesh within her. He knew that hunger. He found himself trembling all over and his sex was once more erect, aching with complex desire. He wanted Charlie. He wanted to make Martha moan and cry out for him. Her fingers were clawing Charlie's back, her cries were growing shriller. At some unseen signal Charlie seemed to take complete control. Her body was locked to his. She rocked to the hard rhythmic thrust of his hips. She began to keen. This was more than sex as Peter knew it and less than love. It was a ritual of power that perhaps could be performed only by a man and a woman. He wondered if she could generate the power in him that he felt in Charlie now. If so, perhaps he would discover something in women after all. Her keening rose in pitch and broke off with a sharp cry and then she was sobbing as all her body went limp. Charlie released her and propped himself on his arms again and thrust hard into her a half-a-dozen more times until his body was convulsed and he dropped down onto her again. A thrill ran through Peter as he realized that Charlie hadn't uttered the cries of ecstasy with which he was always rewarded but only a few satisfied grunts. In a moment, Charlie's hand reached out across the bed and fumbled for him and found his erect sex. He grunted again. After a few more seconds, he gathered himself together with an obvious effort and withdrew from Martha. His chest was still heaving and his sex still nearly erect. "Come on, baby," he said, perching on the edge of the bed. "She really wants it."

Peter felt Charlie's hand on his buttocks as he moved into position on his knees as Charlie had done.

"Look at him," Charlie said proudly. "I wish I was going to have it."

Peter felt Martha's eyes on him. He still couldn't look at all of her, but kept his eyes fixed on her breasts. She held his sex and ran her expert hands along it. Charlie waited until he started to drop down on her and then he rose and went into the bathroom. This was the real initiation and he wanted him to find his way alone.

Martha felt Charlie's absence as she guided his lover into her. He was forcing her to give herself unrestrainedly to this second invasion. He had been right about their being the same person in the sense that she had felt no embarrassment at having Peter lying beside her while Charlie took her. Their identification with each other communicated itself so strongly that his being there had seemed perfectly normal.

She found his body exquisite as her hands learned its contours. She drifted into a delectable lethargy as his sex reached into her almost as deep as Charlie's. It didn't fill her as his did, so that its movements were more clearly defined, a precision instrument of pleasure. She held his hips and worked him into her and found a movement that made her cry out with astonished delight. All of her body was coming alive to him; his sex was a conjuror's wand. His open mouth was on her breast, drawing it in with electrifying lips and tongue. He nursed at her breast, but his mouth was soft and sensual and provocative, a mouth that kissed as it devoured. She cried out again as his mouth opened wider. He did extraordinary things with his tongue.

Her heart beat wildly as she thought of his mouth moving down over her, knowing all of her. She felt in him a sweet, responsive playfulness as if he consciously sought to give pleasure, unlike Charlie's masterful indifference to anything that didn't please him. He offered her the key to how she could make Charlie hers.

He mastered the movement of his hips and added variations

of his own so that his sex whipped sleekly through her, applying pressure precisely where she wanted it. She could see it in her mind's eye; it moved so freely in her that she knew exactly its shape and dimensions: long, slim, sword-straight and steel-hard, with a probing head that was teaching her to desire him for himself rather than as a surrogate for Charlie.

She moaned ecstatically and continued to moan as she slipped her hands flat, palms up, against his abdomen, rising and falling over her, and moved them down until her fingertips encountered tight little curls of pubic hair and the hard flesh that sprang out from the base of his belly. "So beautiful," she moaned. "You're—oh, you're doing it, my darling."

He surged proudly into her. He had heard that it took some skill to give a girl an orgasm. Maybe Charlie was right. Maybe he was good at it. He laughed out loud at himself. His nervousness was gone. He had found an unfamiliar comfort in the way their bodies fitted together so easily. There were none of the moments of strain that were an essential part of his experience. He was pleased that the techniques he had learned with Charlie satisfied her.

He was driving into her for the sergeant. He was fucking her for his father. He was taking her for all the sneers and snubs and humiliations that had accumulated over the years. As he did it, a great weight of guilt he hadn't even known was in him seemed to lift from him. He had lost his virginity at thirty. High time, but he felt none of the power of conquest he had sensed in Charlie. He was proud to be having a girl and giving her pleasure. He was proud that Charlie wanted him to share in fatherhood. He felt no completion in it; it led to nothing except, if that was part of Charlie's program, to a few more times with Martha to confirm in him this exhilaration he supposed must come from feeling a part of the normal world.

Charlie dawdled in the bathroom, he showered lengthily, he laughed quietly when he heard the cries from the other room. He dawdled a few more minutes after they were over. When he came out, Peter was approaching the bathroom door. Golden hair fell over his eyes; he looked adorably spent and disheveled. They moved automatically to each other and Charlie put his arms around him and kissed his mouth briefly. Peter found in the embrace more promise and excitement than anything else that had happened to him during the evening. He had done what Charlie had expected of him and now he was back where he belonged. He didn't quite understand what it had been about, but he was ready to forget about it. The fact that Charlie was holding him again in front of Martha was reassuring. It emboldened him to move his hands over his shoulders and down to his waist and pull him in close and exchange another kiss.

Charlie laughed. "You look as if you'd had a real workout, baby," he said as he smoothed the hair back from his forehead.

"I got pretty frisky as I went along. Ask Martha." He threw his head back and echoed Charlie's laughter.

They broke apart and turned to her, keeping their arms around each other. She rose from the bed and stepped quickly to where Charlie had left her robe and put it on. She approached them with a loving smile for both of them. "You're making me behave disgracefully," she said, surveying them frankly. "Two such perfect lovers. Two such beautiful bodies. Two—well, you know what I'm thinking. I've told Charlie I'm in love with him, but perhaps I meant you both. I never dreamed anything like this could happen to me, but it's thrilling. I can't even pretend to be ashamed of myself."

Charlie dropped his arm from Peter and took her hands. "Little mother. If anything can make you pregnant, you're certainly pregnant now."

"Oh, I am. There's no doubt about that." She looked into his eyes, telling him there was no doubt who was responsible. She broke the eye contact with evident reluctance and turned to Peter and kissed his lips lightly. "I'm going to leave you. I really do want a real rest in a real bed. I'm green with envy that you two have been living in such luxury all this time."

Charlie put his arm around her and led her to the door and gave her a hug as he let her out. He turned back to Peter with a happy grin and went to him and mussed the hair he had just smoothed. "She's marvelous, isn't she? Tell me about it."

"About what?"

"For God's sakes, you've just had a girl for the first time. Wasn't it good?"

"It was all right, I guess, if you happen to like girls. Everything *we* do together is a lot more exciting and satisfying and—well, you name it." He went and poured wine for them and handed a glass to Charlie.

"Well, sure, baby. But still. Didn't you feel there was something sort of special about it—I don't know—natural, and the idea that you're doing it to have children?"

"I thought that was the only point—your wanting me to be a father with you because you'd already done it. That part's nice. I didn't know it was supposed to make me want to rape every girl in sight." He dropped down on the end of the bed. "I'm all fucked out. I don't like that, not when it could have been with you."

"But we have each other always, baby. This has to do with life and the future. Don't you want to have children?"

"I've always loved the idea of little Charlies. I don't seem to feel any great procreative urge in myself. I don't know. Maybe the idea of little Charlies is a bit silly, we being what we are. I mean, if two people who love each other can't have children together, they should probably learn to get along without them."

"Now *you're* being silly. What about adoption, for God's sake?"

Peter stretched out on the bed and laughed. "Can you see us, Mum and Dad, being allowed to adopt children?"

"No, but there are other ways. Like tonight."

"Yeah. Like tonight." Peter sipped his wine. The more he thought about it, the less he liked it. It had been forced, extreme, basically uncharacteristic of all of them. Martha was too sensible and nice to get involved with a couple of queers who didn't pretend to care about her particularly. Charlie was too good to allow it. As for himself, he had simply gone through motions that were totally alien to his nature. The only excuse he could find for himself was that he had had to try it to make sure. "What it boils down to is that I don't see much sense in having children unless you're going to bring them up yourself."

"I quite agree with you." Charlie brought the bottle of wine and refilled Peter's glass and sat at the head of the bed.

"Bringing up children means giving them a normal home life, and 'normal' in this case means something. It means a woman in the house and the maternal element and all that. So." Peter shrugged.

"You're absolutely right. I'm thinking of all that. Martha wants the baby. We could sort of look after them, have them live near us. It all depends on how it works out. I could marry her if there was some reason to. Or you could, as far as that's concerned. We don't know what might happen. We'd always work it out so we'd be together."

Peter sat up. "You must be completely nuts," he protested. Some of it seemed to make a little sense momentarily, but he was sure that if he had time to think about it, none of it would.

"It's not as nuts as all that. Tonight was only the first time for you. After you've done it a few more times, you might find you like it."

"You expect me to do it a few more times?"

"Of course. There'll be lots of opportunity before the trip is over. Martha obviously loves it."

"Thanks a lot. You can have my share."

"But think of the alternative, baby. Doesn't the future scare you sometimes? We've known enough old queens. In another few years, we might not find it so easy to turn down pretty boys like your Dimitri. In another few years after that, they won't be offering themselves any more. That's when the horror begins. We've seen it. How can we know we'll be exceptions? We've already seen how easy it is to be tempted."

Peter looked at him and the open, happy animation drained from his expression. "I see. I should've known you hadn't forgiven me. I suppose that's what this is all about."

"I have, but that doesn't mean it didn't happen. We've got to accept it as a warning. It doesn't matter which of us it happened to. I'm trying to find something that'll give more stability— no, a broader base for our lives so that we'll be better prepared to cope when time catches up with us. What's wrong with having a normal home life? Having a woman in the house that we both get along with wouldn't kill us."

"Maybe not. But what would it do to the woman, especially if she happened to be in love with you?" Peter noted that the unnamed woman had already moved into the house.

"People can make adjustments. Women don't get as emotionally involved as we do. There'd be children. Yes, plural. Yours and mine. It would hold us together. I'm not talking about tomorrow or even next year. It's something to keep in mind and maybe work toward. I'd never want to do anything that you didn't agree to."

Peter gazed into his glass. Charlie was speaking persuasively, even pleadingly, but there was the melancholy he had noticed before that neutralized it. He felt a great sadness in him, and something else he couldn't quite define. A tightly controlled, undirected rage? Something intense and potentially dangerous. This sharp swing from his earlier exuberance suggested an instability of mood that was unusual even for Charlie. All his instincts were alert to defend his own; he couldn't bear even the suggestion of the intrusion of a third person into their lives. In a brief instant of panic, he thought of refusing to go on with the cruise, but caution prevailed. The experience with Martha was obviously reviving in Charlie all the old conflicts about his sexual tastes. He would help him through it as circumstances indicated. He couldn't stand Charlie being sad; he felt his responsibility for it so deeply that it made him want to cry. He forced himself to speak. "When you put it like that, there's not much I can be against, is there?" He looked up at Charlie with a little smile.

"No, there isn't. That's what I'm trying to tell you, baby. I think there's something good in what's happened with Martha. Please don't cut yourself off from it. I want it for both of us. I don't mean it's going to make us straight but your having sex with her is part of everything else I've been talking about."

Again, Peter felt he was being offered a freedom he didn't want. Perhaps he had to take it before Charlie would understand what it could lead to. He didn't feel Martha as a real threat, but it might not be a bad idea to take steps before all this went too far. "We'll see. I just wish you wouldn't talk about being scared of the future. Faggots are always carrying on about *old* faggots. What about old anything? What about Jack when Martha leaves him? He'll probably start running after little girls. The fact that he won't dye his hair and wear a little eye makeup doesn't make him any less pathetic, just less conspicuous. People who don't make something good of what they've got are bound to end up desperate."

"Sure, baby. I just want us to keep open to experience, and growing. I know it can't be good for us to be sealed off hermetically from everything outside us. I left you on purpose that night in Poros. I wanted you to have your chance with Dimitri."

"Thanks a lot. Honestly, darling, what is a quick fuck with a little Greek boy going to do for my future? Come on. Let's finish the wine and sink inert into the sheets. I'm going to have to take pills or something if you're going to go on shoving all this extramarital sex at me."

They went back on board the next evening to be ready for the predawn lull the following morning. It came and they set off once more. They were trending south now, their course set for fabled islands, Naxos and Paros and Ios and Santorin, with Crete their ultimate destination. Within hours, they had left the fierce wind behind them and encountered gentle southerly breezes that doubled the distances but made for relaxed sailing. It took them all day to reach Naxos and by noon the next day, they were ready to make the short run to Paros, having found nothing of great interest to keep them.

They stayed over a day in Paros and visited the ancient marble quarries. The wind was still light and southerly when they set off for Ios. By choice, Charlie was almost always on the wheel, while the others came and went, sunned themselves, napped. He was bringing them into Ios on what he hoped would be the last tack of the day when Peter came aft wearing brief swimming trunks and flopped down beside him.

"She's really something, our Martha," he said, keeping his voice low. "I was lying down in my bunk a while ago and she came along and insisted on going down on me. I tried to stop her because of Jack, but she swore he was sound asleep. She's no amateur. I almost choked trying not to make any noise when I came."

Charlie felt his smile freezing on his lips. He glanced down at the object of Martha's attentions where it made a trim, appealing bulge in his trunks and was outraged by what she had done. But why shouldn't she? he demanded of himself angrily. He was reacting with the blind possessiveness he wanted to break them both of. He had asked Martha to make Peter feel that she wanted him. He forced his smile to become more genuine. "I told her she'd be crazy about you."

"Did you? It seemed a bit funny without your being there, but I figured it was all part of what you were talking about the other night. I certainly felt no pain once she got started."

"Is that the first time since Mykonos?"

"Of course. Oh, she wanted me to kiss her boobs yesterday or whenever, when we were sunbathing forward. She seems to be nuts about that, but it was only for a second when the coast was clear. I have the feeling she'd like me to go all the way down. Have you ever done that?"

"No."

"I don't see how anybody could. All that hair and—" Peter made a little face. "Still, if she's going to do such dreamy things to me, I suppose I ought to reciprocate. I'd just as soon not get the chance."

"Play it the way you feel it, baby." Charlie congratulated himself for having overcome his brief, quite unreasonable displeasure.

An hour later, they sailed into a lovely wooded bay that they could identify as Ios by a light tower and a small church mentioned in the pilot book, but there was no town in sight, nor were there any mooring facilities. They anchored off a long sandy beach and when the boat was shipshape, Charlie and Peter rowed ashore, having been assured by Jack that a town was clearly marked on the chart, slightly inland. When they came back, they reported that the town was, indeed, in front of them, hidden in a fold of the hills. There was no hotel but a *taverna* with a few rooms above it. Charlie and Peter had rented all six beds in one so that they could have it to themselves.

"Well, if the accommodations leave something to be desired, I'll tell you what I'd like to do," Jack said. "We can stay here for the day tomorrow and leave in the evening. That'll give us the next day for Santorin and I'd like to leave there in the evening, too. Crete's a good day's haul and we don't want to arrive there after sunset. You'll have two nights in a row on board. You don't mind?"

They agreed to the schedule and Jack rowed them back to shore. The next morning, they had towels and trunks with them and were wandering through the town on the way to find a place to swim when they ran into Martha.

"I was going to see if I could find some fresh supplies," she explained after they had greeted each other happily.

"I've seen a couple of vegetable shops," Charlie said.

"We're going for a swim. Come with us," Peter suggested. "There's plenty of time to shop later."

"I haven't anything with me."

"We can probably find a place where that won't matter," Charlie said.

They wandered on together to the other end of the town, Charlie and Peter greeting everybody they encountered. "We had the usual welcoming party last night," Peter said. "We know every man in town." The road dwindled away and they took a path leading in the direction of the sea. It descended steeply through a pine wood and came out into a cove with a curve of sandy shore enclosed between rocky promontories. It reminded Charlie of something and he remembered Porquerolles. A world away. Anne had perched over there on the equivalent of that point.

"How about this?" Charlie said as they strolled toward it. "We don't have to wear anything here." They spread out their towels side-by-side when they reached a place that pleased them.

"You're turning me into a nudist." Martha stepped out of her simple cotton dress and with a few quick movements was naked. Charlie stripped, noting with satisfaction that all trace of her white patches was gone, except for a slight paleness along the upper edge of her pubic hair. Peter was undressing slowly.

"Well," he said, "I guess we all know each other well enough for you to see what this is doing to me." He peeled off his undershorts and his sex sprang out straight in front of him, slanting downwards.

"Look at the cocky one," Charlie cried. He ducked down and took it in his mouth and felt it leap up instantly with a lively life of its own. He released it and straightened.

Peter's eyes were wide, staring at him in wonder. "Jesus," he muttered. For an instant he wanted Charlie to go on and take him in front of Martha.

"Martha love, there's a gentleman here who appears to want a word with you." Charlie laughed and slapped Peter on the back and ran down the beach and plunged into the sea. He swam hard until he was winded. When he turned back, he could see them locked together on the towels. His Peter. He could hardly believe it. They weren't playing fancy games; Peter was on her, riding her hard. Even at a distance, the working of his body delighted him. He thought again of Porquerolles; this was better than hiding around the corner with a vicious boy. Clean and healthy. His grand design was filling out; soon Peter would be even more in favor than he was of keeping Martha near them.

He swam lazily and lay on his back in the limpid water. In a little while, he saw Peter come trotting down to the sea and dive in. He swam in to him and they glided up to each other and kissed.

"That's my Slugger. You're beginning to like it, aren't you?"

Peter looked flustered. "*She* seems to like it so damn much. What's a guy to do? But you, God, I almost fainted."

"Sure. I wouldn't mind showing her how you fuck me. That would really give her a jolt."

"Are you going to do it with her?"

Charlie laughed. "We're not all sex maniacs." He splashed water at him and swam in to shore. He found Martha stretched out on the towels, apparently just as Peter had left her. "Aren't you going to swim?" he asked, standing over her.

She lifted a hand to shield her eyes from the sun. They wavered over his body and came to rest where they always did. "I was waiting for you. Won't you—"

"Not so soon after him. I want you when you're all alive for it. You're absolutely limp with satisfaction now. You should see yourself."

"I only do it because you want me to."

"Of course. But you don't exactly hate it, do you?"

Her eyes lifted slowly to his. He sounded amused, but she thought she detected a faint hint of sharpness underlying it. "No," she said. It was a risk, but it might have the desired effect.

He dropped down beside her and lay back propped on his elbows and watched Peter swim in and go wandering off down the beach. He rounded the point where Anne might have been sitting. Jeannot could have been waiting for him farther along. He wanted to follow Peter, but he felt Martha's presence beside him and thought it would be unkind to leave her. When he realized that he was being governed by a sense of obligation to her, he sat up. This was the sort of intrusion in their lives that he couldn't permit; he had promised Peter that nothing would change.

"I should be getting back soon," Martha said to his back.

"We'll take you back in a little while. I'll go find Peter. Go ahead, if you don't want to wait." He rose and snatched up a towel in case of unexpected encounters and ran off after Peter. He climbed over rocks and teetered down into another smaller cove with a big outcropping of rock at the water's edge. For a moment, he didn't see Peter and then he emerged from beyond the rocks wandering on away from him. Charlie ran after him. Peter heard him and turned quickly, looking startled and dropping his hands to cover his sex, and then offered him a radiant smile of welcome.

"Hey, am I being pursued?"

"As a matter of fact, you are."

"Then you must be Zeus. My name's Ganymede. Seize me."

Charlie laughed and grabbed his wrists and held his hands away from his body. "OK. You're seized." His eyes dropped to Peter's sex. "I started something I want to finish. It felt good." He dropped down and took his sex in his mouth again and began to nurse it erect.

"Oh, God. What bliss. Being out of doors where people could see us drives me crazy." Peter ran his hands through his hair as his sex grew and lifted.

In a moment, Charlie let it leap free and stood and surveyed him. "God, baby. You're unbelievable. Standing like that against the rocks and sky. It's too beautiful for mortal eyes."

Peter laughed, and took Charlie's sex in his hand as it rose heavily between them. "When you get like this, I don't want anybody to see. I want it all for myself. Come on down here where we can get at each other." He pulled Charlie to the ground with him and they automatically fell into position so that each could take the other with his mouth. "Charlie darling." Peter's voice was thick with love. "This is what *I'm* all about, no matter what. Oh, God. You."

Charlie felt as guilty as a schoolboy for doing it. It was a retrogression, a return to everything he had been moving them away from for the last weeks. Did he want to prove that he could do it as well as Martha? Lacking her zest for it, he doubted very much if he could. He felt Peter's orgasm gathering and was grateful for its rapidity. When it was over, he lay back and surrendered to the rapture of Peter's miraculous mouth.

Jack rowed them back to the boat in time for an early dinner at sunset and they set off once more. The sea was calm, the breeze light, a waxing moon was setting.

Martha stopped Charlie as he was passing through the galley to get a sweater for Peter. Her eyes glowed with contentment.

"Do you realize what day it is tomorrow?" She stood close to him as she dried a plate. He shook his head. "My period.

I'm so sure I'm going to miss that I'd forgotten all about it. Tomorrow it's official."

"Mightn't you be late?"

"I never am. Besides, I'd be almost a week late. It always starts several days before in various ways. I'll spare you the tiresome details, but none of them has happened. If it's still the same tomorrow, we'll know."

"I'll be damned. That's pretty exciting." Charlie realized that she had so convinced him of her pregnancy that he felt no surprise or additional thrill at the news.

"Do you want to go on with the cruise?"

"Of course. You don't have to start taking care of yourself yet, do you?"

"Good heavens, no. I just wondered about telling Jack. I'm dying to. Of course, I won't until you leave the boat. I want so to talk to you. Both of you. Have you told Peter about suggesting I live near you?"

"Sure. He thinks it could make sense. I even talked to him about your maybe moving in with us and possibly getting married if we want more children. All that remains to be seen, naturally."

"Naturally." She touched his arm. "You know, I'm beginning to think he's no more queer than you are. He probably will find a girl."

"Very possibly," he said, not meaning to make it sound dismissive. Everything was fine. Everything was turning out as he had hoped. There was certainly no doubt about his potency. About Peter's potency? What difference did it make? He gave her hand a pat and went on to get Peter's sweater.

They picked up a breeze from time to time that carried them a few miles. They drifted. Sometime after midnight, Charlie told Peter to go below.

"Why don't you?" Peter countered. "You never get enough sleep. Let me sit there for a while."

"No, honestly, baby. I like it. You'd be bored out of your wits, but I actually enjoy it. God knows why. Get a decent night's rest."

"If you say so." He kissed Charlie and went below.

Time drifted with the boat. An hour or two later, his eye was caught by movement in the companionway and he assumed that it was Peter returning. When he looked again he saw Martha stepping out on deck wearing her long dressing gown. She came aft and moved in beside him where Peter usually sat.

"What are you doing up here?" he asked in a muted voice, making room for her.

"I wanted to be with you." Her hand went to his fly and began to unfasten it. His sex stirred and began to harden uncomfortably. He let her disentangle it from the confining folds of cloth. By the time she had done so, it was standing upright. She ran the tips of her fingers along it while it swelled and locked into immobility.

"All right," he murmured. "You've seen what you can do to me. That's enough."

"No," she whispered. "Not nearly enough. I want to kiss it till you come."

"Are you crazy? Jack could come up at any minute."

"He won't. He sleeps like a log. Peter let me."

"Sure, but he wasn't in charge of the boat. Besides, I don't want it that way. Nobody can do it right but Peter. I fuck you, remember?"

"Then fuck me." She held his sex with both hands and bent toward it.

He put a hand under her chin and lifted her face. "How can I? You see how much I want to."

"Yes. It's too big and hard not to now."

"Where can we, damn it? It's not possible."

"Below. Where we did before. Peter would if I went to him."

"You stay away from Peter. I mean, we've all got to stop this while we're on board."

"How can we stop when you're like this? Look at it. Your monumental phallus. You're a taker. Take me with your monumental phallus."

"All right, damm it. Go wake Peter and tell him to come up here. But I warn you. If we do it, we'll do it with no holds barred. I'll fuck you till you holler."

"How marvelous." She laughed softly. "I want you to make me holler. I feel like hollering just looking at it. Hurry!" She brushed his hand away and bent down to it and took the head in her mouth. Her teeth and tongue made him jerk up in the seat. She let him go and rose and hurried back to the companionway.

He got himself back into his trousers somehow and buttoned

his fly with difficulty. His heart was beating rapidly. He felt in some obscure way that he was breaking the rules he had himself laid down. He was ashamed to face Peter, which made him angrily defensive. Peter appeared in a few moments, pulling on a sweater.

"You want me?" he asked, joining Charlie at the wheel.

"Yes. Take over here," he said curtly. "We're headed for those lights. I won't be long." He could feel Peter recoil from him as he took the wheel.

"What about Jack?" he asked after an instant's silence.

"You didn't let him stop you," Charlie said accusingly. Peter said nothing. Charlie hated himself for having said it. Again, he felt a wrench deep within him as he sprang up and moved quickly away so that Peter wouldn't see his erection.

Martha whispered his name as he entered the dark saloon. She stripped him below the waist while he was pulling his jersey over his head. She tangled her fingers in his pubic hair and cradled his testicles in her hand. She held his sex and lay back and he climbed in on top of her. She was already making her little moaning sounds. She cried out as he entered her and cried out again as he completed the long thrust of his penetration. Their bellies ground together.

"Does Peter make you scream for it?" he demanded. He kept his voice low but he didn't bother to whisper.

"No. Oh, no. Only you, my precious." She had made him jealous. The moment was coming when he would want her all for himself. After that, perhaps he would want only her. "You do it all this time. Everything. I won't stir the soup. Make me come by just being there. You can, my lover. Only you. Your magnificent great cock. It's so huge after Peter. Use it. Fuck me hard, precious."

He did as he was told. They drove each other to a moaning, gasping, shouting paroxysm of desire, but the fierceness of the engagement didn't dislodge from his mind the image of Peter sitting alone at the wheel. He had never left him before. He shared his hurt and loneliness. His pride was engaged in achieving Martha's orgasm, but he longed to be sitting with Peter.

The sun was up when they sailed into the great circle of the bay formed by Santorin and its outlying islands. It was like sailing across the crater of a volcano, which was more or less what it was. One of the islands that formed the circle was smoking like a dump heap. They motored in toward a sheer cliff at the foot of which they could see caïques tied up. High above, a town seemed to balance on its edge. Jack and Peter went forward to prepare for mooring.

"Today's the day," Martha said, standing beside Charlie at the wheel. She was gazing forward, prepared to help him with the motor. "I think Jack heard us last night. He's acting a bit odd. It doesn't matter. I've missed my period."

He eased up on the helm in response to a wave from Jack. "You wanted to, didn't you?" he asked.

"Heavens, yes. We're going to have a baby. We can start to plan now."

"Cut the motor down a bit. That's good," Charlie said.

"I've been thinking. You said you didn't want the baby to have Jack's name. I'm sure a good lawyer could manage it. I can get doctors' certificates to prove he can't be the father. There's no reason why he should fight it. That is, if you want to marry me."

"We'll have plenty of time to talk about that. OK. Neutral." He swung the wheel and sprang to the rail to fend-off.

They were all busy for the next fifteen minutes getting the boat tied up and in order. When it was done, there was no further opportunity for private conversation. They discussed their plans for the day and agreed to meet back at the boat at sunset. Martha looked at Peter and Charlie longingly as they prepared to leave.

They had a dizzying ride on donkeys up the face of the cliff. Peter was quickly aware that Charlie was in a difficult mood. He was silent and unresponsive. He had been even more remorseful about the night's incident than Peter felt he had any reason to be. It was the sort of thing that demonstrated the impossibility of their all living together, but he could put up with it for a few more weeks. When Charlie had returned from Martha, he had been angrily solicitous, obliquely apologetic. Peter hadn't felt reproachful. He had made the most of Martha's advances as a calculated challenge to Charlie. He had known the day before on the beach when Charlie had followed him that he had won.

The island had been a cult center in antiquity, celebrated for the beauty of its naked dancing boys; dedications to them from their male suitors remained, carved in stone. When they reached the town at the top of the cliff, Peter tried to make him laugh with joking references to "their" shrine and naked dancing boys in general but he failed.

"Come on, Peter. Cut all the camp talk, for God's sake," Charlie said shortly.

The unfamiliar use of his name told Peter that his mood was blacker than he had realized. Men surrounded them when they stopped to inquire about the site of the ancient city. There was much talk of food and they gathered they should take something to eat with them. They were escorted to a bare little shop where they bought bread and cheese and a bottle of wine and a tin of sardines. Back out in the street, they found donkeys awaiting them. Before they knew where they were going, they were astride and being led off, plodding daintily, by a small boy on a third donkey.

It was the sort of expedition they usually liked—impromptu, haphazard, novel, stimulating to the eye, with a nice touch of the absurd to keep them guessing—but it failed to lift Charlie's spirits. He made a few comments on the island landscape, high hills and glimpses of sea everywhere, and relapsed into silence. The mood lasted through a long donkey-ride, a visit to the ruins where Peter refrained from making any further references to the dancing boys, their meager lunch under an olive tree, the long ride back. Since he could think of nothing he could have done to cause it, Peter allowed him to brood in private. Charlie would tell him about it when he was ready.

When they returned to the boat at sunset, they found the Kingsleys finishing off a shaker of martinis. Peter saw Charlie pointedly snub Martha when she started to tell him about their day.

"That fucker Jack is really drunk," he said when they were below changing their clothes. His tone was ugly.

"Not much more than usual," Peter said placatingly. "Anyway, we don't need him to get out of here."

They returned to the deck and set about casting off without consulting the Kingsleys. When Martha saw that they were ready, she started the motor.

For the first time, Jack was definitely unsteady on his feet. They went forward to raise sail. The day's northeasterly wind was dying. When they had the sails up, Jack swung the helm and cut the motor and headed south. Charlie and Peter stayed forward watching the sun set on the curiously menacing circlet of rocky outcroppings.

"It's really spooky," Peter said. "I'm glad we got off before it blew up. Did it depress you? You've seemed sort of funny all day."

"No, I'm OK." He saw some breeze coming in from the west. He started to call back to Jack, but it was so clearly visible that it would have been bad sailing manners to mention it. When he decided he couldn't wait any longer, it was too late. A puff of wind hit them. The great boom swung in a heavy arc across the boat and crashed to the other side in a wrenching jibe. Charlie raced back along the deck, crouched down in case the boom swung again. He flung Jack out of the way and seized the wheel.

"You drunken bastard," he shouted, trimming the main and getting the boat steadied. "Where do you expect to find another mast around here? Christ Almighty! Why don't you stay below where you belong."

"Really, Charlie—" Martha began.

"You shut up. Get the jib in."

"Don't you order her around," Jack protested, sitting on the bench where Charlie had shoved him, looking dazed.

"I'll fucking well order her around if I fucking well feel like it," Charlie roared.

Peter had come aft and was staring at him with startled, protective eyes. Charlie turned to him. "Get us drinks, will you, baby? We all might as well get drunk."

Peter was blushing as he hurried below. He returned with bottles and glasses and poured them whiskies and sodas while the Kingsleys watched in silence. Charlie drank thirstily.

"Good. Maybe Jack has something. We'll go careening all over the Mediterranean. How about getting the mizzen up, baby."

"What is all this faggy 'baby' stuff?" Jack demanded nastily.

"That's us—a couple of fags. Still, we're probably better men than you'll ever be. If you only knew."

"I think we'd better go below, Jack," Martha said hastily. "Charlie's in a nasty temper."

"I'll go before this goes too far," Jack said, "but I think there'd better be a serious talk when we get into Heraklion."

"Any time, any place, but preferably sober," Charlie snapped.

He finished his drink in another swallow and handed Peter his glass for a refill. Martha stood and waited for Jack. He stumbled slightly as he crossed the deck. They disappeared down the companionway. Charlie pulled Peter to the wheel without saying anything and left him there to work in the stern. When he had the third sail set, he returned to the wheel and elbowed Peter out of the way. Peter sat on the bench near him, waiting for him to speak. He had no clue what to expect next; he had never seen him quite like this. He knew his temper on the rare occasions when he lost control, but now his control seemed to be still operating. He seemed disgusted rather than angry; Peter felt outside it and was still content, therefore, to bide his time. They sat in silence as darkness gathered in around them. They finished their second drink.

"I suppose we ought to eat something," Charlie said finally. His voice sounded normal but tired. "Would you go see what you can find?"

"Sure, darling." Peter stood and moved toward Charlie and put a hand on his shoulder. Charlie held his knee and leaned his head against his hip. Peter could feel a tremor in the body resting against him. "I'll fix you another drink." He did so and went below. He was back in a moment. "Martha's bringing us some sandwiches and soup."

Charlie didn't speak. Martha appeared in the hatch and lifted food onto the deck. Peter went to collect it, but she came on up and moved aft to the cockpit.

"Do you think it was a good idea to go quite so far?" she asked.

"There's just one question I want you to answer and then you can go below," Charlie said coldly. "Did you have that normal fuck with Jack we talked about?"

There was a long silence during which he could feel her struggling to decide whether or not to lie. "Yes," she said at last. "I had to. We haven't been able to talk seriously about the future. You haven't known what you wanted. I had to think of the child. I thought I might have to convince Jack that he was the father. I haven't known what to think. I've been waiting for you to tell me."

"No, you didn't wait. You've got yourself covered all the way round. Very smart. You were right, of course. I never pretended you could count on us. Anyway, that settles it. Get the hell below."

"Settles what? Please, my precious—"

"Shut up, goddamn it," he roared. "You've done the one thing I told you not to do. I was sure you would. As it turns out, it doesn't matter a damn, if that's any comfort to you. Go below. I don't have anything more to say to you."

Her eyes glittered in the moonlight. Tears? She hestiated and then her shoulders sagged resignedly as she turned and went.

"Jesus!" Peter said when she was out of sight. "How are we going to go on with them after this?"

"Who said we're going on with them?"

"We have to. We can't ditch them now. What's the matter, for God's sakes?"

"You know what's the matter. Jack for one."

"There's more to it than that. What were you saying to Martha?"

"You heard me. All that crap about being in love with me and she lets Jack fuck her just to be on the safe side. It makes me sick."

"That's not all. There's been something wrong since this morning. Please tell me."

"There's nothing to tell. Drop it, for God's sake." How could he tell him of the extent of his failure? He had already said too much about the hopes he had pinned on Martha. Now that they were dead, they seemed ludicrous and perverse. He longed to blot everything he had said about her from Peter's memory. He didn't want her in their life: he didn't want their child. He had known it the minute she had mentioned marriage this morning. If marriage hadn't been touched on before, he could understand it better, but she had only been echoing his own words. He had been entirely responsible for the whole situation. Every minute all three of them had spent together should have told him that his vision of their living together could never be realized to the satisfaction of any of them. Why had a chance, harmless word of hers opened his eyes at last? He had battled with himself all day, clinging to his vanishing hopes, but the image of Peter alone at the wheel vanquished reason—or perhaps restored it to him. His dream of fatherhood was dead. The baby would be the Kingsleys'; he had renounced his own child. All his natural instincts were blocked by a beautiful, effeminate young man. Not effeminate, some more judicious corner of his mind corrected. His beauty and exquisite youthfulness set him apart from other men, but there was nothing effeminate about him. There was nothing effeminate about the way they had both taken Martha. It would all be more understandable, perhaps, if there were. He was raw with failure. He had failed in whatever he had been trying to attain with Peter; now that it was all over, he hardly knew what it had been all about. The grand design was wrecked and blurred. His attempt to be a man like other men had failed. He hated the way he had spoken to Martha. He thought of what he had done on the beach the day before and hated Peter for driving him to it. He hated himself.

"Give me another drink, will you, baby?" he said quite calmly. "I'm sorry if I sounded cross with you. I'm not."

Peter sprang to do his bidding. As he passed the drink, he leaned over and kissed Charlie on the top of his head. "Don't worry about it any more. Jack's drunk enough so he probably won't remember anything about it tomorrow."

"So much the worse for him. I don't know why he hasn't sunk the boat long ago."

"Don't you want me to take over for a while? You should rest. You haven't slept since I don't know when."

"No. I'm fine. The wind's coming around more southerly. We'd better get the sheets in."

When they had trimmed the sails, Peter crowded in on the seat behind the wheel. He felt no response in Charlie's body, only the tremor he had felt before. Something was still wrong. He couldn't imagine what had affected him so deeply. Was it possible that he cared more about Martha than he had supposed? He had the impression that the brief, cruel exchange with her just now had been a farewell. He couldn't be sorry about that but he didn't want Martha to be needlessly hurt. He felt a surprising possessive tenderness for her. Even he had given her a few moments of ecstasy. She had been his girl. It created a tie. He was beginning to see some sense in Charlie's plans. Of course, they couldn't have her in the house but they could keep in touch with her, watch the child grow up at a distance, do things for it. There was something special about being a father, after all. To his astonishment, he found himself getting an erection as he thought about her. He switched his attention back to Charlie. Should he insist that he go below and get some sleep? He must be on the edge of total exhaustion after all the weeks of brief,

286

interrupted sleep. Peter put his arm around his chest and hugged him close, trying to soothe the odd tremor he felt in him.

The wind freshened and whipped up the sea. Sailing close to the wind, the boat heeled like a racer and leaped through the water.

"The old tub is really moving again," Charlie said after a long silence, with only a faint echo of the excitement he had always displayed when he was pleased with the boat's performance. An almost full moon gilded the plunging sea. Charlie went on drinking slowly and steadily, taking slugs directly from the bottle. The alcohol contained his emotions and gave weight and depth to his depression. Peter could feel a stubborn determination building up in him that told him he would never get him to rest now. He kissed the side of his face and stretched out on the leeward bench and slept.

Charlie was a machine attached to the wheel, swaying with the movement of the boat and driving it on. He had no idea how many hours he had been holding it when he became aware of a solid shape outlined against the pale sky on the distant horizon. He could see no lights. He had noted on the chart a tiny island off Crete to the east of their course for Heraklion. The wind had been pushing them eastward. If this was the island, it was getting on toward dawn and they had made good time. He was heading straight for it. He looked for the heights of Crete behind it but could see nothing. He decided to get in closer before taking the long tack back to get into position for the approach to Heraklion.

He watched the rock grow bigger slowly as he seemed to rush toward it. He began to make out a line of white at its base. He recognized this as the foaming sea breaking against it. It caused a little tightening of his nerves and he shifted in his seat. He had never liked sailing too close to land. In this case, it was perfectly safe, he reassured himself. The wind would blow them off it. He probably had nearly an hour before he would be really in close. By then, if this was the island he thought it was, he should be able to make out the headlands of Crete and establish their position.

He began playing a game with the boat, heading it up with every small favorable shift in the wind to see if he could pass to windward of the rocky mass in front of him. It would be nip--

and-tuck. His hands gripped the wheel hard as he saw them being flung up on what appeared to be steep cliffs if the wind played tricks on him at the last minute or he made the slightest miscalculation. This was silly; games weren't for boats. Even if he could make it to windward, the risk was unjustifiable. Good sailing sense required that he regard it as an obstacle and keep well clear of it. He held the helm steady. The cliffs drew him. The thought of running up on them recurred and its terror slowly passed. Why not? An easy end to a sad story. The Kingsleys were sleeping. They would never know what hit them. His unwanted child would be obliterated. He savored the peace he had found before in the thought of death. Peter couldn't live without him. They would all go in one great smash. He thought of the magical moments of the last weeks—the nights at sea under star-filled skies holding Peter close against him, the kiss exchanged unashamedly on the beach at Siros, Peter naked on another beach, his voice clotted with love, saying, "This is what I'm all about, no matter what." Moments filled with a joy he knew could never be recaptured. His failure, the collapse of his grand design, had crushed some vital element in him. He was tired, so damn tired, tired deep in his marrow. He could never care about anything again. End it. End it all.

He leaned forward and peered ahead. The light was changing. The islet looked much closer. He could just make out the movement of the crashing surf. His heart began to beat more rapidly, but his hands were relaxed on the wheel, exerting only the pressure necessary to guide it. It should be quite painless. If the rocks were as sheer as they appeared to be, there would be the smashing impact as they raced upon them, perhaps a brief battle with the sea, and then nothing. He felt in competent control of the boat and quite rational.

As the night paled to gray, he began to make out the conformation of the steep rocks ahead. He was coming in to windward of a promontory. Beyond it was the headland he had been trying to clear earlier. He couldn't have managed it; the wind was bringing him right in on it. He leaned forward and touched Peter's hair. He sat up immediately and smiled and yawned.

"How're we doing?" he asked sleepily.

"I'm going to smash the boat up," Charlie said in a matter-of-fact voice.

Peter looked at him and his breath caught. The words meant nothing to him, but Charlie's face frightened him. It was composed, but in the gray light his eyes looked dead, his mouth was grim, his expression strangely set. He looked old. He had never thought of age in connection with Charlie. It scared him more than what he had said. "What're you talking about?" he asked when he had taken a deep breath.

"Just what I said." He nodded forward. "Look."

Peter stood and looked forward and whirled back to him. "Where are we? What is this?"

"It's a pile of rock. I'm going to run us up on it."

Peter tried to smile and his breath caught again as he looked into the dead eyes. "Come on. What're you doing? What's the joke?"

"It's no joke. I've had it."

"Had what? You don't want to go on with the cruise?"

"I don't want to go on with anything. This is the way it's going to end."

"For God's sake, have you lost your mind? You mean, you want to kill us all?" Peter started to put a hand out to him, but something about the odd, set expression made him draw back. He sat, his back turned to the land looming up in front of them. "Please, darling. Tell me what it's all about."

"I wish I knew. Dying is so simple. Don't you want to die with me? You've often said you did."

"But the others."

"I don't care about them."

"But you've got to. You're crazy. If you want us to kill ourselves, we'll take pills or something. Not this."

"I just don't care about anything. It's all over."

"But why? For Christ's sake, tell me," Peter pleaded. "If it's something I've done, I've got to know."

"You haven't done anything, baby. Neither have I. That's the trouble. I wanted something better for us. It's no good."

"I don't understand what you're talking about. We've got to get somewhere we can make sense together. Then it'll be any way you want it." He spoke lightly and persuasively, struggling against the tripping of his heart. He didn't want Charlie to feel his fear or do anything that would create a sense of conflict. If his mind had slipped, if this was some sort of breakdown, Charlie might be capable of anything to win a battle of wills. He must make him feel unopposed. Out of the corner of his eye, he caught a glimpse of land closing in on the port side. "You can do anything you want with us. Don't you see? You can't get the others into it."

"Why not?"

"You don't have the same rights with anybody else that you have with me. It's not fair to act as if you had." He reached out to Charlie's hand on the wheel to test its determination. "Please come about. Damn it; if I'm going to die I want it to be with you, the way everything's always been. They're not good enough to die with us." He saw a flicker of interest light the dead eyes.

"Take your hand off the wheel," Charlie said flatly.

Peter did so and his heart skipped a hammering beat. For an instant, he thought he might have won. He saw Charlie ease the helm. He was apparently just testing it. He held to his collision course. "Damn it," Peter burst out in desperation. "I don't want to do it, but if I get the Kingsleys up here maybe you'll see how impossible it is." Perhaps they would shame him into sanity. Peter wondered if he could bring himself to use force as a last resort.

"Do anything you like," Charlie said. He reached down to the locker under the seat where tools were kept and pulled out a wrench.

Peter watched with growing fear. He sprang up and ran forward. He paused for a chilling moment, looking ahead. The sea hurtled itself onto jagged rocks. The force of it flung water into the air, curtaining the steep cliffs behind. He could hear the deep pounding of it. He could feel in his bones the impact they would make. There would be a great splitting and crashing. They would all be hurled against rocks, torn, battered, crushed. How long did they have? Five minutes? Surely, ten minutes at the most. He dropped down the companionway. He was back in a moment. Jack followed. He clambered out on deck looking bleary and aggressive.

"What in hell's going on?" he demanded. He looked forward. "Jesus Christ!" he shouted. He came rushing back toward the wheel. Charlie lifted the wrench.

"Watch your step, Jack," he said as if this were an ordinary occasion.

Jack gave him an instant's calculating scrutiny and turned and ran back to the hatch. He disappeared and was back with a knife.

"I'm going to count ten," he shouted. "If you don't come about, I'm going to cut all the sheets loose."

"You would, you poor idiot," Charlie called back. "Can't you see what that would do? We'll be washed up on that point over there. Do you prefer going slowly?"

Jack hesitated for a second and then made a rush for him. Charlie swung the wrench and clipped him across the side of his head. He crumpled into the cockpit. Peter hurried to him and pulled him forward out of the way and stretched him out on his back. He picked up the knife and put it on one of the benches. He turned back to Charlie.

"I'm going to take over," he said quietly. His eyes sought Charlie's. Charlie was looking fixedly forward. His regard shifted and their eyes met. Peter's voice broke as he burst out, "You're not a murderer, goddamn it! You're out of your head. I won't let you do this. It's all right for me. Maybe even Martha. But not Jack. We hardly even know him. It would be plain pointless murder." He started toward him.

Charlie lifted the wrench. "You saw what happened to him."

"We don't hurt each other," he asserted staunchly. He made a grab for the wrench.

Charlie yanked it up and brought it down, sideways and out, and flung it into the sea. "Get the jib sheet," he snapped. Peter scrambled to obey. Charlie made a lunge for the main sheet.

"Ready about. Hard alee!" he called. He planted his feet and spun the wheel. Unexpected dangers were suddenly all around them. The momentum of the speeding boat brought them sliding up and around to within a few feet of barely submerged rocks he hadn't noticed. For a shuddering moment, they hung in the wind, bucking and rolling while they edged toward disaster. Then the sails took the wind on the other tack, the bow lifted and surged forward and they fell off heavily while Charlie eased the main sheet, adjusted the helm and set them on their course. He saw Martha hovering in the companionway, looking pale and in substantial in the ghostly light.

"Take over," he ordered Peter curtly without looking at him. "Crete's off there somewhere. I'm through." Jack was stirring. He stepped over him and brushed past Martha as she emerged from the companionway, and went below.

291

He lay in his bunk trembling from head to foot, his eyes open, staring at nothing. It kept him from thinking. It didn't prevent the feeling of failure from spreading deeper and deeper into him. He had come so close. His body still vibrated with the pounding of sea against rock. Peter had found just the right words to cripple his will, as always. It all remained now to be picked over and sorted out and arranged into neat manageable patterns for the future. He closed his mind to it; he had nothing new to contribute. He had failed to achieve the resolution of death. Somebody would have to find a new point of departure.

He lay in his bunk for several hours. The trembling stopped and a great inertia followed it. He was aware of activity above. Several times, he felt a small urge to go up and see if everything was in order. It was a reflex reaction; it didn't mean that he really cared. Several times, he was aware of Martha passing back and forth to the forward cabin. He could tell by the way she dragged past him that she would have been glad for a word from him, but he didn't move a muscle, isolating himself in his inertia.

At last, he registered that the motor was running. His mind maneuvered the boat into position as it reversed and idled and churned forward. The motor was cut and the boat was silent and motionless. In a little while, Peter was beside him, bending down and touching his knee.

"Are you all right?" he asked with cautious concern. "I think we'd better go ashore. I'll do something about a bag later."

Charlie sat up and threw his legs over the side of the bunk. Peter handed him a fresh shirt and trousers. Charlie removed the things he was wearing and dressed. When he was ready, Peter put a hand on the waistband of his trousers and rocked him cajolingly. Charlie lifted the hand away and went aft through the galley and climbed up the companionway. There was no sign of the Kingsleys. Ashore already? Peter put a hand on his arm and he went to the gangplank and teetered down it. He was aware of being in a crowded, dirty, citified port. Trucks and trolleys clattered by. After the weeks of sunbaked, whitewashed, sea-girt villages, he had forgotten that this was the way the world looked. They crossed a street and a square and entered a building where Peter conferred at a counter. They climbed stairs and entered a bare, hot bedroom. Peter locked them in. There was a chair. Charlie sat in it. Peter moved around behind him and touched his hair. He put his hands on his shoulders and pressed them.

"So. Here we are," he said after a long silence. "Do you still want us to kill ourselves? I'm almost ready to when I see you like this."

"It's too late even for that."

"What are we going to do? Jack won't allow you back on board."

"The feeling is mutual."

"The trouble is, I can't let them down. They'd be stranded here without at least one of us. We've talked about it. I've offered to go back to Piraeus with them. They can find a professional captain there if they want to go back to France. It was always understood that we might have to leave them in Piraeus."

"Poor Peter. Aren't you bored having to clean up after me?"

"I'm just doing what I know you'd want when you can think about it straight. We don't let people down. No matter how much they know about us, they can't understand it's like being married. If one of them was put off a boat, the other would go automatically, but it can't be like that for us. They take it for granted that I'll stay with them. I think I have to."

"Why not?" Charlie sprang up and took a turn around the room. "You talk about being married as if there was something good about it. Look at the Kingsleys."

"We're not like that. That's what makes it so hard to take. Can you imagine what it's going to be like being alone with them?"

"Everything passes." Charlie slumped down on the end of the bed and subsided once more into lethargy. "Nothing ever matters very much. When are you leaving?"

"I told them I wouldn't go until I'm sure you're all right."

"You're apt to have a long wait. I feel as if I'll never be all right again."

"Oh, God, can't you try to help me understand it? All I can think is that I'm to blame somehow. Was it wrong of me to react the way I did to Martha?"

"Of course not. I wanted you to. Don't ask me why."

"I know I wasn't very encouraging about having her living with us. I was thinking about it last night. I'm beginning to see what you were getting at. We can talk about it some more later. I think she really is in love with you."

"Oh, God. You don't understand anything. Well, there's no reason why you should. I don't understand very much myself. I don't want Martha to be in love with me. If you think I was getting at something worth talking about, you take over. She gives you a good time in bed. You'll have the trip back to work on it. Maybe you'll manage to make some sense together. I certainly couldn't, but she's still pregnant. It's your child as much as it is mine, no matter what she thinks. Take it from there."

Peter dropped into the chair Charlie had vacated. "Where would I take it? You say she gives me a good time, but that was only because you were there and you seemed to want it. You do know that, don't you? If you want the truth, the thing that really excited me was being naked with you and having erections and kissing each other and everything in front of somebody else. It was like making a public announcement at last of all we mean to each other."

"God. Bodies. I'm sick of them. They don't tell us anything we need to know."

"Ours have always told us a lot we've wanted to know. About each other. Don't forget that."

"I think maybe I want to. I honestly feel as if I never want to touch you again."

Peter took a quick deep breath and swallowed hard and clenched his jaws to hold back the tears that started up in his eyes. "Then I really will kill myself," he said in a strangled voice. "Is Martha that good?"

"Martha? Can't you understand? I certainly don't intend to touch *her* ever again."

"But why? What happened? I've never been afraid of losing you to a woman, but you've liked her a lot. You've told me what it means to you to be having a baby." Peter looked at him and again was scared by what he saw. The expression Charlie had worn on the boat had returned. He stared through Peter.

"I don't want the baby," he said slowly. "I never want to see it. That's what I found out last night."

For a moment, Peter was riveted to the chair. Then he was kneeling in front of Charlie, gripping his hands. "Oh, Christ! Why didn't you tell me? No wonder you wanted to kill us all."

Charlie gazed into the devoted eyes with a rekindling of interest. "You understand?" he asked incredulously.

"I don't understand what's made you feel like that, but I understand what it must've done to you. I suppose you hated me just for existing and hated yourself for not really wanting something you thought was so important. I don't know the rest. I can guess things but I wish you'd tell me."

Charlie withdrew his hands from Peter's grip and sat back, removing himself from contact with him. "I probably shouldn't. You're apt to draw conclusions that will make everything worse, if that's possible. Try to listen carefully. I minded so terribly your being unfaithful to me." Peter flinched and lifted himself and backed into the chair. Charlie nodded. "Yeah. It knocked everything to pieces, everything I thought I knew and wanted and believed in. I've tried, but I still can't put it all together again. I knew I was wrong to take it like that. I know it shouldn't have meant so much. I tried to open everything up for both of us, to see how these things work. I've failed. I'm right back where I started from. I *want* us to be sealed off hermetically from everything else. I knew it when I wanted to suck your cock on the beach the other day. I don't want the baby. I don't want anything that might let in a little air. For God's sake, baby, don't sit there all full of light and love. Don't you see what it means? It means I'll kill us just as surely as I would have a few hours ago if you'd let me have my way. I'm sick. I mean it. I'm sick with love. Life might be possible if everybody were like you, but we're not. Least of all me. I think we're going to have to leave each other, baby."

Peter sat very still in the chair and the tears that had brimmed up in his eyes before now spilled over and ran slowly down his cheeks. "Ouch," he murmured. "It's pretty terrible to hear you say that when you're not even angry with me. Listen. You must know you're not yourself right now. You're worn out. You can't think straight until you've had a real rest. Please let it ride for the time being."

Charlie nodded dully. "I don't see how anything will change, but I'm not in the mood for melodrama any more. I'm not trying to prove anything—it's all being proved *to* me. I promise that whatever happens, we'll do it in whatever way is easiest for both of us."

"All right. But don't try to decide what's easiest for me. Talk to me." Peter brushed tears from his cheeks and went and sat on the bed beside Charlie, being careful not to touch him. "There're lots of things. Don't close your mind about the baby yet. We don't have to decide anything now. Later, it may turn out that we can play some part in his life. We'll only be about fifty when he's twenty. He's bound to be a boy. I wish he'd hurry and grow up. I'd like to know him."

Charlie rose and took another turn around the room. "That's just what I don't want. I don't want to think about it."

"I'm sorry. I meant later, of course."

"Work it out the way you want it, baby. I think you might really make something of it. Don't *you* close your mind to the possibility. It's just as well you're going with the Kingsleys."

"There's no hurry about that. I told them we might stay here for several days."

"No. The sooner I clear out the better. I've got to be alone. I think I'm going to have to be alone for a long time. Always, maybe."

"Please. Don't say any more now. I can't stand it." Peter rose and stood in front of him and looked him in the eye. "Are you sure you're ready to be alone? Can you promise you won't think any more about—about killing yourself or anything?"

"I've always told you I wouldn't die without you."

"All right. This is going to be hell for me. You do understand why I have to do it, don't you? It shouldn't take more than three or four days. Less than a week at the worst. We've been dawdling all this time."

"Be careful. I know you can handle the boat, but it's not going to be easy with Jack. Make him use the motor." Talk of the boat restored some sense of the familiar to them both. They were hurt and helpless, but they were still a pair. "I've got to find out about boats to Piraeus. I can probably get one today."

"So soon? You'll wait for me in Athens?"

"Yeah, I'll be around. If I go anywhere, I'll leave word at the Grande Bretagne."

"Promise not to worry about me. I'll be all right. Jack has agreed to get back any way I say. I'll probably motor all the way. I'll bawl my head off out there all alone at night. I know you don't want to touch me but does that include not kissing me goodbye? We may not get a chance later."

"Oh, God, baby. I've—" Charlie choked on a word. He pulled Peter to him and their mouths met in a long, deep, oddly sexless kiss, fervent with love. Tears were running down Charlie's cheeks when they broke apart. "I guess I was wrong about not feeling anything any more," he said.

Peter lifted a hand and touched the tears with love and gratitude. It was going to come out right somehow.

They left the room and went out and found a travel agency. There was a boat for Piraeus in a few hours. Peter left Charlie in a café and went back to *Cassandra* and packed a bag for him.

"I told them I want to leave tonight," he said to Charlie when he came back. "Since we've come all this way, I suppose I'd better go out to Knossos this afternoon. I don't really see anything when I'm not with you."

They had a silent lunch. As they set out for the Piraeus boat, Charlie took Peter's hand in his.

"Thanks," Peter said. "That helps."

There was a departure building where the Piraeus boat was tied up. Charlie set down his bag outside it.

"Don't let's make this a big farewell," he said.

"No. It isn't one, anyway. I feel as if we were at the ends of the earth, but I checked the chart again. We'll make Milos by day after tomorrow. It's only another day or two from there." They stood holding each other's elbows. "You're sure you're all right? Take care of yourself. Rest, darling. You need it. I'll see you at the Grande Bretagne. I love you. If I stand here another minute, I'll do something that even the Greeks might mind." He squeezed Charlie's arms and tore himself from him and hurried away.

Charlie stood, watching him go. He moved with jaunty grace, the golden head gleaming in the sun. Charlie wondered if he would ever see him again.

When he reached Athens the next morning, Charlie had decided what he was going to do. At Peter's insistence, he had kept the name and address of the owner of the Hydra house with his passport. After he had checked in at the hotel, he went out to hunt him up. He turned out to be a courtly old peasant living with his son's family. When his mission was understood, Charlie was welcomed as the bearer of great good fortune. Lawyers and notaries were visited. Two hundred dollars changed hands. Charlie was presented with an enormous iron key. When the deed had been registered at the title office in Hydra, he would become the official owner.

He found out with some difficulty that there was a boat for Hydra the following day. He didn't want to sit around a grand hotel in this dusty, unfamiliar little city. He would go to Hydra and take possession of the house Peter had wanted so much. It would give him something to do, and it would give them something to talk about. He had reached the point where he welcomed anything that suggested a new departure, a fresh start. He felt that he had run through his capital, that everything that had seemed important in the past was worn out and ready to be discarded. He had no idea what they would do with a house in Hydra, but at two hundred dollars it didn't matter.

When he was checking out of the hotel the next day, the moment came for him to leave a message for Peter. He started to speak but said nothing. It was unpremeditated. He felt the need growing again to be cut off and on his own. Alone. That would be something new. It might tell him things he should know about himself. He had bought a small bag to carry a change of clothes. The suitcase Peter had packed he left with the concierge.

"And when shall we expect you back, sir?" the man behind the counter asked.

"I don't know. You can tell my friend Mr. Martin that the bag's here. Give it to him if he wants it. Tell him I haven't left Greece."

He hadn't crossed the lobby to the door before the impact of what he had done hit him. He had severed the ties of all his adult years. He was completely alone. Anything he did or thought or experienced would be for himself. He was uneasy but determined. It was an essential move. If he came back now it would be because he had to come back. He wondered what Peter would make of it. He would be bewildered and angry, but he wasn't one to panic. He might easily guess where he had gone. Or he might simply sit with the suitcase and wait for him to come pick it up.

The boat to Hydra took him past remembered landmarks. Salamis. Aegina. He looked at the sea and the sky and wondered where Peter was. The weather was fine; would it be, all those miles to the south? He thought of Peter battling the treacherous sea alone and his chest ached with anxiety and longing to be beside him.

Eventually, he realized with a start that they were heading in toward Poros. He went out and stood on deck as they entered the long lagoon and thought of the first time it had opened out before him. The white town gleamed beckoningly in the sun. He thought of Peter's Dimitri with a tensing of his muscles. Promiscuity had nothing to offer him, but he had found the boy in Poros enormously appealing. He didn't know what he wanted any more; perhaps a purely physical experience, by breaking through his loneliness, would help him think clearly again.

The boat was steaming in close enough for him to see crowds gathering on the quai for their arrival. He hurried back to his seat and collected his bag and returned to the rail to watch, prepared to go ashore if he saw the boy and responded to him as he had before. The small ship eased in broadside to the quai with a great swirling of water and wild clanging from the ship's telegraph on the bridge. Lines were thrown. The gangplank was down and passengers were spilling ashore. Others were pushing forward to get on board. There was a great deal of shouting and milling about, so that Charlie found it difficult to concentrate on individual faces. He began to wonder if he would recognize the boy.

There was a lull as some nondescript bundles were unloaded. Charlie had started to turn away from the rail when he saw him. His flimsy shirt (his only one?) was open and clung to his spare hairless boy's torso. His face had all the fresh innocent ardor Charlie had found so irresistible; it reminded him of Peter when they had first met. His big dark eyes were darting animatedly over the ship. Charlie let out a shout as Dimitri saw him. His mouth widened in a dazzling delighted grin and he shouted in reply. Charlie flung himself aft toward the gangplank. Passengers blocked his way. He heard a whistle and the ship's telegraph clanged again. He made a lunge through indignant passengers and yanked his bag free from some obstruction and reached the place where the gangplank had been. It was already up. Lines had been cast free. Charlie saw the water widening between him and the eagerly shouting boy on shore. For a mad instant, he considered jumping overboard. His body was pressed against the rail as he shouted "Hydra" helplessly and pointed.

The ship was gathering way. The boy broke into a run as the distance between them grew. Charlie's eyes lingered on the curve of his throat and on the slim chest heaving with exertion. He saw Dimitri stop and his body slump with disappointment as he lifted an arm and waved farewell. Charlie stood with his body pressed against the rail and waved until the boat followed a turn in the channel and he was blocked from view.

He found himself churning with excitement and frustration. He wasn't dead after all. He could still care. Briefly, he had felt poignantly what it must have been like for Peter with Jeannot. Watching Dimitri run after him, he had been ready to sacrifice anything to possess the fleet young body. There had been such yearning in every straining line of it. Could one deny such a gripping urge without loss of some revitalizing life-force? The question had plagued him all summer and he was no nearer to an answer. When did one say yes? Never? Always? Sometimes? When the circumstances were propitious? None of these seemed to provide his disciplined mind with a guide to rational behavior. His excitement subsided and with it his regrets and he returned to his seat for the remainder of the trip to Hydra. He had learned something new. He had learned that what he had only half-believed in his last talk with Peter was true: he had to remain alone. He would be of no use to Peter or himself or anyone until he had caught at least a glimpse of the solution to the riddle. Since it appeared insoluble, the prospect was at best disheartening.

Taking possession of the house presented no problems. It dominated the eastern arm of the port, a big, square, plain block of masonry that looked more dilapidated than it was. News of his arrival spread quickly and a considerable delegation, determined to be helpful, accompanied him on his first inspection of it. It was habitable in the most primitive sense of the word. Much was made of the fact that there was a cistern full of water under it, which didn't particularly interest Charlie until he finally understood that there was no water supply on the island. There was a well-head in what had once been a kitchen and he bought a bucket to drop down it. He bought a bed and some rough sheets and a lamp and a single-burner kerosene stove. A table and a few chairs came with the house. He moved in.

Even after his unexpected decision about not leaving word for Peter, he had more or less assumed that he would go back to Athens in a few days but now he was committed to staying. Something was happening to him. He was getting through to the core of himself; he had to stay until the uncomfortable process had run its course. He missed Peter agonizingly, his nerves were raw with worry about his safety, but this was the price he had to pay to find out what had gone so disastrously wrong.

The day of his arrival and the second day spent settling-in passed quickly enough so that he was almost able to believe that he could cope with solitude, even though he couldn't stop referring everything to Peter in his mind. Would Peter want the bed here or over against that wall where there was a view of the sea? He wouldn't like not having any place to hang their clothes. Would he want a real stove or would he be glad not to bother with cooking here? Being with him was a condition of living.

On the third day, he realized that, counting the day he had spent in Athens, it would be four days that evening since Peter had been due to leave Crete; with luck, *Cassandra* might be nearing Piraeus. Immediately after breakfast, he went down to the town and learned that a boat was scheduled the next day at noon. The possibility that Peter might be on it filled him with hope and panic. He longed to see him and to know that he was safe, the balm of his presence would relieve him of much of his torment, but it was too soon. What could they say to each other? He feared being forced somehow into making the break final.

The sense of not being whole, of being less than a man, that had grown out of his rejection of Martha and her child, still filled him with shame and self-loathing. He was a faggot, playing at being a man, yet the summer had rid him of every vestige of his reticence about his sexual nature. If he had lived with Peter right from the start as openly as he had for the last month, as openly as Peter had always wanted to, he might not have fooled himself into thinking that parenthood was possible for him. In the unlikely event that somebody organized a campaign to erase the stigma from homosexuality, he would gladly lend a hand. He was what he was; he wasn't breaking any laws. He felt sure of so few things that it was a comfort to have got this much straight in his mind.

Will What's-his-name had shown them before where the foreigners swam, so, after finding out about the boat, he took swimming trunks and towel in the opposite direction and found rocks that offered access to the sea and where he hoped he would be undisturbed. He found that lying out languidly, voluptuously under the sun was an added torture: when he rolled over expecting to brush against a familiar body, when he opened his eyes expecting to find Peter's eyes on him, the shock of solitude was even greater than when he woke up alone in bed.

The surge of the sea around him reminded him of his brief flirtations with death. Even that escape was closed to him; Peter had made him realize that he had somehow forfeited his right to such a simple solution. He had to live if only to demonstrate to Peter that they couldn't live together.

He lay just long enough to dry off after his swim and then fled the enormous vacant eye of the sky. The crumbling house was a little part of Peter, his choice, perhaps his destination.

The next day, he was waiting at the landing stage when the boat came in. His eyes swept over the disembarking passengers as they were rowed ashore. It took only an instant to see that Peter wasn't among them. There was a strong element of relief in his stabbing disappointment. It was still too soon. Besides, four days was barely enough time for *Cassandra*'s voyage. They would more likely be getting in this evening. He didn't know if there was a boat tomorrow, but he resolved not to inquire. Counting hours, meeting boats was an indulgence, distracting him from the confrontation with himself that was the purpose of his being here.

As he came to this decision, he found himself searching for another face as the new arrivals began to climb out of the small boats onto the quai. Dimitri had surely heard his repeated shouts of "Hydra." The boy's wild gestures had probably been intended to urge him to stop at Poros on the way back, but they may have indicated that Dimitri might follow him to Hydra. The boy's ardor suggested he would be capable of it, especially if he had mistaken him for Peter.

He lingered until he was sure he knew no one among the travelers and then dragged himself back up the hill, moving stiffly. His muscles were still knotted with the desire that had swept through him at the thought of seeing the boy.

He stopped abruptly halfway up the stepped road and stood stock-still under the blazing sun. A devastating knowledge crashed through all the barriers of his mind; he was nearly insane with jealousy of Peter. That was his sickness. He had been ridden by jealousy, not love, all these years. It was suddenly, blindingly obvious; he couldn't understand why he felt the need to formulate it in coherent thought. It was basic, something he must have known about himself all along. Jealousy was the monster that possessed him. It was suffocating him from within. He had pretended, even to himself, never to have been attracted to boys with the hope that Peter would adopt a similar indifference. Jeannot, the plots and plans involving Martha, his giving her to Peter (safe, since she wasn't a boy) had all been sops to appease the monster, all offered in the name of perfect love. He wanted Dimitri only because the boy had flung himself at Peter.

He stood for a stunned moment and then forced his feet up the remaining steps and sank into one of the rickety straight-backed chairs.

Now what? Somewhere in the wreckage of the monument to self-love he now seemed to inhabit, the mind went on searching relentlessly. Perhaps they could save their deep, loving friendship by attempting to achieve the Socratic ideal. Sexless love. Physical satisfaction in casual encounters, the Jeannots, the Dimitris, the Tonys. It would probably kill him if Peter took happily to such a life, but he would kill them both if he didn't curb the demon that was in him. He had known that much in Crete. He had learned it could drive him to murder.

How did you conquer jealousy? It was lodged in the ego, perhaps in his goddamn cock. Was it simply that he couldn't bear anything to challenge its supremacy?

He wasn't prepared to put himself through intensive psychoanalysis. He had to come to grips with an immediate problem: now that infidelity was an issue between them and could become increasingly so, how could he love Peter, how could he live with him without destroying them? He had found the source of his despair. Could he transform himself, or was there more about himself he had yet to learn?

His waking hours lost whatever shape they had had, given significance only by the hoot of a boat in the harbor, sometimes during the day, sometimes at night. The days when there was none simply dropped out of time. Because he had refused to learn their schedule, he was in a state of constant alert and expectation while he continued to search within himself for a clue to the future. Everywhere he looked in the past he was confronted with self-love.

His altered attitude toward the public acknowledgment of their relationship might help, but it carried with it the danger of greater exposure to all the things he feared. The party at Capri, the evening at Poros had been a defiance of all his instincts.

Renounce the physical in their lives. His mind kept coming back to it. They had so much together that went beyond sex. He thought he could train himself to bear the thought of Peter with others if it were no longer a question of infidelity but an understanding they had reached together. With time, the hunger of his own body must ease.

He had progressed no closer than that to a resolution of the conflicts that seemed to be threatening his sanity when he realized that he had been there a week. Panic immediately paralyzed thought. Had he pushed tolerance too far? Had Peter finally rebelled and left him to his fate? Even worse was the possibility that something had happened to him. He was sure that Peter could handle *Cassandra* and he had confidence in the boat, but there were always dangers at sea. How could he find out if he was safe? Even if they weren't together, he couldn't live in a world without Peter in it somewhere. He wanted to rush down and find out when there was a boat for Piraeus. Frantically, he counted the days once more. Something might have delayed the departure from Crete. Peter's mention of four days had been whistling in the dark. Five or six days was much more realistic. They might have got in last night. If they had had engine trouble, seven or eight days would be good time. There had been no storms or big winds recently.

Slowly, he calmed himself. No matter how he tried Peter's patience, he knew he wouldn't go off without him. He might not come look for him if he were angry, but he would wait for him, at least until they were due to go home. Give it a few more days. Something might yet come clear in his mind. He had promised Peter to make it easy for them. If he had just arrived, or was about to, letting him wait a few days was not too much to ask of him.

He was reading by the light of the kerosene lamp the next night after dinner when a boat hooted in the harbor. As usual, he tried to pay no attention. As usual, he couldn't resist the urge to go out to the perilous terrace overlooking the port just in case he might catch a glimpse of the golden head. As usual, he went back inside and began to go through the movements in his head that anybody looking for him would have to go through: finding an interpreter, asking for a blond American, learning how to get to the house. After enough time had passed so that he could reasonably expect to hear someone coming, he steeled himself as usual against disappointment.

When he heard Peter's unmistakable hurrying footsteps, he leaped up and his heart felt as if it would burst his chest with joy. They were getting near. For a terrible moment, he thought they might have taken a wrong turning. He couldn't hear them. Was that the sound of voices? One brief feminine note. Martha? Oh, no, his mind protested. He forgot it as the footsteps came clear again, louder, almost here.

At the knock, he rushed to the door and flung it open. Peter stood in front of him. They looked at each other without moving. Charlie longed to seize him and hold him in his arms, but as soon as the first rapturous shock of his presence passed he knew he mustn't get them off to a false start. He was aware immediately that Peter was holding back, too.

"I'm in a blazing rage," Peter said sharply, "but that doesn't change the fact that I can't stand not knowing where you are."

"I'm glad you found me. Don't you have a bag?"

"I left it below. I wasn't sure I'd be invited to stay."

"You're invited, with qualifications maybe. I still don't know what they are."

"I see. Well, my acceptance is apt to be pretty damn qualified, too. Did the goddamn hotel lose your message or didn't you really leave one?"

"I didn't leave one. Well, I told them to tell you I was still in Greece."

Peter swept past him into the house, lighting it up with a blaze of vitality. "What's it supposed to be, a treasure hunt?" he demanded. "Usually they give you clues."

Charlie closed the door, realizing that he was thrilled by him in a way he had never been before, thrilled in some unfamiliar feminine part of himself that was quickened by the virility that had been growing more pronounced in Peter and now made him a commanding presence. "I knew you'd guess," he said, almost apologetically. "I left my bag."

"What was that supposed to tell me? God, what a trip. I'd have gone out of my mind if you hadn't been here."

"I'm sorry. But you must've been pretty sure I would be. This is the only place we talked about buying a house. Where else could I have gone?"

"How do I know? I don't know what to expect any more. Did you buy it?"

"In both our names. There're some papers you're supposed to sign."

Peter looked around him at the big bare room and a glimmer of a smile twisted his lips. "I'm glad you haven't overfurnished it. All right. Tell me. What's it all about this time?"

"What? Coming here without leaving word? I had to do it that way. I had to make a complete break. I had to find out what it felt like. It was the only way to discover what's been wrong with me."

"Wrong with *you*?" Peter sat in one of the chairs at the table and looked up at him, a challenge in his lively eyes. Even when he was angry, there was too much love and interest in his face for his anger to seem hostile. "I thought I was the one who was always wrong. I was once, God knows."

Charlie sat across the table from him and nodded briefly. "That's part of it. The essential part, I guess. There are more important things than sex, but it certainly causes most of the trouble. I've been wondering if you *were* wrong. I've been trying to look at myself and us and everything. I've been going around in circles. I don't know if you should stay, but seeing you has certainly lifted one load off my mind." He put his hand out to him on the table.

Peter looked at it but didn't move. "What if I'd just given up and gone home?"

"I knew you wouldn't."

"You're pretty sure of me, aren't you? I'm proud of that."

"You have the right to be. I wish I had as much to be proud of. Did all go well with *Cassandra*?"

"Sure. It was unmitigated hell. Thanks for asking. We got back day before yesterday. There wasn't a boat till today. It's been nice in Athens, wondering about you."

"Will you please believe me? I cracked up. Surely that was obvious enough. Wrecking the boat. Jesus. If I hadn't come out here or somewhere and tried to come to grips with myself, I don't know what would've become of me."

Peter's eyes filled with solicitude, although everything else about him remained tough and unyielding. "Are you all right now?"

"More or less. It helps to find out things." He paused, looking at Peter with fresh eyes. He saw a hard strength in him that hadn't been there before. He had hardened physically and his youthfulness seemed less a phenomenon than the natural emanation of thriving health. It occurred to Charlie that perhaps he hadn't been a total failure after all. "I think I've found out things."

"Such as?" Peter's tone was demanding. The soft dependence was gone.

Charlie wondered if it would end with his pleading to retain a place in his life. This, too, gave him an uneasy thrill. "I know I've had to be alone. I may still have to be alone, even though it's wonderful being with you now."

"Well, I suppose you might as well be alone if you don't want to touch me."

"It isn't just a question of wanting. I wanted to the minute I opened the door and saw you."

"Why didn't you say so?" Peter put his hand out and Charlie took it in both of his and leaned over and kissed it. Peter moved his fingers in a brief caress. "That feels better. What else do you know?"

"I know I'm human. I've given up trying to play God. Being human presents me with a new set of problems." Charlie paused and then plunged in more abruptly than he had intended, not sure that he would be able to define the basic problem but determined to try. "I saw your Dimitri on the dock at Poros the other day. If I could've got off the boat, I'd have stayed with him. For a minute, I would've given up everything just to be with him for an hour. I gather that's what you felt about Jeannot. How can we *not* give in to things like that and stay alive? The fact that maybe you weren't wrong has led me to some pretty strange conclusions."

"Just a minute, before we get to conclusions," Peter said, his look hardening. "How about this? One of the best-looking guys

I've ever seen picked me up at a bar last night. American. Sensational. Damn nice, too. Intelligent. Everything. I could have had him—in the time-honored fashion. He made that clear enough. You, Martha—all right, start with Jeannot—well, I didn't know what I've been missing all these years. It's still new enough so that it does things to me that are pretty hard to resist. If I'd been on my own, I might've fallen for the guy in a big way. Once would've been better than never. Is that the sort of thing you're talking about? Are you trying to say I should have had him?"

"Yes. *No.* When it happens to me, I can understand it. When it's you, I can't take it. There, by God. Now we can get down to brass tacks." He slammed his fists down on the table and leaned forward. "You tear me apart. My being so sure of myself and knowing what's best for us is a goddamn act. I'm rotten with jealousy. I've found out that I'm literally capable of killing you. That's why I say I have to leave you. The only hope I can see for us is to stop having sex with each other and find it somewhere else."

"What *are* you raving about?" Peter demanded.

"Stand up."

Peter looked at him as he leaned intensely across the table. There was a wild gleam in his eye. Peter shrugged and did as he was told. Charlie sprang up and swung his fist. It connected hard with Peter's jaw. He went careening back across the room.

"That's for Jeannot." Charlie roared. "That's what I want to do whenever I think of him. That little tap I gave you in St. Tropez was nothing. I want to beat the shit out of you when you even look at anybody else. Do you want to live with that?"

Peter shook his head and steadied himself. He flung off the light jacket he was wearing. "I'll answer that question later. Right now, I'm going to do something I've been waiting to do for years."

He went for Charlie with fists flying and crowded him back into a corner of the room. Charlie was hurting before he realized that Peter was in earnest. He fought back, smashing his fists into the hard body. He was careful not to land any punches near his eyes or mouth. Peter observed the same caution but they were hurting each other. Their breathing became labored. They grunted as their fists hammered each other.

Peter landed a strong blow to the side of Charlie's jaw. His head snapped back and for a moment his sight failed. Peter followed up his advantage with a blow to his solar plexus and another hard one under the heart. This is a *man*, Charlie thought with wonder as his breath was cut off; I'm in love with a man. He flung himself forward and felt Peter catch his weight and support him as he waited for his body to recover.

"Had enough?" Peter asked cheerfully despite the heaving of his chest.

Charlie nodded. As he began to breathe more easily, he was shaken by helpless laughter. Revelation had descended on him once more: this was what he had always wanted—a man he could cling to, who could beat him into his senses when he lost his bearings. He didn't know why it should take him so by surprise; all the history of their lives pointed to it. Peter had chosen his career and had guided him through it. Peter had kept him. Peter had always provided the solid foundations; he, only the dramatic flourishes. He had been misled by the sexual role he had played. The reversal he had initiated in Athens hadn't been a passing whim but the expression of a long-felt, unrecognized need. And it had worked for Peter too. He could tell by the way Peter held him that it had worked. As his strength returned to him, his laughter redoubled.

"What's so funny, you shit?" Peter demanded with a chuckle. "You hurt me. It was sort of fun but I don't see that it gets us anywhere."

Charlie pulled himself up and settled his weight on his own feet and looked at him. "It gets us through life, Slugger darling. God, what a man. Thank God, I didn't hurt that mouth."

"Is this the traditional clinch?"

"Why not?"

Their mouths met and they kissed at length, holding each other close in spite of their drained and aching bodies. Their mouths parted and Peter laughed.

"How D. H. Lawrence can we get?" he said. He moved his hips against Charlie's. "Mmm. Everything seems to be working normally. What was all that about not having sex together?"

"More of my brilliant analysis of a nonexistent situation. I overlooked the fact that you're the man in the family."

Peter looked at him with a sly smile. "I guess maybe we both are. At least, I'm not as much one of the girls as I thought. I was really steaming at the idea of letting that guy have it last night. He was very butch, too. How's that for a switch? It's amazing the things you know about us, the things you know about me that I don't even know myself."

"Feminine intuition, my darling."

"Look who's calling me darling. What's wrong with baby?"

"You're nobody's baby now."

They laughed and Peter gave him a quick kiss and broke away from him. "Come on. Show me our house. I hope there's a good strong bed that'll hold both of us. I intend to put it to a rude test. What's out here?"

"Be careful. Part of it doesn't look very solid." They went out onto the terrace overhanging the port.

"My God, how beautiful," Peter said in an awestruck tone. "Just the way I imagined it."

"This is where I wait for you to show up."

"Of all the nutty ideas. I still don't see why you were so sure I'd pick this place."

"I wasn't. I figured if you couldn't find me, you didn't deserve to have me."

"Bastard." He took Charlie's hand. "Always keep 'em guessing. It makes life interesting. Things happen to us. I've been wanting to tell you how amazing it was, being with Martha and knowing you were there growing inside her. Don't let's kid ourselves. It's you. I almost fell in love with her. There wasn't any question of sex again after you left but—well, I'm glad there's a little Charlie at last."

Charlie squeezed Peter's hand. "If I'm not mistaken, you're thinking it would be nice for there to be a little Peter, too."

"There you go again. Yes, the idea's beginning to make sense to me. You've started something that's pretty fascinating. I even understand what you meant about the sex part of it. As far as I'm concerned, sex will always be you, but there *was* something special about doing it with Martha—simple and natural, thinking about having a baby. How's that for a queer? Honestly, all the fuss about male and female! It's a wonder it hasn't turned us both into screaming queens. Speaking of which, there's more about Martha."

Charlie remembered the voices and he stared at Peter in the

dark. "For God's sake. Don't tell me you've brought her with you."

"The old intuition is working overtime. Yes. I was in such a state that she offered to come in case I didn't find you and went off my rocker. She was marvelous to me on the trip back. Always there when I needed her."

"You mean, we're going to have to have her up here?"

"Not tonight, idiot. I showed her the hotel and brought her partway up here so she'd know where we were. I told her if I didn't come back, it would be because you were fucking me silly."

"Or vice-versa?"

"Well, yes, now that you mention it. Maybe vice-versa."

They looked at each other, just catching the glitter of eyes in the light from the lamp, and burst out laughing. Charlie knew that he was given to extremes of optimism and despair, but he felt that even his jealousy would be manageable now that he saw Peter in the light of his real need. In spite of his talk about the boy last night, or perhaps because of it, he didn't think he would stray in that direction again. There might well be girls. He found it exciting to think of sharing him with girls. He tangled his fingers in the golden hair and held on. "You're my Slugger."

After another burst of laughter, Peter sobered. He put a hand on Charlie's arm. "Martha was hit pretty hard by what you said to her on the boat. She's going to make a clean break with Jack. I want to try it like you said. I love her. I want her near us as long as it fits in with her life. I want little Charlie. Maybe she'll have one for me later. I'd marry her then unless you find out you can make Charlie officially yours. I hope you're not going to make any trouble."

"No, darling. I'm not afraid of a little air now. You're the boss."

"A likely story, but I intend to take advantage of it while it lasts. If any of this is going to work, we've got to help her get over being in love with you. We've done just about everything else with her, maybe we should let her see us making love. That might do it, especially if it's vice-versa."

"I had that idea first."

"I know. I don't want to stage a performance, but we could arrange it so she sees us. It can't come as a shock to her. We've talked about everything, but it might make her realize we're for real. I have this weird hankering for a witness, anyway. It's probably because we didn't get married in church."

Charlie tugged his hair. "What a nut."

"Talking about it is doing things to me. Oh, God, to be with you again at last. Where's that bed?" Peter began to unbutton his shirt as they stood side-by-side, looking down at the still circle of harbor and up at the star-filled sky.

"I have an idea this is going to be fairly spectacular," Charlie said with a chuckle. "I want to make you feel how much I love you."

"Oh, darling. Me too. With all of me." Peter pulled off his shirt and tossed it aside. "The hell with the bed. Let's bring a mattress out here, damn it." He laughed as he unbuttoned his trousers. "How's this for doing it in public? I don't guess the town can see us but I'd like to show that gang on Mount Olympus a thing or two. This one is for the gods."

Books 1 and 3 of Gordon Merrick's beloved Peter and Charlie trilogy!

In **THE LORD WON'T MIND,** Merrick explored the coming-out of a young homosexual and the stormy, painful, and abiding love he finds with another man. When the book was first published, Merrick's startling frankness and open affirmation caused shouts of praise and howls of protest, but *The Lord Won't Mind* rode out the storm securely lashed to *The New York Times* best-seller list.

FORTH INTO LIGHT concludes the saga of Peter and Charlie. In a sandstone villa on the windswept beaches of a Greek isle, Peter and Charlie—and Martha—have settled into a harmonious and passionate life together with their offspring. When a lovely Greek youth enters their lives, a tangle of affairs—and bodies—ensues, with the tension building to a heart-stopping crescendo on the windy cliffs of Mykonos.

These books and other Alyson titles are available at your local bookstore. If you can't find a book listed above or would like more information, please call us directly at 1-800-5-ALYSON.